Love of a Cowboy

He leaned in close and took her face in his warm hands. "Don't you see there's a lot more going on here and it has nothing to do with the fact you work here?"

She didn't know what to say, except to be honest. "I feel something."

"That's the phone in my pocket vibrating with a string of texts. Probably from Tate." He teased, but her words had made the intensity in his eyes sharpen. "What else do you feel?"

"You."

He leaned in another inch. Their noses almost touching, their breath mingling. The same pull she felt earlier when they'd collided drew her in and made her want to get closer.

He asked, so she gave him the truth that came straight from her heart. "I feel the way you look at me. When you touch me, it's like a burst of sunlight shoots through me. When you're not touching me, I'm hoping you do it again."

"Do you want me to do it again right now?"

"Yes."

His lips pressed to hers . . .

LOVE OF A COWBOY

A McGrath Novel

JENNIFER RYAN

AVONBOOKS

An Imprint of HarperCollinsPublishers

Excerpt from *True Love Cowboy* copyright © 2021 by Jennifer Ryan.

LOVE OF A COWBOY. Copyright © 2021 by Jennifer Ryan. All rights reserved. Printed in the United States of America. No part of this book may be used or reproduced in any manner whatsoever without written permission except in the case of brief quotations embodied in critical articles and reviews. For information, address HarperCollins Publishers, 195 Broadway, New York, NY 10007.

First Avon Books mass market printing: April 2021
First Avon Books hardcover printing: March 2021

Print Edition ISBN: 978-0-06-285198-7
Digital Edition ISBN: 978-0-06-285187-1

Cover design by Nadine Badalaty
Cover photographs © Rob Lang/roblangimages.com (cowboy); © dsteller/
iStock/Getty Images (barn); © MarekUsz/iStock/Getty Images (orchard);
© George Stone/Shutterstock (background)
Author photo by Steve Hopkins

Avon, Avon & logo, and Avon Books & logo are registered trademarks of HarperCollins Publishers in the United States of America and other countries.

HarperCollins is a registered trademark of HarperCollins Publishers in the United States of America and other countries.

FIRST EDITION

21 22 23 24 25   BVGM   10 9 8 7 6 5 4 3 2 1

LOVE
OF A
COWBOY

Chapter One

SKYE KENNEDY snuck toward the master bedroom, drawn by Gabriel's harsh voice and the ominous feeling she couldn't ignore. She peeked through the ajar door and stared, horrified by the anger blazing in his eyes. Gabriel held Lucy trembling in front of him, his hands fisted in her linen shift dress, his body bent toward her as she leaned away, his face an inch from hers.

Skye didn't recognize who Gabriel had become.

The boy she grew up with had turned into a very dangerous man.

Poor Lucy. She couldn't get away. Not that she tried. Fear held her wide-eyed and docile.

Lucy's fear echoed through Skye.

"What will my bride think if you bring that bastard into this world?" Rage and disgust filled Gabriel's unbelievable words.

They stopped Skye's heart.

If she wasn't mistaken, in this case, "bride" referred to *her*.

Skye didn't like being told what to do, which is why she'd never agree to be *his* wife.

But several of the other Sunrise young ladies couldn't wait to marry the men Gabriel—in an unprecedented dictate—handpicked for them. They thought it an honor to marry into his inner circle of tried-and-true, trusted friends.

Believers in his new vision for Sunrise.

She didn't believe in Gabriel's new direction. It led them down a dangerous road. And if the rest of the Sunrise Fellowship community outside Gabriel's circle of friends knew what he was doing behind their backs, they'd cast him out once and for all. But for the sake of the community and all they believed in, Skye worked in the shadows to find a way to take down Gabriel without him turning the tables on her for going against him.

Right now, she feared she'd taken too long to oust him, and Gabriel was about to do something else to prove how far he'd strayed from their ideals.

Tears streamed down Lucy's pale face. "I didn't mean for it to happen."

Skye had no idea, nor did she care, that Gabriel had been sleeping with Lucy.

Gabriel pulled Lucy even closer, their noses nearly touching. "Who did you tell?"

Lucy patted Gabriel's chest with one shaking hand, trying to soothe him, but nothing, not even the child she carried, seemed to calm Gabriel's ire. "No one. Just you. Please, Gabriel, he's your son."

"Skye will give me strong sons. *She's* the only one worthy to be my wife."

He'd always had a thing for *her*. She avoided him when possible. When that didn't work, she tried to be kind like she'd been taught, but careful about how much attention or interest she showed Gabriel.

She didn't want to give him the wrong idea.

Not that he cared what she wanted either way.

"*She* will stand beside me. Not *you*."

Never. Not going to happen.

A desperate plea filled Lucy's eyes. "But you said *I* was chosen."

Gabriel sneered at her. "You were. To serve me. And you've served your purpose."

So cruel.

He was one of those people who thought everyone loved him and you were lucky to be *his* friend even when he was unkind.

He held himself in high regard, thinking himself better than everyone else.

Tonight he proved to be far lower than the worst of them.

"You will not have this baby."

"I won't give him up," Lucy wailed.

Gabriel shook her. "You'll do as you're told!"

Lucy's gaze dropped and she shook her head. "You can't make me." Her defiance set Gabriel off.

He shook her again, making her head snap back and forth like a rag doll's. "You will!"

"No!" she shouted right in his face.

He shoved Lucy to the floor and kicked her right in the stomach, sending her body sliding across the hardwood toward the dresser. "Why are you trying to ruin everything?"

Skye pressed her hand over her mouth to cover her shocked gasp.

Lucy screeched, then let loose an agonizing wail.

In a blind rage, Gabriel kicked her again, then stomped his big booted foot right into her thigh as she tucked her legs to her chest to protect herself from further harm.

Too late.

Lucy's piercing scream echoed in Skye's ears.

Bright red blood spread and saturated Lucy's white dress.

Gabriel stood over her, his breath heaving in and out with the fury still tightening his muscles and etched in his face.

Lucy stared up at him, her teary eyes wide and wild. "Why?"

Gabriel gave no answer for his horrendous behavior. If he felt any remorse for his child and what he'd done, it didn't show.

Lucy clawed at the material, dragging it up her thighs, and stared as blood spread and pooled on the floor between her legs. She clutched her belly. "No!" Pain etched lines on her distraught face.

Skye wanted to rage. She wanted to help Lucy, but fear locked her in place, witness to the horrifying tragedy. Stuck in this terrible nightmare, her mind couldn't make her body move.

Lucy stared up at Gabriel, her eyes huge and filled with grief and blame and unimaginable sadness. "Y-you k-killed him."

Gabriel stared down at Lucy. "He was never meant to be." Those flat words left Skye cold.

He squatted next to Lucy. Skye hoped he'd finally help her. But no, he gripped her jaw tightly in his fingers and glared at her. "My son will be born to my *wife*, not some whore."

How had so much malice corrupted his heart?

Shame washed over Lucy's face, but she retaliated. "Skye w-won't have you. When she f-finds out . . . you plan to m-make her . . . m-marry y-you . . . tomorrow, she . . . she'll . . . re-refuse you."

That truth narrowed Gabriel's eyes and filled them with renewed fury. He released Lucy's face and back-handed her, splitting her lip and sending her sprawling on her back. Her head cracked against the floor and her tear-drenched eyes fluttered.

Gabriel pointed his finger in Lucy's face. "No one refuses me. I am the supreme leader of Sunrise."

No, he's not!

There was no such thing here. They worked in cooperation with each other.

But Gabriel wanted to be treated like some patriarch. He demanded people's respect, but hadn't earned it through his words or actions.

Tonight, he'd proven he'd lost all reason.

Lucy's head rolled to the side and her eyes locked with Skye's through the crack in the door. "Love is free." Lucy's breath slowed. "Love is kind." Lucy sucked in a shaky breath as the blood pool between her legs grew wider and she looked up at Gabriel. "You will never have love, because y-you're cruel." Air whistled as she inhaled. Then Lucy exhaled, "Ruunnn," though barely a sound left her lips.

Lucy bled out and didn't breathe again.

Skye watched the soul disappear from Lucy's beautiful hazel eyes. Her heart broke and her mind reeled. She should have done something. Anything to stop this.

But her brain found some reason and whispered the disturbing truth: *Get out of here before you're Gabriel's next victim.*

He couldn't be reasoned with or deterred from his deadly path.

Ever since his dad died two years ago, he'd changed. Grief gave way to acceptance of his leadership role at

Sunrise Fellowship and morphed his childish selfishness and tendency to push the limits into destructive subterfuge.

He lashed out at those who didn't go along.

Anyone who questioned or defied him suffered his punishing disapproval, fury-fueled tantrums, and petty retribution.

What had once been a peaceful community of people living a quiet, simple, self-sustaining life had become corrupted by power and greed. In one short year, Gabriel had tainted their community-first home, built on cooperation and the farm everyone worked to sustain them.

She took Lucy's last request to heart, found that her frozen limbs loosened with her resolve to do what she'd been planning for the last few weeks. She backed away on silent feet, and though she didn't run, she left the man who stared down at the young lady he'd used like she was nothing. The man who in cold blood killed his child and an eighteen-year-old girl and talked as if he ruled the good people who lived their lives in peace at Sunrise.

She tiptoed down the hallway to the home office she'd worked in since she was fourteen, when Gabriel's father noticed her aptitude for math. He taught her accounting and gave her a purpose greater than the farm chores she'd performed her whole life.

She didn't bother to go to the phone and call the police. Gabriel's corruption had spread to them as well and it disheartened her to know she couldn't turn to the authorities for help. Which left her only one option: run. There had to be someone outside their community and town who could help her stop Gabriel and what was coming.

The threat of discovery made her heart thrash, but she tried to stay focused, fought the fear, and did what needed to be done. Otherwise she'd never be able to take Gabriel down.

She went to the rug in front of the sofa, folded it back, and pushed it away. She pressed her shaking hand on one of the boards and the secret panel popped loose, revealing the safe embedded in concrete. She spun the dial, her trembling fingers barely working. She didn't know how much time she had before Gabriel left Lucy and called for his trusted "guards" to help him cover up his crime. Every beat of her heart amped her anxiety as she twisted the dial to each number, gripped the handle, turned it, and lifted the door open. She didn't sort through folders and envelopes, just pulled everything out.

For a split second she stared at the stacks of cash, disgusted by how Gabriel earned them. She thought about the other women he was hurting and the people who'd get hurt if he carried out the plans she'd spent weeks uncovering.

She hadn't stopped him from killing Lucy, but she would find a way to stop him from hurting anyone else.

She wasn't a thief. She believed they were all better off when they worked together and shared the rewards with everyone.

But if she was going to get away, she needed help.

She snatched one of the thick packets of cash and stashed it in her cargo pants pocket.

As she'd uncovered Gabriel's elicit activities and the threat of being caught meddling in his affairs drew ever closer, she'd feared she'd have to run, but she never thought it would happen like this.

There was no time to cover her tracks. She stuffed the files and papers into the messenger bag hanging on the back of Gabriel's desk chair, pulled the strap over her head and across her body, stared at the picture on the desk, and wished the man she'd admired had been a better father. If he'd disciplined instead of spoiled and coddled, maybe Gabriel would have turned out to be a better man.

With little to no consequences ever imposed on him, Gabriel had become entitled. Now he wanted to be some "Supreme Leader."

She rolled her eyes at the absurdity of it.

Ironic when Sunrise taught cooperation and equality for all.

No one person, not even Gabriel, dictated their lives. His ego had grown to astronomical proportions. Lucy paid the price for his belief that he could say and do whatever he wanted without repercussions.

Skye planned to teach him a lesson he should have learned long ago.

But to do that, she needed to get out of here before Gabriel discovered what she knew, what she'd done, and came after her.

Even with the police on his side, Gabriel would not get away with Lucy's murder. She'd find a way. And she knew someone who could hopefully help her. And the others.

Infused with fear and desperation, she ran from the office for the front door and snuck out with barely a click when the door closed behind her. She leaped down the porch stairs and hit the gravel path leading back to the great hall and other cabins. She wanted to follow Lucy's command, but she kept her head and walked like she had not a care in the world when she had a million thoughts and fears circling her mind.

She didn't want to alert any of the guards who patrolled the property. No one but her questioned why they needed them. Did everyone think someone was out to steal their bumper crop of apples?

No. Gabriel hid something much more valuable and dangerous on the property.

If he discovered what she'd done with it, she'd suffer the same fate as Lucy.

If Gabriel succeeded with his campaign to brainwash everyone into thinking his way would bring them unimaginable prosperity, she feared for everyone's safety.

What she saw for Sunrise's future frightened her.

What used to be home, a simple life on this thriving farm, now felt like corruption of everything she'd been taught to believe in and trust.

Gabriel had always pushed the boundaries. His father had tried to reel him in with reason and appealing to his better nature.

Too bad Gabriel didn't have one.

Now, no one even tried to steer Gabriel away from the dangerous path his compass pointed him down.

No one dared.

So she'd have to be the one to put up the roadblocks and stop him before he reached the point of no return and more innocent people got hurt.

She arrived at the cabin where Gabriel had ordered the young women who were to be married off tomorrow to gather for their last night as bachelorettes. She had been told to join them and enjoy the treats Gabriel had arranged for the ladies before their morning weddings and the reception brunch.

She wondered how Gabriel planned to get her to walk down the aisle.

Didn't matter now. She wouldn't be there.

Neither would the other women. She hoped. They deserved to make up their own minds about whether or not they really wanted to marry Gabriel's men—his guard, as she thought of them.

She rushed into the cabin and stopped short when she spotted the ladies sitting in a group, enjoying tea and cake. Such a sweet scene compared to the gruesome one she'd left at Gabriel's place.

The young ladies stared up at her, shocked by her sudden entrance, worry and resignation in some of their eyes.

Sue stood and took a step toward her. "Skye, what's wrong? Has something happened?"

She didn't have time to explain. If Gabriel caught her with the files she took . . . if he knew she'd seen what he'd done . . . she didn't want to think about what he'd do.

Maybe some of these young ladies wanted to get married. She'd bet, given a chance to really think things through and make their own decisions without Gabriel's influence, they'd choose differently.

"Skye, are you okay?" Sue took another step toward her, wanting to help.

They all did. They were all so eager to help, so eager to please.

And that would be their downfall if they continued to just go along without questioning Gabriel and his motives.

"Would you like to leave?" The broad question raised some eyebrows.

Alice surveyed the spread before them, then looked up at her. "But what about our party? We don't want to upset Gabriel by leaving without finishing after he did this for us."

No. No one wanted to upset Gabriel.

"Gabriel suggested we see a movie." It was a treat they weren't likely to pass up. Once she got them away from the farm and Gabriel's influence, she'd explain what had happened and let them decide if they wanted to return and get married—or not. She hated to lie to them, but telling them about Lucy's murder would only delay them longer. They'd panic. "If you want to go, we have to go now." She waved them to come along.

Finally, they abandoned their cups and half-eaten plates of food and headed for the door, happy to get away for another special treat.

Alice stopped next to her and smiled. "Gabriel has been so kind. He's given us so much. I worried about marrying Michael. He's so much older than me."

Yeah, the twelve-year age gap should make Alice wonder what they really had in common and if they could make it long-term.

"I barely know him," Alice went on. "But Gabriel has done so much to make this a wonderful experience. I know it's meant to be, just like he said." Alice uttered the words, but a lot of fear and reluctance filled her eyes.

Skye wondered if she'd been that naïve and stupid at seventeen. Had she ever blindly followed without question?

No. Which is how she got herself into this predicament.

"Alice, Gabriel can't force you to marry Michael."

"My parents want the match, too."

That was a lot of pressure for a young lady.

She didn't understand how Gabriel managed to dupe everyone into believing his grand plans.

Yes, Gabriel had spent weeks pushing his agenda and convincing the Fellowship that the matches created stronger family bonds and guaranteed future generations of Sunrise stewards.

The other members didn't know Gabriel was just covering his ass.

"As his wife, I'll help him to become his best self and give him children, a family, and stability so he can fulfill his purpose."

Gabriel liked to spout big ideas like that, but his words held no substance. They sounded good, especially to the young, impressionable women who wanted a fairy-tale life.

If she asked the other four women why they'd agreed to get married without a lengthy courtship, she'd probably get the same exact answer.

None of them were prepared for reality.

Back when Gabriel's father headed the Sunrise council, she might have agreed to a similar match if he'd suggested it, but she'd have wanted time to get to know the man first, to be sure. A man and woman should be tied together by their shared beliefs. They should be best friends as well as lovers.

She figured that out when she was sixteen and fell madly in love with Joseph. She tossed reason to the wayside and went to great lengths to see him as much as possible. She even snuck out for their romantic rendezvous. But like all young love, it was fleeting—especially when she caught Joseph kissing Renee.

And looking back now, she realized she'd never had another serious boyfriend because Gabriel had always been lurking in her life, trying to keep her all to himself. And it worked, because the other boys accepted there was something between them. Like Gabriel, they believed she was meant for him.

She'd simply put guys on the back burner and focused on her job and making Sunrise the best it could be.

"Alice, you're only seventeen. Do you really want to be a wife and mother so young?"

"Babies are so sweet. I would love him or her so much."

Of course she only thought about a cute baby, not what it would be like to take care of an infant day in and day out. Yes, a baby brought a lot of joy into your life, but taking care of them was a lot of hard work. And a husband . . . Alice had no idea what it meant to take care of and be a partner to a man. To have her life and decisions tied to that person.

She hooked her hand around Alice's arm and tugged her out the door. When she got the girls out of here, she'd have a talk with Alice and the others about the reality of marriage and family, so they made an informed decision about the rest of their life without pressure from Gabriel or their families.

The others had already piled into the van down the road.

Skye wanted to find her parents and sister, but feared she'd already taken too long to get away before Gabriel discovered her. She needed to get out of here before he found her and killed her to keep her quiet.

This was so much bigger than Lucy's murder.

Her family didn't know anything. She hoped they'd be safe. Gabriel couldn't get rid of them without explaining or raising suspicions. Not now.

Ten feet from the van, Joseph stepped out in front of them, rifle hanging down his back by the strap over his shoulder. Guns at the compound were new, too. "Hey, Skye. Where are you going?"

Skye tamped down her rising panic, pushed Alice to keep walking to the van, and tried to talk her way out of this. "Gabriel suggested I treat the girls to a movie tonight." The false brightness in her voice didn't seem to alert him that anything was wrong.

Since their relationship ended in disaster, all their encounters were fraught with tension. She hoped he took her anxiety as remnants of her resentment toward him.

Joseph stared past her down the road to the girls. "Are they excited about their weddings tomorrow?" Hesitation filled his voice and skepticism filled his eyes.

"Why wouldn't they be?" She wanted to know if Joseph was still blindly going along with Gabriel or if he'd finally started thinking for himself again and saw the reality of what Gabriel was doing to Sunrise. To all of them.

"I wonder if they really know what they're getting into." His cynical expression answered that and made her think he didn't wholly go along with the impending marriages.

She took a chance on the slim hope that he finally had doubts about Gabriel's new plans for Sunrise. "I'm going to make sure they know they have a choice."

Joseph gave her a firm nod.

And she took another shot at getting through to him in case it would help stop Gabriel. "Go to Gabriel's place. You'll see who he really is."

With that, she rushed off to join the girls at the van with hope in her heart that exposing Gabriel to Joseph would have a domino effect and he and the other men would finally stand against him.

She climbed behind the wheel knowing that was a long shot. She shifted the bag of evidence onto her lap. It and the other things she'd hidden were probably her only hope of putting Gabriel in a cell where he belonged if she got them to the right authorities.

Alice leaned over. "I'll hold on to that if you'd like."

"I've got it. But thanks." Skye put her shaking hand on the bag, turned the key in the ignition, and hit the gas to get them out of there. Everyone fell back in their seats, then let loose a holler.

They thought they were out to have fun.

She knew better.

No telling what they'd say or do when they realized where she was really taking them.

As she drove through the gates, she took a moment to think about what she was leaving behind, but it only made her heart ache more, so she shut off her brain and drove.

Lucy deserved justice and she planned to get it for her. One way or another.

Alice leaned forward, staring out the windshield. "The movie theater is the other way."

"I'm going to make a stop. I think you'd all benefit from talking to someone about your upcoming marriages." She hoped she was doing the right thing.

"Like a counselor?" Bess asked.

"Very much like that." A legal counselor, who could advise the fourteen-year-old, who of all the young brides needed the most help because she already had a baby on the way.

"I'm nervous," Julie confessed. "But the flowers are going to be so pretty." She covered her complicated feelings by talking about pleasant things.

"My bouquet is filled with pink peonies." Alice beamed.

"I made this really pretty floral crown with baby white roses and orchids," one of the other girls chimed in.

It seemed easier for them to follow Julie's lead and stick to the simple things.

They grew all kinds of fruits, vegetables, and flowers on the farm and in the green houses and sold them at farmers markets along with the other goods produced at Sunrise. It's how they sustained the compound.

"Mine has pink roses and blue hydrangeas." Beth's voice didn't sound as exuberant as the other young women caught up in the weddings. At nineteen, maybe Beth was one of the ones unsure of sprinting down the aisle.

The others responded to her restrained tone and fell silent as if Beth's quiet resistance amplified their unspoken fears.

They should be afraid.

Skye had gathered pieces of the odd things happening at Sunrise. Taken one at a time, they didn't seem to be anything more than a ramp up to increase production for much-needed repairs, renovations, and expansion. But put together with the slow changes to the culture and philosophy they'd lived by for decades, alterations that Gabriel forced with his persistent ways, it painted a picture that went against everything she'd believed in her whole life.

Lucy's death proved someone had to stop Gabriel before it was too late.

Chapter Two

GABRIEL STOOD over Lucy, his hands shaking with the adrenaline still running through his system. Her dead eyes stared into nothing, devoid of life and the sweetness that had drawn him in and made him want to feel it.

Her devotion fueled him. Her obedience made him feel powerful.

Her betrayal set off a wave of rage he couldn't control.

He hadn't meant to kill her, just teach her a lesson. He simply couldn't let her derail his plans.

How dare she defy his order to get rid of the baby!

He'd warned her.

This was her fault. Not his.

No one, not even a good lover, would deter him from having and getting what he wanted.

He was chosen. He decided the others' fate. He knew best.

And no one would question that without swift reprisal.

If he didn't take control of Sunrise, others would move in and take it all. Sunrise didn't know it, but he stood between them and losing everything.

They'd thank him later.

For now, he'd reap the rewards he deserved. And that included the woman he'd craved his whole life.

Skye would be *his* tomorrow. She'd stand beside him as his obedient wife and the future mother of his children. She'd personify everything the women of Sunrise should be.

But first, he needed to get Lucy out of his house, clean up the mess, and complete the final preparations for moving Skye in tomorrow. He'd hoped to have one last night with Lucy before he dedicated the next days and weeks to getting Skye pregnant. Then he could go back to partying with the boys at their private hideaway.

He walked out of the bedroom, away from the mess, to call Joseph to help him clean up. Two steps past the office door, the hairs on the back of his neck stood on end. He abruptly halted, backed up, turned, and stared at the rolled up rug and open trap door.

The same uncontrollable rage he'd felt earlier raced through his system, tightening every muscle in his body until his hands were fisted at his sides, arms locked straight.

The urge to punish and kill surged through him again.

Someone had stolen his private files.

Only two people had the combination besides him. And the one who violated his trust would face his wrath and reel from the pain, because no one got away with betraying him.

"What happened?"

Gabriel turned to Joseph and grabbed him by the jacket, his fists clenched in the material. He shook Joseph, making his head whip back. "What did you do?"

"Nothing." The genuine shock in Joseph's voice temporarily mollified Gabriel. Joseph pushed him away. "What's wrong with you?"

If Joseph had to ask, he didn't do it, and that left only one other person who could be responsible. "Skye betrayed us." He tried to think of a reason why she'd do this to him.

How did she even know to look for the files in the safe?

"What are you talking about? She just left."

Gabriel's jaw clamped down so hard his molars hurt. "What?" He needed to find her. Now. Before she ruined everything. Before she got him killed.

"She and the other girls left in the van."

His ears burned with the rage racing through him. "What other girls?"

Joseph winced. "The brides."

Why the hell would she leave with them?

He stepped closer to Joseph, whose eyes went wide and worried. "Where did they go?"

"I don't know." Joseph stepped back. "But she told me to come here."

That surprised him. "Why?"

Joseph's gaze darted away, then came back to meet his. "She said I'd see who you really are."

It took him a second to reason that out.

If she'd come into the house and opened the safe, then she must have heard . . . She must have seen him with Lucy.

She knows.

And now she was gone and she'd taken the files and the brides with her.

She needed to be stopped.

And he needed Joseph and the others on his side. "She stole the files."

"What? *The* files? That means she knows . . ."

"Everything!" He raked his fingers through his hair.

Joseph's eyes went wide with fear.

Good. They needed to work together to stop her.

Because he wasn't going down without a fight—and making sure she got what she deserved.

She thought she could take him on, but she'd find she had nowhere to turn for help.

He took Joseph's arm and pulled him out of the office and down the hall. "I'll show you who *Skye* really is."

Joseph gasped the second they stepped close to the bedroom door and he saw Lucy sprawled on the floor in a pool of blood. He covered his mouth. "What happened? Is she . . ."

"Dead. Yes. By your sweet Skye's hand. She killed Lucy and stole from us. She wants to punish me and take us all down."

He'd turn Joseph and the others against Skye and save himself.

"No." Joseph shook his head. "She wouldn't hurt anyone."

"She did." And then a flash of brilliance struck him. "After what you did to her when you were seeing each other, she couldn't stand to find out I was seeing Lucy. She went nuts and attacked Lucy."

He'd wanted to give her everything and she'd turned on him. She deserved what came next.

His friends had warned him about Skye not being a true believer in the new order at Sunrise. They'd hinted that she wasn't that into him. He didn't want to hear any of it because she'd be lucky to be his wife and partner in what was coming. Once she knew the full extent of his plans, she'd believe in him and embrace the power and status she'd have as his woman.

This betrayal revealed her doubt. She was a traitor to him and Sunrise.

And when he got his hands on her, he'd teach her to obey and never turn her back on family and home— or him.

"Poor Lucy." Joseph stood transfixed, grief and disbelief with some guilt mixed in shone in his eyes. "I can't believe Skye would do such a thing. I know I hurt her . . . I just . . . I can't believe she'd do this."

Gabriel didn't want to give Joseph too much time to think about Skye, Lucy, and how this all happened. "She did. And we need to stop her. Find her and the others. Now."

"But Lucy."

For a second he'd regretted what he'd done, but now Lucy would serve his needs one last time. "Lucy's dead. If you don't find Skye, you'll wish you were, too."

Joseph took the threat seriously and turned to carry out his order, but Gabriel called him back. "Start with Gordon Banks."

"The lawyer?" Joseph looked and sounded surprised.

"He's been helping with the new contracts."

"Yeah, so we can partner with other businesses to sell the flowers and harvest so everything's legit." Joseph glanced back at Lucy. "He probably can't help with this."

He'd better not.

"If she isn't there, she'll go to him soon. Find her fast. Before the cops get here. We don't want them talking to the girls."

Joseph understood why that wasn't a good idea with a shocked look and agreeable nod.

He couldn't take the chance that the cops who were friends to him spoke to a few of the underage brides, had an attack of conscience, and called in social services. He'd have them and several disgruntled families on his case then.

Joseph's eyes went wide. "Why would you allow the police onto the property? Even the ones we know. It's too dangerous." Finally, Joseph was getting it. Lucy's death and everything Skye stole exposed their other enterprises and they'd be caught. He didn't worry about the cops locking them up. He feared their dangerous and deadly partners.

Joseph's concerns were more than warranted.

Gabriel's rage grew, but he kept it in check. Nothing and no one would derail what he'd spent months planning. "Find her before she hands over what she stole to Banks. Get those brides back here. If you don't, I'll have no choice but to call the police and let them apprehend Skye for killing Lucy in a jealous rage."

The color drained from Joseph's face.

Gabriel pushed him toward the door. "If you want to save us all from your precious Skye's impulsive and hateful deeds, you better find her fast, or we all go down. Go! Now!"

Joseph ran to do his bidding.

Gabriel walked back to his bedroom and stared down at Lucy, his fury building with every passing minute he got no word from his men that they'd found Skye, until finally his phone rang.

He answered without saying a word, breath held.

"We found the girls."

Finally some good news. And one disaster averted.

Joseph waited a long pause before he dropped the bad news. "Skye got away."

He hung up on Joseph, sucked in a breath, and silently seethed.

Skye. The one threat he never saw coming.

I will make you regret this if it's the last thing I do.

With the brides secured, he dialed 911, happy to set them after Skye. He didn't even wait for the dispatcher to ask about the emergency. "Help me! Help me! There's blood everywhere. Sh-she k-killed her," he pretend-sobbed. Just to make it look good when the cops arrived, he rubbed at both eyes to make them swollen and red despite the fact that he didn't shed a single tear.

When the cops he knew heard the call go out from the dispatcher, they'd come. Gabriel had to make it look good, but also make it clear he expected them to help him if they wanted to keep themselves from getting exposed. In their small town, there were few cops to deal with in the first place.

"Sir, please calm down and explain what's happened."

"She killed Lucy! Why? Why would she do this?" He added a bunch more fake sobs and ragged breaths.

"Is the victim breathing?"

"No. She's dead!" He paused, then wailed, "Oh God, she's dead."

"What is the address of the emergency?"

"Sunrise Fellowship. Please. Send help." He hung up, glared at Lucy, went back to the office, closed the safe, put the carpet back, then ran to Skye's cabin for what he needed. On the way, he ordered one of the guards to warn everyone the police were coming and to keep their mouths shut.

Skye would regret crossing him.

And she'd spend the rest of her life in jail for doing so unless he got his hands on her and killed her himself.

She deserved no less for her treachery.

THE COPS FOUND Gabriel with Lucy lying across his lap and in his arms as he pressed his face into her hair and cried for all to see. None of them knew he'd used a little hot sauce in the eyes to make the tears flow. All they saw was a display of overwhelming grief when he looked up, satisfied to see that at least one of the responding officers was sympathetic to Sunrise. "She's gone."

Officer Hogan squatted in front of him and looked Lucy over. "Who killed her, Gabriel?"

"Skye. Skye Kennedy."

Hogan's eyes narrowed. "Your fiancée?"

He nodded. Better to stick as close to the truth as possible and let the cops believe this was some love triangle that turned deadly than for them to suspect Gabriel.

Officer Hogan knew him and would take his word, but he still had to sell it for him and the other officer. Because of what he had on Hogan, the cop would cooperate. Or else.

"I didn't think she knew about Lucy." He rocked Lucy in his lap. "But I guess she found out. I meant to end it. I told Lucy it was over, but Lucy said she was pregnant, and I didn't know what to do." He let the tears fall and embraced the burn that helped him appear wrecked.

"Did you see Skye attack Lucy?"

"I came in and saw her standing over Lucy. The rage in her eyes . . ." He shook his head, filling the gesture with all his dismay. "She ran." He nodded to the bloody shoe prints he put there using a pair of shoes from her cabin leading out of the room.

He had to admit, they looked pretty damn convincing. Combined with strands of Skye's hair he took from her hairbrush on Lucy's dress, they'd have no reason to look further than the obvious suspect.

"Joseph told me she left with some of the other women who were going into town. It was the fastest way for her to get away."

Hogan took note of everything he said and nodded to the other officer, who spoke into his radio, relaying Skye's name and description to the dispatcher before he walked out of the room.

"Coroner is on the way. We need to process the scene. It's time to let her go."

Gabriel looked up at Officer Hogan with a plea in his

eyes. "I can't. She can't be gone. The baby . . ." He looked down at all the blood and pretended to be torn that he had to leave her. But, in reality, he had bigger, better things coming his way.

Hogan's eyes filled with understanding. "I'm sorry, Gabriel. But we'll find Skye and she'll pay for what she's done."

That's all Gabriel needed to hear.

The other officer stepped into the room again. "They located the van, including several women, outside the home of Gordon Banks. A few of the men from Sunrise were there looking for Skye. They're bringing the women back now."

"Thank God. I didn't want her to hurt anyone else." Gabriel played his part, but silently raged that his men hadn't captured Skye. "Are they all right?"

"Scared. Surprised." The officer didn't seem concerned about the women.

Gabriel wanted to accuse Skye of kidnapping them, but that might lead to them questioning the girls and that's the last thing he wanted to happen.

He thanked God his men got to the girls before that happened and he faced some tough questions and further scrutiny about what was going at Sunrise.

The officer spoke up again. "The ladies had no idea what happened here. They thought Skye was taking them to a movie."

Officer Hogan asked the question Gabriel needed the answer to also. "Did Mr. Banks have anything to say about Skye and why she went to him?"

"Skye rushed into his home, upset and ranting that Lucy was dead, but as soon as the men from Sunrise arrived, she snuck out the back and ran. We have officers searching the neighborhood." The officer Gabriel didn't know as well as Hogan pinned him in his gaze. "How did you know she'd go there?"

"She's been working with Mr. Banks on some business contracts. Maybe she thought he could help her."

"Then why run? The lawyer could have simply contacted the police and arranged her surrender."

He threw up his hands and let them fall limp. "She killed Lucy. She's out of her mind. How do I know what she's thinking?"

Officer Hogan got things back on track. "Join the search for the suspect. I want her found and questioned immediately."

The officer stared down Gabriel for another long moment, waiting to see if Gabriel tripped himself up and said something stupid, but he did the smart thing and shut up. The suspicious officer waited another beat, then left to do as Officer Hogan ordered.

Gabriel let some of his anger show. "What the hell is wrong with him?"

"He's doing his job."

"He better do the job the right way." Gabriel eyed Hogan, letting him know with a look that this better go his way. "She took something I need. When you find her, I expect you to hand it over, no questions asked."

Hogan heard the unspoken threat to his job and health and quickly reassured Gabriel, "Don't worry, I'm on it. We'll find her."

If I find her first, no one will ever see her again.

Chapter Three

DECLAN PULLED his coat closed against the chilling breeze, crossed his arms, and walked down to the barn. His endless to-do list ran through his mind. The number one item remained outstanding because he could never find the time to hire more help, which meant he and his brother Tate had to do all the other items on the list themselves. The truck sat loaded and ready to go so they could feed the cows in the west pasture.

Where the hell was Tate?

"Hello! Is anyone here?" The woman's anxious voice stopped Declan in his tracks.

How long had it been since he heard a woman's voice? This one was unfamiliar.

His brother Drake and his new wife, Adria, moved into their new house last month. His sister, Trinity, moved into the apartment over her *Almost Homemade* shop weeks before that, and Tate and Liz were back in the cabin now that the renovation was complete after their whirlwind wedding and honeymoon. Thank God he didn't have to listen to all that hammering anymore.

Liz started her new job at *Shady Trails Retreat* like three weeks ago, and he hadn't seen her in about that long because she and Tate spent their evenings in wedded bliss, holed up in bed judging by the perma-grin on his brother's face.

Had it really been weeks since he'd heard a woman's voice?

He needed to get off the ranch and spend some time in town, at a bar or restaurant, anywhere with a woman.

He'd prefer in a bed, naked.

But right now, he needed to see who was skulking in his barn.

Declan let his eyes adjust to the stable's darker interior. Several horses poked their heads over their stall doors and whinnied a hello to him, but Declan only had eyes for the woman standing at the other end of the long building, a strip of her belly exposed as she held the hem of her shirt up, loaded with something he couldn't see.

He closed the distance to get a better look at her and find out what she was doing here.

She spotted him coming and a huge sigh of relief whooshed out of her. "Thank God. I was told in town that you were looking for help. I need the money. I haven't eaten in two days." Desperation filled that melodic voice.

It tightened his gut to think the poor thing hadn't eaten in days. It made him wonder what happened to her.

Finally close enough to see her clearly, he spotted the apples tucked in her shirt and the strap of her messenger bag across her chest. The heavy bag hung down her back at her ass. "I found them on the ground in the orchard. I hoped you'd let me have them. They're overripe anyway." She longingly glanced at them, then him, with a plea he couldn't ignore.

At the end of the season, the only thing left in the orchard was rotten or mush. The fruit wrapped in her shirt had to be the best of the pick.

Declan had never gone hungry a day in his life. The woman's desperation got him right in the chest. It was his business to feed people. The cattle he raised right here on this ranch put food on his own table as well as others'.

"I'm here to work, but I need some food to do it. I'll work it off. I'll do anything."

The woman tried to hold on to the apples and adjust the messenger bag strap across her body while eyeing him warily. "Please."

That *please* tore at him.

About to finally say something to put her at ease, he opened his mouth, then rushed forward just as she swayed on her feet, her eyes rolled back, and she started to drop, the apples spilling and rolling in all directions.

Declan caught her before she was laid out flat on the dusty cement and cracked her head open. He hooked his arm under her knees and picked her up just as Tate walked into the stables.

"What happened?"

"She's so fucking hungry and weak she passed out." Unexpected but wholly appropriate rage swept over him. No one should go hungry. "I'll take care of *her*. *You* feed the cattle."

Tate gawked. "Um, who is she?"

"Got me." Declan headed for the house with his awkward load, walked right past his brother, and didn't stop until he reached the house. He brought her inside and tried to lay the poor woman on the sofa. The heavy bag ended up stuck behind her back when he set her rump on the cushion. He slipped his arm free from under her long legs, lifted the strap from her shoulder, brought it over her head, and tugged it out from under her. He set the bag at her feet and gently lowered her onto the pillow.

He stared down at her, hoping she'd move. Twitch. Something to indicate she was okay. The soft rise and fall of her chest gave him some comfort, but he wanted her awake, fed, and not so pale and sickly-looking.

He wondered if he should check her bag for ID and a phone to call someone for her. He didn't even know her name.

Pale, thin, her hair a mass of tangles, dark brown and shot through with red streaks, she lay perfectly still. Worn clothes, dusty from her near tumble in the barn, highlighted her soft curves and just how down on her luck she was. The tear in her dirty canvas shoes with the worn soles made him think she'd been just trying to get by for a long time.

With lots of questions circling his mind and no answers forthcoming, he covered her with a blanket and headed for the kitchen. If she didn't wake soon, he'd get her to a doctor.

Trinity was the chef in the family, but he could whip up something edible. He grabbed the eggs, cheese, and salsa from the fridge. He took a pan out of the cupboard, cracked two eggs inside, scrambled them with a fork, added salt and pepper, then flipped the soft eggs. He topped it with shredded cheddar and folded the eggs in half. While it finished cooking, he stuffed two slices of bread in the toaster and pulled the butter out of the fridge.

The coffeepot had gone cold, so he poured a mug and put it in the microwave to heat.

He slipped the cheese omelet onto a plate, poured the salsa in the hot pan, swirled it around to warm, and emptied it over the eggs.

He turned and spotted the woman standing in the dining area, her arms wrapped around her bag against her chest like a shield.

She jumped when their eyes locked.

"Hey. I'm Declan McGrath. This is my house. I own the ranch." Happy to see her back on her feet, he set the plate on the breakfast bar between them. "Sit. Eat." He grabbed a fork out of the drawer and set it beside the food.

She didn't move, except to glance at the hall that led to the living room where he'd left her passed out on the sofa, and then at the front door. He expected her to bolt any second, but her gaze shot to the food and her stomach grumbled.

He gave her a second to decide, though he suspected she'd need a bigger threat than him before she gave up a hot meal in her weakened condition. She probably wouldn't get far before she passed out again.

To put her at ease, he went to the fridge, pulled out the milk, and poured her a glass to go with the coffee if she wanted it. "Food's getting cold."

"You didn't have to go through all this trouble."

"No trouble. You said you're hungry. I made you a meal." He stepped back until his ass hit the counter across the kitchen from the breakfast bar. He leaned back and crossed one leg over the other, trying to appear at ease so she'd ratchet down her guard and come closer. "I'm Declan," he repeated, because she didn't look like she'd registered anything he'd said since she smelled the food and couldn't decide if she should eat or run now that he had her in his house.

She finally met his gaze for more than a second without looking for an escape. "Skye." She didn't give a last name, but he let it slide for now.

"Nice to meet you."

Her gaze fell to the floor. "I'm sorry about stealing the fruit."

"From what you said, you planned to barter some work for food." That made her relax. "This is my family's place. My brother Tate and his wife, Liz, live in the cabin across the way. He works with me here at the ranch. We've got a few other guys on the crew." His rambling finally made her feel comfortable enough to take a seat, set the bag on the empty stool beside her, and pick up the fork. Before she ate, she changed her mind and downed half the glass of milk. He kept talking. "I need the help. You said you wanted a job. So, what are your qualifications? What can you do?"

With half the omelet devoured during those few sentences, she held up a finger to ask him to wait while she chewed the huge bite she stuffed into her mouth. She swallowed and washed everything down with another chug of milk. "Sorry."

"Don't be. You scared me when you passed out."

"Sorry."

He raised an eyebrow at the second unnecessary apology.

She sighed like the weight of the world pushed all the air out of her and raked her fingers through her tangled hair. "I've been on the road for a week. Yes, I need a job. I ran out of money a couple of days ago and gas on the road about a mile from here. I used to do the books for a large farm. Flowers. Fruits. Vegetables. Eggs. Hay and alfalfa."

"In Montana?" Produce was harder to grow this far north with the shorter growing season.

It took her a second to answer. "Wyoming." She took

a more reasonable bite of the omelet. "I don't know much about cattle, but I'm smart and a quick learner. I'm decent with horses. I'm used to working hard and doing what needs to be done. I'm not averse to getting my hands dirty. I'll give you an honest day's work for a decent wage."

"You said something about eggs."

"We kept one to two hundred laying hens at any given time. The farm was self-sustaining. We ate and sold what we grew or raised."

Nice. She had some of the experience he needed. "My sister and sister-in-law own a store in town. *Almost Homemade*. They make prepared meals and meal kits with fresh, wholesome ingredients for people to cook at home. Think lasagna, other pasta dishes, pizza, soups, salads, sides like mashed potatoes and roasted vegetables, everything ready-made. All you need to do is cook and serve."

"Cool idea."

"Yeah. We supply the beef to the shop, but my sister wants us to do chickens now, too. I've held off because I've had to increase the cattle herd and we are undermanned."

"You'll need to build a structure for the chickens and heat it in the winter."

"Exactly. What I don't know is whether or not it's worth it for me to do it, or have the girls use another supplier."

"I can work up a cost analysis, including the building costs, food, water supply, startup costs, and potential sales price."

He needed that, but didn't have the time to pull the information together. "You can do all that and give me a ballpark number?"

"I try to keep things conservative, but the last few times I did an analysis, we came in between ten and fifteen percent higher."

"I'll keep the short in mind."

"No. That was profit. I add a buffer for unforeseen costs. As long as there's no need for the contingency funds, profits come out higher than I anticipate."

"Smart. Maybe I could get you a job with my sister at her shop in town. Might be more to your liking."

She shook her head before he finished speaking. "I prefer the ranch if you're willing to take a chance on me. I won't let you down. I promise, I'll work hard." When he didn't answer right away, she tried to sell herself again. "The orchard is overgrown. I can work on it and up your yield. You can sell the produce to your sister's shop, too. She could make pies, stuffing with apples, pear tortes. I'm not sure what else you've got out there, but it could make you some money. Any overripe fruit can be given to the chickens along with the alfalfa you grow. Red clover in the chicken run will give them something to forage and attracts the bugs they like."

"You know a lot about chickens."

"The chickens had some acreage to roam. It's cheaper to seed in plants than buy feed, but you'll need to do that, too. The structure will need to be strong enough to keep predators out. Raccoons are strong and smart. Skunks and coyotes can dig under fencing. I haven't seen one here, but you might think about a dog to deter predators."

Declan missed having Sunny around. "Drake, my other brother, took his dog with him to his new place. Maybe it's time to adopt another one. Or two. With this much land, the dog could have a friend of his own."

Her soft, sweet smile caused some sort of strange lightening in his stomach, like the weightlessness when a roller coaster raced down a steep dip. He needed to keep his attraction to Skye in check if she was going to work here. For him. But damn, that smile lit up something inside him. And those guileless light brown eyes, they held a weariness that made him want to make everything better. She seemed so fresh and innocent. Like she needed someone to take care of her, but at the same time, he'd seen her strength in the way she made it clear she'd earn what she needed. She didn't want a handout.

He liked the contrasts.

"I love dogs."

"Me too. Until Drake needed the puppy to get him out of his head and keep him from getting lost in his flashbacks, we hadn't had one on the ranch since we lost Morris when we were teens."

Skye finished off the last bite and tilted her head. "Your brother has flashbacks?"

"Waking nightmares. Whatever you want to call them. He's ex-military. He, uh, faced some bad shit overseas, came home banged up and lost. But Adria changed everything for him."

"How so?"

"She got him. She loved him, flaws and all. He wanted to be better for her, so he worked his ass off to heal and accept who he is now." Declan couldn't help the smile. "And she didn't take any of his shit. She shot down all his excuses. When he said he couldn't do something, she dared him to try."

"We all need someone who cares enough to push us in the right direction sometimes."

"Drake needed a heavy-handed shove. And because he wanted Adria, he knew he needed to stop punishing himself."

Skye's eyes went soft. "She's lucky to be loved like that." Her mouth tilted into a half frown, erasing the dreamy look in her eyes. "In my experience, people don't change." Something dark crossed her eyes, but whatever it was she shook off.

Maybe it was too painful for her to think about.

Declan somewhat agreed with her assessment of people in general. "What happened to Drake changed him. He found a way to be the best of what he used to be and stop fighting the physical and emotional changes and learn to live with them without hurting himself or others."

"I bet that took a lot of strength and determination."

Declan set his hands on the counter at his sides and sighed. "You have no idea."

The front door slammed. Skye jumped and turned toward the sound, her eyes wide and watchful as Tate walked into the kitchen.

Declan introduced them. "Skye, my brother Tate. Tate, Skye. She works for us now."

Tate eyed him. "Uh, no offense, but she doesn't look like she can handle the labor."

Skye didn't take that silently. "I've worked hard my whole life. Just give me a chance. I'll show you. I need this job. I'm out of money and options."

Tate looked at him again.

Declan offered a reason for the hire. Even though Skye wouldn't necessarily be able to take any of the load off his or Tate's shoulders, she offered something they did need. "She knows a lot about raising chickens."

Tate's eyebrows went up with surprise and interest. "Really?"

"Yes, I can help you get the whole operation set up, including planting cover crops for them to forage."

Declan held up a hand to stop Skye from going over all of it again. "She knows what she's talking about and can even work up a cost estimate. She's got some good ideas and wants to rehab the orchard, too."

"Didn't Trinity say something about using the fruit at the shop?"

Declan nodded toward their new employee. "Skye's made some suggestions for that, too."

"Apple pie." The enthusiasm and hope in Tate's voice made Declan and Skye smile.

"If I can find enough good apples out there now, I'll make you one myself."

Tate didn't hesitate. "You're hired."

Skye stood next to the stool, still keeping a safe distance away from them. Her caution didn't bother Declan. She didn't know them. The longer she spent with them, the more she relaxed. But he couldn't help but feel like she held something back. Or was hiding something.

He wanted to ask a dozen questions.

What was she doing in Montana if she used to live in Wyoming?

Why did she leave home?

Did she leave someone behind?

With the way she kept him and Tate in front of her, was she running from trouble? A man?

The thought that someone had hurt her made his blood boil.

"I've delayed you long enough. Let's get started."

Tate cocked his head and eyed Skye. "Uh, no offense,

but maybe you want to get cleaned up before you start work."

Skye took Tate's wrinkled nose in stride. "I smell that bad, huh?"

Declan stepped in before his brother stuck his foot in his mouth and really offended Skye. "You don't have to start today. Get settled and come back tomorrow morning."

Skye's gaze dropped to her worn shoes. "I, uh, don't have a place to get settled. I was hoping you'd pay me at the end of the day so I can get some gas for my car, maybe a room for the night to shower. And sleep." The hopeful look on her face did him in.

He glanced at Tate, who acknowledged his unspoken decision with a nod. "Tate and I will go get your car. There's a room with your name on it upstairs. Tate took his stuff to the cabin, so the room is pretty bare, but it's got a bed and it's right next to the bathroom." Because she was already shaking her head, not wanting to take advantage—he liked that about her—he added, "To earn your room and board, help keep the house clean and take on some of the cooking duties."

"Especially if you want something good to eat. Declan probably won't kill you, but, trust me, you'll eat better if you make it yourself."

Her eyes narrowed with suspicions. "Why are you guys doing this?"

That was easy for Declan. "We have a sister. If Trinity needed help, we'd want someone to step up and give it to her. No strings attached, Skye. I wouldn't hire you and do all this if I didn't think you'd put in the work and appreciate it."

Relief filled Skye's beautiful eyes. "I don't know what to say."

Tate, always so easygoing, put Skye at ease. "Deliver on the apple pie and we'll call it all even."

Declan added, "Lunch is at noon. Tate hates mayonnaise on his sandwich."

"Declan is a five-year-old and loves peanut butter, grape jelly, and nacho cheese chips. You don't have to cut off the crust."

Skye tried to hide a smile, but failed.

Declan took his brother's teasing in stride, because he knew Tate was just trying to score points with Skye and get her to like him and be at ease here. Tate would never cross a line when he'd already put a ring on the love of his life's hand. He and Liz, they were everything to each other.

Still, he checked the urge to shove his brother away from Skye.

He acknowledged the jealousy for what both his brothers had found with the women in their lives. He wanted something like that for himself.

He couldn't deny Skye got to him. Something about her drew him in. Maybe it was as simple as the fact that she needed help and he was hardwired to protect and provide.

"There's some roast beef and sliced sharp cheddar in the fridge."

Skye nodded. "Got it. And dinner?"

Declan pushed away from the counter and took a couple steps closer to her just to see what she'd do. It pleased him that she didn't back away, even if she did carefully eye him. "It's my night to head into town and pick up our meals at *Almost Homemade*. And check on our sister. Don't tell her that, though. It pisses her off as much as she loves having overprotective brothers."

"Can I tag along? If you're serious about advancing me some pay, I need to pick up a few essentials." She pointed to her tangled hair. "Like a brush and shampoo."

"Did you leave home with nothing?" The intrusive question popped out of his mouth.

"It's been a rough week." That's it. That's all she gave him.

He and Tate exchanged another look, both of them wondering what she didn't want to tell them.

Declan decided to give her some space and time to settle in and get to know them better before he pushed for more background on her and whatever happened to bring her here.

"Let's get to work. We've got a long day ahead of us. We'll start by getting your car while you get cleaned up."

Her head dropped. "Thank you." The depth of feeling and gratitude conveyed how much she meant it. She looked up at him again. "It's on the side of the main road." She pulled the keys from her pocket and tossed them to him. Of course she kept her distance. "I'll just wash the dishes and take a quick shower, then meet you down at the barn."

Declan nodded and followed Tate toward the front door. His name on Skye's lips stopped him in his tracks.

"Declan."

He turned to her.

"Thank you. For the food, the room, the job, getting my car, everything. I really didn't know what I was going to do if you d-didn't . . ." Her lips trembled and tears filled her eyes. "Thank you."

He hated the desperation in her eyes and words beneath the sadness that called to him to help.

"You're safe here, Skye." He didn't know why he said it, but it seemed she needed to hear it.

The words seemed to ease Skye. She nodded and looked toward the living room.

"Up the stairs. First door on the right is yours. You'll see the bathroom. I'll put your stuff in your room for when you're done showering." With that, he left her to find her way and settle in because he needed to get out of there before the images of her naked in the shower filling his head showed on his face.

He wanted her. The way it overtook him surprised him, yet he couldn't deny it. But more than that, he wanted her to feel safe and like she belonged here.

He didn't think too hard about why or what that really meant to him.

Chapter Four

SKYE WASHED and dried the dishes and put them away after opening and closing most of the cupboards to find where they went. Nervous and uneasy about wandering around Declan's home, she made her way upstairs, smiling at the family pictures lining the wall up the staircase. Smiling faces aged in regression from happy high schoolers back to baby photos as she ascended the stairs.

She stopped on the landing and turned to the open door on the right. Declan promised a bed and not much else. The bare mattress called to her. She'd been sleeping in her car for a week, staying on the move, trying to outrun the nightmare in her mind.

She'd barely escaped Gordon Banks's home before the men from Sunrise showed up. She hated that she hadn't been able to facilitate discussions between the girls and Mr. Banks. She hoped he stepped in and helped the girls before it was too late and they were used and married off to men they didn't love. Men who wanted them for a purpose, not as true partners.

Her thoughts turned to Declan.

She'd never met a man like him outside of Sunrise. His compassion and gentleness surprised her. The generosity he showed, giving her a job and a place to stay . . . she didn't know what to do with that, especially with how so many of the men at Sunrise had changed. It had been too long since she'd experienced something so pure and genuine.

It reminded her of what Sunrise used to be before she discovered Gabriel's secrets.

But not anymore.

A ball of regret rolled in her stomach. Grief flared in her sad heart.

She made her way to the bathroom, found a towel in the cupboard and leftover shampoo and soap, presumably from when Declan's brother lived here. She stripped off her dirty clothes, turned on the spray, and stepped under the hot water, letting it wash away the grime and the tears that fell for all she'd left behind.

She missed her sister and parents. She prayed they were safe.

Thoughts of Lucy and the brutal way she'd been murdered overwhelmed her again.

She needed to do something, but what?

She needed to contact someone at Sunrise or Mr. Banks and find out what happened after her escape.

Gabriel's men nearly caught her at Mr. Banks's home, which meant Gabriel had to know she took the files and that she'd probably watched what he did to Lucy. Luckily, she'd seen them pull up and had run while Mr. Banks went out to try to get the girls to stay and not go back to Sunrise.

What would Gabriel do when he discovered what else she'd done to thwart his plans?

She wanted things to go back to the way they were just a couple of years ago when the focus had been on the farm and working as a group.

How had something so simple and wonderful become so corrupt?

Evil had worked its way into Gabriel's heart and he'd spread it through the community. He didn't appreciate the life they'd lived at Sunrise. He'd wanted power. He'd wanted easy money and didn't care who got hurt.

He thought he could get away with anything. Forcing her to marry him. Even murder.

Lucy had been closer to Skye's sister, Meadow, because of their age, but Skye remembered how sweet Lucy had always been, and how her smile and open heart drew people to her. She'd had her whole life ahead of her. Gabriel stole that from her.

Even though Skye had lived her life on the fringe of society and didn't know how everything worked with law enforcement, she had to find a way to stop Gabriel before others suffered poor Lucy's fate.

She'd found a safe place to stay and hide, but how long could she do either?

How long before Declan and Tate started asking questions?

She cupped her hands and filled them with water, then splashed it over her face, erasing the last of her tears. She didn't have time to wallow in self-pity and the past. She needed to figure out what to do next.

First, she needed money, which meant she needed to get to work.

Hair and body washed and rinsed clean, she shut off the shower, grabbed the soft towel, and dried off. She wrung her hair in the towel, wrapped the towel around her middle, then spent a few minutes combing her fingers through the long, dark strands. It took some time to work out the tangles, but she managed for the most part.

She folded her dirty clothes and stacked them in a pile. They weren't much. Just a few things she picked up at a thrift store in one of the small towns she passed through on her mad dash out of Wyoming. She'd had no plan, just a prayer that none of this was real and she'd wake up from this nightmare soon.

She'd used most of the money she took from the safe to buy a used car. The rest went to her few clothes, food, and motel rooms until the last dollars she had went into her gas tank.

Determined to make the best of this amazing opportunity, she walked out of the bathroom and nearly ran right into Declan coming up the stairs. She stopped short and pressed her hand to the towel at her breasts to make sure it didn't slip. Heat burned her cheeks that he'd caught her in such a state.

Even with the towel covering her, she felt naked.

She expected Declan's gaze to dip, but it remained locked with hers. "Your car is in the driveway. I left the keys on the counter downstairs. I didn't find a purse or anything but these." He held up the two plastic shopping bags from the thrift store.

"Thank you for bringing them up."

"Is this seriously everything you have?"

She nodded, held her dirty clothes to her chest, and reached out to take the bags from him, but he walked into her room and dropped them on the bare mattress. She remained standing in the hallway. She'd never had a man in her room and didn't know the protocol here, especially when she wore practically nothing and he was her new boss.

Declan went to the hall closet, pulled out a set of sheets and a blanket, walked back into her room, and dropped them on the bed.

He stood in the doorway, taking up most of the wide space with his broad shoulders and tall frame. "Tate and I are headed out to feed the herd. We'll be back in an hour or so." He stared at her like he wanted to ask her something, thought better of it, and dismissed it with an almost imperceptible shake of his head.

He left as abruptly as he arrived and she let out the breath she hadn't been aware of holding this whole time. She went into the sparse room, set her pile of dirty clothes on the dresser, and noticed her hands shaking after all her dark thoughts sent her into tears.

Declan probably noticed her puffy eyes.

She needed to pull herself together. Sleep would help, but if she hoped to keep her job and this place to stay, she needed to get moving and prove her worth. She'd give her all to earn her place here.

She closed the door, wishing there was a lock on it, even if she knew Declan would never walk in unannounced. He'd proved to be a gentleman by not leering at her in the skimpy towel.

He'd been kind, giving her food, the job, and this room.

She pulled the towel off, found the pack of plain cotton bikini underwear she'd bought at a Walmart, pulled out the last clean pair, and shimmied them up her legs and hips. She'd scored a pretty lace-trimmed bra on sale and wore that instead of the old one she'd been wearing when she made her escape. The thrift store offered a variety of hand-me-downs. She'd kept her picks to simple T's and a couple pairs of jeans. Good thing, too, because she'd need the heavier denim here on the ranch. She pulled on a purple T and a pair of jeans. She didn't have any more clean socks, so chose the ones that looked the best and stuffed her feet into them before she slipped on her canvas shoes. They would be trashed by the end of the day, but it's all she had for now.

She raked her fingers through her still-damp hair and

left the bed unmade. She gathered all her dirty clothes and took them downstairs, found the washer and dryer in a mudroom off the kitchen, and set her clothes down to take the load of jeans out of the washer and put them in the dryer. She threw in a dryer sheet and dumped her clothes into the washer, filled the soap dispenser, closed the lid, and set the cycle.

One chore done, she headed out to the stables to get to work.

Declan hadn't given her a list of chores, but on a ranch there was always something that needed to be done. She went with the obvious and checked the first horse stall. The big brown horse stared at her just as he let loose a brand new pile to add to the others.

"Looks like you're up first." The stables were well appointed with tools, buckets, and wheelbarrows. She gathered what she needed and opened the stall gate. She had some experience with horses, so the big animal didn't make her nervous at first, but then he tried to take a nip out of her when she dumped the third shovelful into the wheelbarrow. She caught his head just before his teeth sank into her rump. "Hey. Be good."

Declan or Tate had picked up the fruit she dropped earlier and put it on the table next to the sink. She went out and fetched one of the apples and brought it back. She took a big bite to peel off a chunk and held it out in her flat hand for the horse. "Go on. Take it. I'd rather you eat it than me."

The horse finally reached out his head and gently nibbled the morsel off her hand.

"That's a good boy." She bit off another chunk and handed it over.

He didn't hesitate to take it this time. She stroked his long neck, trying to make friends. His soft coat made her want to pet him more. He wanted another apple chunk. She gave it to him and leaned her head against his. "You're really a sweetheart, aren't you?"

He swung his head up and down and searched for another bite of apple. She gave him the last bit. "That's all, big guy. Now let me finish your stall."

She grabbed the shovel and got back to work. The horse stared at her and shifted out of her way when she nudged him. He didn't try to bite her again.

Finished with his stall, she gave him a hug and a pat down his long neck again, closed up his stall gate, and moved down the row to the pretty chestnut mare.

"Hello, sweetheart."

The mare didn't mind the cleaning job and Skye fell into a routine, working her way down the stalls, emptying the wheelbarrow, and going back to complete the job, one stall at a time.

Sore. Tired. She headed back up to the house for a short break. Kinda. The guys hadn't come back yet, but when they did, they'd probably be hungry for lunch. She stopped in the kitchen, washed her hands, and went to the mudroom to fold the load of jeans and transfer her clothes from the washer to the dryer. She wanted Declan to see that she could be useful and didn't take this opportunity for granted.

The refrigerator had all the makings for sandwiches. She found the bread in the breadbox. Obviously. She put together some mixed fruit and roast beef and cheddar sandwiches, no mayo for Tate, found a couple of plastic containers, and put them inside the fridge to keep until the guys returned.

She took the stack of folded jeans upstairs and felt a little intrusive going into Declan's room and laying them on his bed, but that didn't stop her from grabbing the damp towel from his bathroom, loading it with his dirty clothes from the hamper, and carrying the whole thing down to the mudroom. She sorted it, put in a load of darks, started the washer, grabbed her sandwich off the counter, and headed back down to the stables and the office, looking for something to do.

The desk was cluttered with papers stacked on top of a laptop. Other papers were piled and falling over on a wide file cabinet behind the desk. She opened the cabinet and filed away papers in between bites of her sandwich. Once she figured out the filing system, it was easier to sort the papers and drop them in the folders.

Satisfied the office work that she could do without getting into anything confidential on the computer system was complete, she tossed her napkin in the trash and went back into the stables to find the tools she'd need to tackle the orchard.

Declan and Tate had been gone quite a long time. She hoped nothing had happened and they were simply waylaid by work they hadn't anticipated when heading out to check the herd.

She hoped when they returned they found lunch and enjoyed it. She hoped it put a smile on Declan's face. From the short time she'd spent with him, it seemed smiling didn't come easy.

She didn't have anything to smile about either.

She pressed her hand to her heart as thoughts and images of poor Lucy assailed her. She wondered about her parents and sister.

Sick with worry, she wondered for the thousandth time, were they safe?

Not if Gabriel still ruled Sunrise.

Not if he still wanted retribution because she'd escaped with the evidence to take him down.

Chapter Five

Declan rolled his sore shoulders, easing the aching muscles in his back. He'd thought this morning would go a whole other way. But, of course, his best laid plans took a detour when things went sideways.

"What's wrong?" Tate sat beside him with his head laid back against the truck seat, eyes closed. At least Tate had a good reason for being so tired this morning. He'd spent the night with his beautiful wife.

Declan tamped down the uncharacteristic jealousy that evoked and tightened his grip on the steering wheel. "Doesn't she have a family? Someone she can turn to for help?" Declan's hand ached, so he loosened it on the wheel.

"I don't know, man." Tate went quiet for a moment. "You think Skye will stay a while?"

Declan tried not to show how much he wanted her to stay. Something about her intrigued him. He also had a lot of questions about how she'd ended up at the ranch in her condition.

"Right now, I don't think she's got any options. She said she's out of money." It still tied his gut in knots to think she hadn't eaten in days, had run out of gas on a long stretch of road, and had been desperate for help.

"I'm surprised that piece of shit car of hers got her out of Wyoming."

"Everything she had came from a thrift store or Walmart. Seems like she left wherever she came from in a hurry."

Tate rolled his head and opened his eyes. "You think she's running from someone? A boyfriend or husband, or something?"

Something. But Declan didn't want to think of her with some guy who treated her like crap. She hadn't been looking for a handout. She hadn't used her considerable beauty to get what she wanted. No, she'd made a deal to earn what she needed.

He admired that kind of integrity.

"Something is going on with her. After she passed out, I wanted to give her a little space to get used to us before I started asking questions."

"You didn't seem to have a problem moving her into the house and leaving her alone there."

He didn't respond to Tate's amusement. But he did hear a question in there somewhere. "It seemed like the right thing to do for someone who needed food, shelter, and a job. I can supply all three."

"Yeah, but she can't do the job we need three people to do, so when do you think you'll finally hire some ranch hands?"

"I've got some prospects. Until then, she can pick up some of the slack and do the stuff we keep putting off because we're too busy doing the heavy lifting."

Tate closed his eyes again. "And she's nice to look at."

Declan backhanded Tate's chest. "That's not why I hired her."

"It's a perk." Tate grinned. "You're the one who's al-

ways saying you can't get a date because you never leave
the ranch. Now you've got a woman living *in your house*.
Pretty convenient if you ask me."

Declan felt a glimmer of hope, but remained silent.

Tate didn't. "Or maybe it's fate. You're too busy to go
out and meet someone, so someone came to you."

Yeah, right. Because that's how it worked.

Declan didn't even entertain the idea something would
happen between him and Skye. She worked for him. She
wanted a job and a paycheck, a means to get back on her
feet.

And that sounded very much like an excuse and a reason why she'd shoot him down. Maybe he shouldn't be
attracted to her, but he undoubtedly was, one hundred
percent. And he was damn tired of watching his brothers
with their wives, so happy and in love.

He'd been alone a long time now.

But Declan wasn't about to admit that to Tate. "Fate.
Love. You're so sentimental these days."

Tate grinned again. "Who said anything about love?"

Declan had stumbled right into that one.

"She works for us now." Maybe that would shut
Tate up.

"I wonder what she's been doing since we left this
morning."

Declan did, too. He hadn't stopped thinking about her.

Like the immediate desire that swept through him
when he met her, that surprised him, too.

They'd fed the herd, then spent what seemed like an
endless amount of time checking fences, and rounding
up seven wayward cows who somehow made their way
into a narrow ravine and couldn't figure out how to get
back out. A calf wandered away from mom and got stuck

in some brush. Mom stood by bawling and moaning for her babe. Declan scrambled his way through the twisting branches, picked up the hefty calf, and carried him out, not without a few bruising pokes to his legs and one nasty gash from a broken limb that tore open his jeans and leg.

All the while he took care of business, he thought of Skye—wrapped in nothing but a towel, fresh-faced, pale skin glowing and dotted with freckles, breasts mounded at the top of the towel.

He'd tried to keep his eyes locked on her brown, watchful ones, and not make her uncomfortable, but damn, she'd had his full attention. He took her all in and wanted like he hadn't wanted in a long time.

The shyness in her weary eyes had stirred the protective streak in him. He'd wanted to make her feel at ease and at home, so he'd tried to focus on the mundane tasks of getting her settled and not how badly he'd wanted to strip that towel off her and kiss every inch of her creamy skin.

"Declan."

"Yeah."

"It's okay to want her. But you should find out what she's hiding before you get in any deeper."

She was living in his house and had somehow taken up his thoughts. Deep? He feared it might be too late to get out now and hoped whatever she was running from wasn't too serious.

Chapter Six

DECLAN WALKED into the stables with his stomach grumbling and his head scrolling through the list of to-do items he'd hoped to tackle this morning before his day got derailed. While the horses got fed and watered, he still had to clean out their stalls. He stopped by the first gate and peeked in at Bingo, who usually greeted him when he wanted his stall done and to get brushed. Bingo looked at him, but didn't come forward. Declan stared amazed at the clean stall and Bingo's gleaming coat.

"Let's eat lunch before we tackle the stalls," Tate called from the wide-open doors.

Declan glanced down the alley and spied something else off. Someone had swept it clean, including brushing the dust off all the gates.

"Hey, you coming or what? We don't eat now, it'll be dinner before we get a chance again."

Declan walked along the next three stalls, checking each one. He turned to his brother. "They're all done." Just to be sure, he crossed the alley and checked several of the stalls on that side.

"All of them?" Tate called.

"Yep." Impressed, he walked back to Tate. "She said she'd earn her keep and she meant it." He didn't know what else to say. Inside, he appreciated her so much for being true to her word.

Some days he felt like he was drowning in work. She not only did the job, she did it well and went above and beyond.

Tate didn't hide his admiration. "Damn. She must have worked her ass off to get that all done."

Declan agreed and wondered if they'd find her taking a nap up at the house after all that hard labor. Before he followed Tate up to the house, he dashed into the office to pick up the business cell phone he'd left charging this morning, so he could check the messages. He stopped in the doorway and stared at the immaculately clean cabinet top. His gut tightened as disbelief settled in him.

He opened the file drawer and stared at the noticeably fatter folders. He checked one, then another, elated to see that everything had been filed correctly. She'd saved him at least an hour's worth of work, if not more.

How the hell did she get this all done?

He hurried up to the house. He wanted to thank her for doing a great job, but when he entered the kitchen, she wasn't there.

Tate sat at the table eating a sandwich out of a plastic container. "She left one for you."

He opened the fridge and took out the tub, popped the top, and stared at the sandwich and mixed berries she tossed together from the bins of strawberries, blackberries, and blueberries. He thought it a nice touch. He usually ate the berries by the handful right out of the plastic containers. "Where is she?"

Tate shrugged and chewed. "Not here," he said, mouth still full of food.

Declan set his lunch on the table and ran upstairs,

wondering if he'd find her in her room taking a break. Nope. But her clean clothes were folded and stacked on her bed. He turned to go back downstairs and spotted the stacks of clothes on his bed. He walked down the hall and stood in his bedroom doorway, wondering how the hell she had time to wash all his jeans and a stack of shirts.

He went back downstairs and sat at the table across from Tate.

His brother stared back at him. "What's eating you?"

"She did the stables, filed all the paperwork, did the laundry, and made lunch."

Tate sat back in his seat and relaxed. "Yeah?"

"She's only been here for like six hours."

"And put in a good day's work so far." Tate's head bobbed up and down with approval. "We're paying her to do a job."

"I know, it's just, I didn't expect her do so much right out of the gate."

"Seems to me she wants to make a good impression. Done. I'm impressed. You should be, too."

"I am." He just never expected to be. He thought she'd help out, but he hadn't expected her to work so hard. He admired that kind of dedication and work ethic.

"You don't know what to do with yourself now that she did part of what you thought you'd have to do today along with the thirty other things you think are your sole responsibility."

Declan glared at Tate, but the expression quickly faded with the first bite of his sandwich. God, he was hungry. And she'd made the sandwich just the way he liked it.

She paid attention.

She made sure to do everything just right.

He appreciated that more than he could say. It meant

he didn't have to come back around and fix things or worry that she wouldn't do something the way he wanted. "The ranch is my responsibility."

"It's ours," Tate snapped. "I live and work here right beside you. Yes, you took the lead, but that doesn't mean I'm not giving a hundred percent."

Declan swallowed the sweet strawberry and his sour retort, because Tate was right. He didn't treat Tate like a partner. They were brothers. And partners. Declan should try harder to treat him that way. "I know you do. It's just . . ."

"You've got nothing but this ranch. It's your life."

Those words stung, but Tate wasn't wrong. Declan had been feeling how right that was for months. He wanted something more than the day-to-day on the ranch. What exactly that meant, he didn't know.

Tate popped a fat blackberry into his mouth and spoke as he chewed. "You want to see this place continue to grow and succeed. I do, too. But you're a perfectionist. And it's slowing us down."

Declan stilled with the blueberry in his fingers a couple inches from his mouth. "What do you mean?"

"You keep saying you're going to hire more help. You interviewed two people, but for whatever lame reason, they didn't make the cut. Yet you hire her on the spot."

Declan didn't deny it.

Tate wiped his mouth with a napkin. "She's proving to be a good hire so far. Frankly, I'm surprised you gave her a job without a background check, ten references, and a blood oath that she wouldn't do anything around here without your permission and explicit instructions."

"Shut up." Declan usually took the ribbing in stride, but right now, he didn't want to hear it. "I'm doing what I think is right for the ranch. I don't want to hire someone who can't do the job."

"You brought her on, no questions asked."

"What do you want me to do? Fire her? She has no money and no place to go."

Tate held up his hand. "All I'm trying to say is that you took a chance on her and it paid off. Maybe if you took a chance on a few of the other people who have applied to work here, we'd have the help we need and you'd have the time to figure out what is making you so damn unhappy."

"I'm not unhappy." The automatic response didn't ring true to him, or Tate, judging by the eye roll he got.

"Then what are you? Because all I see is you hiding behind work to avoid dealing with whatever it is that's eating you."

He was . . . unsettled, maybe. And to his mind, that was a whole other kind of thing. He went through most days content with his life. But lately, in the quiet hours late at night when he thought about the day's accomplishments and what needed to be done the next day, he wondered what he was doing it all for.

He saw Drake with his new wife and the security business he'd recently bought. Happy didn't begin to describe him.

And Tate. Ever since he and Liz got together and moved into the cabin, he seemed settled and at ease like Declan had never seen him. It was like everything made sense for him now.

Declan got it but didn't. Yes, Adria and Liz brought something new into his brothers' lives. Love. Companionship.

It seemed his brothers had also found something

deeper and more profound that made everything else in their lives make sense.

Declan wanted those things and more in his life.

More than work.

More than the few meager dates he'd had over the last year that didn't turn into anything more meaningful than a few hours of fun. And as he thought about it, it had been months since he'd even attempted a simple date with anyone.

Tate leaned forward on his arms on the table. "Give yourself a break."

He didn't know how to do that. "There's an endless amount of work to do."

"Exactly. But you don't have to do it all yourself." Tate fell back again. "I feel like a broken record. So, what is the most pressing thing on your mind right now?"

"I need to put in the order at the feed store and call the vet to come out and check on the cow we penned with the sore on his back leg."

"I'll do both those things right now. You go find Skye, because I know that's what's really bugging you."

"Where the hell is she?" He hadn't realized he spoke that repeating question in his mind out loud until Tate grinned.

"Go find her."

Instead of pretending his brother was wrong or denying it with some transparent lie, he stood and left the house intent on finding the woman who'd moved into his home and took up far too many of his thoughts.

Chapter Seven

SKYE WISHED she'd found some ear plugs in the shed before she started this project. The chainsaw loudly revved as she cut another thick branch from the overgrown apple tree. With fall setting in, the trees would go dormant for the long cold winter and come back better than ever in the spring. This wasn't the optimal time to prune them, but she'd been careful not to thin them too much.

The branch fell and caught on another limb. She hit it with the chainsaw again and let the two pieces fall the rest of the way down to the ground. Her reach didn't quite meet the next branch she wanted to cut, so she leaned over the top of the ladder, resting her knees against the top rung, planted her hand on the main trunk, and extended her arm and the heavy chainsaw to get it. When the branch gave way, she nearly dropped the chainsaw as the weight of it made her fall forward.

A strong arm banded around her middle and caught her wrist before she let the chainsaw swing back toward the ladder. She caught her breath and glanced over her shoulder at Declan's very angry face.

"What the hell are you doing?"

With her ass pressed into his gut, his chest at her

shoulders because he was so tall, and his warm hand on her arm, she really couldn't quite think of anything to say with his heat and strong body short-circuiting her brain.

Declan took the chainsaw out of her hand, leaned away, put his hand on her lower back, climbed down, and steadied her as she followed him to the ground.

"Are you crazy?"

The unexpected concern and angry snap in his voice made her find her voice. "No. Are you? I had it under control."

"You nearly fell off the ladder. With a chainsaw in your hand!" He shut it off and set it down, stood tall again, then held his hands out to her, but dropped them before he touched her. In fact, he looked like he wasn't sure what he wanted to do. Strangle her or run his hands over her to make sure she was okay.

It hit her then. She'd scared him.

Her heart softened at the concern he had for her. "I'm sorry. You're right. That was stupid. I should have moved the ladder so I could get the branch without leaning over like that."

"I didn't know where you were. And I find you out here . . . what if something happened? How would I know you needed help?"

She appreciated that he cared. "I'm sorry. I'll be more careful."

His eyes narrowed again. "You're not using that thing again."

She scrunched her lips, feeling the anger spark and trying not to let it show, because she really needed this job. "Would you say that if I was a guy?"

His head tilted. "What?"

"I appreciate that you want to protect me."

"You need it if you're doing stupid things like this," he snapped.

"I'm not stupid. I made a mistake."

Declan sucked in a breath and held his hands up. "I'm sorry. That's not what I meant at all." He raked his fingers over his head. "Damn. My heart is still pounding." He pressed his hand to his chest.

She eased up on her defensive attitude and tried again to understand his reaction came from fear and not some backward stance that women weren't capable. "You hired me to do a job. I'm doing it. The second that chainsaw got away from me, I knew I got lucky and needed to take better precautions. I will."

The intensity in Declan's eyes diminished. "You better."

She glared at him. "Did you want something? I've got a lot of work left to do." Since he kept staring at her, she walked past him and started dragging the cut branches into a pile like she'd done at the other five trees she'd finished.

Declan helped her. "I don't expect you do everything in one day."

She used the loppers to cut a long limb in half. She stopped and stared at him. "This orchard is going to take a least a week for me to do on my own."

"I would have guessed two, but your efficiency is off the charts."

"You didn't give me a list of tasks, so I jumped in and did what I saw needed to be done."

"Horse stalls, laundry, filing, making lunch."

She didn't know why he listed it all off like that. "Did I miss something?"

He chuckled under his breath. "On the contrary. I thought maybe you'd clean up the rest of the spoiled fruit on the ground out here, or simply wait for me to get back to tell you what to do. Instead, you jumped right in."

"I appreciate what you've done for me, giving me food and a place to stay. I'll earn it." She didn't know how else to assure him she wouldn't let him down.

"It's not just that I underestimated you."

"Then what is it?"

He seemed to hide a grin. "You surprised me."

They stared at each other for a long moment. Skye didn't know what to say. She thought they were talking about the work she'd done, but his simple words seemed to go deeper. They felt personal. Like *she'd* surprised him. *Her.*

For some reason, tears pricked her eyes. She blinked them away. She'd spent the whole day trying to focus on the job and not let thoughts of Sunrise, Gabriel, Lucy, and her family intrude. She missed her sister. She wondered what her parents thought of her sudden departure.

The worry she carried wondering about their safety flared in her heart and gut.

She didn't know anything but the life she'd had at Sunrise.

Working on the McGrath ranch was familiar, but not.

Declan was a man like any other, but not. He seemed familiar in a way that made her feel oddly connected to him. Maybe it was just that she needed someone to help her and he'd done so without knowing anything about her. Generosity like that was rare. Declan was special.

"Skye, are you okay?"

She stopped her thoughts from turning too personal. She'd just met Declan. He needed her to keep her mind on work. Not him. "Yeah. Fine."

"Thanks for making lunch."

The simple statement made her belly flutter despite the fact she assured herself he was just being nice. "No problem."

"Did you eat?"

Her stomach grumbled even though she ate her lunch. It wasn't enough to make up for the two days she'd gone without any food. "I did, but I guess I'm still hungry."

"You did a lot of manual labor today. It builds an appetite."

Her arms ached from using the heavy chainsaw. "What do you want to do with all this wood?"

"We'll cut and stack the bigger pieces in the wood shed to use as kindling. The smaller stuff we can mulch."

She nodded. "I think I'll hold off on trimming more trees for tomorrow and work on that. If it's okay with you?"

His gaze dipped to her feet. "Are those the only shoes you have?"

She stared at what used to be perfectly good white canvas shoes that were now brown with dirt stains and wet from the dewy grass. The worn spot had turned into a full-fledged hole and if she could feel her toes, she was sure they'd be cold as ice. She wished she'd been wearing her work boots when she left Sunrise. "Yeah. I can probably put them in the washer with the bathroom rugs when I get back."

Declan looked as dubious as she felt about salvaging the shoes. He didn't say so, but picked up the chainsaw and laid it next to the pruning tools she'd stacked under one of the bigger trees.

She noticed the bloody tear in his jeans. "What happened?"

Declan barely glanced at his leg. "It's nothing. Just a scratch."

With that much blood, she didn't think so and kneeled to get a better look. The second she tugged up his jeans and touched his bare skin, Declan went completely still.

She looked up at him. "This is bad. You probably need stitches."

"A couple bandage strips will get me by. I'll take care of it later."

She shook her head, annoyed he dismissed the injury. "The blood is dried. You didn't even clean this. It'll get infected." She stood and went to where she'd set the tools. She found the first aid kit she'd taken from the stables and brought along. Just in case.

"Really, Skye, that's not necessary."

She glanced at a nearby tree stump, then back at him. "Sit."

He stared at her for a good ten seconds, sighed his reluctance, but ended up following her order. He pulled his pants leg up to his knee, exposing one lean, strong leg and the long gash.

She grabbed her bottle of water, squatted in front of him, opened the med kit, and pulled out several gauze pads. She hooked her hand under his solid calf, pulled his leg out straight, and poured water over the cut, washing away most of the blood. She carefully wiped the cut clean, drying it, then used an alcohol swab. It had to sting like hell, but when she glanced up at Declan, she caught him staring at her with an awareness and intensity in his eyes that had nothing to do with any hurt she caused and everything to do with her nearness to him.

It took her a second to break eye contact and finish tending his leg.

She was all too aware of the warmth of his skin under her fingertips as she applied the antibiotic ointment and affixed several small bandage strips across the cut, pulling the sides closed. She did the best she could with the limited supplies, knowing he had no intention of having a doctor stitch it up.

She checked her work, then rose on her knees in front of him. All of a sudden, she found his face inches from hers. Their gazes locked and she caught her breath. His eyes were so blue. His lips tempting. He smelled like the wind, crisp and clean. She was aware of all of that and so much more.

"Not that I want you to necessarily stop, but if you keep doing that, you'll pull the cut clean apart again."

It wasn't easy to tear her gaze from his, but she glanced down and stilled her hands the second she realized she was gently rubbing her thumb along the gash, her fingers wrapped at the back of his calf.

She immediately released him. "Sorry."

Their gazes locked again. He didn't look at all like he wanted her to stop touching him.

The look in his eyes drew her in and made her want to lean in and kiss him. Crazy as that seemed, the urge nearly overtook her.

Both of them remained still and close and let the moment stretch.

He broke the rising tension. "Thank you." His deep voice only tempted her more.

"For what?"

His hand covered hers on his knee. She hadn't even realized she'd put it there. "Fixing up my leg."

"Oh, right. Sure." Embarrassed by her actions and lack of brain function, she abruptly stood and put some distance between them. Maybe that would allow her to think rationally again. "Keep it clean and put the ointment on it a couple times a day and it should be better soon."

Declan carefully pulled his pants leg over the cut, then stood in front of her. "Come up to the house. Wash up, and we'll head into town."

"Why?" For the life of her, she couldn't follow the conversation.

Mirth filled his eyes as he held back a smile. "You need new shoes."

Oh, yeah. Duh!

She tried to regain her composure and tamp down the overwhelming attraction she felt. She reminded herself she needed this job, so she refocused, looked up at the position of the sun, and gauged it was late afternoon, but not quitting time. "I've got a couple more hours of work to do." She needed a little space from him so she could stop thinking about kissing him.

"You work for me, right?"

"Yes." She eyed him.

"Get cleaned up. I'll meet you at the truck in fifteen minutes." He gave her one last long look, then headed across the pasture and back to the stables.

She watched him, drawn to his quiet intensity, taking in his tall frame and long stride, thinking about how he made her feel when he was close. She'd never felt anything like it.

Just when she was about to have her heart rate and thoughts under control, he glanced over his shoulder, caught her staring, and smiled.

It hit her like a beam of light in the dark. Bright. Welcome. A beacon.

She smiled back before she caught herself because

that smile made everything about the big man more approachable. And even more appealing.

Oh sure, she'd thought him handsome. Who wouldn't? But he intimidated her. It's why she'd tried so hard to do a good job. She didn't want to disappoint him. She didn't want to give him a reason to turn his disapproval on her. He seemed to be focused and driven. He hadn't asked her anything really personal. He'd been more concerned with being shorthanded and getting the massive amount of work on the ranch done.

She understood that and admired how he took his responsibilities seriously.

Maybe too seriously if he couldn't find time to smile and have fun.

But what did she know? She'd only been here a few hours.

In that time, he'd shown her he could be kind, generous, and protective. He was a good man.

Unlike Gabriel, who showed none of Declan's finer qualities.

A piercing whistle brought her out of her thoughts. She jumped and stared out toward the stables, where Declan stood and waved his arm for her to come on. She got a move on and headed to the house, anxious to get to town. And to be near him again, though she tried really hard not to let that thought overshadow what she needed to be focused on instead of her boss.

Maybe she could find a library and use their computer to look up information on what happened at Sunrise after she left and if the police knew about Lucy's murder.

Not that the cops would necessarily be helpful.

She wanted to call the compound and speak to her sister or parents, but she couldn't take the chance. Not yet.

The last thing she wanted to do was let Gabriel know how to find her. But the constant worry for their safety gnawed at her gut.

Had he retaliated against them? Had he hurt them?

And what about the girls she left with Mr. Banks? Did he get them help?

Did the girls understand the danger they were in and how they'd been used?

Her stomach knotted with all the answers she didn't know and her fears that she knew all too well what Gabriel was capable of doing to them. To her. As much as she missed home, she couldn't go back until Gabriel was locked up.

A cold chill ran up her spine at just the thought of facing him again.

Gabriel would kill her if she did.

Chapter Eight

WHEN I get my hands on her, I'll kill her.

Gabriel stared down at the two men he'd tasked with finding the traitor who'd made a fool of him.

Skye would pay dearly for it.

"Do you have any news?"

Joseph spoke for both of them. "The cops don't have any leads. No one in town has seen her. It's like she disappeared."

"It's not like it. She did!" The shouting made the men lean back in their chairs and drop their gazes to the floor. Gabriel tried to hold it together, but if the cops couldn't find Skye, he didn't know how he'd find her. She didn't have a cell phone or a car. But she had something far more valuable than the money she stole from him. And he wanted the files back as much as he wanted to get his hands on her.

"Have her parents said anything?"

Joseph frowned. "They're devastated. They can't believe Skye would kill Lucy in a jealous rage." Joseph didn't meet his gaze, but Gabriel saw and felt his skepticism. Not that Joseph would voice it. Not if he wanted to stay in Gabriel's good graces. Joseph was in as deep as him. If he went down, so did Joseph and the other men in his inner circle.

"I hope you made it clear to her parents that finding Skye and bringing her to justice is the only way they will have closure. And that it's in their best interest to help."

The harmony at Sunrise had been disrupted. While he'd laid the blame on Skye, it had naturally transferred to her family as well. They didn't understand why Skye voiced objections, though subtly, against the changes at Sunrise and that it had led to her doing something so drastic and reprehensible. Theft of community funds. Murder of a beloved member.

To them, it made no sense.

But he knew what she was trying to do. She'd undermined his plans and he'd had to put them on hold. For now. That made his inner circle, who were in the know of what was to come, nervous. They wanted to see action. So did he. But he needed to stop Skye before she ruined everything—or got him killed.

She'd spoiled his plans for the weddings that would have quieted suspicions and distracted the community from looking too closely at the changes coming and why they were necessary. They'd had to postpone. Another disappointment for the community.

"I hope you've kept a guard on Skye's family."

Joseph nodded.

"Good. I want to know if they try to leave or contact her in some way."

Joseph's gaze narrowed. "How would they do that?"

"If she's still nearby, they could sneak out to see her, which is why I want them followed. If she tries to call here, I want to know if they are in the offices taking calls.

If they send out a letter, or speak to someone outside the compound, I want to know about it."

Did he have to do their thinking for them? Did he have to think of everything?

"I still can't believe Skye killed Lucy." Joseph's head hung down.

Gabriel didn't care if most of Sunrise Fellowship didn't believe it. He'd chosen Skye to be his because he wanted her, but he also knew that nearly everyone at Sunrise adored her. They believed everything she said. They followed her lead. They worshipped her and did what she said. As his wife, he'd make sure she steered them along the path he chose for them.

Together, they could have accomplished anything.

Now he had a lot to lose if she divulged his secrets.

But she had a lot to lose, too.

And he knew her greatest weakness. "Find Meadow."

"Why?"

Because he wanted to keep a close eye on Skye's sister. And if he couldn't make Skye his bride, the younger version of her might work out to his advantage in more ways than one. Meadow wanted to please. He'd teach her to please him in and out of bed. And the people of Sunrise would see that he didn't hold a grudge against the family. He'd elevate Meadow to the highest rank among them and squash their suspicions that Skye hadn't killed Lucy by convincing Meadow she did.

They'd believe her own sister.

Chapter Nine

Skye sat beside Declan in the truck, completely aware of how his presence filled the space. Something about him made her wholly focused on him. Maybe it was his intensity. He'd made her a meal, took care of her car, got her settled in her room, and left to work, all with a get-it-done attitude. He'd shown her compassion, and his trust and faith in her that she'd not take advantage and would do the job he'd hired her to do eased her mind about moving in with a stranger. He checked off tasks and kept moving to the next one with little emotion. But then they'd had that intense moment when she bandaged his leg, and he'd suddenly smiled at her when he caught her staring at him from the orchard. She'd gotten a glimpse of a whole other side of him.

He might be the most handsomely rugged man she'd ever seen. And he seemed completely unaware of it. Or so it appeared until that devastatingly gorgeous and knowing smile.

What could she say? So she'd been caught gawking at the handsome man. Oh, he had her attention in that department. Any woman would admire his lean, strong body and those intense blue eyes. But his character hit something deep inside her and compelled her to take a deeper look.

He had integrity.

Which made it so hard to lie to him. Even by omission.

She'd had to evade answering his questions. She'd probably do a lot of that if she stayed on the ranch for any length of time. And that made her think of how she'd deceived him in a small way. Yes, she needed the job and money, but she couldn't promise to stay long. And he needed the help.

"Do you have any family?" Declan's deep voice made her jolt out of her thoughts.

"Um, yes." Her stomach tightened with thoughts of them.

He turned that intense gaze on her. "So, you're married? Have kids?"

She shook her head. "No. Sorry. I misunderstood. It's just my parents and little sister."

Declan accepted that with a nod and a look in his eyes she couldn't quite read. "What are you running from?"

Her stomach dropped. She should have expected the blunt question. "I just needed to get away." Her quick answer made his eyebrows draw together.

"How'd you end up in Montana without any money and no place to go?" He had her there.

Damn. "There was some trouble back home. I needed to get away and figure out what to do next."

Declan side-eyed her. "Trouble with a boyfriend?"

Is he fishing?

Of course he is. He thinks I'm in trouble.

You are! that voice in her head shouted.

She focused on what he asked.

"No boyfriend." Even the thought of Gabriel seeing

her that way made her stomach knot. She couldn't believe he'd wanted to marry her. It wasn't like they had a deep connection, or even an infatuation with each other. Not like the spark of attraction she tried to hide from Declan.

She didn't feel anything for Gabriel. She didn't think he felt any affection for her either. He tended to have an agenda for everything he did.

"Trouble with your parents?"

"No."

"Sister?"

"No." She hoped Meadow and her parents were okay. She hated to think Gabriel would take out his anger on them.

"I know you're hiding something." His deep voice held a lot of concern.

She appreciated it, but . . . "I simply wish to keep my personal life out of . . . this. We barely know each other."

Declan had enough on his plate without her adding a heaping helping of her troubles to it.

"I'm trying to get to know you. You're living and working on my ranch. So if you don't want to tell me what sent you on the run, tell me something else about *you*." At first, it sounded like an order, but then he glanced at her, all interest and openness in his eyes. "Favorite color?"

She gave in to the simple inquiry and the charm she found in him despite the fact he wasn't trying to be endearing in his direct way. "Every shade of green." She stared out the window at the beautiful trees and hills. "Just look at it."

"I love being outdoors," Declan admitted, his voice soft, like they shared a secret.

"Where I grew up, being outdoors most of the day, helping out in the fields, and doing chores was just how we lived our lives." She wished life were as simple now as it had seemed when she was a child.

"That's why you know how to trim the trees. You did a better job than I expected."

She didn't mind that he underestimated her. She'd shown up out of the blue without giving him concrete proof or even a reference she could do what she promised. She'd had to work hard her whole life. She'd prove herself to Declan.

"We grew all our own fruits and vegetables. Tons of flowers we sold at farmers markets."

"Were you homeschooled?"

"Yes. My father and mother were both teachers. They wanted a simple life, but working in public education had them struggling to make ends meet. They believed in community and found a place where they could raise me and Meadow in a life that wasn't all about having more but being connected to people, the land, and love for all."

"Sounds like an idyllic childhood."

It had been. But now that life was in jeopardy for her and everyone else who still believed in the Sunrise of her childhood. "For the most part I loved it. I didn't know any different. But as a teen, I noticed the things other people had that we didn't."

Declan settled back in the seat, eager to hear more. "Like what?"

"TV."

His gaze shot to hers filled with surprise. "You didn't have a TV."

She chuckled at his shock. "No."

"No watching football or baseball games?" He sounded like he just couldn't fathom such a thing.

"We played in the field. Soccer, too. Several people played instruments, so we had music, but not like what's on the radio." She waved to the dash and the country song playing low in the background. She didn't know the artist or the song, but she liked it.

"Did you have electricity?"

She found herself laughing at his amazement and in-credulity. He must have thought she grew up in some re-mote cabin. Close. "Yes. And running water." He gave her a sheepish grin, so she gave him a break and told him more. "No internet. Until recently. We only used the computer for spreadsheets and documents to run the business. Only a couple of us learned to use it. We lived a simple life on the farm."

"So you never went camping or swimming or to a movie?"

"We'd camp out on the property in the summer and sleep under the stars. There was a big pond. Everyone learned to swim. Going to the movies was a treat a couple times a year, usually a kids' movie."

"Wow. It seems so strange in this day and age."

Yeah. Which is why Gabriel, and the others in his circle, rebelled against their way of life. With him in charge, they'd gotten more technology aside from the two computers they used in the offices that were strictly for operating the business, not for surfing the internet. Gabriel insisted they needed satellite TV in his home and a couple of the communal cabins. Rumor had it they watched a lot of risqué movies during their parties.

"Do you have a driver's license?"

She took pride in that. "I'm one of the few from home who do, though most everyone learns to drive despite not getting a valid license." She clenched her hands together in her lap. "The thing is, when I left, I didn't have my bag, so I don't have it with me."

"Can you ask someone to send it to you?"

She turned to stare out the window at the beautiful landscape, homesick and feeling lost in this big world. All she wanted to do was go home, but the home she once knew didn't exist anymore.

"I don't know." She didn't know if she could ever go home again. As long as Gabriel was there, no way. She needed to figure out what to do with what she'd taken from the safe.

Who could she trust to do the right thing with it?

She needed to contact Mr. Banks. But she didn't know if it was safe to do even that.

Declan side-eyed her again. "Well, that's a problem we can solve with a trip to the DMV. You can get a copy."

She nodded, but felt compelled to ask, "Why are you going out of your way to help me? Like you said, you don't know me."

"What I do know tells me you're worth helping."

"Because you know my favorite color?"

He scrunched his lips. "You're not a thief. You want to earn what you're given. You work hard. You multitask better than anyone I've got working on the ranch. You don't half-ass anything so far as I've seen. I think you've got a great deal of strength and courage."

Stunned, she wished she felt the way he saw her.

"You worry that you're asking too much when something is offered to you. And while I don't know what happened to you, I can see it weighs on you. You're worried about someone, and I don't think it's yourself. Though you've been vague and careful about what you've said, I don't think you've actually lied to me."

"Lies only make things worse." She went with her gut and confided—a little—in him. "You're right, something terrible happened. I'm not sure I can fix it. Someone else is trying, but I'm afraid I'll have to come forward. I'm afraid I won't be able to stop . . ." She couldn't say anything more, not without risking Declan firing her because he didn't want any part of her drama. She'd have no place to go if he made her leave.

She clasped her hands so tight her knuckles ached.

"Are you afraid someone will hurt you?"

She propped her elbow on the door and stared out the window. Her non-answer said it all.

Declan's warm, work-roughened hand settled over hers on the seat between them. "We just met, so I'll give you time to get to know me and trust me, but eventually, you will need to tell me what's going on."

She didn't want to bring him into her mess or put him in danger.

"Until then, I promise, you will be safe on the ranch."

Tears pricked her eyes. She needed that assurance even if it wasn't true. If Gabriel found her . . . she didn't want to think about it. She'd leave before anything happened to Declan or his family.

But for now, Declan made her feel safe.

The grateful words she owed him clogged in her throat. She simply turned her hand, linked her fingers with his, and squeezed to let him know she appreciated the sentiment even if she didn't believe anyone could keep her safe if Gabriel, or the others, came after her.

Chapter Ten

Declan didn't know what possessed him to take her hand. Whatever it was kept him from releasing her. The spark that shot through him when they touched spread a warm buzz along every single one of his nerve endings. It had been a long time since he'd been this aware and drawn to a woman. It started when he had her in his arms as he carried her up to the house and she fit so perfectly there. He hadn't acknowledged it at the time. He didn't want to be reminded of it now.

She worked for him. End of story.

But something about the vulnerability mixed with fear and uncertainty in her eyes woke up all the protective drive in him. Whatever happened to her that left her spooked and on the edge of running again made him want to do a hell of a lot more than reassure her that she'd be safe with him. He wanted to slay all the demons lurking in her mind and stop anyone who dared try to hurt her.

He told himself he'd do it for anyone in trouble. True enough. But it quickly became clear the longer he spent with her, and from the simple touch they shared, this was developing into something personal. And intimate, judging by the way her hand felt so perfect in his.

It had been a long time since he'd been with a woman,

and the urge to draw her close and kiss her overtook him hard and fast. The desire running through his veins stunned him. He rationalized it away with how long it had been since he'd kissed a woman, let alone slept with one. It wasn't her, but a desire to slake his lust.

No it's not.

That little voice in his head irritated him.

He didn't want to take advantage of her. She obviously needed help and comfort after something happened to her.

He'd give her that and remember he wasn't the kind of man who expected something in return for doing something nice.

He pulled into an open spot right in front of the mercantile. He didn't look at her, but gave her hand a soft squeeze before he reluctantly released her. He couldn't help it or deny himself the pleasure of feeling her skin slide against his like it had when she patched his leg in the orchard and his whole body had become aware of her.

He hopped out of the truck and went around to her side to help her down, but she was already out and closing the door when he got to her. He held his hand out toward the shop's door and walked beside her with his hand at her back. Manners. Nothing more. He'd do it for any lady in his presence.

Yeah, right!

He dismissed that with a frown and led her toward the clothing section. "What do you need?" He stared at the stacks of sweaters and pants, the hanging shirts, and wall of shoes, thinking she needed a little of everything. He hoped she'd hurry because he hated shopping.

She walked through the clothes to the rain boots. "These should work."

Yeah, but they wouldn't be comfortable for working in all day. "You'll need some regular boots, too."

She chose a pair of green rain boots and the least expensive brown cowboy boots, both in a size six. She kicked off a canvas shoe and pulled on the ugly boot. She stood on it and half her mouth dipped in a frown.

He checked out the rest of the selection, found a pair he thought would work better, grabbed the size six box, and handed it to her. "Try these."

"They're three times the price."

"And probably a hundred times better fit and comfort, not to mention better-looking."

She narrowed her eyes. "It's not about how they look. I can't afford them."

He just wanted to get the stuff and go. "You work for me. You need proper gear. Try them on."

"Declan, I can't let you spend that kind of money on me."

"Why not? I can't have you running around the ranch in bare feet. What good will you be to me if you're wearing those uncomfortable boots and you can't stand or walk in them after a couple hours?" He planted his hands on his hips and stared down at her, waiting for her to see reason.

She needed the stuff, so why didn't she just let him buy it for her?

He wanted to do it to make her happy.

She rolled her eyes and tried on the boots. She stood in them and rocked back and forward. It didn't take a genius to recognize the look of satisfaction in her eyes.

"Feel good?"

She stared down at them, then looked at him through her lashes and reluctantly admitted, "Yes."

"Great. You need a couple pairs of jeans, shirts, and

a jacket." He waved his hand out toward the array of clothes and waited for her to get a move on and make her selections.

She repacked the boots in the box. He took it and stacked the rain boots on top, ready to be her mule and carry the load. She walked among the racks, surreptitiously checking prices on tags before she made a choice.

"Skye."

She brushed her hand over a sweater that looked super-soft and comfortable but cost more than the boring cable knit she plucked off the sale table. "Yeah."

"Are you going to make me pick up all the things you really want and passed up like you did the boots?"

He hated that she denied herself what she really wanted just to save him a few bucks. He appreciated it, but he'd rather she be happy with the items and comfortable in them than save him money he could afford to spend for the few things she needed.

"I don't need that much." She held the sweater and a single pair of jeans.

He rolled his eyes and plucked the super-soft green sweater from the rack. He didn't know what it was made of, but he'd never touched anything so soft. "You want this one, don't you?"

Her too-tempting lips pressed into a crooked line. "It's really nice."

"Awesome." He pulled the same one in blue and purple from the rack. "Put that other one back and grab two more pairs of jeans and a few T-shirts."

It took her a second to move, but she finally gave in and picked out the things she really wanted, surprising him by walking by and grabbing a hooded sweatshirt and a heavy jacket to go along with everything else.

"Is that it?" he asked, genuinely ready to buy her more if she wanted it.

She frowned but dashed over to the sundry aisles and grabbed some personal items: a brush, toothbrush, toothpaste, razors, deodorant, and lip balm.

She met him at the counter. "You have no idea how much I appreciate this." It was written all over her face. He heard it in every syllable she spoke.

"Like I said, you need proper gear." He hoped that benign answer relaxed her.

If she'd left without grabbing her purse and wallet with her license, then she really didn't have a dime to her name. He'd fix that with a paycheck, but he had a feeling she'd always feel uncomfortable accepting a helping hand.

Everyone needed one once in a while.

He was happy to help. It made him feel exceedingly good to do this for her.

He'd never bought a woman clothes. He wasn't big on gifts for women he dated either. He'd done the flowers thing a couple times.

With Skye, he wanted to do whatever would make her happy.

She laid her hand on his arm and electricity shot through him. Her eyes brightened and went wide for a brief second.

Yeah, she felt it, too.

"Thank you for being so kind."

"My pleasure." It would be his pleasure to do a hell of a lot more. His long-dormant sex drive revved up and he tried to tamp down thoughts of peeling off her faded jeans and stripping away any and all barriers until he had her laid out below him.

Maybe he thought about it, but he didn't act on it, and notched his chin toward the counter. Her hand slid from his arm, and he missed it and felt the echo of her warmth all at the same time.

The saleswoman gave him a knowing smile as he handed over his credit card. He'd been in here a lot over the years. She'd probably spread the word that he'd bought Skye clothes through town before they ever reached *Almost Homemade* to pick up the food order from his sister. Small towns. Everyone knew everything. And the smallest thing, like doing a favor, could be misconstrued and blown out of proportion faster than a wildfire spread across a dry field.

He signed the sales slip, dropped the pen, put his card back in his wallet, turned to Skye, and took the bag from her. "I'll carry it. Let's go." He waited for her to head for the door first.

"You two have a good day, now," the saleslady called after them, amusement in her voice.

He rolled his eyes. Of course she had them paired up in her mind.

His gaze landed on Skye's swaying hips and sexy ass and his mind had them doing all kinds of things together, too. All he wanted to do was spend time with Skye. He wanted to know so much more about her.

He wanted to explore the feelings stirring inside him.

He opened the truck door and waited for her to climb in. Before he closed it, she snagged the bag handle and held tight. "Um, mind if I pull something out?"

"It's your stuff." He bent at the knees so she could reach into the huge bag.

She pulled out the green sweater, rubbed the soft material against her cheek, and gave him a huge, beautiful smile. "I don't think I've ever worn anything so soft. Thank you for pushing me to get it."

Her happiness felt like a punch to the gut. It woke him up and made him take notice. All he wanted to do was make her smile like that again. Tongue tied, he tried to get his words out. "Uh . . . I'm glad you like it."

She slipped it over her head, pulled her long brown hair out of the collar, and shook out the waves.

He watched, transfixed.

She pulled the tag off the cuff and held it up while she rubbed her free hand over the material again. "Worth it."

Yes, you are.

He handed her the box. "Put the boots on. Those other shoes are toast."

She set the box on her lap and opened it. Her eyes lit up, seeing them again. Her fingers trailed over the soft brown leather and the rose-and-vine pattern. "They're so pretty."

You'd think he bought her diamonds.

"You deserve pretty."

Their gazes locked. He couldn't look away, but fell into the light brown depths of hers. For a long moment they simply stared at each other, letting the time stretch and what they were feeling build. Neither of them said a thing.

They didn't need to.

He caught himself leaning in to kiss her and reluctantly pulled back before things went too far. It took him a second to find his voice. "Buckle up after you put those on." He closed her door, opened up the back one to stow her things, then went around to the driver's side, climbed in, and started the truck.

She bent her knees and pulled her feet up to show off the boots. "You like?"

He didn't even look at them, but answered, "Yeah. I do."

He liked her a hell of a lot more than he should.

SKYE GOT THE distinct feeling Declan was talking about more than her pretty new boots. At least, she thought so until he spent the drive to his sister's shop completely ignoring her. She felt the wall he'd put up between them. Maybe they both needed it to keep the undeniable attraction in check. They barely knew each other. They worked and lived together.

While she'd dreamed of someday finding someone to have a real and lasting relationship with, right now wasn't the time or place.

She'd been completely in the dark about what happened at Sunrise since she bolted. She needed to find out what happened, so she could figure out what to do next. Though she could tuck away her worries and fears for a little while at a time, they lingered in the background, gnawing at her gut, pushing her to do something. Fast.

They drove by a police officer who'd pulled over a huge four-wheel-drive jacked-up truck to give the driver a ticket. Skye turned her head to watch the guy behind the wheel waving his hands out the window, obviously pleading his case even as the cop ignored him.

She wondered if he'd ignore her if she told him what she knew.

"Pete gets a ticket for driving too fast in town about every other week." Declan shrugged his wide shoulders and pulled into the parking lot of a beautiful brick building painted white with black shutters and an *Almost Homemade* sign.

Declan parked the truck, slid out, walked around to her

side to help her out, then closed the door for her. She appreciated the manners, but missed the touch of his hand on her back he'd used at the downtown mercantile. She didn't know what she'd done to shut him down—maybe it was for the best—but he held himself away from her as they made their way to the front door. He held it open and stood back to let her pass. She stood in the entry, took in the amazing smells: garlic, cheese, biscuits, and chocolate all hit her nose in different notes that made her stomach grumble and her mouth water. "Oh, wow. This place is amazing."

She'd often thought about opening a shop on or near Sunrise. A place for them to run a business that invited the town people to embrace them instead of spread silly rumors about the place they didn't wholly understand. She wanted to take what they grew and sold at farmers markets and have a year-round location to sell flowers, produce, meals, and baked goods.

Declan stopped short beside her and glanced around the shop, looking at it like he hadn't seen it in a while. "They do a really good business. I eat well." He sauntered off toward the counter just as a beautiful blonde came around and threw herself into his chest, wrapping her arms around his neck and hugging him close.

Skye didn't recognize the instant wash of emotion for what it was until the urge to pull that woman away from Declan hit her. Living and working together her whole life with the people at Sunrise, she hadn't experienced jealousy more than a few times in her life, and never like this. Not an all-out, hands-off, stay-away-from-him kind of thing.

It shocked her.

She barely knew him.

And yet . . . when he released the woman and waved

Skye over, she walked in the boots he'd bought her, wearing the sweater he'd known she wanted, and somehow that made her feel connected to him. Like he was hers.

"Skye, this is . . ."

"Your girlfriend," she finished for him, understanding why he'd pulled back from her all of a sudden. He was taken.

"Ew." The woman scrunched up her face and glared at Declan.

"Yuck," he shot back, then cleared things up. "This is my sister. Trinity." He pointed to the pretty blonde behind the counter. "My sister-in-law, Adria. She's married to my brother Drake."

It all made sense now. "That's right, you have two brothers."

He nodded. "And one bratty sister."

Right. Why couldn't she think properly around him?

"And who is this?" Trinity asked Declan, nudging his arm.

Adria chimed in. "Yeah, Declan, who's your friend?"

Declan rolled his eyes, clearly not happy to be put on the spot. "This is Skye. She started work at the ranch this morning. I brought her into town to pick up some stuff. Do you guys have my order?"

Trinity held up a finger. "Wait. Back up. She works at the ranch? You"—she poked him in the chest—"hired someone. Her."

"Yes." Declan rolled his eyes.

Trinity turned to her. "Um, who are you?"

"Skye. I work for him," she repeated lamely. "Well, both your brothers, I guess."

"And what do you do, Skye?" Adria asked from behind the counter, both women checking her out.

"Whatever needs to be done." Declan hadn't given her a list of responsibilities, so she wasn't quite sure what else to say.

A smile bloomed on Trinity's face as she turned to Declan. "What exactly do you need her to do for you?"

Declan's eyes narrowed and turned hard with a warning. "She's working on the orchard so you and Adria will have fresh fruit from the ranch. She was raised on a farm and knows all about growing stuff. And"—he paused for dramatic effect, then continued—"she knows everything about raising *chickens*."

Trinity's eyes went wide. "Really? Truly? That would be amazing, if we could buy direct from the ranch."

Skye felt much more comfortable talking about business. "I'll put together a prospectus for Declan on building the structure and everything required to feed and care for the birds."

That raised an eyebrow on both women.

Adria leaned on her arms on the counter. "You can do a cost analysis on all that?"

"I used to do the accounting for the farm and business."

"What kind of business?" Adria asked, though she had Trinity's full attention, too.

"We raised the chickens for eggs and grew produce and flowers. We sold everything at local farmers markets, along with some baked goods, like pies, cakes, and breads. The apple, pear, and cherry trees on your ranch will provide you with plenty of fruit to do all that here."

Declan stared down at his sister. "Satisfied?"

Trinity gave him a mischievous grin. "Not yet."

"God help me." A long-suffering sigh escaped his parted lips.

"Do you have family in the area?" Trinity asked.

"No. I'm, um . . ."

Declan stepped in. "Look, sis, she's got nowhere to go and needed a job. I gave her one. Double my order, so we can get home."

Trinity's eyes went wide and she exchanged surprised looks with Adria.

Skye knew, just like Declan, who tilted his head and stared up at the ceiling, that they'd gotten the wrong idea. "Uh, listen, really, I'm working at the ranch for room and board and . . . whatever."

Declan's sisters' broad smiles and giggles only intensified.

"Knock it off," Declan ordered, then glanced at her. "Sorry. They're messing with *me*." He took an intimidating step toward his sister. "Just get the food."

"Happy to help."

Declan looked like he wanted to strangle Trinity. She knew the feeling well. She'd often wanted to stifle Meadow's needling.

That thought brought up all her fears and anxiety about her family and what was happening back at Sunrise.

To hide her rising concerns from Declan and his sisters, Skye turned her back to them. She hoped he took it as a sign she knew his sisters were teasing and nothing more.

The shop really was wonderful. And after not eating for several days, the smells and temptation to try everything, especially the sweets, sent her hunger into overdrive.

"Ready to go?"

She jumped, not realizing Declan had moved right up behind her. She spun around to face him and stared up into his brilliant blue eyes. "Sure."

He handed her a plastic container filled with brownies,

an apple tart, and two cinnamon rolls. "If your stomach growls any louder, you'll scare little kids away."

The belly laugh came out of nowhere, just like Declan's amazing smile. "Thank you."

"I thought you might start drooling all over your new boots."

She laughed at that, too.

"I love your sweater," Trinity said. "It's a great color on you."

"Thank you. Declan bought it for me."

The second Trinity cast her surprised and knowing gaze on her brother, Skye knew she should have kept that tidbit to herself.

Declan spun on his heels and headed for the door. "Let's go."

"I'm glad you won't be eating alone anymore," Trinity called as Declan held the door open for Skye.

She passed him just as he groaned and followed her out. He held the truck door for her, too, and leaned in to set the food on the seat beside her.

Before he shut the door, she blurted out, "I'm sorry I made them think something was going on that isn't."

He stared at her for a long moment, and though his gaze didn't leave her face, she felt it everywhere and wondered if what she'd just said was a total lie.

"Like I said, my sister's a brat sometimes."

Skye got that. Declan took his sister's teasing in stride, but she wondered if it bothered him on a deeper level.

"If my staying with you is a problem—"

"It's not." His quick response surprised her. "Besides, you don't have anywhere else to go. Do you?"

She hung her head and clasped her hands in her lap. "No. Not right now."

"Then let's head home and have some dinner after you spoil it with one of those treats I know you're dying to eat."

Her lips quirked into a half smile and she side-eyed him. "Want some?"

Heat and desire filled his eyes. "Yeah. I do." He closed the door after those telling words.

She sucked in a breath and tried to wrap her mind around a man like *him* flirting with *her*.

Unless she was completely wrong, because let's face it, growing up at Sunrise, separated from the outside world for the most part, she had little experience to draw from to determine someone like Declan's motivations and intentions.

"Are you okay?" Declan sat behind the wheel, staring at her.

She met his inquisitive gaze with one of her own. "Do you like me?" She couldn't believe she blurted that out. Heat rushed up her face and made her ears burn. But in order to know she had to ask.

Declan chuckled and smiled at her. "Yeah. I do." He started the truck, pulled out of the parking lot onto the main road, and drove them out of town.

She hoped her soaring heart didn't fly right out of her chest. To distract herself from staring at Declan, she opened the plastic container and pulled out the brownie, broke off a big chunk, and held it out to him.

He took it, his fingers brushing against her hand. Whether by accident or on purpose, the effect was the same: an electric little zing shot through her and made her heart race.

He liked her.

She liked him. She tried to think of something to say to get him talking so she could get to know him better.

"I love it out here." She stared at the gorgeous landscape. "Nothing but nature." She loved watching the rolling hills and trees pass by as the setting sun turned the sky pale gray and peach. Town had too many people rushing to get from here to there, buying things they didn't really need, trying to impress others instead of finding what really made them happy.

At least, that's how it seemed to her.

"I barely spend any time in town anymore." He took a bite of the brownie. "And I like you even more for sharing this with me. They're my favorite."

"Mine, too." The blush heating her cheeks this time didn't embarrass her, but did make her aware of how much Declan affected her on a physical level.

She liked that they had a few things in common and hoped she'd find more. If she had time.

Maybe it was crazy to . . . This whole thing was crazy.

She'd experienced so many new things since running from Sunrise. She stole, ran away from a problem instead of standing up to Gabriel, experienced unimaginable fear, hunger, loss, and sadness.

She'd finally found a man who turned her head and made her wonder what could be.

Why him?

Why now?

Why was any of this happening?

Her very structured life had been turned upside down. She missed that life and her family. She missed feeling like she was a part of her community, instead of hiding in the shadows, trying to fix what most of them didn't even know was broken.

She loved living at Sunrise until things slowly changed.

She wanted more of that sense of belonging and being just as important to everyone there as they were to her.

It wasn't like that anymore.

Gabriel elevated some and made others feel left out.

He was setting them up to serve others outside the group and a purpose so far outside their beliefs it forced her to act.

He may have wanted to make her his wife, but he hadn't intended to make her an equal partner.

She wanted that with a man. To be important in his life. To know she was loved and valued.

Declan's hand settled on her shoulder. "It's going to be okay, Skye."

How did he know she needed to hear that?

She appreciated the sentiment, even if she didn't believe it. Everything in her life had changed and it would never be the same again.

"If you tell me what's going on, maybe I can help." Yeah, Declan was the kind of man who took a problem, figured out how to solve it, and did what needed to be done.

He'd been so kind and giving. Involving him in her problems meant exposing him to potential danger and worse. She couldn't do that to him.

"I appreciate all you've done, Declan." She left it at that, because she couldn't stomach the thought of something happening to him because of the trouble she brought with her.

Chapter Eleven

DECLAN SAT on the sofa, feet on the coffee table, a football game on TV, his laptop on his stomach, and a stack of bills and invoices beside him. He entered one of the bills into the finance spreadsheet, caught a glimpse of an interception on the TV, and winced. "Come on." The Cowboys were giving away the win tonight.

Disgusted with his team, he dumped the laptop on the cushion beside him, stood, and headed for the kitchen and another beer to wash down the bitter taste of impending defeat.

Skye walked around the hall corner as he walked out. They slammed into each other.

Her forehead smacked his chin. "Oh my God, ow!" She reached up and brushed her fingers along his jaw. "Are you okay?"

"Fine." He pushed the single word that came to mind out because she'd short-circuited his brain the second her body pressed to his. He'd instinctually grabbed her by the waist when they collided. To steady her. Yeah. That's why he still had his hands on her.

Truth be told, he didn't want to let her go.

Her gaze met his. He fell into the depths of wonder,

interest, shyness, and that dark thing she carried with her ever-present in her eyes.

For a split second, they both leaned in for the kiss he desperately wanted and that interest he saw in her eyes tempted her to take, but at the last second, her shy reserve came back and her gaze dipped to his chest.

She stepped back, making him drop his light hold. His hands felt as empty as his life felt lately.

He wanted to pull her back in.

She stood very still, making him wonder if she wished she was back in his arms, too.

Out of nowhere she held up a fresh beer. "For you. Uh, the floor is wet in there, so give it ten, fifteen minutes to dry before you walk on it."

He took the beer, his fingers brushing hers. He couldn't help himself, even if he should. "Thanks."

Neither of them moved. They simply stood close, staring at each other, the tension building between them.

Her gaze dipped to his mouth and the need to kiss her swept over him once more.

She looked away again. "Um, you're missing your game."

He didn't care about football. Her scent, something fresh and sweet, tinged with . . . lemon—probably from whatever she used to clean the floor—wrapped around him.

She did things like mopping without being asked. Yesterday she'd stripped his bed, washed all the sheets and blankets, and remade it before he went to sleep last night. It made him feel odd to know she'd been in his room. And the second his head hit the pillow, he swore he could smell her. When he slept and dreamed about her, he felt her move against him, her skin next to his, until he woke up reaching for her and found nothing but a cold, empty spot beside him.

He felt exactly that way right now after he'd held her close a moment ago and now they stood a foot apart.

She moved past him and picked up the laptop from the sofa along with the paperwork he'd abandoned.

"Hey, I'm working on that."

She notched her chin toward the widescreen TV. "Watch the men beat each other up. I'll do this."

He'd never met anyone who put things like football in such weird terms. "It's football, not boxing." Everyone he knew binge-watched some show or was obsessed over sports. Not her. She didn't know *The Bachelor* from a *Real Housewives* of whatever. She had a vague idea about *The Big Bang Theory* and laughed through a rerun with him last night. But she'd never seen a *Star Wars* movie. What the . . .

She had seen two of the *Harry Potters*.

Last night she snagged a book on cattle ranching he didn't even know was buried in the bookshelf and took it up to bed with her.

He could think of a hell of a lot more interesting things to do in bed. None of them included reading.

Unless it involved reading her every sigh, moan, gasp, and desire.

It would be his pleasure to do that kind of reading every damn night.

He shifted his position to accommodate his throbbing erection. With her living in his house and underfoot all the time, his hand was going to get a workout. With Skye here, all he thought about and wanted was her.

Skye didn't exactly flirt. It seemed to him she always had something on her mind. But then he'd catch her gazing at him, the way she did moments ago, and he thought . . . but the expression came and went, and she hesitated, and he pulled himself together.

He wished he knew what had her so distracted and if those looks meant what he'd like them to mean.

She settled in the recliner that made her seem small and vulnerable and set the laptop on her thighs. "I'm teasing. I know about football. You worked hard today. You deserve a break."

He took his seat on the sofa, propped his feet on the coffee table, tugged his shirt over the erection-that-wouldn't-quit, and rolled his sore shoulders. "You worked just as much, made dinner, and mopped the floor." He couldn't keep up with her. But he'd tried to keep his eye on her the last few days because he didn't like the thought that whatever trouble she'd left behind had followed her here.

It seemed she spent each day trying to outrun her thoughts. He thought he worked hard. Skye spent the last three days on the move. One task after the next. She didn't shy away from getting her hands dirty and pitching in wherever she was needed. The horses were well taken care of despite that she didn't know much about caring for them to begin with. She learned fast and retained all the little details of what he told her.

The orchard was coming along.

The house hadn't been this clean since his mom and dad moved out. He bet he could eat off the floor in the kitchen now.

"Thanks for the beer." He needed it to cool off after their . . . whatever it was that sparked between them and set him on fire.

But her doing all this stuff for him at home after work

hours seemed weird, especially when he wasn't thinking about her as an employee but something more.

"You always have two. One with dinner. One while you watch TV." She opened the laptop and stared at the spreadsheet.

"Seriously, you don't have to do my work, too."

She gave him a shy smile without really looking at him. "I don't mind. Paperwork relaxes me."

"It's boring as hell." But watching her wasn't at all.

If she wanted to do it, fine. But he thought there might be more to it. He'd seen her trying to be inconspicuous about wanting to get into the office. Why? He didn't know. But he suspected she wanted to get her hands on the laptop.

Why not just ask?

He'd let her use it, no problem.

He'd do just about anything to discover what had her so jumpy all the time. The longer she was here, the worse it got.

To save his sanity, he stopped watching her, mostly, and focused on the Cowboys being thoroughly trounced by a better defensive strategy. Skye settled into entering information into the laptop, giving him a chance to memorize the slope of her cheek and spot the tiny freckle at the corner of her mouth.

Her gaze kept darting to him, the clock, and back to the laptop. He knew exactly when she found whatever she was really looking for and all the color drained from her face.

His stomach knotted. He wanted to jump up and demand she finally trust him with whatever made her eyes fill with horror.

He worked fast when he wanted to, but she input the

rest of the bills and invoices in record time. Unable to hold his tongue any longer, he asked, "Are you okay?"

"Fine." She slammed the laptop closed, stacked the papers on top of it, and rolled out of the recliner, sending it rocking back and forth. "I'll take this down to the office."

"It's fine, Skye, just leave it on the coffee table and"—he was talking to the back of her as she passed in front of the TV and headed for the front door—"I'll take it down in the morning," he called after her.

The front door slammed.

It took everything in him not to rush after her. He wanted to know what the hell was going on, but every time he asked about it, she shut him down. He'd give her a minute to collect herself before he confronted her. And this time, he was going to get an answer, because the devastation and terror that filled her eyes when she read whatever she'd looked up on the laptop said clearly what she'd been denying to him since she got here: she needed help.

He watched another play, but the football game meant nothing when Skye was obviously going through something serious. Unable to wait another second, he went after her.

He didn't hide his intention as he walked down to the stables, but he did stop short just outside the office door when her words beat into him like a jackhammer with every sentence she uttered.

"I did not kill her!"

"I would never marry him."

"Yes, I stole the money to get away."

"He forced those men on the girls. A couple of them weren't even eighteen."

"Please tell me you're safe."

"He's having you followed! What the . . . What about Mom and Dad?"

"You need to leave there. Now. Please."

"I'm safe, but you can't know where."

"Because then he can't make you tell him where I am."

"Please, Meadow, I'm begging you, get out now."

"No!" She sobbed. "Meadow! Meadow." She tossed the cell he kept in the office drawer on the desk. Her head came up and she spotted him standing in the doorway. She hadn't turned on the lights and stood in the glow of the outside floodlights that filtered through the window.

She looked wrecked with tears glistening in her eyes. He'd never seen anyone seem so lost and desperate.

He stepped inside and stood across the desk from her.

She crossed her arms under her breasts and narrowed her eyes, trying to look strong and defiant. "You followed me."

He took the accusation in stride because he didn't care what she thought of him following her on *his* ranch. But because he wouldn't like someone sneaking up on him, he tried to make her understand his concern. "You were upset when you left. I wanted to make sure you're okay. Obviously, you're not. What can I do?"

"This is none of your business."

He hated to admit how much she felt like his business and how much he wanted that to be true.

Hell, she lived in his house, worked for him, ate with him. In just a couple days, he'd seen and experienced what it would be like to have a partner. Someone who touched every part of his life. He liked having her around. She worked hard, spoke her mind, added her two cents when decisions had to be made, and took care of him like he mattered. She went out of her way to show him that when she made sure he ate and took a break from work. She generally added to his well-being just by being here.

Three days and she'd changed everything for him.

Maybe he was just desperate for a woman. Except he'd been with other women. None of them felt quite like Skye did. She filled a space inside him. And with each passing day, she became more imprinted on him and more necessary.

He'd never gotten used to having any of his other girlfriends around so much. He hated to admit it, but he'd enjoyed their company on *his* time.

Probably why none of them lasted. He'd never really committed to them like he'd dedicated himself to the ranch.

Superficial relationships had been enough. Until lately, when he'd watched his brothers fall for their wives and find a kind of happiness and contentment that had always eluded him.

Could he and Skye become more than employer and employee?

Would he even have a chance to find out?

Someone accused her of being a killer.

Who would think *she'd* do such a thing?

Not me.

Not anyone who looked into her eyes and saw the vulnerability and kindness.

She didn't get upset with Trinity and Adria for hinting about something going on between him and her and teasing them about it. She took it in stride.

She wasn't prone to temper tantrums or outbursts.

He'd never seen her be aggressive with anyone on the ranch or the animals.

It didn't make any sense.

But what did he really know about her?

He liked her and having her around. He wanted to get to know her a hell of a lot better. He wanted her to open up to him. He had a million questions but went with what seemed the most important to her. "Is your sister in trouble?"

"Yes. No. I don't know." Sorrow and fear thickened her voice. Her gaze fell. "How did this happen?" The question wasn't for him.

"*What* happened, Skye?"

Her gaze flew up to his. "It's not your problem. Leave it alone." The words croaked out and tears trickled down her cheeks. She ran past him and flat out to the house.

He could have stopped her, but he wasn't one to manhandle a distraught woman. He didn't want to force her to talk to him. He wanted to help her, not push her away. And the way she looked, like a rabbit about to bolt, he knew if he kept at her before she was ready to talk, she'd leave.

The thought of never seeing her again, never knowing if the trouble she ran from caught up to her, it tightened his gut and made him ill at ease just thinking about it.

He grabbed the spare cell phone off the desk and headed up to the house. He'd give her time to calm down and think. She was smart and practical. She'd come to the right decision and ask him for help. If nothing else, he hoped he'd shown her the last few days that she could count on him to give that much and more.

Chapter Twelve

SKYE SLAMMED her bedroom door and fell on her bed, worried sick about Meadow and their parents. They needed to leave Sunrise. They weren't safe there. Not anymore.

Meadow had been ready for her call just like they planned. Gabriel made Skye paranoid the last few months she'd been at Sunrise. Meadow thought she'd gone out of her mind, planning for something that would never happen. But Skye knew she'd eventually have to leave Sunrise and their little town to find some authorities to help her take down Gabriel. So she told Meadow if she ever unexpectedly left to wait for her call in the office each night at the designated time. She wanted a way to check on her family and warn them about what was to come if she couldn't get them to leave with her.

Meadow thought plotting secret late night calls was ridiculous. Until Skye disappeared and Gabriel spun a fantastical tale about how she'd betrayed him and Sunrise.

Thank God, Meadow didn't believe the lies, even though she hadn't told Meadow everything about Gabriel's plots and plans. Like everyone outside of Gabriel's inner circle, Meadow believed Gabriel's changes at the compound were to keep them all safe.

Meadow had such a sweet heart, she wanted to believe everyone was good.

Skye wished that were true. She wished Gabriel was like Declan. He said what he meant. When he offered something, he didn't expect anything in return. He believed in helping others.

He'd helped her, a perfect stranger.

He'd given her a place to stay, a purpose here on the ranch, and a place in his home. He made her feel welcome and appreciated.

And she'd repaid his kindness tonight by yelling at him and basically telling him to stay out of her business.

But how could she tell him her sister took a huge risk sneaking into the office? That she'd heard someone coming and cut the call short before Skye could convince her to do what needed to be done? He wouldn't understand her urgency and desperation to get her family out of there. Not without her telling him everything.

Would he believe her?

Where would she go if he kicked her out?

How would she get back to Sunrise to save her sister with no money or a plan that didn't end with her in jail for a crime she didn't commit?

If something happened to her family, she'd never forgive herself.

She should have stayed and spoken to the police.

She scoffed at that idea. They'd take Gabriel's word over hers to save their own necks. Meadow confirmed it tonight. They'd believed his fantastical tale and wanted her for Lucy's murder.

Most of those living at Sunrise now naively followed Gabriel. They believed his lies. Her parents included, based on what little her sister was able to tell her before their call abruptly ended.

She didn't want to believe it, because how could her parents think for even a second she'd kill Lucy?

It was so absurd.

And felt like a betrayal.

Her parents were more connected to each other than the two girls their love brought into this world. They loved her and Meadow in their way, but this made her feel like she'd been pushed out and left in the cold.

She wrapped her arms around herself and gave in to the tears that wracked her body.

It took her a second to hear the soft tap on the door.

"Skye, can I come in? Let's talk."

"I'm fine." The words sounded hysterical and desperate even to her.

"Skye."

The way he said her name warmed her heart, but she couldn't drag him into this.

She wiped her hands over her eyes and wet cheeks. "Thank you, Declan, but I'll be okay." She held her breath, wondering if he'd come in and demand answers he had a right to because she was staying here. She'd put him in danger. If Gabriel or his men found her, well, she didn't want to think about what they'd do to her. Or Declan.

She had to leave first thing in the morning. He was too good a man to put at risk like this.

The quiet and her seized lungs threatened to suffocate her, but then she heard the creak of the hardwood as Declan walked away.

Selfishly, she wished he'd come inside and held her. It

had been easier than she thought possible to get through the last couple days because Declan's quiet strength and formidable presence made it easy for her to pretend everything was fine.

But she couldn't pretend anymore. She needed to come up with a plan. With little experience with the police and the laws that didn't really intrude on or affect life at Sunrise, she needed to figure out who could help her.

Gabriel had convinced the local police she'd killed Lucy. How? She didn't know, so how could she convince them otherwise? It would be her word against Gabriel's.

She needed to contact Mr. Banks and ask him if he'd been able to help the girls escape Sunrise and the arranged marriages that most of them didn't want. The others thought they wanted them, but reality might have proven how incompatible they were for each other. Most of the girls barely knew the men they were marrying. And from what Skye could see, Gabriel wasn't the only one who'd changed for the worse over the last many months.

What would become of her sweet sister if Skye didn't save her?

She lost herself in the whirlwind of horrible thoughts, fears, and helplessness until the tears faded and she fell into the nightmare that haunted her sleep every night.

Gabriel, his eyes filled with hate and rage, kicked poor Lucy, who held her hand out toward Skye, her eyes imploring her to do something. And in the dream, Skye ran into the room, trying to get to Lucy in time, but Gabriel kicked her again and blood poured across the floor.

"Lucy!" Skye kept running, but she never got any closer to her. She ran and ran and ran, screaming, "Lucy!" over and over again.

Strong hands clamped onto her shoulders and pulled

her up. In her dream, Gabriel caught her. She fought to get free.

"Skye, it's me. Declan. Wake up!"

Her eyes flew open. She caught the red imprint of her hand on Declan's cheek and the worry in his eyes. Safe with Declan, she threw her arms around his neck and held on for dear life, afraid Gabriel would get her even though he wasn't here.

Declan's strong arms went around her and he held her close, one big hand rubbing up and down her back in soothing strokes. "You're okay. You're safe. It's all right." The soft words helped ease her mind and racing heart, until she realized she was pressed up against his bare chest and warm, tempting skin.

He sat on the edge of her bed and smelled fresh and clean, like the wind with a hint of soap.

The few times she'd fooled around with Joseph, it had been all heavy petting, overwhelming sensations, and a truckload of embarrassment and insecurity. One night, he found her alone in the office. He'd surprised her with a flip of the lock, a smile that melted her heart, and a kiss that stated clearly what he wanted. His passion and eagerness thrilled her. It made her believe he felt things for her that she'd never experienced. She thought he felt all those wild emotions filling her heart.

Caught up in the rush, everything moved too fast for her to really savor each moment. The kiss ended with him fumbling to undo his pants and hike up her dress all at once. The thrill of his hands on her bare thighs and her panties sliding down her sensitive skin turned to awe when his fingers skimmed the soft flesh between her legs. She wanted more, but he spread her thighs and thrust into her. Before the initial shock wore off and she processed the wonder of being full of him, he bucked against her, grunted, then laid his head on her shoulder for barely a few seconds. She wanted to embrace him, but he stepped away, leaving her unsure and adrift from his sudden departure. She'd quickly pushed her dress down her legs and stared at him from her seat atop the desk, hoping he said something, waiting for the words of love she desperately wanted to hear.

They never came.

She didn't regret what happened. Not really. But the memory, like the experience, always left her wondering—and feeling like she'd missed something.

Being held in Declan's strong arms made all those imaginings come back for the first time in a long time. She wondered what it could be like to have every inch of her bare skin pressed to his. What it would be like to feel his hands move over her, to have him fill her, and take the time to enjoy each other and the experience of being close and connected.

Would he let her look at him? Touch him?

She'd barely had time to think, let alone explore, when she was with Joseph before it was all over.

She'd like to take her time with Declan and learn everything about him. She wanted to discover all the ways she could please him. More than anything, she wanted to know if sex could be different with someone like him. Because something told her Declan wasn't the kind of man who rushed anything. She'd seen the way he worked. Every task, big or small, got his full attention.

He saw to every little detail.

Joseph liked her, but in the end, she'd been a conquest. One in a string of them. Her mother had consoled her by saying boys were like that at that age. That didn't mend her broken heart, but it did teach her to look for something more than attraction in a partner.

The electricity and sexual tension between her and Declan was palpable every time they were near each other. It was all she could do to keep her hands to herself.

That near kiss earlier . . . She'd wanted it so badly she'd nearly dived in and taken what she wanted, but that wasn't fair to Declan. Not when she couldn't stay.

And she'd never treat him the way Joseph had treated her, taking what she wanted without any thought to his feelings and what he wanted.

Declan was a man, not some randy teenage boy.

She had no idea what he wanted. From her, or any woman.

He was her boss. And this was inappropriate.

"I'm sorry." She tried to pull away, but he held her still.

"You scared me. I thought someone was hurting you." He shifted and she swore she felt a soft kiss brush her hair. His hands swept up her shoulders to her face. He cupped her cheeks and stared into her eyes. "What happened?"

"It was a nightmare. That's all." If only. Lucy's murder was all too real.

"Who is Lucy?"

She clamped one hand on his wrist and tried to escape his penetrating gaze, but he didn't release her from his light hold.

"I know we just met, but can't you trust me even a little bit?"

She sighed and fell into the sincerity and plea in his eyes. She needed to tell someone, because holding it all in was too much.

"Lucy . . . she's dead." Tears welled in her eyes and

the words fell from her lips. "I watched him kill her. I didn't do anything to stop him. I should have done something." The words ran together, she hyperventilated, and the tears fell in earnest again. "She told me to run. So I did. I ran. And I didn't s-save h-her."

Declan hugged her close, brushed his hand down her hair over and over again, and whispered soothing words that barely registered but eased her anyway as she cried for poor Lucy and silently berated herself for not doing what she should have done. Lucy told her to run, but Skye never intended to hide. Yet that's what she'd been doing since she left Sunrise. She'd found this wonderful place, a man who made her believe in good men, and let Gabriel get away with setting her up for the murder *he* committed.

She gave in to the tears, her fear, and dug deep for the resolve to set this right come daybreak.

And if that meant leaving Declan to keep him safe and out of her troubles, then that's what she'd do.

The tears subsided as Declan's strength and warmth seeped into her. He gently laid her back on the bed and stared down at her in the dim light filtering through the blinds she hadn't quite closed. "Do you know who killed her?"

Skye nodded, seeing Lucy's deathly pale face and empty eyes all too clear in her mind.

Declan didn't give up. "The man you were supposed to marry?"

"I was never going to marry *him*. I hate him, and he knows it."

The satisfied look he gave her bolstered her resolve to do the right thing as soon as possible. For Declan's sake. For Lucy. Her family. For all those under Gabriel's thumb at Sunrise.

And for the people whose lives were still in jeopardy if she didn't stop Gabriel and his cohorts from following through with their deadly plots.

She stared into Declan's eyes, hoping he saw that she wanted to stay and explore this strange but tempting connection between them but that she also had to go.

He suddenly stood beside the bed. "We'll talk about the rest in the morning. Try to get some sleep."

Impulse was a dangerous thing. Especially when she went with it.

She reached out and grabbed his hand. Her eyes traveled up his thick toned legs, over his really nice ass, up his lean back, and right to the intense gaze staring down at her from over his shoulder. Before she thought better of it, she tugged him back down beside her because she didn't want to miss an opportunity to spend a little more time with him. "Stay."

Exhausted, she needed to sleep, but she was too scared to face the night alone. And Declan had this magic way of banishing all her dark thoughts.

Declan squeezed her hand. "You're safe here."

She relaxed into the pillow and stared up at him. "Will you stay? Just until I fall asleep."

His lips pressed together and indecision filled his eyes. "Please."

He shifted on the bed, stared down at her, and placed their joined hands on his warm, bare thigh. The hair on his legs brushed the back of her hand. The heat from his skin seeped into her. And that wonderful zing of electricity that vibrated through her any time he touched her hummed to life and eased her heart.

"Close your eyes."

She really liked looking at him. Maybe that's what

put that something extra in his gaze as he stared down at her. Whatever he was thinking or feeling he kept locked down. She wished she could read his thoughts. She didn't have enough experience with men to guess, but hope bloomed in her heart that maybe he was as attracted to her as she was to him, and somewhere down the road, maybe, when things were different, she'd find her way back to him.

When he said she was safe here, she heard *you're safe with me.*

She believed that.

Some men had a core of dominance they used to bend others to their will. Like Gabriel.

Others, like Declan, protected, encouraged, and took care of people, even if it meant putting themselves at risk.

"I need to leave," she whispered.

His hand contracted around hers and just as she fell asleep, she heard the quiet response that made her lose her heart. "I want you to stay."

Chapter Thirteen

Declan stood in the kitchen, his back to the counter, drinking his third cup of coffee after a long night and little sleep. His mind was on the woman quietly tiptoeing down the stairs at this godawful hour. He'd known she'd try to bolt, but he'd hoped she'd confide in him, trust him, and stay.

He'd sat beside her last night watching her sleep far longer than he should have, but he couldn't seem to stop staring at her. Or thinking about the way she'd looked at him and what she'd told him.

The urge to lie beside her and hold her through the night was so strong he'd had to force himself to leave. But not before he brushed his hand down her soft hair and gave in to the overwhelming need to kiss her, though he'd kept that tame with a press of his lips to her forehead.

He didn't know where this strange tenderness came from, but she brought it out in him.

When she headed for the door, his sensitivity evaporated.

"Where do you think you're going?" The gruffness in his voice had more to do with lack of sleep than his anger, but he couldn't ignore the pang of disappointment laced in the words.

It took her a second to muster her courage and step into the kitchen entry, her bag held protectively against her belly. "I can't stay."

"And yet, you have nowhere else to go."

That took what little spunk she'd had this morning and drained it away. "You don't understand."

"Only because you won't give me the whole story."

Her lips pressed tight.

He sighed and set his mug on the counter before he let his frustration loose and threw it against the wall. "You watched someone murder your friend Lucy. That same someone is looking for you to keep you quiet. Is that about right?" He'd spent the whole night thinking about someone hurting her. The thought turned his stomach and reinforced his need to keep her safe.

Her gaze sank to the floor, but she gave him a hesitant nod.

"And your plan is to run away from here, where he doesn't know you are, and what? Keep running without any money or anyone to help you?"

"You've been very kind. Which is why I don't want to get you involved. I'll find someplace else to earn some money until I can figure out which authorities I can trust to help me."

"You don't need to leave to do that. I can help you talk to the police."

"And put yourself at risk." She shook her head. "I don't want that. My family is already in jeopardy because of what *I* did. If something happened to you . . . no." Regret and remorse filled her eyes.

"But you think I'll let you leave and face whatever it is you're up against and not think twice about it? Come on,

Skye, you've got to know me better than that." He hoped he'd shown her better in the few days they'd known each other.

"He's planning something big. He has to find me and stop me before he's facing more than just his messed-up plans."

His gut tightened with those ominous words. "Then it sounds like we don't have time to squabble over mundane things like I'm not involved when you already know I am invested in *you*." He didn't know how to make it any clearer than that, because he obviously sucked at talking about his feelings and their attraction and wanting her so damn bad he could barely contain the urge to pull her into his arms.

Right now, he'd like to hug away all the pain in her eyes.

"I'll pay you back for the clothes and shoes and stuff."

Anger rushed through him and he had to clamp his jaw shut on the swear words he caught in his throat before he spewed them at her. "Do you really think I care about the money?"

Her shoulders slumped. "No. It's just . . . I don't know what to do, how to do it, but I need to do something."

"Great. Let's figure it out." He waved his hand toward the table. "Sit down. We'll talk it through."

"But . . ."

"Skye, I haven't slept and am a breath away from losing my temper over you not trusting me, so sit."

Her whole body went rigid. "I do trust you."

Well, that was something, and great news to him. And it mattered to him more than he thought when it felt like a weight lifted from his shoulders.

A plea filled her sad eyes. "I don't want to dump my problems on you when you've been so good to me. Can't you see I'm trying to protect you?"

"I'm trying to do the same for you. So since we want the same thing for each other, let's figure out how to fix this and both stay out of danger."

She stared back at him for one long moment. He held his breath because he really couldn't make her stay, and damnit, he wanted her here.

She took the few steps to the table, set her bag on one chair, and dropped into the other.

"Coffee?"

"Please." She stared at the wood, not looking at him, but she didn't leave, so he'd take it.

He poured her a mug, added a dollop of milk from the fridge just the way she liked it, grabbed his mug from the counter, and joined her at the table. He took the seat closest to her, turned it so they faced each other, and cupped her face in his palm. "Let's make something clear. I want to help you. Not because of some obligation or because I expect you to pay me back for anything. I'm doing it for you."

"Whoa!" Tate stood behind Skye, wide-eyed, and taking in Declan touching Skye in a non-employee-employer way.

"Get out." He didn't even look at his brother, but kept his eyes locked on Skye's.

Tate spun around and left without another word.

Skye leaned into his touch for a moment before she sat up straighter and he pulled his hand back. "Okay."

"Okay, what?"

"I'll tell you everything. But you can't do anything

without asking me. My family is still there. Gabriel could retaliate. If he hasn't already."

"Deal. We handle this together."

She shifted and faced him more fully, then sucked in a breath and started with what she'd revealed last night. "I witnessed a murder."

He hated that she'd seen such a thing and that it haunted her day and night. "Your friend, Lucy."

"Yes." The sadness in her eyes made his heart clench. "But for you to understand what happened, I need to tell you about Sunrise Fellowship."

"Is that the church you attend?"

She shook her head. "No. Not a church. It's where I was raised."

That intrigued him. "Like a cult?"

"No," she snapped, relieving him that there wasn't an added disturbing layer to her troubles. "It's like I told you. We're a community of like-minded individuals who believed in self-sustained living that included a large farm, on-site school, community dining area, and family cabins. It takes a village, right? That's what it *was*." She painted a nice picture, but the last word held a note of scorn.

"It's not that anymore?"

"The community has a council to oversee things for the group headed by the founder, who directed the community and controlled the finances. He passed away two years ago. He taught me computers and accounting. I worked with him on the books and also oversaw the business side of the community."

"Selling your produce and goods at the farmers markets."

"And to small shops in town. We didn't rake in the dough, but we made enough to sustain the community and pay for things like gas and doctors for the sick when the nurse who lives there recommended more care for someone. We aren't opposed to the outside world, we just believe in trying to live without all the waste and excess."

"Is there a religious component to the group?"

"We had Bible study as part of our history courses. Morals, kindness, responsibility to self and community, generosity, having a work ethic, these and more like them are the things we focused on. We believed in family. Not just the nuclear family but the community family."

"It sounds like an idyllic life." Not so different from the one he knew, and not so out there he couldn't relate. Family was important to him and everyone else in his family. But it was a smaller circle than her much wider one.

"You mean naïve."

"Maybe a little bit. I mean, your eyes popped when you pulled the grocery bill out of the bag Tate left on the counter."

"Cereal is outrageously priced. And ice cream. Oh. My. God."

That and the other things, especially her lack of knowledge about pop culture, amused him.

"But my opinion and imaginings of your life are based on my growing up here on the ranch and experiences, not yours."

"Then I'll say life at Sunrise was very peaceful and filled with friendships and a sense of security. I mean, the worst things that ever happened to me were silly in retrospect. Arguments with my sister. Butting heads with my parents about being allowed to go into town for movies and pizza like other teenage girls got to do. A boyfriend who decided he liked someone else more than me."

He barely hid his grin. "I find that hard to believe."

Her shy smile sent a swarm of butterflies fluttering in his belly. He liked her this way. Open. Honest. Sweet.

He tried to show her they had more in common than not. "Life on this ranch was a lot like that. My brothers and I had our squabbles. We wanted to be with friends in town rather than doing chores out here."

"And as a teen, you probably would rather have been off chasing girls." Her knowing smile made him grin back. "I'd imagine a lot of them found their way out here looking for you."

He couldn't deny it happened a few times to him and his brothers, but he wasn't a bragger and he'd never kiss and tell. "Maybe."

"It's easy to see why." Her cheeks pinked and it just made her look so damn cute. "Gabriel grew up spoiled and entitled because his father was the founder. Everyone dismissed his rude and entitled behavior because his mother died when he was four. His father indulged him, hoping that as he got older and took on more responsibilities he'd settle down."

"But he didn't."

"He's a bully who thinks his word is law and everyone should do what he wants. If you don't, there are tantrums and consequences no one wants to deal with, so going along is so much easier." She stared at the wall, then back at him. "After Joseph dumped me for another girl, Gabriel made it known that I was off limits to the other boys."

Declan didn't like the sound of that. "Did you date

Gabriel?" The disgust in her eyes said no, but he wanted the whole picture.

"I couldn't stand him. But I also couldn't alienate him, so I simply ignored him."

"Which only made him try harder to get your attention." *You always want what you can't have.* Declan wondered how annoying Gabriel had been to put Skye off even more.

"I kept my head down, studied hard because my parents made it clear education was more important than anything else, and worked with Gabriel's father to learn a job that made me an important part of the community."

"I take it in the community, everyone is assigned a job at some point based on their skillset."

"Yes. For the most part the person chooses what they want to focus on, but in some cases they're assigned a job if they don't take the initiative. The community tries to be fair and equal. It's the same with marriages. Most of the members find partners within the community. A few have met outsiders and brought them into the fold. In a few cases, families have set up matches by simply putting the two people together and seeing what happens."

"Did the families force the match?"

She shook her head. "Never. Choice is a part of our teachings. If you want to be happy, you must weigh the gains and losses of your choices."

"Everything has consequences," he agreed. He'd made his fair share of bad decisions. Who hadn't?

"Harmony at Sunrise is important. No one wants anyone to be unhappy. It sows discord."

"You're only as strong as the weakest link in the chain." Declan nodded. "My father used to say that to us all the time."

"A mother is only as happy as her most unhappy child," she added. "The farm sustains us. The people are charged with maintaining the land and crops. If the people are unhappy, unproductive, then everyone and everything suffers." She stared deep into his eyes. "When you don't allow others to help, you take on too much, and the consequences add up."

Declan didn't like the rebuke, but he knew she pointed out his shortcoming to get him to see how her life connected to his. "Trying to tell me I work too much and try to control everything when what I really need to do is accept help and allow others to do their jobs?"

"You already know that. You just need to put it into practice before you work yourself into an early grave. Working as a team, dividing responsibilities, allows everyone to reap the rewards and avoid taking on more than they can handle." She gave him a pointed look. "What happens if you get hurt or sick? You've taken on so much of the responsibility here that without you, the operation breaks down. If you evened out the workload and responsibilities, the operation would run smoothly with others covering with minimal extra effort."

"It's annoying when my brothers and sister harp on me. Coming from you . . . the way you put it . . . making so much sense . . . it's maddening." Though he didn't mind that she had his best interest, and the ranch's for that matter, at heart. Hearing it from her allowed him to take it in instead of trying to justify himself to his siblings.

"They see what I see. You can't do everything the way you do and sustain it. Something will have to give. They don't want it to be *you* who breaks."

Right now, only his personal life suffered. And that made him restless and lonely, which made him work more so he didn't have to think about what was missing in his life. "I've been doing it so long, I don't know how to do it any other way."

"Set yourself up for success, instead of chasing it all on your own."

That was it. He didn't want to do it all by himself. He wanted a partner is his life like his brothers had found with their wives. He didn't have anything else in his life, so he dove headfirst into his work to fill the gaping hole inside him. Being busy used to make it easy to ignore what wasn't working in his life. Now he spent not just his off hours thinking about it, but all day thinking about one thing: Why did he work so hard?

The ranch was profitable. He lived a comfortable life. Even if they faced some future lean times, he'd banked enough money to sustain the ranch, barring any catastrophe.

"I'm sorry, Declan. I'll stick to my troubles, not yours." She'd only been here a few days, yet she understood him well.

"I know something has to change. It's just been hard to stop what I've been doing so long and take the time to make the necessary adjustments." He appreciated that she nodded and didn't harp on him even more, the way his family did.

"So. Gabriel. He took over. At first, the changes he made were subtle. He replaced some of the older council members with his buddies. Everyone hemmed and hawed about it, but in the end it seemed a good idea to have a fresh perspective from the men who were now doing a majority of the work. Work didn't necessarily drop off, but the men spent more time at leisure or directing others than doing their jobs."

"It threw the balance off in the community," he guessed, trying to understand.

"Yes. But Gabriel didn't allow any pushback. No one wanted to set off his volatile temper. So those who needed to, worked harder. Others picked up the slack."

He understood all too well. "For the good of the community." When Drake joined the military, Declan had to step up and work harder on the ranch.

Her soft smile never failed to make his belly flutter. "Gabriel talked about getting into new business ventures. Something that would make more money. For the community." She rolled her eyes on the last part.

Declan caught on fast. "He got greedy."

"Our community has always been about having what we *need*, not going after the excesses that have corrupted the world."

"I don't think you're giving up rocky road ice cream anytime soon," he teased.

She'd taken one bite the other night and devoured two bowls. He'd thought she'd give herself a stomach ache indulging in that kind of gluttony, but damn if she didn't look simply satisfied when she finally set her spoon down.

It had been a long time since he discovered something new and got that excited about it.

"Treats now and then are a happy part of life. The expansion Gabriel proposed was one thing, but it's what I discovered him doing behind the scenes that proved he no longer had the collective in mind." She traced her fingers across the table and over the wood grain. "Girls started gossiping about how the guys on Gabriel's council started having private get-togethers. At first, it seemed innocent enough. Everyone wanted to be part of the group, but the men kept it small and quiet. Rumors started about girls trying beer and liquor for the first time. Alcohol had always been banned."

Their clean life had been tainted. "The downfall of many." Declan could attest to a few morning hangovers and a head full of regrets for the bad decisions he'd made under the influence.

She nodded. "It soon became well-known that the private parties got a little out of hand. People became concerned. Especially when a couple of the girls got pregnant. Gabriel took care of the talk with hasty marriages. A couple were good matches. One was not. The girl showed up with bruises she passed off as clumsy accidents."

An alarm went off in Declan's head. "You keep saying girls."

Skye's lips pressed tight and her eyes narrowed with disheartened distaste. "Of those girls, the youngest was seventeen. The oldest just twenty."

"I take it the men were older."

"Late twenties, early thirties. One of the older council members, who had recently been widowed, was in his midfifties. I believe his age and acceptance of what Gabriel and the others were doing emboldened Gabriel."

She fell silent for a moment. "Gabriel and the men made it appear they'd settled down and stopped the parties, but really they just got better at hiding it. The other girls who participated learned to keep their mouths shut. Really, they feared Gabriel's wrath."

"But?"

"Suddenly, the men were gone for long hours of the day. Gabriel told everyone they were working on a project. Gabriel started spending money. Receipts came in for lumber, electrical fixtures, furniture, and more alcohol. When I raised questions, Gabriel ordered me to do my job and keep my mouth shut. He swore that the new business would pay back the funds and be self-sustaining just like the farm. I didn't approve of it, but like everyone else, I reluctantly went along. Then the men started coming back from their trips with new girls who wanted to join Sunrise." Her sad gaze met his. "Gabriel was recruiting."

Declan's stomach soured. He didn't want to know, but asked anyway. "For what?"

"I didn't know." She shook her head. "That's not it. I didn't want to be right." Anguish wrinkled her brow. "But I followed Gabriel one evening to a remote part of the property, closer to town but still far enough away that it was secluded and easily disguised on the outside as something other than what it really was on the inside."

He covered her hand on the table. "What was Gabriel doing?"

"He turned an old barn into a . . . club of sorts."

Declan tried to read between the lines. "A man cave?" At her confused look, he tried to explain. "A place for him and the guys to hang out, maybe bring the girls, and party?"

She nodded. "That's what I thought. At first. But then Gabriel paid the farm back the money he used to fix it up."

"How?" Declan had a sinking feeling.

"The new girls didn't get integrated into the farm or the community. Within days of them showing up, Gabriel put them to work. He just never said doing what."

"And when you followed him again, you figured out what they were doing." A sense of dread settled in his gut like lead.

"I didn't have to follow him. I knew where he'd taken

those girls and I didn't like what I thought he was doing with them. Turns out, my imagination didn't take things far enough. I just didn't know someone could be that . . . awful."

He had a feeling it was a lot more terrible than that when she couldn't think of how to explain the dark and twisted things she'd discovered and seen. "What did you do?"

"I snuck into the barn two men were guarding."

"Are you crazy?" He dragged his hand over his head, thinking of a dozen horrible things that could have happened to her. "What would have happened if they saw you?"

She shrugged that off. "I didn't really think about it. Up until I saw Gabriel kill Lucy, I'd never seen anyone be violent at Sunrise. That just wasn't part of our life there."

He had a hard time remembering her life experience and knowledge didn't match his. "I can see why you thought you were safe."

"Naïve," she admitted. "Ignorant about the darker side of life. But I got an education when I went into the barn and discovered that the twenty stalls had been turned into small rooms with locked doors. At one end was a bar with stools and all kinds of alcohol. Tables and chairs with cards and poker chips." She shook her head. "I believe some of the money came from their gambling."

"Maybe, but if this was just their hangout . . ."

"Sorry. I'm not explaining well. Yes, the men went there, but it was more than that. I didn't understand the locked rooms. I could hear rustling inside, but I couldn't be sure if someone was living in there, until one of the women from Sunrise caught me sneaking around. She grabbed my arm and wouldn't let me go. She dragged me into the room, which turned out to be a small office with a desk and safe. I didn't understand what was going on, until she threatened me. She said if one of the men found me, or Gabriel discovered I knew what he was doing, he'd kill me. Or worse."

"What's worse than death?"

"Being one of the girls locked in those rooms." She stared down at her hands. "Gabriel sent the men out to find desperate, lost souls and bring them there to be . . ."

"Prostitutes." Declan finally understood what she had tried so hard to explain.

"I think that implies they had a choice and got paid. Right?"

"Yes." He rubbed two fingers over his tense brow. "So you're saying he held them as sex slaves?"

"His new business was abusing those girls and women. He forced Anne to oversee their care and keeping. She hated it, but Gabriel had said if she didn't do it, she'd be extricated from Sunrise. She'd been there most of her life. She didn't know what she'd do if he kicked her out with nothing. Where would she go? How would she survive?"

Gabriel's behavior disgusted him. "He used fear and intimidation to get her to cooperate."

"It works for him."

"So where is the money coming from if it's just Gabriel and his boys abusing the women?"

Her deep frown said there was so much more. "Gabriel and his guys went out and quietly spread the word." Disappointment and helplessness filled her eyes. "Once people knew about that place, they came. I went back one night just to see. The sheer number of cars in the parking lot sickened me until I spotted one and hoped it would end, but then the officer walked out with Gabriel. He handed the policeman a bunch of cash, they shared some words and laughed, and then the cop drove away. And that's when I knew there was nowhere to go for help."

Declan put his hand on her knee. "I'm sorry, Skye. That must have been really hard to take."

"I felt helpless. I didn't know what to do. So I kept trying to find a way, but Gabriel and the men became more assertive. Everyone simply tried to avoid them. Again, to stifle rumors and questions, Gabriel plotted to make everything seem normal again. He and the men spent more time with the Sunrise women. And then Gabriel announced the marriages he arranged and an impending wedding date that was days away."

"But that's not how things were normally done at Sunrise."

She'd already explained that. "Not at all. But Gabriel thought this would make the men seem dedicated to Sunrise, and make others see them as committed husbands and family men."

"Gabriel wanted to clean up their reputations."

"Hard to do when the youngest girl was fourteen and pregnant by a thirty-one-year-old man Gabriel wanted her to marry."

"Oh God." Declan didn't like that one bit. The girl was half the guy's age, hadn't even finished school, or had enough life experience to know what she wanted for the rest of her life. Now she faced being a mother and wife when she was still a child herself.

That man took advantage without any thought to how it would change her life. And his. Now he was responsible for both of them. He needed to be held accountable for his actions.

"Gabriel told the men to court the girls. This guy had

gotten so used to getting what he wanted at The Stable, as that place became known, that he didn't date the girl so much as seduce her. She had no idea what she was getting into, and just like that, her whole life is changed. Gabriel wanted the girls swept up in the whirlwind of it. Once they were married, they'd have little to no say in what their husbands did. I think most of the men figured they were young and malleable, so they'd get the women pregnant and keep them busy with babies, and then the men could do whatever they wanted." She smacked her hand on the table. "The calculated way they went about it disgusted me."

He pressed his forearms on the table and leaned in close to her. "Did Gabriel do the same to you?"

"Hell no!"

He'd never heard her swear or use harsh language, so it threw him to hear the ferocity behind those words.

"He planned to have me simply brought to the altar where I would of course be overwhelmingly grateful to marry him." Sarcasm and anger coated those words along with her disdain for Gabriel and what he was doing, how he was destroying the place and life she'd loved at Sunrise. "And the night before he expected me to marry him, I went to the office to get something, heard him in the back bedroom, and went to investigate." She choked up.

He squeezed her knee, letting her know he was there. "You found him with Lucy."

She nodded and swallowed hard. "He was yelling at her. How dare she get pregnant with his baby? There was no way she would ever tell anyone it was his. He ordered her to get rid of it. He was destined to marry me. I would be the mother of his golden children. Whatever he and Lucy had was over." Her watery gaze met his. "She was barely eighteen, his child in her belly, and he turned his back on her and the baby. They didn't fit in his plans. He didn't want them, so he shoved her to the floor and kicked her in the stomach until she . . ." Skye hyperventilated, trying to hold back the tidal wave of tears and sorrow.

Declan's heart slammed to a stop at the thought of what poor Lucy endured and Skye witnessed. The trauma and fear she'd suffered, but she'd still found the strength to run and save herself before it was too late.

He hooked his hands at her waist and pulled her out of her chair and right into his lap. He held her close, her back to his chest, as the tears wracked her body.

"How could he do that? Just kick her like that. The blood . . . it poured out of her." Skye's nails dug into his skin where she clamped them down and held his arms tight to her middle. "She was in agony. She mouthed for me to run, her eyes pleading with me to go, and then nothing. Her eyes went blank and she was just . . . gone."

"You did what you had to do. If he saw you, knew you'd seen what he did, he might have killed you, too."

"I left her there, taking the girls who were supposed to get married the next day with me. I thought I'd be able to get them help and make Gabriel pay for what he'd done. But he sent men after us. They got there too fast for me to really do anything. I had to run again. I left them. I don't know what happened to them."

He didn't like the fear and anguish that filled those words.

"We'll figure it out," he assured her, though he didn't really have a plan for how they'd do that.

She wiped her eyes, settled deeper into his chest, and leaned her head against his cheek and dropped a bomb.

"He pinned the murder on me. There's a warrant out for my arrest."

It took everything he had not to jump up in indignation and dump her off his lap. "What? That's ridiculous."

"Remember the cop I saw at The Stable . . ." She didn't need to finish that statement.

Gabriel blackmailed the cop, or something, and screwed Skye.

"Fuck."

She sighed, then sucked in a breath, trying to regain her composure. "So what do I do? My family is still there. Still under Gabriel's reign. Meadow refused to leave because she thinks she can help me from the inside, keeping track of Gabriel, who has taken particular interest in her now. She's nineteen. My parents don't know what to think and are leaning toward the fact the police have evidence against me."

That got his attention. "What evidence?"

She shrugged. "Gabriel is diabolically smart. He found a way."

"Then we'll find a way to stop him."

Chapter Fourteen

Skye fell silent, lost in the nightmare that had become her life. She'd always tried to be good and nice and kind to others. She offered a helping hand when someone needed it. She worked hard to do her part and better herself, so she could be better for others.

Yes, she'd wanted something more in her life, but that had been more of a dream for her future. A husband who lived the kind of life she lived. A man who loved her. Children. A family filled with happiness and years of sweet memories.

If Gabriel got away with pinning Lucy's murder on her, she'd have nothing. They'd lock her in a cell and the life she loved would be nothing but a memory.

What would happen to her family? To Sunrise?

"I need to contact Gordon Banks. He'll know what to do." She needed help, and that meant a lawyer who understood how to navigate the trouble Gabriel caused.

"Who is that?"

"Sunrise's lawyer. We'd begun contracting with other businesses and individuals. While the accounting stuff comes easy to me, contracts were a bit more complicated. He helped me understand them and how to protect Sunrise's interests. When rumors about underage girls getting pregnant made it to town, he asked me about it. I thought he was as concerned as me, but he was reluctant to send child protective services out to Sunrise because . . ."

"Why, Skye?"

"Gabriel befriended a very dangerous man. I only know him as Jeremiah. Mr. Banks had heard of him. He described the group Jeremiah heads as militant separatists. They believe the government should be abolished and everyone should be armed."

Concern drew lines on Declan's forehead. "I've heard of groups like that."

"It's the other reason Gabriel needs to silence me."

Declan's hand settled on her cheek. He gently turned her head to face him. "Why?"

"I stole the evidence of what they're plotting."

Declan ran a hand over his face. "It just keeps getting worse."

She tried to stand, but he took her by the hips and pulled her back down on his thigh. "Where are you going?"

"You hired me to do a job, not bring all this mess into your life."

"Do you really think I'd turn my back on you, let you walk away and face this all on your own?" He leaned in close and took her face in his warm hands. "Don't you see there's a lot more going on here and it has nothing to do with the fact you work here?"

She didn't know what to say, except to be honest. "I feel something."

"That's the phone in my pocket vibrating with a string of texts. Probably from Tate." He teased, but her words had made the intensity in his eyes sharpen. "What else do you feel?"

"You."

He leaned in another inch. Their noses almost touching, their breath mingling. The same pull she felt earlier when they'd collided drew her in and made her want to get closer.

He asked, so she gave him the truth that came straight from her heart. "I feel the way you look at me. When you touch me, it's like a burst of sunlight shoots through me. When you're not touching me, I'm hoping you do it again."

"Do you want me to do it again right now?"

"Yes."

His lips pressed to hers, and what usually felt like a beautiful sunny day when he kissed her turned into a fireworks explosion of heat and need.

The brush of his thumb sweeping across her cheek sent her eyes closed on a sigh. He took advantage of her parted lips and caressed his tongue along hers, slow and easy, letting them both get used to the intense intimacy. She fell into him, the moment, the immense feelings stirring inside her.

His hands went to her back and pulled her close. She wrapped her arms around his neck, pressed her heavy breasts to the solid wall of his chest, and held on as he took her on a daring ride into temptation.

His hands swept up and down her back, then to her sides, where he held her with his thumbs brushing softly back and forth on the outside of her breasts. She wanted his hands on them, but she didn't want to put any space between them. She didn't want to break the magical spell or make him stop kissing her like nothing else in the world mattered but this.

Because right now, nothing else did.

All her troubles and fears and anger toward Gabriel washed away.

She wished she could feel this good every second of the day.

And then Declan slipped a hand inside her shirt. Skin on skin and her brain short-circuited. But he wasn't done making her body sizzle. His other hand slid between them, covered her breast, and he squeezed and molded it in his wide palm. She moved against him, her hip rubbing his thick erection.

He wants me.

That thought went from unbelievable to powerfully emboldening in a split second. She didn't stop kissing him, but lifted off his lap.

"Where are you going?" he asked against her lips, pulled her back, and kissed her deeper.

She straddled his legs and settled into him again. "Right here," she said and rolled her hips against his.

"Damn, that's brilliantly better." His hands clamped onto her hips and pulled her tighter against him, his hard cock pressed right up against her soft center. One hand went up the back of her shirt again like he needed to touch her skin as badly as she needed his hands on her. The other one settled on her breast, his thumb sweeping over her tight nipple. The sensation made her moan. "Mmm. I like that. Do it again." He pinched her nipple between two fingers and she instinctively rocked against his hard flesh and involuntarily moaned again. Those two things urged him on and they lost themselves in the kisses and sensations overwhelming both of them.

A loud bang sounded, but she paid no attention to it or anything else. Her whole world shrank to Declan and how he set her body on fire.

"Declan!" Tate's insistent voice penetrated the lusty haze surrounding them.

Declan growled against her mouth, broke the kiss, and turned to his brother standing in the kitchen entry. "I don't care what it is. Handle it and get the fuck out. Now."

"Okay." Tate turned and left, calling out, "Get a room."

"The whole fucking house is mine!" Declan shouted back, frustration and a touch of humor in his voice.

She sat back on his lap, her hands on his shoulders. "I've kept you from work long enough."

His big hands clamped onto her ass and he pulled her snug against his erection. "Honey, I'm ready to beg you to keep me."

A soft laugh bubbled up and she smiled at him, her cheeks on fire. "He saw us . . . like this." She shouldn't be embarrassed, but this had been more intimate than anything she'd experienced, including her fumbled time with Joseph. She hadn't felt as close to or lost in him the way she was with Declan.

"He won't say anything, if that's what you're worried about. Except maybe to his wife. And the rest of the family." At her frown, he added, "The only thing Tate cares about is that I'm happy."

"Are you?" It mattered to her more than she imagined.

His fingers slipped into her hair and he pulled her in for another kiss that was warm and sweet and just as sexy as all the others. It ended far sooner than she liked when he pressed his forehead to hers and stared into her eyes. "This ranch has been my whole damn life for too long. Just you being here has changed me. It used to be all I thought about. Now I find myself thinking about *you* all the time."

"Really?"

"When I'm out working, I'm wondering why I'm not with you. I look forward to coming in for lunch and dinner, because I know you'll be here, smiling that sweet smile."

One bloomed on her lips because his words overjoyed her.

His hand slipped down to her face and his thumb brushed over her lips. "Yes, I'm happy. I wanted to kiss you that first day." He did so now, with another soft press of his lips to hers. "I just plain wanted you, Skye. I still do. And it keeps getting stronger the more I get to know you. So the thought of someone hurting you . . . I won't let that happen." He crushed his mouth to hers. His arms banded around her.

Tight in his protective hold, locked in a searing kiss, she felt safe and hopeful.

She didn't want to lose this. Or Declan. She'd do everything possible to stop Gabriel from taking any of this away from her. Which meant she had to overcome her fear, take a chance on a system she didn't wholly understand, and ask for help, all while facing the man who'd killed her friend, ruined her life, and put Sunrise and others at risk.

Declan broke the kiss and stared deep into her eyes. "Stay. You don't have to do this on your own."

She pressed her palm to his stern jaw. Golden stubble tickled her skin. "I want to be here with you, but I have to stop him."

"We can do that together."

Uncharacteristically bold, she brushed her thumb over his lips, leaned in, and kissed him softly. Reluctantly she stood and backed away.

His hands dropped from her waist to his thighs. He

shifted in his seat, clearly uncomfortable and still wanting her.

She went to her bag and pulled out the cell phone he'd left in her room last night after he comforted her and helped her find peace after the terrible nightmares. He'd wanted her to have a lifeline to her sister.

She dialed the number she'd memorized, hoping it wasn't a mistake. At this point, she didn't know who from her other life she could trust besides her sister.

"Mr. Banks?" he asked, reading her mind.

She nodded and held her breath, waiting for him to answer.

"This is Gordon."

"Hello."

Mr. Banks's relief came through the line on an exhaled whoosh of air. "Skye. Are you okay?"

"I'm fine."

Declan held out his hand. She took it and felt better than fine.

"Where are you?"

Something told her to keep that to herself. She wanted to protect Declan. "I'm someplace safe."

Declan waved his free hand toward the phone. She held it out to him and he put the call on speaker.

"Sunrise is on lockdown. No one is allowed to leave the property."

"I spoke with Meadow last night. Gabriel has someone watching my family at all times. She managed to ditch her shadow and get to the phone, but she had to cut it short when she heard someone coming."

"Then you know."

"That Gabriel framed me for the murder? Yes. But how did he do it?"

"They have your bloody footprints leaving the room. Your hair. Fibers they think they can link to your clothing."

She shouldn't be surprised at all by Gabriel's deceptions and lies, but that took her aback. "I was never in that room."

"That's what you say. And I believe you," Mr. Banks quickly added. "But the evidence says otherwise."

"And what about the girls I brought to you? What did the police say about them?"

"I'm sorry, Skye, the men from Sunrise took them back before the police questioned them. I tried to tell the officers about them, but they were only interested in finding you."

"So you told them about Bess, that Adam was having sex with a fourteen-year-old girl and got her pregnant?" Skye's heart pounded. "Please tell me they arrested him and stopped the marriage between them."

Mr. Banks sighed again. "I was told no such girl lives at Sunrise."

"She was in the van! The girls should have been enough to get a warrant to the property. You promised you'd help! Those girls aren't safe!" Panic and rage shook her.

"I'm sorry, Skye. Corruption is a dirty business that hurts a lot of innocent people."

Her sheltered life led her to believe good always won. But not when those perpetuating evil suppressed those fighting for what was right. "What about the girls still being hurt?"

"I can't get the police to help without any proof. They're reluctant to investigate a group like Sunrise and stir up past mistakes and tragedies without something solid and a warrant."

She didn't know exactly what he meant by that, but it sounded bad and hindered her from getting the help she needed. "They won't even send someone in to check on the children?" Declan asked.

"Who is that?"

"A friend," Skye answered, hoping to keep Declan out of this if she could.

"Local police were on site investigating the murder. They found no cause to believe anyone was being mistreated or held against their will."

Declan's deep frown matched her own.

"The police want to talk to you."

"You mean they want to arrest her for Lucy's murder." Declan shook his head, letting her know that was a bad idea.

"They're open to hearing her side of the story and knowing what else she has on Gabriel."

"If they take her into custody, she may not get the chance to prove Gabriel framed her. We need someone in law enforcement not connected to Gabriel or the local police who can't be swayed by either."

She agreed with Declan.

"I've spoken to the FBI."

Declan raised a brow and sat up straighter.

Mr. Banks added, "I hoped they might step in because of who is guarding Sunrise now."

Dread washed through Skye's whole body and settled in her gut. She'd hoped she could prevent this from happening.

Mr. Banks delivered more bad news. "The agent I spoke to needs some kind of evidence to get involved. If she turns herself in, that will go a long way to them listening."

"If she turns herself in, the local police will back up Gabriel's story. How do we get the FBI on Skye's side?"

"Skye will have to be a cooperative witness in another ongoing investigation into another group."

Declan raised an eyebrow, asking her what Mr. Banks meant with just a look.

"Are *they* after me, too?"

"One has to assume that Gabriel enlisted their help to find you."

"Who?" Declan's deep voice made that single word a demand.

"Prosperity." Gabriel posed a threat that made Skye nervous and cautious, but Prosperity terrified her.

Declan's eyes went wide. "That group in Wyoming who call themselves a ministry, but they're really a militia group who clashed with federal authorities over some land dispute like two years ago?"

"Prosperity is registered as a legal nonprofit church. The government can't touch them." Mr. Banks filled in information she didn't know about the group. "Wyoming has laws against militia groups, but the church classification insulates them. With the current political climate, their numbers have grown over the last couple years because some people feel like there's been a call to arms by those in power. With popularity increasing, they've become emboldened. You know just how much, don't you, Skye?"

Declan looked to her to explain, though she didn't like that Mr. Banks seemed to want her to admit just how much she knew. She filled Declan in on the background that led them here.

"Several of the men from Sunrise who were looking for something more . . . meaningful and . . . bolder than farm life, joined Prosperity. Gabriel wanted to join, but his father forbid it, because of their hate speech and rhetoric. His father said if Gabriel joined up he would not be welcomed back at Sunrise. He made it clear to all that that kind of ideology was not in line with what Sunrise stood for and wanted for the future. It may sound corny and simple, but we preach peace and kindness. Prosperity says they want that for all, but they breed hate against those who aren't like them or believe differently from them.

"Over the last two years, Gabriel has slowly started to change things at Sunrise, gauging just how far he can push the boundaries of what has been the norm. The more pushback he got, the more secretive he became. Only the men around him are made aware of all the decisions Gabriel makes for Sunrise."

"And you," Declan guessed.

"It's hard to get anything done without it somehow involving the finances."

"But Gabriel disguises it in some way." Declan was two for two.

"Yes. He thinks I'm stupid, naïve, or that I'll just blindly follow along."

"Probably all of that." Declan was too smart and savvy to believe anything else. "I, for one, know not to underestimate you." And he'd only known her a short time.

Gabriel didn't know her at all.

She appreciated that Declan saw her as she was, not as how he wanted her to be. "When things didn't make sense, I investigated. Quietly. Sometimes without even trying to hide it because no one believed I'd do anything about it anyway."

"But you did."

She smiled at Declan's confidence in her. "I did."

"Does anyone else know what you did and what you have on Gabriel and Prosperity?"

She shook her head. "No. I didn't want to get anyone else involved. Too dangerous. If Gabriel or anyone else caught me . . ." She didn't know for sure what would happen, but it seemed clear nothing good would come of her interfering in their plans.

At best she feared being ousted from Sunrise and separated from her family. At worst . . . She simply didn't know how far Gabriel would go—until he killed Lucy in cold blood.

Declan eyed her. "Do you know whether or not anyone knows what you did and what you took?"

"Gabriel knows I took the evidence from the safe. He might not know what else I've done. Yet."

"We need to meet. You've got to give me that evidence and tell me everything." The desperate plea in Mr. Banks's voice made her want to comply, but still she didn't say anything. "I can help you, Skye. I will. If Gabriel or Prosperity catch you before the authorities are involved, they'll kill you. The FBI agent I spoke to said he'd agree to a meeting and hear you out."

Maybe they could help. "I'm not in Wyoming anymore."

Declan lurched forward and pressed his finger to her lips, stopping her from saying more, though she'd never put Declan at risk.

"Where exactly are you?"

"She's safe," Declan assured Mr. Banks. "And so is what she has on Gabriel and Prosperity. That's all you need to know."

"Skye, you know I'm on your side. I'll meet you

wherever you want. We don't have time to wait. Those girls . . ."

That's all it took for her heart and mind to be reminded of the immediacy and urgency that had been riding her these last days. She'd waited long enough and wasted too much time already. She took Declan's hand.

He shook his head again, imploring her with his eyes not to tell Mr. Banks anything about her location.

She understood he wanted to protect her, but it seemed an overabundance of caution if they were going to meet the FBI and Mr. Banks could help her turn everything over to them. "I know what needs to be done. Let me get everything in order here. I'll call you as soon as I'm ready to meet."

Declan nodded, agreeing with her stall tactic, even if she didn't understand why he wanted her to wait.

"We can't put this off much longer. Every day, those girls are still there. And Prosperity . . . there's no telling what they'll do if they discover what you've done."

She knew exactly what they'd do. They'd eliminate the threat. Her.

"If you're afraid to come forward, you can turn over what you have to me and I'll take it to the authorities. I can act as your agent as well as your lawyer."

"She'll call you and let you know when she's ready." Declan terminated the call.

"Why did you do that?"

"I get that he's worried about you. He wants to take what you have and go to the cops. Great. But because he works for Sunrise, you have no idea if he's looking out for you, or trying to get information for someone else."

"What do you mean?"

"The cops know you went to him that night. Are they using him to get to you? Is Gabriel?"

"Mr. Banks wouldn't do that." He'd seemed sincere.

"How do you know?"

She didn't want to believe one more person she thought she knew would do something to harm her or others. "I've worked with him for the past year. More than that. He's a good man." But how did she really know for sure?

"Maybe he is. And maybe he's being coerced into helping those corrupt cops and Gabriel." He had a point. "What if Gabriel had some of his men threaten Mr. Banks? What if one of them was standing over Mr. Banks, forcing him to try to get you to say where you are and go to that meeting where they could get their hands on you?"

She pressed her hand to her stomach. "I've put him in terrible danger, haven't I?"

"No one would ever think that's what you intended, sweetheart."

The endearment warmed her heart. "We should call someone to check on him."

"If someone is pushing him to get to you, they won't hurt him. They'll want him to try to get in touch with you again."

She glanced at the phone. "He has the number now. Can't he find me?"

"It's a prepaid cell."

She raised her shoulders and let them fall. "What does that mean?"

"It can't be traced. At least not easily."

"If there's even a small chance, I should leave before you get even more involved in this."

Declan just stared at her, waiting for her to dismiss her own declaration. "Did the impulsive feeling pass?"

She smacked his shoulder. "Yes."

He leaned in and gave her a quick kiss. "Good. Now stop talking about leaving and let's figure out what to do next."

"If the local police are corrupt, is the next likely agency to go to the FBI?"

"I'd think it would be the state police, but in this case, since Prosperity is a known militia group and has already crossed paths with the FBI, I'd bet they're still monitoring, if not investigating, the group. So yes, they're probably our best bet."

"That's what I think, too, but I don't have a lot of experience with how things are run outside of Sunrise, or our little town, so, yeah, let's call them."

Declan sighed. "The minute we start this, we risk the FBI, police, Sunrise, and Prosperity finding you."

"Are you saying you don't want me to come forward with what I know and the proof I've collected?"

"It's the right thing to do."

She thought so, too. "It was always my intention to give it to the *right* authorities."

"The question is, is what you have enough to keep you out of jail for Lucy's murder?"

"One doesn't have anything to do with the other. Does it?"

Declan rolled his eyes. "I forget sometimes that you don't watch TV. You've never seen a *CSI* or *Law & Order*."

"Are those some kind of tutorials on the justice system?"

He laughed, though she didn't take offense. She often found she said something others in town or at a farmers market found humorous.

"Sorry, sweetheart. No. They're entertainment based on how the justice system works. Police procedurals."

She bit her lip, tried and failed to ignore how that *sweetheart* made her belly flutter and her heart melt, and tried to understand what he meant. "So based on these shows, you know what we should do?"

"I have a good idea. But most of what I'm thinking is based on the news."

She stared at him, not understanding.

He squeezed her hand. "Do you trust me?"

"Yes."

"Just like that?" Gratitude and appreciation lit his blue eyes.

She shrugged. "You gave me a job based on nothing more than my word I'd work hard and let me live in your house without knowing more than my name. You bought me what I needed to get by and spend most of your time watching out for me because you knew I ran away from something bad. You heard me scream last night and came running to my room in nothing but your underwear. Then you held and comforted me, and even stayed until I fell asleep again, all without asking for anything in return."

"I left you alone in bed last night, even though I wanted to stay."

"I know. You're a good man, Declan. Maybe the best man I've ever known. I believe you have my best interests at heart. I know you'd never do anything to hurt me. So what do you think I should do?"

"Make a deal."

"What does that mean? Don't I just give the police or FBI what I have and they do their job?"

"In an ideal world, yes. But you're facing a murder charge, and you can bargain with what you have to get them to investigate Lucy's death and prove you didn't do it."

"Oh. Really? I can do that?" Who knew she held so much power?

"*We're* going to do that."

She liked the sound of that, because going at this alone seemed daunting. And without Declan's help, she'd probably make a mistake. "Okay." She picked up the phone. "So let's call them."

He put his hand over hers. "Not from here. Let's go into town. We'll buy another phone and call from there."

"I thought you said they couldn't find me with this one."

"Maybe I'm being paranoid, but . . ." The worry in his eyes made it clear he didn't want to miscalculate anything they did.

"Okay. Let's go to town later tonight."

"No. We'll go now."

She felt guilty for taking so much of his time. "Are you sure? You never miss work."

"And yet, I've kicked my brother out twice to be with you."

"Why?" She blurted it out, unfairly putting him on the spot.

He tugged on her hand, pulling her into his lap once again, and kissed her with a desperation she didn't wholly understand but felt within herself, too. He ended the kiss and pressed his forehead to hers. "Does that answer your question?"

"Yep." The *p* popped on her lips.

He hugged her close. "Good. Now will you please take your stuff back upstairs?"

She slipped off his lap, though she would have liked

to stay right there and forget everything else going on in her life. But she couldn't stall any longer. Not when lives were on the line.

"I'll head down to the stables and let Tate know we're leaving for a little while."

Skye grabbed her bags and stared at him as he stood to leave.

"What is it, sweetheart?"

She smiled at the endearment. "You keep calling me that."

His head tilted to the side. "It just came out. Why? You don't like it?"

"I do. I've never been a guy's . . . anything."

His eyes narrowed. "Lucky me they were idiots, and you didn't look twice at them."

She eyed him up and down. "I like looking at you."

He chuckled. "Good. Because I can't take my eyes off you. And all I want to do is this . . ." He leaned down and kissed her again. The soft, sweet kiss melted her heart and made her want more. Eyes locked with hers, he added, "And a lot more." His hands contracted on her hips, though he didn't pull her closer. "But I get it if you need time."

"My life hasn't been like yours. Dating. Relationships. I don't have a lot of experience with it." She had one single unfulfilling experience to draw from, but felt everything would be different, more meaningful, with Declan.

"You don't need to, to know what you want and what works for you. Let's just go with what feels right."

That made it seem so easy and made any lingering nerves evaporate and turn to anticipation.

"There's no right or wrong answer, Skye. If something

doesn't feel right, say so. Faster, slower, I'm in, because I want to be with you."

"That sounds so amazing and unreal."

"I think the same thing about you. Everything seemed to change when I met you."

Her hand found its way to his chest, and it felt like the most natural thing in the world to land there over his thumping heart. "I appreciate the honesty."

"But?"

"No but. After everything that's happened, I appreciate *you*, Declan. You've made this all so much easier to bear."

He pulled her into his chest, hugged her close, and pressed his cheek to her head. "It's going to be okay."

She hoped so. Because she really wanted to see if the feelings building inside her brought them closer together. She dreamed of a life with a man who loved her, children, and a future filled with joy and love. Right now, in his arms, on this ranch, she felt that dream coming to life.

Whatever happened with Gabriel, Sunrise, and Prosperity, nothing would stop the pull inside her that would always lead her right back to Declan.

Chapter Fifteen

DECLAN WALKED into the stables, heard somebody in one of the horse stalls, and walked over, ready to take a ribbing from Tate for heating up the kitchen this morning with Skye. He couldn't remember the last time someone caught him making out with a girl. Not that he cared. But Skye didn't have a whole lot of dating experience, and the last thing he wanted was for her to feel uncomfortable or embarrassed.

He liked that everything seemed new and unique to her. It kind of felt that way for him because she was so different from other women he'd dated. The way he felt about her, how fast and deep it hit him, surprised him. *Special* described her and the way he felt about her.

He didn't know what it meant, except that he hoped it lasted, because he liked this feeling. Anticipation mixed with need and caring about her. So much so, he wanted to know everything about her. He wanted to get her out of this mess so he could just be with her.

He'd been attracted to other women. This thing with Skye, it went deeper. It felt bigger.

He wondered if this was how Tate and Drake felt when they fell for their wives.

But he was getting ahead of himself and letting his

desire for having what his brothers had found come true for him right now.

Relationships took time.

Unless you were Drake and Adria. They met and got married in like a split second.

Tate and Liz were friends practically their whole lives, so it didn't seem odd for them to go from friends to lovers to married in a heartbeat. Not after what they went through with Liz's ex stalking her. Tate wasn't about to lose her right after he finally allowed himself to love her.

Declan felt the same way about Skye. Now that he'd found a woman who got under his skin the way she had, he didn't want to lose her before he found out what this could really be between them. Because it felt urgent and important.

"Tate," he called out, then glanced over the stall gate and locked eyes with someone he'd never seen. "Who the hell are you?"

"Brad. You must be Declan. You look like your brother." The guy nervously rambled on. "Tate hired me this morning. I'll have the stalls done in another hour or so, unless you need me for something else."

Declan vaguely remember getting an email request for an interview with a Brad. "Where's Tate?"

"Office, last I saw him."

Declan walked away without a second thought to Brad, the job he was doing, or the hundred other tasks Declan could assign him. He didn't care about anything right now, except getting to town and contacting the FBI and finding a way to help Skye out of this mess.

He ignored Tate's broad smile when he walked into the office. "I'm taking Skye into town. I don't know when we'll be back."

"You made your point this morning, man. If you two want to be alone, I'll stay away from the house."

Declan didn't regret kicking his brother out—twice—but he felt bad about the way he did it. "Sorry I yelled at you."

Tate laughed. "I loved seeing you lose your shit over her."

He wanted to deny it, but couldn't, so he gave it to Tate straight. "Here's the deal. I like her."

"I got that from the way you had your tongue down her throat and your hands on her ass."

Declan expected the teasing and lewd comments, but Skye might take offense. "Don't say shit like that around her. She's embarrassed enough. She grew up very sheltered. I think she's only ever had one boyfriend."

"Seriously?"

"Yeah." He ran his hand over his hair, realizing Skye messed it up raking her fingers through it while they made out. He stopped the smile that thought brought out before Tate saw it. "She grew up at a place called Sunrise. It's a kind of communal living place. A farm slash self-sustaining community."

"A cult?" Concern filled Tate's eyes.

"No. More an idealistic way to live isolated from surrounding communities or the influence of society and technology. She's seen very little TV, had limited access to the internet, doesn't know what social media is, that kind of thing. Her view of the world is very small. She's educated but in a more focused than broad way." Declan waved his hand. "None of that matters right now. She ran away because she witnessed a murder. The guy who did it pinned it on her. Her family is in danger and so is she. She has evidence of a conspiracy of some kind between

Sunrise and a Wyoming militia group called Prosperity. The cops are on the take with Sunrise, and Gabriel and the folks from Prosperity are looking for her and will probably kill her to keep her quiet. I'm taking her into town so we can call the FBI and see if we can make a deal of some kind to take them down and keep Skye safe." Declan sucked in a breath after that long-ass explanation.

Tate stared up at him, jaw dropped, eyes wide. He shook himself and found some words. "What the fuck."

"Exactly. So who the hell is Brad and why is he here?"

Tate tried to catch up to Declan's racing train of thought. "Um. He showed up this morning, said he's desperate for work, had emailed you about the job posting at the feed store, and wanted to see if you'd be willing to hire him on for a trial run or something permanent. I tried to ask you about it, but—"

"I told you to handle it."

"You were busy and had your hands full."

Yeah, Declan got the joke. He wanted his hands on Skye again. "Where's this guy from? What's his story?"

"He's from up near Missoula. He broke up with his girlfriend, got in a fight with his dad, landed on a buddy's couch in town, and is looking for work. He's twenty-two and seems legit. His dad runs cattle on a place called River Rise. I looked it up. It's exactly what he described."

Declan appreciated that Tate didn't take the guy's word for it and did some digging before hiring him. "Okay. But keep an eye on him. If he takes an interest in Skye or acts out of the ordinary, I want to know about it."

"You want to keep her all to yourself, got it," Tate teased.

"I want to keep her *alive*."

Tate needed to understand the gravity of the situation.

All the humor left Tate's eyes as he leaned forward and braced his weight on his forearms on the desk. "Are you sure you want to get involved in whatever trouble Skye's in?"

"I'm all in, Tate. Whatever it takes to keep her safe." To prove how much he meant it, he added, "I'm leaving the ranch in your hands until this thing with her is settled. I'll probably be around some of the time, but I need to focus on her. Can I count on you?"

"I've always had your back. Don't worry about the ranch. I've got it covered." Tate sat back again and held his gaze. "And if you need help with Skye, I'm in for that, too."

"Thanks." He relaxed and his shoulders sank. "I can't let anything happen to her," he admitted, having a hard time making that confession while looking at Tate.

"Then we won't let anything happen to her. I'll keep my eyes open here. I'll talk to the crews and make sure they report anything out of the ordinary, especially any strangers showing up on the property."

"Good."

"Want to call in Drake, have him do some security shit up at the house?"

"Not a bad idea." He should have thought about it already, but his mind was reeling with all he'd learned this morning and thinking about how to handle the FBI and not get Skye arrested on the spot.

"On it. Anything else?"

"Is this crazy?"

Tate held his gaze. "Love makes us do stupid things. I went after Liz with a concussion and broken ribs to save her from toppling off a bridge." Tate shrugged. "Totally worth it."

Declan found this quest to help Skye and handing off his responsibilities to Tate completely reasonable and necessary. Worth it? Yes. Especially if it meant having Skye in his life.

"I don't know when I'll be back, but I'll call and text to let you know what's happening."

"I hope it works out." Tate meant a hell of a lot more than getting Skye out of this trouble.

Declan appreciated his brother's support, both with the ranch and with the woman who somehow became more important to him with every passing second.

Chapter Sixteen

SKYE SAT in the front seat of the parked truck, enjoying the sun on her face. She stared out the window and tried not to think the doom and gloom roiling in her gut and fears cluttering her mind would come true with one simple phone call. She tried to remain calm, focusing on her breathing and the bird flitting from here to there across the grass in the park.

She believed in moments.

The joy you feel when you're a child and someone hands you a soft puppy.

The safety you feel when you tell a best friend a secret and know they'll take it to the grave.

The first time the boy you like smiles at you.

The first time he kisses you.

The difference you feel when the right man kisses you and you feel the fireworks go off just like people talk about but you never believed in until they burst inside you.

The moment when you understand that death can be just a breath away and you don't want to waste another second.

How a smile that seemed so rare the first time you saw it comes so easily every time the guy who likes you sees you and you know that smile is just for you.

Declan made her sigh with pure contentment. Just watching him walk down the sidewalk, his gaze locked on her, that sexy smile, telling her he was happy to see her, all of it just made her happy.

He opened the truck door and handed her a paper bag before he climbed inside and closed the door against the cool breeze. He leaned over and kissed her softly, his lips cold but still able to light a fire in her.

Another great moment.

"Sorry it took so long."

She pulled the prepaid phone trapped in plastic out of the bag and smiled when she spotted the candy bar at the bottom.

"How did you know I like chocolate?"

"You ate all of what was in the house." He tipped the bag toward him and pulled out the bottle of water.

The moment when you realize the guy you like likes you so much he stores away all the tidbits of things he knows about you so he can find little ways to show you he cares.

"Declan."

"Yeah, sweetheart?"

She leaned in, put her hand on his face, and kissed him. "You're not just a good guy, you're a great guy."

One eyebrow shot up. "Because I got you candy."

"Yes. And because of the *sweetheart* and the smile and being here with me."

His hand slipped up her neck, his fingers sliding into her hair. "You're very easy to please."

She laughed under her breath. "I appreciate the little things."

"I'm just getting started. *Sweetheart*." This time the kiss told her without words how much he wanted her. If this was him getting started, she was in for a huge awakening with whatever came next.

But first, they both had to stop stalling and do what needed to be done.

Declan brushed his lips against her kiss-swollen ones. "I know you're worried. So am I. But this is going to work."

"I wish I had your optimism. And understanding of how the FBI and law work. Maybe I do need a lawyer to help me."

"If it comes to that, I'll hire one. But let's see if we can set the record straight with what you know." He sat back, pulled the knife from his waist, flipped it open, and cut the packaging on the phone. He plugged it into the car charger and turned it on. "Ready?"

"You're sure they can't trace the call."

"They might be able to pinpoint the closest cell tower, but they can't tell who is using the phone or where you live."

"I don't want to get you in trouble."

"I wouldn't take this chance if I thought you'd get arrested or hurt. I know you're scared because you don't know how this all works, but trust me, Skye. I wouldn't give you the go-ahead unless I thought I could keep you safe." He laid his hand on her shoulder and squeezed. "The authorities need to know what really happened. They need to arrest Gabriel and put Prosperity out of business." He had such faith in her and this plan.

She hoped it wasn't misplaced. "I haven't told you everything."

"I know. We have to trust each other. I'll let you know if I think the FBI is trying to trap you or make it appear that you're guilty. You just tell the truth about what happened and what you know. If you're not sure about something, don't answer or guess. Don't say something just because you think it's what they want to hear."

"This is starting to feel complicated."

"It's not. We'll ask to speak to the agent assigned to Prosperity. You'll tell him about the murder and that the cops have been bought off and you want them to investigate. If they agree and ask good questions, we'll go from there." Declan pulled up the number on his cell phone and punched in the numbers on the prepaid phone. Before he pressed the call button, he glanced at her.

She nodded.

He put the phone on speaker and they waited for the call to be answered.

"Federal Bureau of Investigation, how may I direct your call?"

Thanks to Declan's internet search, they'd called the Bozeman office. She let Declan handle the first part of this.

"We have information regarding the Wyoming militia group known as Prosperity. We'd like to talk to the agent assigned to the group." It was a guess on their part, but due to the group's known activities, despite their legal status, it was a safe bet the FBI had them on a watch list of some kind.

"Do you have information relating to a crime?"

"Yes." Declan looked at her for confirmation, because she hadn't told him the details of how Prosperity was involved.

"What type of crime?"

Declan looked at her, so she answered. "Murder. Police corruption. Prostitution. Guns. Bomb-making materials.

And what was that term you used for the girls?" she asked Declan.

"Sex trafficking."

"That, too," she said into the phone.

"Please remain on the line. An agent will be with you in just a moment."

The second the line went quiet, Declan burst out. "Are you kidding me? Guns and bombs?"

"It's a lot, right?"

Declan rolled his eyes. "Jeez, Skye."

She held up her hands, then let them drop. "Why do you think I ran?"

"This is way worse than I thought."

She raised a brow. "What's worse than murder?"

"Mass murder," a deep voice said over the phone. "This is Assistant Special Agent-in-Charge Nick Gunn. Who am I speaking to?"

"I'm a member of Sunrise Fellowship." During the drive to town, she and Declan went over how she'd approach the agent and start the conversation. "I have information about crimes involving an alliance forming between Sunrise Fellowship and Prosperity."

"Do you have proof to back up your claims?"

"Enough to oust the head of Sunrise and take down Prosperity." She hoped that wasn't too big a boast.

"I'm listening," Agent Gunn said, though she wondered if he really was open to what she had to say.

"Almost two weeks ago . . ." She choked up thinking about what Gabriel did to Lucy and her unborn child.

"Take your time." Agent Gunn sounded sincere.

"Gabriel, the leader of Sunrise, murdered my friend Lucy."

"Did you see him kill her?"

"Yes." She lost herself in the nightmare, but Declan brought her back with his warm hands on her face.

"You can do this," he coaxed.

"A lot happened leading up to her death. Gabriel took over Sunrise two years ago."

"We know about Gabriel and that there's been a shift in how Sunrise is operated." Agent Gunn didn't add anything more. What more did he have to say? He'd basically just told her that Sunrise, along with Prosperity, was under investigation. Or at the very least that they had an eye on Sunrise.

She tried to explain. "At first, the change to the council and adopting more modern methods of doing business seemed like good ideas. Until it became clear profit was his goal."

"The people at Sunrise don't want to make more money?"

She supposed to Agent Gunn, Declan, and outsiders, that seemed the way of things. "We have always believed in supporting the group and providing for those less fortunate. Once Gabriel had power and control of the finances, he wanted more of both. He wanted what the group had always fought against: excess. He and his partners eroded our core values. The men were engaging in inappropriate behavior with girls. Drinking, which was never allowed at Sunrise until Gabriel started having private parties with his friends and the girls they lured there. Some of the girls turned up pregnant. The youngest is fourteen. These are men in their late twenties and thirties. One in his fifties. The men went out and brought more girls back, but not to join Sunrise. They set up a place for them on the property called The Stable."

"Were the women brought there expressly for sex?" The agent didn't mince words.

"Yes. They're locked in rooms. Gabriel makes money off them from the men who come from town, including the police officers he's befriended."

"I see."

"No, you don't see. Gabriel locked those girls up. He forces them to have sex against their will. He gets the drugs he uses on them from the friends he has in Prosperity. He makes the girls sell it to their . . . the men who use them. Gabriel is forcing members of Sunrise to take care of the girls and that place against their will by threatening them with expulsion from Sunrise. These are people who haven't lived outside of the community in decades. They have no means of making a life on their own outside the community."

"Do you know where Gabriel and his men are getting the women?"

"They aren't women. They're young ladies. Teens. Runaways from larger cities. I heard one of the men say they promised the girls a new life at Sunrise, where they'd work on the farm and have a good and decent life." She couldn't believe the men sold the life she'd grown up in, one where she was happy and taken care of, to those girls and gave them nothing but more pain. They had to be desperate to escape their old lives. Gabriel and his men promised them a home and gave them hell.

"The people at Sunrise started questioning Gabriel and his vision for our future. To knock down rumors and prove that he and the other men were good, decent, family men, Gabriel arranged matches for the men and several of the girls caught up in the parties no one was supposed to know about."

"Are you talking about arranged marriages?"

"Yes. And unbeknownst to me, Gabriel intended to force *me* to marry *him*."

"Hello, Skye."

Her name felt like a punch to the gut. All the air went out of her.

"I hoped this was you. When I heard the woman who takes care of everyone at Sunrise killed a sweet young girl in cold blood, I wondered what set her off."

She made a grab for the phone to hang up, but stopped a split second before she did.

"Don't hang up! I want to help you."

She didn't believe him. "I didn't kill Lucy."

"Gabriel went to a lot of trouble to make it look like you did." The agent said it so simply. Like ruining her life meant nothing. It didn't to Gabriel, but it meant a hell of a lot to her. It meant her future.

And she didn't intend to spend it locked up behind bars.

"Are you working with him, too?" She feared she'd made a grave mistake.

"No. I'm the man who's going to take him and Prosperity down. With your help, I hope."

"Why should I believe you? Gabriel has the police in his pocket. I saw him pay off the cop who was at The Stable after seeing those girls and doing nothing about it."

"I can see why you'd suspect everyone is working for him, but I assure you I'm not. I know that doesn't mean much right now. You don't know me. I don't know you. But I'm willing to take a chance that you're telling the truth about the girls, Gabriel, and Lucy's murder if you'll take a chance on me."

"I'm not a liar."

"I don't think you are, but I still need proof to back up what you're saying."

"Go to Sunrise. Find those girls. I can tell you exactly where they are."

"I'm counting on it. But first, you have a warrant out for your arrest. Turn yourself in. If what you say is true and Gabriel staged the crime scene, then you'll be exonerated."

"I get that you think because I grew up the way I did, I'm as simple as my life used to be." She tamped down the rising anger and resentment.

"Skye, I don't think that at all." He sounded sincere, but he was also very careful about the way he spoke to her.

"It's okay. I don't blame you. Until a few hours ago, I had no idea what the FBI was or what it did. I didn't know what to do with all the stuff I collected, all the things I've hidden. I'm hoping you'll prove to be smart enough to want that far more than you want me to wait in a cell while you try to prove that Gabriel framed me."

"What did you collect and hide?"

She had his full attention now. "See. That's a smart question. How long have you been investigating Prosperity?"

"We have no evidence that Prosperity is doing anything illegal."

"That's a very diplomatic response to a question I didn't ask."

Agent Gunn smothered what had to be a chuckle.

"I bet you've been on them a long time. Since they know you're watching, it's been hard for them to do what bad people do. So they found another way."

Agent Gunn took a few extra seconds to fill the silence she purposefully left in the conversation. "I have information that suggests something of theirs has gone missing."

"I might know where that something is."

"What is it?" he baited her.

"Dangerous." She waited a beat. "Pull the records on Lucy's death. Take over the investigation. Look at the evidence. I. Did. Not. Kill. Her. I'm five-foot-five and weigh about one-twenty. She and I would have been an equal fight. She could have taken me or put up enough of a fight to get away. How hard could I kick her? What kind of damage could I do? What did her autopsy reveal? Do you know she was pregnant with Gabriel's child?"

"How do you know that?"

"Because I was there when she begged him to accept his child and spare her life. I watched him shove her to the floor and kick her again and again until she bled all over the hardwood. I s-saw her die." Sorrow choked off her words, but then the rage swept through her. "He showed her nothing but cold disdain. I felt his hate. And I will do everything in my power to make him pay for what he's done!" She breathed heavily, ready to fight, but helpless to really do anything, except make the agent understand he needed to act now.

"Where was Lucy killed?"

She sighed, hating to waste time with these mundane questions. "In his bedroom."

"Did you go into the room at any time?"

"I've never been in that room. I worked in the home office, which is right off the main entry."

"What were you wearing when you left?"

"Khaki cargo pants, a gray T-shirt, canvas shoes. My usual attire."

"Did you take anything with you?"

"The evidence I knew was in the office safe, some money, and a satchel."

"What about other clothes, shoes, personal belongings?"

"I ran with the clothes on my back and what I took from the office. I grabbed the girls who were supposed to marry the men in a mass ceremony the next day, told them I was taking them for a surprise trip to the movies, and drove them to Gordon Banks's home."

Agent Gunn didn't speak for a long moment. "Why did you take the girls to Gordon Banks?"

"To protect them. He assured me he'd make sure the police questioned them about what was happening at Sunrise. Bess was the proof that older men were having sex with underage girls and that those girls were being coerced into marriages they didn't really want."

"What happened when the police got there?"

"The men from Sunrise arrived right before the police. They took the girls back to Sunrise. The cops didn't do anything. So I ran. If Gabriel's men found me, they'd have taken me back to him, and he would have either married me and kept me under lock and key or killed me. I couldn't let either of those things happen before I got help."

"Yet you've waited to contact someone."

After what happened, she'd been numb and unable to think and work out a plan. She'd moved around so they couldn't find her and then landed at Declan's ranch. The numbness wore off and . . . here she was trying to make this right.

"I spoke to my sister the other night. She told me Gabriel pinned the murder on me. I don't know how he did that, but I couldn't go to the very police officers who believed him and were on his side. It wasn't until this morning when I talked to . . ." She didn't want to name Declan. "A friend, and we called Mr. Banks to see what he knew because he's a lawyer that I learned the FBI might be able to help. He said he'd contacted someone at the FBI and that they'd listen to me. He wanted to set up a meeting."

"Did he give you a name?" Agent Gunn sounded very suspicious.

"No."

"So you decided to make the call yourself."

"It's too dangerous to let anyone know where I am."

"Is that why you're calling from a prepaid phone? So we can't track you?"

Her eyes went wide, but she relaxed when Declan squeezed her shoulder. His steady presence kept her calm.

"I don't know who to trust or who will help me. If you want me to cooperate and give you what I have, look into Lucy's murder."

"All the evidence points to you. At best you're looking at accessory after the fact. At the moment, I can see about knocking down the murder charge to manslaughter if you prove Prosperity is planning something and help me stop it."

"I didn't kill Lucy. Gabriel killed her. He should pay for his crimes. But he won't unless *you* investigate."

"Cooperate and I will."

"Not good enough. It's your job to catch the bad guys, right? So prove he did it, not me. I've already stopped what Prosperity has planned. For now. But you need to move on what I have soon. There's no telling how long it will take them to find what I hid."

"What are we talking about? The guns?"

"Those. And more. Sunrise is a farm. We order fertilizer on occasion. Nothing like the orders we've been receiving."

"They're making a bomb." Resignation and alarm rang in the agent's voice.

"I may be just the accountant, but I grew up working those fields, learning how to prepare the dirt to yield the most crops. Buying in bulk is cheaper than buying as necessity dictates, but Sunrise wouldn't have been able to use the amount of fertilizer ordered in a dozen years. What was the point? Why stock so much? I went to the library and looked up other uses for it. You can imagine my shock when the computer told me how to make a bomb.

"I put two and two together and figured out Gabriel partnered with Prosperity. They couldn't order that amount of fertilizer and not raise suspicions, but Sunrise could. And an unholy alliance was born. Prosperity paid Gabriel a lot of money to place the order and store it for them. I printed out the list of supplies needed for a bomb and then I stole everything on the list from Sunrise and hid it."

Declan sank into the seat. "Jeez, Skye. What if you'd gotten caught? Why didn't you call the cops?" She raised an eyebrow at Declan, who let his head fall back before he looked at her again. "You really were your own detective. You sabotaged their plans."

"It wasn't easy. It took a lot of late-night hours. While they were partying, I was plotting and carrying out my plans to stop them."

"Does anyone else at Sunrise know where you hid the stuff or that you took it?" the agent asked.

"I didn't tell anyone what I did. If they haven't figured out the supplies are missing, they will soon. I'm sure Prosperity wants their stuff. And when Gabriel can't deliver, that's going to be a problem."

"And put an even bigger target on your back," Declan pointed out, rubbing a hand over his face. "Skye. Damn. I admire the hell out of what you did, but the risks you took . . ."

"What was I supposed to do? Let them build a bomb? Take all those guns and kill people?"

"How many guns?" Agent Gunn asked like he expected a big number. They were dealing with a militant group, after all.

"Crates of guns. A couple dozen of them. Prosperity paid Gabriel to hide those, too."

"How did you move them?"

"Not easily." She scrunched her mouth, then asked, "Did I mention I grew up on a farm?" The sarcasm wasn't necessary, but it helped alleviate her anxiety. "I know how to drive a tractor and backhoe. We have a forklift and flatbed trucks. If you've got the right equipment, you can move just about anything."

"It's a wonder no one at Sunrise found you out."

She didn't tell Declan how close she'd come to being discovered when Gabriel started having the grounds patrolled at night. Lucky for her, most of the people doing the patrolling weren't really looking for trouble because there'd never been any threat at Sunrise. Not until Gabriel brought it to them.

"Agent Gunn, do we have a deal?"

"I've already got agents pulling the records for Lucy's murder."

She shook her head, though he couldn't see that through the phone. "Not good enough. Those records are tainted."

"The coroner's report should give us detailed information about how she died."

Declan leaned closer to the phone. "Would the coroner have done an autopsy?"

"Not necessarily," Agent Gunn admitted. "They're usually elected officials, who use the police investigation to determine cause of death."

She didn't like that at all. "So the coroner will go by what the crooked cops said?"

The question was rhetorical, but the agent helped her out with some details. "If you want a real forensic autopsy, that will take a medical examiner."

"Do you have one of those?" Declan asked.

"Yes." Reluctance filled the agent's voice.

Finally they were getting somewhere. "You need Lucy's body." She hated to disturb Lucy's peaceful rest, but this was important.

"Do you really want me to get a warrant to exhume her body and put her family through that torture?"

"I want you to give Lucy the justice she deserves and that was stolen from her by those crooked cops. I will be the first to apologize to her family for putting them through it, but I will not go to jail for a crime I didn't commit and see Gabriel go free and hurt other people." She picked up the phone and spoke directly into it. "You have my number. Call me when you have the proof and are ready to arrest Gabriel. I'll give you the rest of the nails for his coffin." She ended the call, fell back against the seat, and stared out the windshield, not believing this was her life.

"You did really well."

She appreciated Declan's praise. The call had left her drained.

"Holy hell, Skye. How did you do all that, not get caught, and manage to get away?"

"Luck. Desperation," she added. "I didn't know what to do, but I had to do something. I didn't know who I could trust at Sunrise. Even if they weren't working with Gabriel, I couldn't take the chance they'd say something to him or someone else and ruin my plans."

He hooked his hand at the back of her neck and pulled her in for a kiss. "You amaze me." He kissed her again, long and deep, drawing it out until every ounce of anxiety dissipated from her body. She settled into him and the wonderful way he made her feel, and she forgot everything else. "Let's go home."

She hugged him and said, "That sounds so good."

Chapter Seventeen

GABRIEL FELT something big coming in the air all the way down to his bones. While the cops were looking for Skye, he'd sent additional men out in every direction. None of them found even a trace of her. She'd taken off and disappeared.

Since her escape, the whole place seemed to be falling down around him. He knew she did a lot of the day-to-day management and oversaw the business, but now he saw just how she touched every part of everything on the farm.

When his father died, she'd stepped into his shoes. No one gave her the job, but they all expected her to do it because she'd worked beside his dad for several years.

Gabriel hadn't minded. He'd never really been interested in cultivating and selling produce. Boring as hell. Sure, he'd done his part when he'd been forced to help out. But he'd resented every minute of it. He had bigger, better plans for his life.

And he was on his way to making some real money until she stepped in and ruined it all.

Skye and Lucy. How did the two women in his life fuck everything up?

Why didn't they do what he expected?

And why the hell couldn't the people here do their jobs without direction from Skye, and now him?

"If you don't allow us to leave the compound, how do you expect us to sell the crops we spent all week harvesting? They'll rot and go to waste."

Gabriel couldn't remember the name of the man who'd come to him on behalf of the workers. Didn't matter. Not to him. He just wanted to be left alone to solve the real problems facing them, instead of being peppered with questions and requests every-fucking-where he went at Sunrise these days.

"It's not safe for anyone to leave right now. Skye—"

"—was friends with Lucy," the man dared interrupt him. "She's friends with everyone here. *You* say she killed Lucy because she was jealous. Skye's never been unkind to anyone.

"A lot of us don't like what's been going on around here. We've turned a blind eye to what you and your friends have been doing, the way you've changed things. Some of the men have shifted away from you and are back to doing their jobs and making this place work for everyone."

"If living here doesn't work for you, or anyone else, you're free to leave."

"That's just it, Gabriel. This is our home as much as it is yours. *We* make this place run. We support each other. And those who don't contribute or have the best interest for the collective should leave so the rest of us can thrive as we've always done."

Gabriel glanced at Joseph, who he'd asked to stay for the meeting, to gauge his reaction. Joseph kept his features carefully blank, but couldn't maintain eye contact with him. His gaze shot to the floor as he stood sentry by the door during this meeting.

"My grandfather started this place. You're here *thriving* because he and my father made this place what it is."

"Since your father's death you've begun to slowly dismantle our way of life. You don't hold the same values we do. Unwed girls are pregnant!"

"I tried to set up the marriages they needed to save their reputations."

"You ruined their reputations, seducing them away from the values they've been taught here."

Gabriel rolled his eyes. "No drinking. No partying. No sex. No fun!"

"Yes, you're all about fun. But what about the consequences of your actions? Bess is fourteen. Do you really think she's ready to be a mother? You wanted her to marry a man seventeen years older than her. Is she capable of making a life decision like that, to tie herself to a man she barely knows?"

"She had no trouble fucking him."

The man's mouth pinched like he'd sucked on a sour lemon. "How much pressure and coercion was involved? Did she want to just fit in, or did she really want to be with that man? Was she so drunk she didn't know what she was really doing? And why didn't that older man protect her from getting pregnant? Why didn't you? She may not have known better, but *he* did! *You* did!"

How the hell was he to blame for another guy getting a girl pregnant? That made no sense. "Enough. I run this place."

He *pfted* that away. "You're more interested in organizing late-night parties than the sale of our goods. You don't care about the welfare of the people who live here. You only care about yourself and having fun."

A knock sounded on the door a split second before one

of his other trusted men Ken poked his head in. "The FBI is at the gates. They say they have a warrant for Lucy."

"What?"

Ken shrugged. "They want her body."

What the hell!

"Having fun now, Gabriel?" The man who'd come to put him in his place on behalf of the others turned and left the room.

Gabriel stood stunned, trying to think what to do first. He turned to Joseph. "Gather a few of the men and make sure the crates are secure and that no one goes near them. If the warrant is for Lucy, they can't go anywhere else on the property."

"How do you know they won't try?" Joseph's eyes were filled with fear and worry.

Gabriel didn't have time for either, even if they were warranted.

He didn't like that his men were beginning to second-guess his decisions. He needed to get a handle on the situation and them. "They can try, but if the warrant is specific, then we can deny them access." He'd been advised about that and told to stick to his guns and not let law enforcement of any kind trample his rights.

Ken waited by the door. "What if they don't give us a choice?"

"You've been to the meeting with Prosperity. They told us all about how the cops and laws work when it comes to organizations like ours."

"*We* are not like Prosperity." Joseph's frown conveyed his deep disapproval. His past relationship with Skye complicated things. Joseph still had a soft spot for her.

Gabriel didn't suffer such sentimentality. "If they're here to help put Skye behind bars for killing Lucy, then

I have no problem helping them do it, but I will not let them ruin our other plans." He stared down Joseph. "Do as I said. No one better get near those crates."

Joseph nodded and walked past Ken and out the door.

Ken shrugged. "He misses her."

Everyone on this whole damn place missed her. Right now, he'd give his left nut to get his hands on her, so he could silence her once and for all.

"I assume the men are doing their job and holding the FBI off until I get there."

"Yes, sir." Ken knew his place.

Gabriel liked that. Maybe he'd move Ken up, give him more responsibility. Joseph needed an attitude adjustment and a reminder that he was in this as deep as the rest of them.

He wished he could keep them from taking Lucy. It exposed him, but what choice did he really have if they had a warrant for her? He hoped the evidence against Skye stuck, or he was fucked. "Let's go."

It didn't take long to get to the gate, but it surprised him to see so many of the Sunrise residents clustered together, watching the FBI agents watching them.

Gabriel scanned the Sunrise crowd, grateful they'd followed his orders and kept the children sequestered in the meal hall. The last thing he needed was anyone questioning whether the children were well cared for or not. He'd heard from his friends at Prosperity that the FBI would take their children if they got a chance no matter if they were happy and healthy. Gabriel would have a revolt on his hands if that happened.

He couldn't deal with the FBI and a bunch of terrified and disgruntled parents at the same time.

He walked past the crowd and tried to reassure them.

"Everything is going to be fine. These men are here to make sure Skye is punished for taking Lucy from us."

No one dared contradict him by either gesture or words.

Lucy's parents and younger brother stood in the middle of the crowd, insulated and protected by the group.

He gave them a smile and nod to let them know he'd take care of this.

As he approached the gate, he spotted Skye's parents and sister standing five feet from the man who looked like he was in charge.

"I've spoken to Skye. She sounded okay." The agent's voice reassured Meadow and her parents.

Great. The last thing he needed was them making friends. But if the agent had Skye in custody, all the better. "Have you arrested that murderer?" *Please say yes, so this can finally be over.*

"No." The agent held up a paper. "I have a warrant to exhume and take Lucy's body."

"Why? The police have already investigated and issued a warrant for Skye's arrest. She murdered that poor girl. Shouldn't you be looking for her and let the dead rest in peace? Hasn't her family been through enough?"

Many of the Sunrise residents nodded in agreement with him.

"The FBI has taken over the investigation."

"I didn't know the FBI investigated murders." He blamed Skye for this disastrous turn.

"In this circumstance we do."

"And what circumstance is that? That she belonged to a collective that doesn't conform to your societal norms?" He hoped that's what brought the FBI in and Skye wasn't stupid enough to turn over the documents she stole. If they had them, they wouldn't be here about Lucy. And that meant he had time to find Skye.

"It's my understanding Sunrise Fellowship is a community of people who work the farm and believe in taking care of each other. Nothing about that goes against society or the laws of this land. Someone killed Lucy. We're here to make sure that person is held accountable." The agent turned back to Skye's family. "I'm sorry I can't tell you where your daughter is. I simply don't know. But she's worried about you." The agent eyed Gabriel, then focused on Skye's parents again. "If you would like to come with us, I can put you in contact with her."

"If you can contact her, why haven't you arrested her?" Gabriel loved putting the agent on the spot and showing everyone from Sunrise that the cops weren't infallible.

"I only have a phone number for her. *She* called us."

A collective gasp went up from everyone.

Gabriel's lungs seized. *That bitch!* She thought she could take him down. Not going to happen.

The agent focused on Meadow. "She really wants to talk to you."

Meadow walked over to the agent and leaned in while he spoke into her ear.

Gabriel fumed.

His men stood by the gate, but they weren't close enough to overhear.

They were no match for the twenty agents waiting to get into Sunrise. He'd have to bide his time and hope they arrested Skye for Lucy's murder just like the local cops promised they would. Maybe he needed to remind his contact what was at stake if they didn't.

Meadow turned to her parents and waved them over. They joined Meadow and the agent. Meadow did the talking this time. She put a hand on her mother's and father's shoulders and stared at them for a long moment before she released them, slid the gate open so she could pass through, and joined the agents.

Her parents took a step toward the gate and he knew he had to do something.

"If you leave, you will not be welcomed back. This is our home. We do not follow outsiders."

Another gasp went up from the other Sunrise members watching this all play out. They didn't cast out members lightly.

Skye's parents stood immobile, worried and undecided.

He pushed harder. "Lucy was a member of this community, under all of our protection. She had her whole life ahead of her and Skye killed her. Are you going to side with *her*, or stand with the community?"

The agent leaned over the gate, not stepping a foot on Sunrise land, and said something to the Kennedys, urging them to leave.

Skye's mom's eyes went wide. She shot Gabriel a surprised and disheartened gaze, then joined Meadow on the other side of the gate.

Joseph ran up behind Gabriel and whispered in his ear, "They're gone. The crates. They aren't there."

The agent saw Gabriel's reaction to the news and waved his people forward and onto Sunrise land as an agent escorted the entire Kennedy family away to a van waiting nearby.

The agent handed Gabriel the warrant. "Skye had a lot to say about you." He watched Gabriel absorb that blow and glanced at Joseph, then back at him. "Seems like you got bad news. More is coming."

Joseph put a hand on his shoulder. "Don't say anything."

Gabriel shook off Joseph. "She'll pay for this."

The agent eyed him. "That sounds like a threat."

"I thought you were here for Lucy."

"I am. In fact, I have a few questions for you about the night she was murdered."

"It's all in the police report."

"I'd like to hear what happened from you directly. Is there somewhere we can speak privately? Perhaps the hall?"

Of course the FBI had done their homework about the compound. They wanted access to whatever they could get into, but Gabriel wasn't going to play into their hands. He opened the warrant, read it, and turned to Joseph. "They are only allowed to dig up Lucy's grave and take her body. They are not allowed anywhere else on the property. Make sure everyone knows this and watches to be sure the FBI sticks to the laws that bind them."

"Those laws apply to you, too," the agent pointed out. "My men know their job."

"Then get it done and get off our land."

"On it, but I still have questions for you." The agent waited a beat, then added, "So we can make our case against Lucy's killer."

Gabriel silently ordered Joseph to oversee the agents in the cemetery with a look, then walked to one of the many benches set out by the old apple tree where they sometimes held outdoor services and weddings. It didn't surprise him that the agent followed.

Gabriel sat on the bench like he didn't have a care in the world when all he could think about was the missing crates and what else the FBI knew.

Did the men from Prosperity take them without letting him know?

Did Skye know about them?

How did she know?

What else did she know?

If Prosperity didn't take them, did Skye? How the hell would she even be able to do it?

Did she have help?

Who?

If Prosperity didn't take them back, would he have to return the fortune they'd paid him to store and hide them? What would they do to him if he couldn't deliver?

The agent smiled at him. "I bet you have more questions than I do right now."

Gabriel tipped his head up and stared at the agent. "*Right now*, I'm only concerned with how Lucy's parents must feel having their daughter's grave desecrated." And the death threat hanging over his head if Prosperity didn't get their stuff back.

"My men will do it with respect and allow Lucy's parents the time they need to say goodbye. We will treat her with deference and return her to her family as soon as possible." The agent said all that in the matter-of-fact tone Gabriel had used to declare his concern. "But you don't really care about Lucy's parents, her, or the child who died with her when you kicked her to death."

Gabriel dropped his gaze to the ground and tried to contain the rage building inside him. "That wasn't a question."

"I don't really want to hear the same bullshit you fed the cops. I've spoken to Skye. She tells a compelling story. Very detailed. You had no idea she stood outside that room and watched you kill her friend."

No, he didn't, not until he'd seen the empty safe. "Skye is misguided. She never really fit in here. She thinks she's better than everyone."

"From what I gather about her, she wanted better than what you brought to this place. She believes in helping others and taking care of her family and this community. That's what this place used to be until you turned it into something ugly. Did you really think someone like *her* would marry *you*?"

"Not everyone knows what's best for them. Some people need to be shown."

The agent brushed that off. "You don't know her at all. I had a single conversation with her and I can assure you, no one tells that woman what she thinks or what she believes in. She knows to her marrow what is right and wrong and she's willing to fight for it. You have no idea what she's capable of when she sets her mind to it."

Gabriel had misjudged her. But he wouldn't make that mistake again. "She thinks she's gotten away with this, but she'll see. I'm not the only one she has to answer to."

"Face it, you're in over your head. Do yourself a favor. Tell me everything before things get worse. Make this easy on yourself."

This time Gabriel looked the agent right in the eye. "You're required to operate under the presumption that everyone is innocent until proven guilty." He stood. "Good luck with that." He walked past the agent and didn't stop even when the man spewed even more chilling words.

"I don't need luck. I have Skye, who has all the proof I need to take you and those others down."

Only if she's still alive to hand it over.

Chapter Eighteen

Skye barely slept last night, wondering about the call with Agent Gunn, worrying about her family, and trying to figure out how to make this all work without her ending up in jail. But that's not all that kept her awake most of the night. Declan. He somehow filtered into every one of her thoughts. Her feelings for him felt so big and important and wonderful. They seemed so full of possibility. She couldn't help but spin dreams of a wonderful future with him when this mess ended.

Hopefully, in her favor.

She couldn't imagine jail and being locked away from her family, friends, and the life she'd known. The one she wanted with Declan.

Yes, it was too soon to tell if that's where this was going, but she couldn't help wanting it to work out, because what she felt for him was special.

The connection they shared, it seemed to come out of nowhere.

Was it born out of Declan's innate protective streak?

She believed it was much more than that.

They definitely shared an intense attraction to each other. That part seemed all too real and urgent.

For both of them.

When he was close, he never failed to touch her in some small way. A brush of his hand on her arm or a gentle tug of her hair. He played with it nonstop last night while they watched an action movie with lots of swearing, explosions, and car chases. She'd never seen anything like it. But the good guys won in the end and she sure enjoyed that. And how hard Declan tried to distract her.

She liked movies a lot better than TV. Too many commercials and interruptions. It made her impatient and annoyed. How many types of vacuums, toilet paper, and yogurt did a person need? Or want to hear about? Go to the store, look at the products, and make your decision.

The best part of watching the movie with Declan by far was simply enjoying sitting close to him with his arm around her while his fingers slid through her hair. She'd never enjoyed anything so intimate and comfortable. He'd teased and said she was like a cat, snuggling up to him. She couldn't help herself. He was big and strong and it just felt good to be next to him.

She'd always known her parents adored each other. Their love had kept them together all these years. They had a connection to each other that had always been visible and tangible to Skye. She'd wanted to feel the way they obviously felt about each other with someone special because the other person loved her that much.

She kind of got it now. Being with Declan felt wonderful and right. She had more than a few moments where it simply overwhelmed her.

Like when he walked her upstairs to her door and kissed her with her back pressed up against it. After all the kisses they'd shared, she hadn't known what to do. Say good-night or invite him in. He'd taken the decision out of her hands, ended the kiss with a reluctant groan, opened her door, gently nudged her inside, then closed the door with a brusque, "See you in the morning."

She'd stood there staring at the door for a few long minutes, trying to decide if she should go after him because she didn't want the night to end. But she'd heard the dull hum of the shower in his room and flopped on the bed, disheartened that she'd missed her chance because she didn't have the guts to go after him and what she wanted.

But how many more chances might she have if this whole thing blew up in her face and the FBI found and arrested her?

Two large hands landed on her shoulders and squeezed. She jumped, not realizing Declan had come up behind her in the yard. She'd been headed to the house to get dinner started when she stopped to watch the gorgeous sunset and got lost in thought.

"Sorry, sweetheart."

Her phone rang in her back pocket, making her jump again. She made a grab for it and immediately hit the button to accept the call. "Hello." She hit the speaker button so Declan could listen.

"You sent the FBI."

Relieved to hear her sister's voice, she grabbed a handful of Declan's T-shirt and leaned on him. "Meadow. Are you okay? Are Mom and Dad with you?"

"They're not happy about what you did, but we're all together."

"You got them to leave Sunrise." She really couldn't believe it.

"You know how they feel about relying on outsiders, but Gabriel gave them the last little push they needed to truly believe he lied about you killing Lucy."

Declan frowned at her. "They actually thought you did it?"

"Who is that?" Meadow asked.

"A friend." She didn't want to use Declan's name, because she didn't want anyone to know about his involvement.

"A friend, friend? Or . . ."

"Meadow. We've got bigger things to talk about than—"

"We're more than friends," Declan cut her off.

She locked eyes with him and his twinkled with all the joy in the smile he gave her.

"What? We are." He hugged her close to his side.

Meadow popped her bubble of joy and brought her back to reality. "It's nice to meet you, whoever you are. I'm glad my sister isn't alone in all this."

"I won't let anything happen to her. We're just getting started."

"I was seriously beginning to think you gave up on guys." Meadow thought she worked too much and was no fun.

"It just happened." She'd wished for someone like Declan. She just never expected it to happen like this. A chance meeting. An instant attraction and connection.

She didn't know her heart could speak so loudly until it found what it wanted.

"It's new. We're working it out," Declan added, trying to explain how they both felt about something neither of them expected when she showed up here, desperate and in need of help. She never expected this kind of support, or for him to care so much about her.

"So, here's the thing," Meadow went on. "Your agent friend set us up in a motel with guards."

That shocked her. "What?"

"For our protection because Gabriel knows you're helping the FBI. At least, that's what the agent says."

"Please tell Mom and Dad it is for their protection. There's a lot you don't know. It's not just Lucy's death they're investigating now."

"Care to fill me in?"

"No." Before her sister went off, she added, "I'm trying to protect you. If you don't know anything, Gabriel and the others involved can't hurt you to get the information."

It took Meadow a second to speak again. "Do you think he'd really do that?"

"He killed Lucy because she was pregnant with his child and wanted him to marry her, not me."

"What? You didn't tell me that part."

"You cut our last call short because Gabriel had men watching your every move." She ran her hand through her hair. "Listen, Meadow, now that you're safely away from Sunrise and Gabriel knows I'm coming after him, things are going to get even more dangerous. Promise me you will stay with the agents and not let Mom and Dad leave and go back to Sunrise."

"Kind of hard to do with three babysitters, but I don't think Mom and Dad want to go back until they talk to you."

"Put them on the phone."

Meadow sighed. "I'm sorry but my time is up. Agent Gunn wants to talk to you. Don't worry about us. We'll be okay. And we'll stay put until *you* say otherwise."

"Meadow."

"Yeah, sis?"

"I love you. All of you."

"Love you, too." Meadow's earnest voice eased her

heart. "Don't let him get away with this." She appreciated Meadow's renewed spunk. This upheaval in their lives had taken a toll, but Meadow was hanging in there.

"I'm going to take him down." A tear slipped down her cheek.

Declan brushed it away with his thumb. "You okay?"

"They're safe. That's all that matters." The tightness in her chest released.

In the background, her sister handed the phone off with a "She's all yours."

Agent Gunn's deep voice filled the line. "I held up my end of the bargain. Your parents are out and Lucy's body is being autopsied by our medical examiner. Now tell me where the guns and bomb stuff are hidden."

Declan held up his hand to stop her from saying anything and asked his own question. "How long until the new autopsy results come back?"

"Anywhere from a few hours to a couple of days. I put a rush on it, but it could take a while before some of the tests come back. If you want conclusive, you need to wait."

"Did you get the girls?" They needed to be saved and Skye hoped they were rescued.

"We got Lucy and let Gabriel know we had a hell of a lot more than just your word against his about who killed Lucy."

"You can't just leave those girls there. He'll move them. Who knows what will happen to them?"

"I need evidence for a judge to issue a warrant. I have agents watching the place you call The Stable. I've sent a man in to investigate."

"But—"

"Skye, trust me to do my job. You want the charges to

stick. You want Gabriel to pay for all he's done. I need evidence. I need to be able to build a solid case against him."

"Fine. I just want this to be done."

"You and me both, but we're not quite there yet. So tell me what I need to know."

"The guns and bomb stuff are safe where they are. Gabriel will be desperate to find them, but he won't. He'll try to hide the theft from Prosperity."

"They already know about it."

"How?"

"I made sure they knew about it." He said it so matter-of-factly.

It surprised her and tied a knot in her gut. He'd just upped the stakes.

Agent Gunn stuck to business. "Do you know who they planned to target?"

"Make that plural."

Agent Gunn swore under his breath. "How many?"

"Three that I know of. I have the blueprints, plans, times, dates, everything."

"How did Gabriel get all of that?"

"He probably didn't trust Prosperity to come through on their end without a little insurance. Gabriel may be shortsighted, bold, and impulsive, but he's not stupid."

"We think he and Prosperity are planning to combine the two groups."

She thought about it for a second. "It makes sense from Gabriel's point of view and probably Prosperity's. We supply the food. Prosperity supplies the gun power to keep the government from interfering in either community."

"Prosperity is not a community. It's a well-supplied

army of fanatics who want to eliminate the government. I need those targets and everything else you've got."

"I need my name cleared," she shot back.

Agent Gunn sighed when she didn't back down. "Skye, this isn't a game."

"No, it's not. This is my life. This is about the lives of the innocent people living at Sunrise. It's about those girls. If I thought for a second any of them were in immediate danger, I'd give you everything I have."

"I did what you asked. Your family is safe. Lucy's death is being properly investigated."

"And what about the cops that helped Gabriel?"

"They will be dealt with along with everyone else involved. These things take time. If we rush, we make mistakes. We can't afford to bring these guys in and not have enough to prosecute them."

"As it stands right now, you have enough to prosecute me. Isn't that right?"

Agent Gunn sighed. "Skye, they found your bloody footprints in the room. Your hair on the victim. Gabriel gave them a decent motive for the crime."

"Do you really think after everything I've done to stop Gabriel, I wanted him so badly that I'd kill my competition? That's the motive you think I'd have for killing that sweet, innocent girl, whose only fault was believing in a man who said one thing and did another? He made promises to her. He made her believe he cared about her. Then he kicked her over and over and over again until he killed that mother and child.

"If you can't prove that, how am I supposed to believe you can make the rest of them pay for their crimes? So far, I'm the only one who's really done anything to stop them. You have men investigating. People watching. Do something!" Her anger got the better of her, but she didn't care. She wanted him to stop Gabriel and Prosperity. She wanted everyone to be safe.

"I'm trying." His frustration helped ease her ire.

"Try harder. Until you clear my name, you're not getting anything more." She hung up, frustrated and hoping that lit a fire under the agent to hurry up and do the right thing.

Declan hugged her close again. "Damn, sweetheart. Remind me to never piss you off."

"Why can't people just do the right thing?"

"The same laws that protect the innocent can be used by the guilty to circumvent justice."

"It's not fair."

"Well, you've been accused of a crime. Technically, you could be sitting in jail waiting for your day in court. Instead, you're holding evidence hostage that the FBI could use to take down Gabriel and Prosperity until you're cleared."

"The evidence against me isn't right."

"Yet you expect Agent Gunn to take your word for it and believe you have the evidence against Gabriel and Prosperity that he hasn't seen or corroborated and act on it against other people who may or may not be guilty."

She frowned up at him. "I thought you were on my side."

"Always." He pulled her in for another of his really great hugs. "I just want you to see things from both sides."

She rubbed her cheek against his hard chest. "Fine. I'll give him what he wants tomorrow even if he hasn't proven I didn't kill Lucy."

Declan gripped her shoulders and held her at arm's length. "I'm not saying to hand it all over without them doing their part. The last thing I want is for you to spend a single second locked up for something you didn't do. I'm just saying to give the guy a break. He's doing his job the best he can."

She sighed out her frustration. "He did get my family out."

Declan gave her a lopsided smile. "I liked your sister."

"She's cool. We've always been close, despite the seven-year age difference. Sometimes I was more the parent than Mom and Dad."

"What are they like?"

"They're . . . parents. Nice. They focused on educating us and making sure we contributed to everything and everyone around us."

"That sounds . . . normal."

She laughed under her breath. "They weren't the tuck us into bed, read bedtime stories, kiss on the head kind of parents. Other kids had that. I'm not saying they're cold. They weren't. But affection was spare. Except between them."

"That seems odd. I mean, I have tons of memories of my mom and dad kissing in the kitchen . . . and lots of other places. But they were affectionate with us, too."

"I can tell. You have no problem showing me how you feel."

A sexy grin lit Declan's face. "Honey, I haven't even scratched the surface of showing you how much I want you."

"I kind of figured that out, but you've been . . . considerate." At this point, she wanted him so badly, she didn't know if she appreciated it or not.

"I've been dying," he teased, then took her hand. "I'm not in a hurry, Skye. I like what we have. I want more, and I'm willing to wait until you're ready."

She scrunched her lips and stared up at him through

her lashes. "You should know that I'm not very good at the whole flirting, seducing thing."

"Not true. You've got me spending every second of the day wanting to get my hands on you."

An unexpected smile made her giggle. "Really?"

He cupped her face and leaned in close. "You tell me." He pressed his lips to hers, slid his hands down her back to her hips, grabbed hold, and pulled her up and snug against him. On tiptoe, her body aligned with his, and she felt every inch of him against her front, especially one long, hard part of him. The kiss spun out with his tongue sliding along hers. She locked her arms around his neck and rubbed her breasts against his chest, and her hips rolled into his. She had the overwhelming urge to climb him and find a way to get closer.

He blazed a trail of kisses across her cheek to her ear and whispered, "Do you have any doubt how much I want you?" His hand gripped her ass and his thick erection pressed against her belly.

"No. Not one."

"Good," he growled and took her mouth again in a searing kiss that made her knees weak. Luckily, Declan had a firm hold on her, or they'd have ended up rolling around in the dirt.

A truck honked, startling both of them. They turned their heads, but didn't let go of each other.

Tate and Liz stared at them from the truck, matching knowing smiles on their faces. She'd worked a little with Tate over the last few days and seen Liz from a distance, but they hadn't officially met.

The pretty woman leaned out the window, her arm braced on the ledge. "Hey, I'm Liz."

"This is Skye," Declan introduced her.

"Nice to meet you," Skye said.

Tate leaned over to talk past Liz. "You two want to come to the cabin for dinner?"

Declan looked down at her. She wanted to get to know his brother and sister-in-law better, but time seemed to be slipping away, and if Agent Gunn came through with the evidence exonerating her, or arrested her for Lucy's murder instead, then her time with Declan shrank by the second.

"Thank you for the invitation, but I've already put something together up at the house. Tomorrow?" She didn't know if she'd still be here tomorrow, but if she was, she'd love to get together with them. Right now, though, she only wanted to be with Declan.

Liz's smile grew even wider as her gaze dropped to the way Declan still held her close. "I totally understand. Tomorrow, then."

Tate snickered at Declan, then drove the truck further down the road to their cabin.

Declan stared down at her, a question in his eyes. "I didn't think you'd had time to make anything yet."

"I didn't." She bit her lip, knew this was what she wanted more than anything, and went for it. Almost. "Are you really hungry? Or . . ."

"Or what?"

Of course he wanted her to give him a direct answer. "Would you rather do something else?" She went back up on tiptoe, rubbing her body, especially her belly, against him.

His eyes dilated and filled with heat and need. "Desperately." Yet he waited for her to make a move.

"Declan."

"Yeah?" The word sounded strangled.

"Take me to bed."

Chapter Nineteen

DECLAN HADN'T felt this kind of need and desire in a long time. He wanted to dive in and take what he desperately needed, feed his craving, and slake the lust that had been riding him for days. But that meant this would end far too soon. And they had all night.

And tonight started right now.

He slid his hands down her hips, over her plump ass, and hooked them under her thighs, drawing her up to straddle his waist. The surprise move made her eyes go wide and a grin break on her lips right before he kissed her again, letting her know how much he wanted her. It wasn't easy to hold on to her, walk, and feel her center rub against his aching cock while she kissed him back with all the urgency he put into getting them in the house and away from prying eyes.

He wanted her alone, in his bed, naked.

At the top of the stairs, he pulled her shirt over her head and tossed it. He knew the house so well he didn't really need to see where he was going to get there, so he hooked his hands under her arms, pushed her up, and buried his face between her sweet breasts. He pressed a kiss over her heart, then turned his attention to tracing one round breast with his tongue sweeping over her warm skin, across the top of her bra.

His shoulder slammed into the wall when he reached between them and unhooked the front clasp on her bra with one hand. He stalled in the middle of the hall and stared at the two perfect pink-tipped breasts in front of him. He took in the feel of her in his arms, pressed against him, the way her long hair dropped in dark waves over her shoulders, the ends teasing his arm at her back. Her sparkling brown eyes were filled with desire and something that drew him in and slammed into his heart all at the same time. She was too much to take in and still he couldn't drag his eyes off her. "Damn, you're beautiful."

A sweet smile lit her whole face and brightened her eyes, and that warmth in his chest pulsed. "I never thought I'd be lucky enough to find someone like you."

"I'm pretty sure I'm the lucky one." He'd been waiting, hoping, praying for her for so long, she kind of seemed unreal. Even with all the trouble they faced, he'd take it and a hell of a lot more just to be with her.

He finally got his feet moving toward the bedroom again. Holding her in his arms wasn't close enough. He wanted to strip away all the barriers and map every line and curve with his hands, tongue, and lips.

If she was heaven-sent, he planned to worship for a good long time. Forever, maybe.

Right now, he'd start with tonight and dive into this moment knowing everything would be different in the morning.

She'd be his.

Just like she was now, but more.

Because he planned to show her just how amazing they could be together.

He walked straight to the bed she'd remade for him this morning. It drove him to distraction to think of her in his room, putting new sheets on the bed that he wanted to mess up with her.

He put all those thoughts and fantasies into touching her now as his knees hit the end of the bed. He leaned down, laid her on the mattress, and kissed a trail down her chest and belly to the button on her jeans. He stared up at her, past those tempting breasts to her watchful gaze, and undid her jeans, hooked his fingers in them and her panties, and peeled both down her legs to the boots he'd bought her. He loved seeing her in the things he'd gotten her, but he liked seeing her out of them a hell of a lot more.

The boots hit the floor along with the last of her clothes. She lay before him, all pale, perfect skin and curves that made his mouth water.

"Declan."

God, how he loved his name on her lips. "Yeah, sweetheart."

"You're staring." Her cheeks turned bright pink, but she didn't shy away from his gaze or even attempt to cover any part of herself.

"I can't take my eyes off you." He reached his hand over the back of his head, grabbed his T, and yanked it off, tossing it on top of her jeans at his feet.

Her eyes went wide and round as they locked on his chest and swept over his shoulders and arms.

He smiled down at her, hoping to ease any nerves she might be feeling. "Now who's staring?"

"You're solid muscle. Those arms . . ." The cute smirk and appreciation lighting her eyes made his dick twitch.

Ranch work was hard work. It did a body good. And right now, he kind of felt like a god in her eyes.

He undid his jeans, giving his cock a little room behind his boxer briefs. His own boots hit the floor with a thud as he discarded them. He dipped his hands inside his waistband, hesitated for only a second to see if Skye had any second thoughts, then shucked off the last of his clothes and stood before her.

Her gaze drifted all the way down to his aching cock. She bit her lip, then said, "It's not fair to be that gorgeous."

"It's not fair to tempt me the way you have for the past several days and leave me aching for you." He bent and started at her ankles, sweeping his hands up and back down her legs.

She sighed and slowly relaxed, but not near enough. Nervous, her body tensed at his first touch, but quickly melted as his hands ran up her legs again and he kissed his way up one thigh and back down the other.

He wanted their first time together to be perfect. So he took his time working his way up her body, kissing her thighs, bypassing that sweet center that called to him, planting soft kisses up her belly and over her chest until he found one hard-tipped breast and licked the peaked bud. Her hips rolled toward him as her head sank into the pillow and her breasts rose to his tongue. He pressed his body to hers to keep her under him. The sweet contact of skin on skin made her gasp with pleasure and him harden even more. He suckled her breast, then replaced his mouth with his hand, molding her breast to his palm, and took the other tight nipple into his mouth.

Her fingers slid into his hair and she held his head to her breast while he feasted.

She smelled like lemon and honey. Sweet and tart.

And he wanted more.

She liked having her breasts fondled and licked and sucked. So responsive, she offered them up to his every touch, her sighs and moans demanding even more attention. But another part of her called to him as she spread her thighs wider to accommodate his body between her gorgeous legs. He slid one hand down her side, over her hip, and dipped it low between her thighs, finding her sweet center, his fingers tracing her soft folds and one diving deep into her damp core. She was so damn wet for him.

Though he loved all the sighs she gave him as he teased her nipple with his tongue, he wanted to know how she tasted.

He thrust his finger deep in her slick center again, then slipped it free. Her breast popped out of his mouth and he looked up at her, brought his finger to his lips, and sucked her essence right off. Her eyes widened with surprise at the bold move. He thought maybe he'd shocked her, but then she cupped his face and drew him in for a deep kiss, her tongue sweeping over his, tasting herself and saying just how much she wanted him with no words and that sexy-as-hell kiss.

Her hand brushed down his belly. He lifted just enough for her to wrap her hand around his dick and stroke him from base to tip, where her questing fingers found the bead of moisture. Her thumb rubbed over the head, spreading it and sending a blaze of heat sweeping through him. He wanted her hand to lock tight around his thick length, but she brought it up and flicked her tongue over her thumb. "Mm."

"You are so damn sexy."

She ran her hand over his shoulders and back, her nails

scratching his skin as they raked up to his neck, setting off every nerve ending. "I love touching you."

"I want to hear you moan."

Confusion lit her eyes, until he laid a kiss on the top of her breast, pulled her leg up over his shoulder as he sank even lower, and licked her seam, then sank his tongue deep inside her.

"Declan." His name was a breathless whisper, more plea than any reservation she had about his intimate attention.

He licked and suckled her soft flesh, driving her up to the precipice, but she still held back, her head rolling side to side on the pillow, her breath coming in soft pants with every tempting lick of his tongue. "Let go. Come for me." He sank one finger deep and circled her clit with his tongue. She pressed into his mouth. He circled that little nub, and she shattered, her body contracting around his finger and pulsing against his lips as she let out a very satisfying and loud, "Yes."

He'd take it and the well-satisfied look on her face, eyes closed, a slight smile tugging at her lips, and her whole body limp and tempting as hell.

He gave her a second to come back to herself and grabbed the packet of condoms from the bedside drawer. He tore one off with his teeth, opened it, and rolled it on.

He needed her so damn bad and settled between her thighs, the head of his dick pressed to her soft entrance. He stared down at her as she looked up at him and swept her hands over his chest.

He didn't move. He wanted her to give him something. What, he wasn't sure, until her soft words—"Please, Declan, make love to me"—made him thrust deep inside her. Seated to the hilt in her tight core, locked together, his heart pressed to hers, a burst of connection, sharing, oneness came over him. He basked in it for a moment.

And then she moved against him, and all he wanted to do was make her feel as good as she felt around him.

He tried to go slow, make it last with long stokes of his body in and out of hers, but he found himself thrusting deep again and again as he lost himself in the rhythm and her. She gripped his ass and pulled him to her. Deeper, harder, he gave her what she wanted and his body demanded.

His release rode him, building in his groin and pulling his balls tight.

Her body locked around his as her head sank into the pillow and her hips rubbed against his, finding the friction she needed to blast over the edge. Her body convulsed, and he thrust deep once, twice, prolonging her orgasm and setting off his own mind-blowing one.

He dropped on top of her, panting hard, his brain misfiring as his body recovered from the best sex he'd ever had.

Completely content, he realized why when his brain found a few cells still working and he took in Skye, lying beneath him, out of breath like him, her sweet breasts pressed to his chest, and her arms around him, her fingers drawing lazy circles on his shoulders.

He loved the way she felt against him and how she held him, content to take his weight and body pressed to hers. She didn't seem ready to let him go or stop touching him.

Her hands went flat on his back and she rubbed them up and down along his spine, in soft sweeps that were warm and loving and soothing to his body and soul.

He brushed his fingers through her hair and kissed her neck. "You okay?"

"Mm. Wonderful."

"That was . . ."

"Worth waiting for."

That got his attention. He'd swear she wasn't a virgin, so . . . he pressed up on his forearms and stared down at her in the gray light that was just enough for him to see her expression. "What do you mean?"

She brushed her fingers up and down his arms and shoulders. "That when it's the right person, it's perfect. Open. Honest. Freeing. I just . . ."

"Let go." He couldn't explain how it made him feel to know that she'd given herself over to him.

"Yes. I don't know, I just trusted in you, me, and everything we felt making love. It all just felt so . . . right."

It should be like that with your partner, but he had to admit, with her, it had been different. The connection they shared brought them closer on a deeper level than he'd ever felt.

He reluctantly separated their bodies, rolled to his back, and brought her up next to him to lie down his side. Her head settled on his shoulder and she snuggled in close.

He didn't know why, but he chose his words carefully. "It's never been that way for me either." He wanted to say more, but held back, because he wasn't quite sure how to explain what he felt. But he had a suspicion he knew exactly what was going on between them. It felt new and heady, and maybe in the aftermath of great sex he was making more of it than it really was, but he didn't think so.

She didn't say anything, just traced her fingers back and forth over his heart that seemed to be two sizes too big for his chest right now.

The quiet settled around them. He enjoyed the easy

silence and the feel of her next to him. His mind wanted to believe they could have this moment every night for the rest of their lives, but he couldn't ignore the fact she had a warrant out for her arrest and there were some very bad men out to silence her.

"I'm afraid this will all go away tomorrow." Her softly spoken fear echoed his own.

He wanted to reassure her that nothing was going to happen to her, or them, but couldn't bring himself to lie when the truth was so complicated.

"No one can take what we have away from us." He shifted to his side and stared into her worried gaze. "Whatever happens, we have this." He kissed her softly, starting the dance all over again. But this time, he made love to her slow and easy, making sure every touch, kiss, push and pull of his body into hers amplified the feelings building between them. He wanted to imprint himself on her, so that if for any reason they were separated, he'd always be a part of her mind, body, and soul.

They didn't have dinner or even leave the bed all night.

In between short naps, he spent the night loving her. And in the morning he stared down at her lying naked on her stomach under the rumpled sheet, her dark hair cascading in waves over one shoulder and spilling onto the bed beside her. Beautiful. His. Everything he'd ever dreamed he wanted in a woman and partner.

And he knew in every cell of his being that he'd never feel about anyone else the way he felt about her.

But would he get to keep her?

Chapter Twenty

GABRIEL HAD questioned every member of Sunrise and gotten nothing but the same glowing response to something he didn't even fucking ask. Everyone wanted to tell him how kind and wonderful and helpful and compassionate Skye had been to them.

They fucking loved her.

They wanted her back.

He fisted his hands and gritted his teeth and silently berated himself for ever wanting her, thinking he could trust her. All the while she'd been working against him. Turning his people against him.

None of them believed this place would be the same without her. Not a single person believed she'd killed Lucy out of jealousy. They all looked at him with their accusing eyes.

Thank God none of them outright accused him or he'd have to show them who was boss around here.

All of them would say that was Skye, but she was gone.

And so were his fucking guns and everything else he'd stored on the property for Prosperity.

They had a plan and a schedule to keep and Skye had well and truly fucked him.

If he got his hands on her, she'd beg for mercy.

If he didn't turn over everything to Prosperity soon, he'd be the one begging for his life.

He stared at the next person sent into his office for him to question about Skye. The older woman stood in front of his desk looking completely clueless, and he had to tamp down the urge to shake the answers he needed out of her.

"When Skye was here, we never were late bringing in the crops. We never missed a market." She wrung her hands. "What's going to happen to us if we can't sell the crops and make the money we need for our other supplies?"

"We don't need Skye to do those things. There are other, capable people here to fill in." Yet no one had stepped up. All of them were looking to him to fix what they all thought he broke.

"Do you think she'll be back soon?"

"No." But he hoped she'd be stupid enough to come back here, as unlikely as that seemed.

"What about her parents and sister? What's happened to them?"

"Just like Skye, they turned their back on Sunrise and everything we believe in. Now, do you know anything about her hiding some of the supplies that have gone missing?"

Her watery eyes met his. "No. I didn't even know you had something stored in that old building. We haven't used it in a long time. Well, the thing is practically falling down."

He and his men had shored it up and used it for Prosperity's guns. No one ever went near it. So how the hell did Skye know about it? How the hell did she move everything without help?

It seemed there was nothing the woman couldn't do on the farm based on what he'd heard today.

Skye does that.

Skye oversees that.

Skye knows about that.

When his father passed and Gabriel took over the council, it seemed Skye took over the operations. The other members of the council bypassed him and went to her for the day-to-day running of this place because she'd been his father's right-hand ma . . . person. His father nagged him to take more interest in the running of the farm and overseeing the people here. Gabriel had wanted his freedom. He'd enjoyed his status and thumbed his nose at some of the strict rules everyone else followed.

He used to think that when the time came, he'd marry Skye and they'd rule this place together. He never once thought she'd usurp him.

But she had without doing anything more than her damn job. She'd pay for that and wrecking his plans.

Gabriel stood and walked around the desk and right out of the office without saying goodbye or anything to the woman. He could barely remember her name, let alone what she did here.

He left the house that served as the office and his home. He barely spent any time in there now. He hadn't slept in his room since the night Lucy died and Skye ruined his plans and his life.

He needed to check in with his men, see if they'd found the supplies Skye took, and figure out a plan to not only find her, but save his ass.

It seemed everyone at Sunrise went out of their way to steer clear of him. As he walked to his truck, every-one went in a different direction. The compound gates had remained closed. No one was allowed to leave without his permission. So far, they'd all complied because they were afraid the FBI would swoop in again and force everyone out. They had nowhere to go if that happened. Not that the FBI would do that, but Gabriel had made it clear that was a real possibility.

He got in the truck and took the road that led through the fields bursting with cauliflower, cabbage, spinach, lettuce, carrots, and pea crops. Rows and rows of raspberry bushes lined the field on his right. The vegetables and fruits gave way to the orchards. Apples and plums in several varieties.

He'd always loved seeing the abundance of crops. He'd hated how hard it was to keep it all growing and thriving. Endless hours plowing, fertilizing, picking, no thank you. And he really hated the chickens.

The smell. Their scratching and pecking. Ugh.

He much preferred the business he had going now. He parked outside The Stable and leaped out of the truck, spotting several motorcycles parked nearby. The guys from Prosperity had arrived before him. He hoped the girls were taking good care of them. If he had time, he'd stick around and let one of them cheer him up.

He loved how they always did what they were told.

Unlike Skye.

The next time she popped off around him, he'd smack her across that lush mouth, just like he did when one of The Stable girls complained.

Thanks to the FBI showing up, they'd had to close down The Stable for the last few days. But he hoped the FBI came to the same conclusion he'd led the local cops to, found Skye guilty of Lucy's murder, and arrested her.

Then he could get back to business.

He slid the side door open and closed it behind him. The music played low, but had a thumping country beat. Several men sat around the tables. One, the guy with the piercing dark gaze and compass tattoo on the back of his left hand, leaned against the bar, his back to the wall. He always made Gabriel uneasy. More so than their leader, Jeremiah, ever did. And just like every other time they met, he eyed Gabriel walking in.

The big man himself, Jeremiah, walked down the hall that led to the girls' rooms, tucking his shirt into his jeans with one hand, the other holding his heavy camo jacket over his shoulder.

Gabriel stopped in his tracks. "Jeremiah." Wide chest, thick arms, Jeremiah was a wall of muscle coming at him. Gabriel imagined one of those beefy hands wrapped around his throat.

Jeremiah pinned him in his angry gaze. "You've kept me waiting."

"Sorry." He didn't even bother to check his watch and remark how early he was for their meeting. He didn't actually expect them to show up with the FBI sniffing around, but if they were here, that meant they didn't think the FBI was a threat. So Gabriel relaxed about that worry but remained cautious about the danger in front of him.

Jeremiah went behind the unmanned bar, grabbed a glass, and poured himself a beer at the tap. He came around and sat at one of the unoccupied tables.

Gabriel moved to the chair across from him and sat, knowing Jeremiah expected him to answer for what happened.

Jeremiah interlaced his fingers and rested his hands on the tabletop, looking as calm as a flat sea, but Gabriel sensed the angry undercurrent. "Is the FBI looking for anything other than the person who killed that poor girl?"

He didn't know how to answer that. His gaze shot past Jeremiah to the man at the bar, staring him down. "Uh, they didn't say anything specific. Agent Gunn asked to see the children, but I refused. I did what you said, and made sure he followed the warrant and didn't see anything that wasn't listed there." He breathed a little easier, hoping that answer appeased Jeremiah.

All of a sudden it felt like Jeremiah had leaned in, though he hadn't moved. "Why would he want to see the children? Are they abused?"

"No. Of course not. It's just . . ."

"What?" Jeremiah's tone deepened, a hint of menace coming out. "A couple *girls* got pregnant because you and your boys got a little overzealous and didn't *suit up* before you set up this place?"

"Look, the FBI didn't see anything. The girls are fine. And you're the one who suggested we set up this place. You don't seem to have a problem coming here and sampling the goods."

"I don't sample. I savor." A gleam lit his eyes before they narrowed again. "And when I told you to get a place with *women* willing to serve, I didn't mean like this. That was all on you." His lips pressed tight. "And you put your own bent on it. You've lost sight of the plan and what we could have done for each other."

Gabriel gulped at that *could have*. "We can still make this work."

"I want what you owe me. You said you'd keep my products safe, yet they seem to be missing."

"They're on the property. She couldn't have moved them far on her own."

"Seems to me she got a hell of a lot done all by herself. Right under your nose." Jeremiah's voice dropped to a menacing tone that sent a chill up Gabriel's spine. "She's talking to the fucking FBI. How long before they're raiding Prosperity? You've put me in a very bad position."

Gabriel laid his hands on the table and leaned in. "Jeremiah, man, I can fix this."

"I don't see how when the FBI is breathing down your neck." Jeremiah checked the text that dinged on his phone. The smile made him seem less intense and intimidating, but Gabriel didn't for a second believe it made him less threatening. "Good news. My men tracked her down. They'll have her in the next hour, maybe a little more." Jeremiah glanced back at the guy at the bar. "Told you Squeak would find her. I won the bet. Pay up."

The guy pulled a five dollar bill out of his pocket, walked to Jeremiah, and slapped it into his hand with a dark scowl on his face.

Jeremiah let out a belly laugh and stuffed the bill into his pocket, then stood. "We're out of here."

All the men headed for the door, the guy at the bar bringing up the rear, typing on his phone.

Before Jeremiah walked out, Gabriel called, "I want her after you get the information from her."

Jeremiah gave him one of those bright smiles that didn't do a damn thing to make him feel better or safe. "Traitors and snitches don't fare well in my organization."

"She's one of *my* people. *I* want her."

Admiration and surprise lit Jeremiah's dark eyes. "Maybe you're not useless." Jeremiah and the others filed out the door.

"Hey, who's going to pay for the booze and girls?"

The guy from the bar glanced back. "You are as stupid as you look." With that he walked out, leaving Gabriel fuming and completely in the dark where Skye was concerned.

"Gabriel." Anne stood in the hallway leading to the girls' rooms.

"What?"

"You can't keep these girls like this. It's not right."

"Do your fucking job or you'll be in one of those rooms, too. If you don't like it, you can leave." Not that she would. He controlled all the money at Sunrise. If someone wanted to leave, they had to come to him for the money do so. Otherwise, they were on their own. Yeah, Anne wasn't going anywhere. No one was.

And if he got his hands on Skye, he'd send all the other girls away and let every man who came in here use Skye until she begged him for mercy. Then he'd send in more men to show her what happened to traitors and snitches.

Jeremiah wasn't the only coldhearted bastard who wanted her to pay.

Chapter Twenty-One

SKYE SHUT off the chainsaw, climbed down the ladder, and set the heavy piece of equipment down next to the trunk, her ears still buzzing from the incessant sound. She gathered the branches she'd cut and piled them next to the tree. She'd been at it for a quite a while and needed a break. She checked her watch, then wiped the sweat from her brow with the back of her hand.

Her phone rang. She spun around, looking for where she'd left it. She found it next to the bottle of water she badly needed. She accepted the call and unscrewed the cap on the water.

"Hello." She chugged the water.

"They know where you are!" Agent Gunn's deep voice boomed through the phone.

She choked out, "What?" spitting water everywhere. Most of it dribbled down her chin and onto her shirt.

"They are coming for you."

A wave of panic shot through her. "Who?"

"Some men from Prosperity. I have men on the way, coming by helicopter, but I'm not sure they'll get there in time."

She turned her head back and forth as she scanned the area. "You know where I am?"

"The general area based on cell tower hits from your phone."

"I'm at Cedar Top Ranch. The McGrath place."

"You need to get out of there. Now. We can pick you up somewhere safe."

Before her brain had time to come up with a plan, she spotted Declan running toward her with one of the rifles she'd seen locked in a cabinet in the office. He yelled her name and pointed behind her.

She didn't think, just lunged forward and ducked at the same time a man's arm swung over her head.

"They're here," she yelled into the phone as she ran toward Declan, who'd very reluctantly left her alone in the orchard to help Tate with a sick cow.

She'd promised him she'd be safe.

She should have known better.

Heavy footfalls pounded the dirt behind her, drawing closer. She tried to outrun the man from Prosperity, but quickly lost ground. His big hand slammed into the middle of her back, sending her stumbling forward until she lost her fight with gravity and fell hard, sliding on the dirt and grass, her hands taking the brunt of the fall. The phone went flying a few feet away as her chin hit the dirt, gnashing her teeth and scraping her skin. The sting made her hiss in pain, but it was nothing compared to the agony of the big man landing on top of her with a bone-rattling *thump*. He flipped her over and straddled her hips, pinning her down. She made a futile attempt to buck him off. With no way of escape, she swung, hoping to at least stun him with a blow to the face, but he thwarted her effort and grabbed her wrist, stopping her from doing anything but look helpless.

He pointed the gun in his other hand right at her face. "Stay still."

The crack of a rifle could barely be heard over the sound of the incoming helicopter, but the blood blooming on the guy's shoulder just above his Prosperity patch confirmed Declan had fired. And hit the mark. The guy's body jerked as blood ran down his chest, but the wound didn't force him off her.

She shoved at him, but he managed to hold her down until her hand landed on a rock next to her. She grabbed it and swung, connecting with the side of his head. More blood oozed out of the gash at his temple as he fell to the side in a heap. She scrambled back, wide-eyed at the three other men closing in on her, all dressed in denim and leather with long hair and patches covering their jackets with their prominent Prosperity badge.

Shit.

Men in black gear ran past her and fanned out, automatic weapons drawn on the Prosperity men, FBI emblazoned on their backs. They went after the bad guys. Someone grabbed her from behind, his arms hooked under hers as he pulled her up and back from the men coming toward her.

The Prosperity men halted in their tracks, hands raised, guns tossed as the FBI drew down on them.

Declan held the rifle on the FBI agent holding her. "Let her go."

The FBI guy behind her turned her out of harm's way, blocking her from Declan as he pulled a handgun on Declan. "Drop the weapon. You are interfering in an FBI investigation."

Declan didn't back down. "I don't care who you are, you're not taking her."

The guy holding her didn't budge or drop his weapon. She twisted and found Declan's desperate gaze. "Declan, it's over. Please put the gun down. I don't want you to get hurt because of me." The FBI may have come to protect her from the Prosperity men, but they still wanted her for Lucy's murder and what she knew about Prosperity's plans. Prosperity and the FBI wanted what she'd hidden.

Declan immediately dropped the rifle in the grass and rushed toward them.

The FBI guy holstered his weapon, took her hands, pulled them behind her back, and cuffed her. "Skye Kennedy, you're under arrest for murder and wanted for questioning in an ongoing FBI investigation."

Declan walked right up to her and cupped her face. "Are you okay?"

Her heart hammered in her chest, but all she could do was look Declan up and down to be sure he wasn't hurt. "You shot that guy." It wasn't an accusation, just her astonishment that he'd do such a thing. For her. To save her life.

"He had a gun. He was going to kill you."

The FBI agent tugged on her arm. "Special Agent-in-Charge Gunn wants a word with you."

"Just one?" Her witty yet inappropriate question made Declan grin. It helped settle her racing heart.

"You're okay." Declan tilted her face up and checked the scrape and blood running down her neck. "This needs to be cleaned. Maybe stitched."

"It's just a scratch." She gave him the same line he'd given her about the gash she'd cleaned and bandaged on his leg in the orchard.

"Don't." He wasn't in the mood to joke. "You're bleeding." It distressed him a great deal, but it didn't stop him from leaning in and kissing her like he hadn't kissed her in forever.

"Mr. McGrath, you're coming with us."

Skye broke the kiss and stared at the FBI agent beside her. "He was only protecting me."

"He'll need to give his statement."

Tate rushed up behind Declan. "You guys okay?"

Declan hadn't taken his hands off her. "She's good." Because she mattered more than his own life, Declan's concern was all for her. "Call Drake. Secure the ranch. Calm the horses."

The herd in the pasture had made a run for it when the helicopter landed.

Declan devoured her with his gaze one more time. "Skye and I will be gone for a while."

"Take care of her. We've got this." Tate smacked Declan on the shoulder. "Nice shooting. Drake will be so proud." Their military brother had seen his fair share, and then some, of action in the army.

Declan finally met Tate's gaze. "That bastard shouldn't have put his hands on her."

The FBI guy had been patient, but that all ended as the three Prosperity men were handcuffed, separated from each other, and sat in the middle of the field, an agent hovering over each of them. "Backup will be here shortly to deal with them. Let's go." The agent held his hand out for Declan to head to the waiting helicopter. The agent tugged her arm to get her moving.

"Are the handcuffs really necessary?" Declan asked the agent.

"Protocol."

Declan and the agent helped her into the helicopter. Two more agents joined them.

"I've never flown before," she told Declan, rambling. "This should be fun." So much happened so fast, her head spun.

He rolled his eyes. "Sweetheart, you took at least a decade off my life today." He hooked his arm around her back and drew her into his side as the agent closed the chopper door. "If you wanted to fly somewhere, I'd have booked us a trip to Hawaii or something."

She leaned into him, rattling the cuffs when she tried and failed to wrap her arms around him. "I've never seen the ocean." Right now, she wanted to forget all this, that guy who attacked her, all that blood, and be anywhere but here.

"As soon as this is over, it's you and me and a beach."

She rested her head on his shoulder as the helicopter lifted up and her stomach dropped. She needed the mundane talk to keep the reality of what just happened from overwhelming her, but the cuffs bit into her wrists and made what came next all too real and daunting.

Declan's beach idea held a lot of appeal. She'd go anywhere with him, but feared the only place she'd end up now was locked in a cell.

Chapter Twenty-Two

"I WANT TO see Skye. Now!" Declan bellowed the second Agent Gunn walked into the interrogation room they'd stuck him in hours ago. "What the fuck is taking so long?"

Agent Gunn set a soda and a bag of potato chips in front of him and sat across from him like he had all the time in the world. "I'll let you see her soon."

Declan huffed out his frustration. "How is the man I shot?"

"Recovering in the hospital before he's booked for a long list of charges."

Declan breathed a huge sigh of relief. "Good." He'd protect Skye no matter the cost, but that didn't mean he didn't care about whether or not the guy who hurt her lived or died. He had a conscience.

Agent Gunn gave him a lopsided grin. "It was a great shot. Through and through. Nothing major hit, but the guy did drop that gun he had on Skye. You impressed the agents on site."

Declan couldn't give a shit. "She's safe and alive. That's all that matters."

"I have a feeling you would have taken the kill shot if he'd managed to go after her again."

No doubt. He'd do anything, including laying down

his own life for her. He was just relieved he'd been in time to save her. If he hadn't seen a man skulking across the property behind the cabin headed in her direction . . . He couldn't think about it. He tried to breathe through the tightness in his chest and remind himself she was safe.

"How long have you known Skye?"

"Not long. Why?" It seemed irrelevant. So much happened and changed for him in the short time they'd been together. Somehow his world—that had previously been about work, the ranch, his family—had become all about her. He used to spend his days thinking about what the ranch needed, the work he had to do. Now he thought about the future and it included her. That family he wanted but that had seemed like a dream became clearer in his mind. He pictured her living on the ranch with him and their children running around like he and his brothers and sister used to do.

"What did she tell you when she came to work for you?"

"Not much."

"Did she say anything about Lucy's death?"

"No. But it was obvious she ran from something. I thought maybe an abusive boyfriend or husband. She talked about growing up on a farm and her life there. I learned about the rest later."

"Do you think she killed Lucy?"

"I'd believe she performed a miracle before I believed she'd hurt anyone."

Agent Gunn pressed his lips tight, but didn't say anything.

"I thought you guys were supposed to have completed your investigation into Lucy's death by now."

"The evidence is contradictory. She's right about not having the strength to have inflicted the kind of internal and external injuries on Lucy's body. But her hair was found on the victim."

"She lived at the compound, worked in the house. Couldn't Gabriel have gone to her room, found some strands of hair, and planted them?"

Agent Gunn nodded. "Her footprints are in the blood."

"Her shoe prints are, but that doesn't mean she walked through the blood."

Agent Gunn ran his hand over his jaw. "You'd make a good lawyer."

"Come on, you can't seriously believe that she'd go through all the trouble to hide those guns and all the bomb-making materials, use her wits and ingenuity to do it, then fly into a jealous rage against the girl who was seeing the very man she was trying to stop, and leave all that evidence behind? Seriously?" Declan shook his head. "She's smart, even if she is a little naïve and in the dark about pop culture, history, and how things work outside of Sunrise. Everyone underestimated her. You. Gabriel. Prosperity. No one saw what she was doing. She may not have known how to stop them legally, but she *did* stop them."

"When we went to Sunrise to retrieve Lucy's body, I asked agents to question anyone they could about her. She practically runs that place on her own. Gabriel is a figurehead, and most of the folks there tolerate him but don't like him."

Declan tried to read between the lines, though Agent Gunn gave nothing away. "Do you seriously think they're covering for Skye?"

"No. All the people who would actually say it out loud believe Gabriel killed Lucy. They know nothing about The Stable, though they are curious about what happened to the girls Gabriel and his men brought to the community. Meadow has been a huge help filling in information about Skye and what she does at Sunrise, which is considerable. But even Meadow had no idea Skye was hiding guns and the other stuff. Her parents are . . . interesting. There's a lot of love between them, but they seem resigned to whatever fate awaits Skye. They feel that she's gone against the teachings of the community by involving outsiders. They don't understand her drive and desire to be a leader and stand out."

"Then they don't understand her at all. She doesn't want to take over Sunrise. She believes in the community and helping others. If she does well, so does everyone else. She puts her heart into everything and expects nothing in return. She's not looking for recognition. She wants acceptance. Maybe because of how you describe her parents. She was raised by a community and not appreciated by her parents for how special she really is because no one is supposed to stand out. But you can't help but notice her.

"From what she told me about Gabriel, he wanted her but thought she was just a means to an end. People there love her. He wanted to marry her, have kids with her, thinking that would make the people accept and look up to him the way they do her. He thought she'd give him the legitimacy that she earned working side by side with those folks."

Agent Gunn held his gaze. "You're in love with her."

He didn't confirm or deny the way he felt. That was between him and Skye. "She's an extraordinary woman and she doesn't even know it. I have no idea what happens next. I just know I don't want to lose her. So get your head out of your ass about her being a murderer and look at who she really is and how she can help you take those bastards down."

"Her lawyer just arrived, so we'll see if she's willing to talk or hide behind him and drag this out."

Declan raised a brow, concerned about who came to see her and why. "What lawyer?"

"Gordon Banks."

"The guy she went to after Gabriel killed Lucy? The one who let the girls go back to Sunrise after Skye tried to get them out so they didn't have to go through with the arranged marriages? That guy?" Declan didn't believe he was here for Skye's sake.

Agent Gunn's eyebrows shot up. "What are you talking about?"

"When she fled Sunrise, she took a bunch of girls with her to Mr. Banks so he could contact child protective services. One of the girls was like fourteen and pregnant and about to marry a much older man."

Agent Gunn leaned forward. "None of that is in the police reports."

Declan went still. "He never reported the girls to the cops?"

"Not unless it's in another report we don't have." Agent Gunn went quiet for a moment. "If Skye took the girls, why isn't there a kidnapping charge along with the murder charge?"

"Because Gabriel didn't want the cops or anyone else asking about underage girls. He didn't want the authorities outside the cops he's blackmailing investigating him or Sunrise. As for Banks . . ." Declan thought something much darker happened with him. "What if he sent those girls back because he's working with Gabriel?"

That got an eyebrow raise from Agent Gunn. "What did Skye tell you about Mr. Banks?"

"She worked with him for a year or so. Something about contracts with venders and retailers. She didn't know much about putting together the agreements and covering Sunrise's interests."

"Who connected her with Mr. Banks?"

"You'll have to ask her."

Agent Gunn stood. "I have some questions for him."

Declan stood, too. "Wait. If he's involved somehow and working against Skye, she'll figure it out. Let me go in with her to talk to Mr. Banks. I can steer her in the right direction."

"Attorney-client conversations are privileged. We can't use anything they discuss."

"He's not *her* attorney. He works for Sunrise."

Agent Gunn understood where he was going with this. "That's a fine line. She'll have to make clear he's not *her* attorney." So long as she did, Agent Gunn could observe, listen, and record the talk between Skye and Mr. Banks because it wouldn't be privileged.

"If that bastard is trying to hurt her, you can bet your ass I won't let him get away with it."

Agent Gunn opened the door. "I'll take you to see Skye."

Declan grabbed the soda and chips in case Skye hadn't had anything to eat. He followed Agent Gunn to the room several doors down, where a guard stood sentry and an older man paced back and forth in front of him, his briefcase tapping his thigh with every step.

He looked up as soon as Agent Gunn approached. "I want to see my client."

"In a minute. Mr. McGrath wants to see her first."

"Who the hell are you?" The man eyed Declan up and down.

"The one standing between her and everyone else." Declan left the sputtering man at his back and walked through the door the guard held open to him but closed to Mr. Banks.

Chapter Twenty-Three

SKYE STOOD without thinking the second the door opened and she saw Declan. Her heart sped up and she tried to reach for him, but the handcuffs, hooked to a ring on the table, prevented her from even taking one step toward him before they bit into her skin.

"Are you okay?" She looked him up and down, desperate for just a glance at him, craving his arms around her.

He set the soda and chips on the table, then cupped her face, kissed her, and wrapped her in the most amazing hug. Nothing had ever felt better than Declan pressed against her. "I'm fine." He rubbed his cheek against her head. "You holding up?"

"I don't know. No one will tell me anything. I've been sitting in here alone for hours. I thought . . ." Tears clogged her throat and choked off her words.

Declan leaned back and looked at her. "What, sweetheart?"

"I thought I'd never see you again."

He crushed her against his chest and held her tight. "No. No. I won't let that happen."

She looked up at him. "Are they going to put me in jail for Lucy's murder?"

"They'll find the proof against Gabriel." He sounded

so sure. "But right now we only have a minute, so I need you to trust me and do what I ask."

"I just want to go home with you."

He pressed his forehead to hers. "I want that, too."

"Give them a second." Agent Gunn's deep voice resonated through the door.

Declan glanced over his shoulder, then back to her. "I need you to follow my lead with Mr. Banks."

His presence surprised her and brought up a lot of questions. "What is he doing here?"

"That's what I'd like to know. How did he know you were in FBI custody? How did he get here so fast?"

She scrunched her lips and didn't like where her thoughts took her. "What do you and Agent Gunn want me to do?"

"I told him you were smart." He kissed her quick. "There is a difference in the privacy laws when it comes to him being Sunrise's lawyer versus him being *your* lawyer."

She thought she understood what he meant. "The work he does is for Sunrise."

"Exactly. So anything you say to him isn't protected under client privilege. He can't be Sunrise's lawyer and yours. It's a conflict of interest. I need you to make it clear to him that you understand he's not *your* lawyer, but don't make him leave. We need to see if he'll talk about his connection to Sunrise, Gabriel, and possibly Prosperity."

She barely had a second to digest that revelation and what it meant before Declan crushed his mouth to hers the moment the door opened behind them.

She tugged at the restraints, desperate to get her hands on Declan, but all they did was clank and hurt more. She sank into the kiss, him, and wondered if this was the last time they'd share something this intense and intimate.

The thought made her heart ache.

She had no idea how this all worked and feared she'd make a mistake and seal her own fate when she'd been so careful to do everything in her power to make things better and keep people safe.

Agent Gunn cleared his throat to get their attention. "Skye, your lawyer is here."

Skye reluctantly broke the kiss, stared up at Declan, then turned to the man she'd trusted, but maybe shouldn't have. "Mr. Banks. What on earth are you doing here?"

"I heard about them bringing you in for questioning."

"It's very nice that you came to check on me, but I need a . . ." She glanced at Declan. "Defense attorney?" They'd had a brief conversation about what might come next this morning before they headed out to work on the orchard. She never expected things to go like this.

Declan nodded, touching her arm, giving her encouragement.

Mr. Banks held his briefcase in front of him, shoulders back, ready to stand his ground. "I'm here. I'll make sure they don't trample your rights."

"But you work for Sunrise, so you can't work for me, too."

Agent Gunn nodded at her from behind Mr. Banks, letting her know that's exactly what he'd needed her to say. "I'm sure Declan can find you a good defense attorney."

Mr. Banks sneered at the agent, then focused back on her. "I don't think you understand the dire circumstance you're in, my dear. Let me help." Mr. Banks took the seat across from her, settling in.

Agent Gunn quietly left the room to them and closed the door.

Declan pulled the chair she'd shoved out of the way to get to him back so she could sit again, then took the seat next to her. "How did you find out Skye was here?"

Mr. Banks tilted his head and frowned at Declan. "I don't know who you are."

Declan sat back and stared the man down. "I'm with her."

Skye would have laughed if any of this was funny. "Mr. Banks, how is it that you're here?"

Mr. Banks stifled his retort to Declan and focused on her. "I asked an officer at the local police department to let me know if you were taken into custody."

Declan's disbelieving face confirmed her thought that the FBI probably didn't go out of their way to notify local law enforcement—in another state—the moment they apprehended a person of interest.

In addition to that, Mr. Banks would have had to get in his car and break every speed law to get here this fast.

And she wondered if one of Gabriel's cop friends was the one who told him the FBI had her in custody.

Declan's hand settled on her thigh, but she didn't need him to tell her something seemed off.

"Why didn't you tell the police what Gabriel had planned for those girls?"

"I told you, Gabriel's men showed up and took them back. I couldn't stop them."

She glanced at Declan. "You know what I don't understand? How they got there so fast."

"They must have followed you." Mr. Banks sounded too sure of that.

She shook her head. "No. I watched to make sure no

one was following. I begged you to call someone for help."

"You said the police were helping Gabriel."

Mr. Banks knew the FBI could help so he set up a meeting for her. Supposedly. Which was why she and Declan went to the FBI directly to get help with investigating Lucy's murder and stopping Prosperity's deadly plans.

So why hadn't Mr. Banks contacted anyone who could help the girls?

Declan squeezed her thigh. "Skye didn't know who could help. But you did. You should have called the state police and child protective services."

"The FBI didn't bring them in when they went to the compound and were refused access to the children." Mr. Banks knew an awful lot about what was going on at Sunrise.

She guessed at what really happened. "You'd already told Gabriel to hide Bess and her family so they wouldn't investigate what I told you was going on there."

Mr. Banks shook his head. "I did what I could, but once Gabriel's men took the girls back, my hands were tied."

"I don't see how the police missed them. There had to be one officer among them who would do the right thing."

"They arrived too late."

She knew better. "No, they didn't. I ran, but I didn't get far before the police pulled up to your place. You and Joseph spoke to the police before the Sunrise men took the girls back." She leaned forward, braced herself on her forearms, and looked him right in the eye. "You're lying. You're helping them. You work for Sunrise. So, why are you really here?"

"To help you."

"How? What can you do for me? I'm charged with murder. You're not that kind of lawyer, nor can you act as my attorney. So unless you know something that will prove I didn't kill Lucy, you are no help to me."

"I can help you use your other knowledge to get out of trouble."

"I. Did. Not. Kill. Lucy."

"I know that." Mr. Banks surprised her with that admission, then leaned in. "But you know other stuff that could get those charges dropped."

She leaned back, pulling her arms straight and clanking the chains on the table. "I don't see how my knowledge about Gabriel and his guys messing around with young girls will get me out of a murder charge." She deliberately left off everything she knew about the girls at The Stable and Gabriel's association with Prosperity because it felt like Mr. Banks was manipulating her. She just didn't know how or why.

Mr. Banks pressed his lips tight and shook his head. "You need to be smart about this."

She pretended to misunderstand. "Those girls need to be protected."

He slammed his hand flat on the table. "Forget about them! They're fine. You need to worry about yourself."

It should shock her that he'd say such a thing, but she'd learned not all men were good and decent like Declan. "We're talking about older men taking advantage of young girls."

Mr. Banks dismissed her again with a shake of his head and a pointed glance at Declan. Then he pinned her in his direct gaze. "Can we speak alone?"

"I've told Declan everything. If you have something to

say, you'll have to say it in front of him because I'm not giving up one second with him before they lock me up for something I did not do!" Frustrated, she rattled the chains, then pressed her hands on the table and sucked in a breath to curb the rising tide of anxiety and frustration before it turned to all-out panic.

Declan reached up, planted his big hand on the back of her neck, and squeezed the tight muscles. "Calm down, sweetheart. It's going to be okay."

She turned to him. "I want to go home, back to the ranch. Anywhere with you." At this point, she'd do just about anything, including beg.

Declan tried to soothe her, brushing his fingers through her hair, though he had no words that wouldn't be some platitude or lie, because things weren't looking good for her.

"Help me get you out of here," Mr. Banks pleaded.

She met his earnest gaze. "You didn't even help those girls."

He put both arms on the table, leaned in close, and whispered, "If you want to get out of here, tell me where you hid the guns, fertilizer, and other things you found at Sunrise."

She went completely still.

The air seemed charged as Mr. Banks anxiously waited for her response.

"I don't know what you're talking about," she lied.

At first, she'd thought it absurd that Declan and Agent Gunn thought Mr. Banks knew anything about Prosperity's association with Gabriel and Sunrise. Now, she wondered if she'd been sent to work with him so he could keep an eye on her because she oversaw so much at Sunrise, including their bank accounts. Had Prosperity wanted to know if she, or anyone else at Sunrise, knew about what was going on?

Mr. Banks often asked how things were going at Sunrise. His interest made her think he cared about her and Sunrise's operation and how they were trying to build the business.

Now, she saw those innocent conversations as fishing expeditions.

If he knew about the guns and other stuff, Mr. Banks wasn't her friend at all.

He slammed his hand down on the table again. "Don't be stupid, girl! You took what doesn't belong to you. And we want it back."

And there it was. Confirmation. *"We?"* Disappointment turned to fury in her gut.

"You have no idea who you're messing with. We are not stupid farm boys looking for a cheap thrill and some easy cash with a few whores. You have complicated and delayed plans that have been years in the making. We will not be deterred by some bitch with a conscience."

She planted her foot on top of Declan's work boot and leaned against him to keep him from slamming his fist into Mr. Banks's filthy mouth.

"Say one more thing like that about *her* and you'll leave this room bloody," Declan warned.

To drive the point home, she added, "He shot one of the guys Prosperity sent after me. I'd think twice about crossing him."

Mr. Banks eyed Declan. "You'll pay for that." Issuing the threat made him grin. It disappeared when he addressed her again. "You have no idea what's coming." His voice took on an angry bite.

"Did you send those girls back to Sunrise with Gabriel's men?"

"You're damn right I did."

She couldn't believe he'd admit it. "You really work for Prosperity."

"Proudly."

Her stomach soured at the fierce loyalty in that single word. He wholeheartedly backed a group that wanted liberty, but not for all. Not for those poor girls. "How long have you been a member?"

He dropped all pretense of being civil, ignored her question, and issued an order. "Tell me where you hid everything. You think things are bad now. They can get worse."

She reciprocated by ignoring his command and asking another question. "Is it just the government you hate, or are you out to destroy people who are just trying to live their lives?"

"The government, this very agency, has suppressed our rights. Prosperity won't stand for it. *We* will see them fall, so we can have the freedom and rights they continue to strip away from us."

She frowned and nodded her head. "So you get freedom while those girls at The Stable are held against their will. Their lives don't matter, but yours does."

"Give us what we want and maybe you'll live."

She leaned in. "More threats?"

"Our members come from far and wide. There is no place you or your family can go that we can't get to you. Tell me where you hid the stuff before someone you love"—Mr. Banks pointedly looked at Declan—"dies."

She stood, leaned on her hands on the table, and stared down Mr. Banks. "You're a despicable man. You deserve everything that's coming to you."

The door opened behind Mr. Banks, who went instantly still.

Agent Gunn walked in and stood beside him, looking down his nose at the hateful attorney. "You should know better than to issue death threats when law enforcement is listening." Agent Gunn pointed to the camera, clearly visible in the corner of the room. "Thanks for making this so easy. And letting us record it."

"This meeting is privileged."

One side of Agent Gunn's mouth drew back. "You work for Prosperity and Sunrise. She clearly stated at least two separate times that you are not her attorney. I heard her, and Declan witnessed it. We have the recording. You didn't come here to represent her. You came to get the information only she knows." Agent Gunn looked at her. "Thank you."

"The girls," she pleaded.

"We're working on the warrant now. Also, the autopsy is back. Lucy's injuries are consistent with a person who is at least five-ten, about a hundred and seventy pounds, and wears a size ten shoe, according to the imprint left on her thigh and the force it would take to do the damage she endured before she died of blood loss. The murder charge against you is being rescinded as we speak. I'm sorry about your friend."

"But there is hair, her shoe prints. She . . . she did it." Mr. Banks tried to throw her under the bus just like Gabriel had set her up.

Agent Gunn simply disputed that with facts. "She doesn't have the physical capability to have inflicted the wounds."

"She didn't report the murder. She's an accessory after the fact." Mr. Banks's satisfied sneer made her heart drop.

Agent Gunn wiped his smug look away. "Based on the lack of investigation by local police and Skye's accusation that they are working with Sunrise to cover up for the real murderer, the district attorney declined to pursue further charges against Skye."

"Does that mean I'm free to go?" She held her breath.

Agent Gunn shook his head. "The murder charges have been dropped, but this is far from over. The FBI is investigating Prosperity as a militia group, and the ATF is very interested in the guns and other stuff you hid instead of notifying authorities."

Which made her an accessory to Prosperity's murderous plans and meant she'd stay in FBI custody and possibly face federal charges.

"We need your help." Agent Gunn pulled a key from his pocket and held it up in front of her.

If they needed her help, she could still make a deal to keep herself out of prison.

Agent Gunn undid her handcuffs, pulled them free from the metal ring in the table, grabbed Mr. Banks by the arm, hauled him up, and spun him around. He handcuffed Mr. Banks before the man really knew what was happening.

"You can't do this. I have rights."

"You have the right to remain silent." Agent Gunn led Mr. Banks out of the room, telling him the rest of his rights as they went.

The second the door closed, she launched herself into Declan's arms. He wrapped her in a tight hug and pressed his cheek to her head. "You are brilliant. You got him to say even more than I expected."

"I can't believe what an arrogant asshole he turned out to be. We worked together for over a year and he always insisted I call him Mr. Banks instead of Gordon. I knew he looked down on me, but I never suspected how little he thought of women in general."

"I can't believe Prosperity had Gabriel use Banks to make sure you weren't on to what they were doing since you were in charge of the accounting for the farm. If you'd said the wrong thing to him . . ." Declan didn't finish that sentence, but she imagined they'd have done anything necessary to silence her.

"I kept what I found to myself." *Thank God.* "I never told anyone what I suspected or what I did because I didn't know who was in on it or who did what, except for Gabriel. He kept things secret even from most of the men who followed him."

"The men who run Prosperity probably coached him to keep things quiet and let in as few people as possible so that what they were doing didn't get out."

"It only takes one person to do the right thing."

He rubbed his hand up and down her back. "The people at Sunrise, those girls, are lucky they have you."

"I'm lucky to have you. What I've put you through . . ." She hugged him tighter. "Are you okay? That man you shot . . ."

"He's fine. In the hospital recovering before he goes to jail. I'm good." He buried his face in her hair. "I have you." He pressed a kiss to her head and they held each other, letting everything that happened settle and taking the comfort they needed from each other.

The door opened behind them. "I can turn the cameras off and come back in half an hour." Agent Gunn's voice actually sounded amused for once.

She reluctantly pressed out from Declan's hold, touched his face, and looked into his eyes to be sure he really was okay. She saw nothing but relief that she was fine and turned to the agent. "Are criminals always that stupid?"

Agent Gunn smiled. "I wish. But you'd be surprised how the little things trip them up and get them caught."

"Like the fact Gabriel stomped on Lucy so hard he left a shoe impression." The thought turned her stomach.

"And that Gordon Banks thinks he can walk into the FBI and say whatever the hell he wants and threaten people in an interrogation room with someone who made it clear he was not her attorney." Agent Gunn took the seat across from her. "You played him perfectly."

"It wasn't that hard once he showed his true colors."

"The next part of this isn't going to be as easy. In fact, it's dangerous for the agents involved. Prosperity is heavily armed even without the guns you hid. Gabriel and his men are an unknown factor."

"Not really. Gabriel killed Lucy in a fit of rage. His men aren't violent. Did they get caught up in partying and . . . being with the girls?" she asked diplomatically. "Yes. They've lost their way, done some bad things, but I bet about now they're looking to redeem themselves. Gabriel is the bad influence. He led them astray. I don't know what's happening there now that you guys showed up, but I bet a lot of people at Sunrise are hoping things go back to the way they used to be. Gabriel, on the other hand, is probably desperate, or getting there."

"I have it on good authority that while the girls are still being held at The Stable, it's been closed down to the men from town. Only the men from Prosperity and Sunrise have been going there."

That was something, but not good enough. "Then it should be easier to get the girls out. What will happen to them?"

"Most of them look like runaways or women who were making their living on the streets. Not all of them are underage. The state police will handle that part of the case as well as the corrupt cops. They've got resources to help the women."

"If any of them have no place to go and want to stay at Sunrise, I will make sure they are welcomed into the community and given a job and a fair wage for their work." She'd make sure everyone at Sunrise earned an income so they had a choice to stay or leave without relying on a payout. And no one, like Gabriel, could hold the money and power or people's fate in their hands.

Agent Gunn nodded. "Until this all came about, Sunrise had never hit the FBI radar."

"Everything was fine until Gabriel took over and invited Prosperity into our community. Gabriel couldn't pass up the money even knowing where it came from and what Prosperity planned to do. The money meant more to him than people's lives."

"Everyone we talked to while we were there said you were the one trying to bring real prosperity to the community. You had increased sales and profits for the farm."

"The collective made that happen."

Agent Gunn's head tilted. "I think you take too little credit for your contributions."

"My reward is seeing Sunrise and its people prosper."

Declan leaned forward. "Is the FBI or ATF going to seize any of Sunrise's assets or land because of what Gabriel has done?"

Shocked, she turned to Declan. "What?" She panicked and implored Agent Gunn, "No. You can't do that."

"Actually, in some cases, we can." Agent Gunn held up his hand. "But that's not what we're interested in doing at

Sunrise. Prosperity is another matter. We want them shut down. To do that, I need your help."

"You have it," she assured him.

Declan put his hand over hers. "Maybe we should get you a lawyer to make sure you're covered."

She looked Agent Gunn in the eye. "Are you a good man?"

"I try to be," he responded honestly.

"Are you willing to make me a straight and fair deal?"

"Yes. I'll recommend to the federal prosecutor that in exchange for your cooperation, you receive full immunity. I don't think we'll have a problem getting it."

She appreciated his assurance, but . . . "You'll get them to put it in writing?"

"Yes."

She glanced at Declan.

He sighed and looked at Agent Gunn. "Are you going to put her in danger again?"

"We just need to know what she knows and where to find the guns and other stuff."

She scrunched her mouth and sat back. "Sure. As soon as I have my written guarantee."

Agent Gunn glanced from her to Declan.

"You heard her. I'll call a lawyer to go over it with her."

She shrugged. "They seem to be a lot of trouble if you ask me. We have an agreement. That should be enough. Right?"

Agent Gunn stood. "Listen to Declan. He's looking out for you." He gave Declan a nod. "I'll get your agreement drawn up." He stared down at her. "You're not like the others I met at Sunrise. They all seemed . . . acquiescent."

"You mistake their deference for others as weakness.

Mr. Banks and the men at Prosperity underestimated me at their peril. I will help you, but if you try to hurt those good people, you'll find I'm not that cooperative anymore."

"This is *you* being cooperative?" The teasing tone made the question rhetorical. "Sit tight. I'll be back soon."

Declan popped the top on the soda can and handed it to her. "You must be hungry and thirsty." He pulled open the top of the chip bag and held it out to her.

She took one and put it in her mouth, savoring the salty goodness. "I love chips."

He chuckled. "You're just starving."

"Have you talked to Tate? Is everything okay back at the ranch?"

"I'll call him later. I'm more concerned about you and ending this so that you'll be safe."

"It sounds like they'll take the information I have and arrest everyone involved."

"I hope so. Eat and I'll see about getting a lawyer in here to make sure you get what Agent Gunn promised."

"Something he said caught my attention."

"What's that?" Declan took a long swallow of the soda they shared.

"He said an inside source told him The Stable was shut down. What did he mean?"

Declan raised an eyebrow. "I think he means they have a man in Prosperity."

"Someone like me, trying to do the right thing?"

"Maybe. Or, more likely, an undercover agent."

She didn't even think something like that was possible. "Do the police do that?"

Declan put his hand on her face. "Sometimes I forget

you've never seen a cop show. We've got some serious binge watching to do."

She cocked her head. "What is that?"

"Where you watch a whole series of shows all at once."

"Oh. Will we be cuddled up on the couch together?" She liked the sound of that.

He leaned in close. "On second thought, screw TV. I'll just take you to bed and binge on you."

She liked that even more, but wondered if and when that would happen. It felt like things were coming to a close, but then again, nothing had been easy about stopping Gabriel and the others.

She missed her friends and family. How long until she could see them?

What happened with her and Declan after this was all over?

Someone needed to run Sunrise.

She couldn't just leave her community without a leader or direction after all they'd been through lately.

Her parents would want to go back, but what about Meadow?

Thoughts swirled in her head, but only one really troubled her: *How will I be with Declan and do right by the home I've always known and loved?*

People were counting on her.

Chapter Twenty-Four

GABRIEL STARED at Jeremiah's text messages and felt the walls closing in on him.

JEREMIAH: They have her in custody
JEREMIAH: Banks is there now trying to get info on supplies
JEREMIAH: Be ready to move as soon as we have a location

Gabriel hoped the damn lawyer got the information they needed. He wanted to hand everything over and be done with this whole thing.

He'd thought life at Sunrise was boring. Nothing but service, work, and endless days of tedium. What he wouldn't give for that kind of monotony in his life right now.

It seemed every part of his life was crumbling. Maybe he should just take the money, pack his bags, and move on. But he had nowhere to go. This place had always been home. These people were family. Not by blood, but by choice and circumstance.

Ever since he could remember he'd been fighting against the system and this place. Now, he saw the secu-

rity and harmony in their way of life. He'd always been
the one to disrupt it. His father had railed against him
many times for not seeing the value in what they did and
how they lived.

He saw it now.

But he couldn't turn back the clock and learn the lesson
sooner, before he'd screwed things up so badly. And for
what? Hoping to modernize Sunrise with TVs. The internet. Travel to places far and wide. No one here wanted or
even seemed to need those things. They resented him for
wanting them.

The front door slammed and footsteps sounded on the
hardwood floor.

He walked out of the kitchen and caught Joseph and
a few others going into the office. "Hey, you looking
for me?"

Not one of the four men responded.

He stepped into the office as they flipped through files.
"What are you doing?"

"Working," Joseph snapped. "The trucks are loaded.
We just need to check the contract and be sure we've got
the order right for the customer."

"What are you talking about?" He really had no idea.
And he should as leader of the council and Sunrise. But
it had become very clear that meant nothing to the people
who lived here or the business they ran since Skye disappeared and everything turned to shit.

If he'd married her, truly partnered with her, he could
have had the respect everyone pretended to give him
up until . . . well, he'd made a lot of mistakes. Partying.
Drinking. The girls. Lucy.

He knew he should feel more remorseful for what he'd
done, but he didn't. He wished he'd gotten away with it.

Then he wouldn't be in this predicament and facing a lot worse. He was more concerned about that than killing Lucy.

He'd always felt different from others and wondered why everyone didn't think like him. He'd always accepted that he was better than them. They wasted their lives worried about what others thought. He simply didn't care.

He'd always hated how his father and the community drilled in the principles they lived by. But they had kept this place and everyone here happy.

Now it seemed there was nothing but discord.

The more he fought for everyone to do what he said and ignore the things he'd done, the worse things got.

"Cal and some of the others have been focused on the fields and crops. No one bothered to listen to the messages in the office."

Gabriel shrugged. "Lucy, Eva, and Meadow usually covered the phone during the day."

"Yeah, well Lucy's dead, Eva is suffering terrible morning sickness because she's pregnant, and Meadow isn't here, is she? Eva is so embarrassed and mortified she's an unwed mother that she hasn't left her family's cabin in weeks."

"That's not my fault." Gabriel was tired of being blamed for everything. He'd never touched Eva. That one wasn't on him.

And Meadow left with her parents, siding with the fucking FBI instead of remaining loyal to him and Sunrise.

"Right. Nothing is your fault. It's not your fault seven girls and women are pregnant because of the parties you threw and the drinking you allowed."

Gabriel glared. "I didn't hear you complaining."

"No. I went along." Joseph looked at the other three men who'd come in with him. "We all did, but not anymore. It's time to put this place back together."

"What does that mean?"

"It means we fulfill the orders we promised to our customers. Thank God Skye kept such good records. We can make delivery on all seven that are outstanding today and tomorrow." Joseph planted his hands on his hips and stared down Gabriel. "When we get back, we need to have a serious talk about the girls at The Stable and getting them home or giving them a proper place to live and real jobs if they want to even stay here. We need to sever ties with Prosperity and get back to doing farm business."

He didn't like this insubordination at all. "Who put you in charge?"

Joseph fisted his hands at his sides and glared at him. "Someone needs to do what's right."

He tried to exert his authority. "I say what goes here."

"You head the council. For now. But it is made up of seven members, including me. We've discussed the things going on here and how to fix them and put things right." Joseph took a step forward. "We're also going to have a talk about Lucy and Skye."

"Skye is in FBI custody right now."

Joseph's gaze narrowed. "I bet that makes you nervous."

"Why should it? I've done nothing wrong." He wished he could back that statement up, but couldn't, not with all he'd done, or what Joseph knew.

"I can see the blood on your hands. Just like everyone else. Just like everyone knows Skye never liked you, let alone went into a jealous rage and killed Lucy because you were sleeping with her. Lucy would have been a good partner for you. She was blind to your faults. But Skye saw right through you. She knew who you really are. And now, so do I. So does everyone else."

Gabriel's phone vibrated in his pocket, startling him. He pulled it out, angry at Joseph for saying such hurtful and too-hard-to-hear truths. They'd been friends their whole lives. But right now it felt like they'd become enemies.

JEREMIAH: Can't get ahold of Banks
JEREMIAH: Something's wrong
JEREMIAH: That bitch must have screwed us again
JEREMIAH: Find what you owe me NOW!!!!!!!!!!

He looked up and saw only Joseph left staring at him.

"Looks like more bad news for you. Do the right thing, Gabriel. Admit what you've done. Turn yourself in. Take responsibility. Ask for forgiveness."

He was looking at spending the rest of his life in jail.

He should run, but all he wanted to do was get his hands on Skye and make her pay for ruining everything. "You're not innocent in all this," he reminded Joseph, who'd helped him store the guns and bomb materials. He'd helped bring the girls to The Stable.

"I'll face whatever is coming. I'm sure Skye will hold me, and everyone else involved, accountable."

Gabriel shook his head. "You love her."

"You wanted to keep her all to yourself because you saw how smart and kind and wonderful she was to everyone around her. You wanted her to shine that light she has inside her on you. It's what I wanted all those years ago, but didn't know it or appreciate it until I lost her because I was selfish and stupid. Yes, I love her. But I don't deserve her. Neither do you. You just wanted to possess her. You wanted people to see her with you and think that you must be really great to have someone like her standing next to you. But they never would think that, Gabriel, because she outshines all of us and we look pale in comparison. If after everything that's happened, you don't see that, you're more lost than I thought."

He held up his phone. "She's talking to the FBI. They're coming for us."

Joseph nodded. "I'm ready to accept whatever consequences come. Are you?"

"She's not taking me down."

"You did that to yourself." Joseph walked out with several papers rolled up in his hand, ready to fulfill orders when they should be planning how to stop Skye and the FBI from raiding Sunrise.

Gabriel feared nothing would stop what was coming, but if he got his hands on Skye, she'd wish she never opened her mouth or crossed him.

His phone vibrated with more texts.

JEREMIAH: They're moving her
JEREMIAH: We have a plan

Which meant he still had a chance to get out of this and make Skye pay, painfully, for everything she'd done to him.

Chapter Twenty-Five

*R*UN.

Lucy's warning rang in Skye's ears as she shot up in the backseat of the FBI SUV.

Declan's big hand rubbed up her back as she tried to catch her breath after the nightmare. "You're okay, sweetheart. Just a bad dream."

She fell back into his side and pressed her head to his cheek, the uneasy feeling settling into her gut and tying it in knots. The dream left her feeling like Lucy had issued a new warning.

Until Gabriel and the others were locked up, this was far from over.

She pressed her hand to Declan's chest, felt his steadily beating heart, and took comfort in his presence and unwavering support.

"I must have fallen asleep." The inane statement only proved how long this day had been and that it wasn't over yet. She couldn't wait to get to the motel where they'd stashed her parents and sister. She desperately wanted to see them.

"It's no surprise you're exhausted. It's nearly midnight."

After she'd outed Mr. Banks as a member of Prosperity and found out she'd been cleared in Lucy's murder, the FBI offices turned into a chaotic mass of people running around and getting ready to raid Sunrise in just a few short hours. Skye hated putting the good people who lived there through one more disruption to their lives, but hopefully this would put an end to everything.

And then what?

Her mind spun with ideas and tasks that needed to be done to get Sunrise back up and running the way it used to and the people living and thriving the way they did before Gabriel turned everything upside down.

Agent Gunn told her it only took a few pointed questions to make Mr. Banks see the bleak future he faced unless he started talking. Last she heard before she and the FBI teams left Bozeman and headed to Sunrise and Prosperity, he was cutting a deal and asking for witness protection. Agent Gunn said he might get it because Prosperity's leaders and followers were determined to see their cause reach the masses. Traitors and snitches regularly died or disappeared.

The thought sent a shiver up her spine, but she believed in doing the right thing and would not be deterred. She thought of Lucy and the girls being held at The Stable, the ones at Sunrise who had been taken advantage of by the men Gabriel led astray.

Gabriel may have made the mess, but she felt obligated to help clean it up.

Though the concerned man sitting beside her in the FBI vehicle might sway her.

Declan did not like the idea of her leaving the FBI offices, but she'd done all she could to help. Now she wanted to see her family.

She missed Meadow, wanted to be sure she was okay,

and speak to her parents and try to make them understand why she'd done what she'd done in secret. She hated that they thought her capable of murder for even a second, but gave them the benefit of the doubt because Gabriel had done a very good job of framing her for the crime.

He'd get what was coming to him soon.

She squeezed Declan's hand and glanced over at him. "I know you think this is a bad idea."

Even Agent Gunn tried to talk her out of it. He swore she could see her family as soon as they had all the players locked up.

Let them do their thing. Her family was in protective custody with agents watching over them. Plus, they'd have the agent driving her and Declan to the motel.

She felt perfectly safe if not a bit nervous. But most of those nerves were about introducing Declan to her family.

Too soon?

Too much all at once?

She didn't know, but her life recently felt fast-tracked and stalled-out all at the same time. In some aspects, she felt like she had all the time in the world, but in other areas, she felt like she needed to get things done before it was too late.

It felt like she and Declan were solid and that she might lose him any second, too.

He hugged her close. "Relax. What has you so on edge?"

"I don't know. I guess it's that I'm not sure what happens next."

He kissed the side of her head. "Everything is going to be okay. It's in the FBI's hands now. You did what you needed to do and got the help that Sunrise needed."

She sat up and stared at him. "It's just . . . what happens with—"

"We're here," the agent assigned to drive and protect them said as he pulled into the backside of the motel and parked in the space outside one of the few rooms that faced this side of the building.

Declan slipped his hand under her long hair and drew her in for a soft kiss. "Relax. We'll figure it out."

Either he knew her well enough already to finish her thought or he had the same concerns as her about how they moved forward once this mess at Sunrise was cleaned up and they found themselves living in two different states and hours apart.

She loved being at Declan's place. The night they'd shared made her want every night to be just like it. As much as she wanted to see her family, she couldn't wait to be alone with him again in their own private room.

Skye needed the connection they shared to chase away all the bad from the day and show her that she had something and someone truly precious in her life.

The agent turned in his seat and held up his phone. "Your sister is awake and anxious to see you. We'll stop by her room first, and then I'll get you settled in your room. Stay close. Be alert. Anything happens, you duck and let me handle it."

She and Declan both nodded.

"Good. Let me come around and open your door. Both of you exit the same door." The agent climbed out and came around to Declan's side, his gaze swinging in all directions as he waited for both of them to exit.

"Are you expecting trouble?" Better to know than be blindsided.

"I don't think we were followed, but there was a lot more traffic heading into town than I expected. Someone could have been watching to see if you passed through town headed toward Sunrise and Prosperity."

The knot in her stomach pulled tighter, but the butterflies fluttering had more to do with seeing her family. She took Declan's hand and followed the agent to the door.

He tapped twice, then once more.

The door opened a crack before it swung wide.

She barely got a glimpse of the older gentleman guarding her family before she rushed in, dragging Declan behind her, and spotted her sister standing by the bathroom sink at the back of the room. She released Declan and pulled Meadow in for a hug.

"You're squishing me." Meadow held her tighter despite her words.

Skye inhaled her sister's sweet floral scent and held back tears. "I've missed you so much."

"Looks like you found some company. Who's the blond hottie?"

"Declan." Just his name made her smile. She released her sister and turned to him. "This is Meadow."

"Nice to meet you. Skye's been worried about you."

Meadow glanced up at her. "You took off without a word."

"I had to get those girls out of there."

Meadow scoffed. "They came right back. Not one of them was brave enough to talk to the authorities about what was going on. Not like you." Admiration filled those last words.

Skye's heart soared with the praise but plummeted when she spotted her mother and father standing in the doorway adjoining the two rooms. "Hi, Mom. Dad."

Her mother looked her up and down. "You look terrible."

She self-consciously ran her fingers through her tumbled and tangled hair. "It's been quite a day."

"None of this would have happened if you'd taken your concerns to the council and kept this in the community." Her mother's disapproval had always stung, but after all she'd been through, it felt like a slap in the face.

"Rely on the very council Gabriel headed, where most of the members were his cohorts? Is that how you wanted me to handle him murdering Lucy?"

"We don't know what happened to Lucy," her father tried to intervene.

"I do. I watched him kill her. I saw the cruelty he inflicted on her. I heard him talk about the calculated way he planned to marry those girls to his buddies to appease the community, all the while they were hiding prostitutes on the property, having sex with them, and making money off them."

Her mother clutched her robe at her chest. "No. He wouldn't." Of course her mother didn't want to believe that. It was easier to believe it was a misunderstanding or never happened and just go on with her peaceful life. "That is not our way of life."

"No, it's not, which is why I did everything I could to stop him from making it a part of our life."

"You got us kicked out of Sunrise." Her mother's voice shook with fear and uncertainty buried under those angry words. With no money and nowhere to go, her fear was real and warranted.

"You weren't kicked out. Everyone will welcome you back. I promise. I'll make this right once Gabriel and the others are taken into custody."

Her father shook his head. "Did it have to come to this? Police, FBI, outsiders trampling over all we've built? Couldn't you have let the community vote him out?" Her father eyed Declan, silently dumping him into that pot of interlopers desecrating their way of life.

"Gabriel and the others working with him would have stopped me before I revealed everything they've done. The police helped Gabriel cover up the prostitutes and Lucy's murder. I had no choice but to find someone else to help take Sunrise back from Gabriel and the others."

"If you'd married him . . . you could have brought him around and back to doing what's best for Sunrise. He's lost. You could have shown him the way." Her mother leaned into her father, who immediately put his arm around her to comfort her.

Gabriel couldn't be fixed, because he didn't want to change. He believed what he was doing was right. She wished her mother could see that.

"Don't you think I deserve to be loved?"

"Of course we do," her mother automatically responded.

"Don't you think I should love the man I marry?"

"We want you to be happy." Her mother was sincere despite what she'd suggested.

"With a man like Gabriel? Not possible. I want some-one who can actually think of others and does the right thing even when it's inconvenient and difficult. A man who wants to protect me and lift me up. A man who sees me as an equal partner. A man who appreciates me for who I am, not what he wants me to be."

Her father stared at Declan. "Who are you?"

She took Declan's hand. "He's the man who turned his life upside down to protect and help me."

Declan squeezed her hand and addressed her father.

"I'm sorry we have to meet under such circumstances. Your daughter is amazing. Strong, resilient, and determined to help the people she loves. You may not approve of her methods, but her heart is in the right place. You should be really proud of her for putting her life on the line to save the Sunrise you helped build and she wants to see thrive for years to come."

"How do you know anything about it?" her mother asked, unsure whether to trust an outsider.

"She told me. I've seen her in action. Everything she's learned, the person she is, comes from her life at Sunrise. She's the best of what you believe in and the life you live there. She believes in truth and justice and helping others. She's kind and thinks of others before she thinks of herself. All she wants to do is free Sunrise from the bad influence that's infected your home."

"We want things to go back to the way they were before all this bad business." Her father finally looked her in the eye. "You could have come to us."

They'd have probably told her to stay out of it and stick to Sunrise business. Her parents lived in a very small world where everything began and ended with the Sunrise community. For them it was nice. Safe. Easy. They cared about others, did their work at Sunrise, but they wouldn't stick their necks out and disrupt the life they'd made for themselves in their happy bubble.

Skye couldn't leave it to the community the way they did to take care of the problem Gabriel created when he partnered with Prosperity. She needed to act. She believed in taking care of others, protecting them and Sunrise. The people there had always embraced her. She wasn't just Meadow's sister, she was everyone's there.

She sighed and gave her father the only answer he'd understand. "I didn't want to put anyone else in danger."

The agents standing guard on the other side of the room trying not to look like they heard every word went still when one of the agent's cell phones beeped. He read the text, then turned wide eyes on them. "Get down!"

Declan shoved Skye to the floor and made a grab for Meadow's hand, pulling her down, too. His body lay mostly over Skye, but he had an arm around Meadow and her body pulled into his side.

Bullets ripped through the door and window in a booming *rat-a-tat-tat* that went on and on.

Her father dropped to the floor, dragging her mother down with him. He bellowed and clutched his chest. Blood oozed and spread over his white undershirt and pooled on the floor.

She tried to get to him, but Declan held her down. "Daddy!"

Her mother pressed her hand over her father's on his chest and wailed. "No!"

The agents in the room returned fire, but one of them fell to his back a second before the other ran out of bullets. The agent scrambled to pull the other clip from his side when two men pushed the torn drapes aside, appeared in the destroyed window, and pointed their rifles at him.

"Get the woman," one said to the other.

With the downed agent's body blocking the door, the guy at the window swiped the glass out of his way with a gloved hand, climbed over, and came for her, his gun trained on Declan. "Don't be a hero, you'll only end up dead."

"Grab him, too," the guy still holding his gun on the

other agent called. "He shot Beetle. Jeremiah will want some payback."

"Get up. Both of you."

Declan reluctantly shifted his weight off her and helped her up as he stood, too. She couldn't take her eyes off her father. "He needs an ambulance."

"Let's go," the guy at the window yelled. "Now."

Meadow scrambled over to their parents and helped her mother press down on the chest wound. Her gaze shot up to Skye's. "I've got them." Tears streamed down her eyes. "Come back."

"Daddy, I love you."

The gunman next to her grabbed her arm and shoved her toward the door. Declan bent down and swung the agent's legs out of the way. The gunman opened the door, pushed her out, then trained his gun on Declan. "Let's go."

Declan followed her out. They were grabbed by the guy by the window and another man, who pulled her toward a waiting van.

She jumped in, sat by the far window, and reached for Declan as he fell into the seat next to hers. Two of the gunmen jumped in the open space behind them and another climbed into the front passenger seat. The sliding side door hadn't even closed all the way when the driver took off, throwing them all back in their seats.

She feared the poor agent by the door was dead, but she hoped the other agent got her father help as soon as possible.

She hoped she'd see him again.

Declan's arm went across her shoulders and he pulled her close. "You okay?"

She spread her hand on his chest and looked him over, not seeing any blood on him, but worried all the same he'd been hit protecting her and Meadow. "Are you?"

"I'm good."

She couldn't believe they'd gotten out of there alive. "Thank you for . . ." Her voice cracked and clogged in her throat.

"I won't let anything happen to you."

"You shouldn't make promises you can't keep," one of the gunmen behind them said. "Now don't move and shut the fuck up."

Skye had a sinking feeling she knew exactly where they were headed and what awaited them when they got there.

She wished she'd never gotten Declan involved, but she was so glad to have him with her. She clung to him, the only good thing she'd found in all this bad, and prayed they made it out of this alive.

Chapter Twenty-Six

FEAR ATE away at Declan's gut. He didn't know what to do, but he had to do something before these men killed them. If they laid a hand on Skye, he'd kill them with his bare hands. Whatever it took to keep her safe.

Silent tears fell down her cheeks and wet his hand where he held her cheek and tried to offer some kind of comfort in the face of her father being shot. Declan prayed her father didn't suffer the same outcome as the agent who'd given his life to protect them.

"It's my fault," Skye whispered.

He hugged her closer. "No, it's not."

"Maybe you should have thought twice before you fucked with us," the guy in the front passenger seat said over his shoulder.

"You got exactly what you deserve," Skye shot back.

"So will you. Just wait."

Declan touched his fingers to Skye's lips before she verbally abused the dickhead up front again. "Let it go."

Dickhead didn't know when to quit. "You won't win."

"I already did. I took all your shit. You shot an FBI agent and my father, asshole. There's a life sentence hanging over *your* head."

Dickhead turned and swung all at the same time.

Declan barely had time to think before he shot his fist out and clocked the guy in the jaw. The guy's head snapped back and Skye blocked his hand from connecting with her face. She leaned back and kicked him in the shoulder when he lunged for her again.

One of the guys in back hooked his arm around Declan's neck and pulled him back. "Stop fucking around," he ordered the guy in the front seat as the second guy in back grabbed Skye by the shoulders and held her in her seat.

None of them were wearing seat belts.

It seemed stupid to think about their safety right now when these guys were armed and could shoot them any second.

The guy holding Declan gave him a shake, then let him go. "Shut up. Sit still. We're almost there."

Declan had no idea where *there* was, and he wasn't so sure he wanted to get *there*.

The guy holding Skye let her go and sat back on the floor behind them. "Who the fuck do you keep texting?"

"Your mother. She can't get enough," the guy who'd subdued Declan shot back.

"You're an asshole," the other guy grumbled.

Skye rolled her eyes, took Declan's hand, and sat quietly beside him, her thoughts turning her face somber and her grip on him tight.

The driver pulled off the main road and drove down a dirt one.

Skye leaned in and whispered, "This is Sunrise land."

One of the guys behind him draped his hand over the seat. Declan glimpsed a compass tattoo on the back of it before he caught the guy's eye. "Thanks to your girlfriend, the state police took the girls from The Stable earlier today. I bet the FBI is coming for Gabriel, his guys, and the guns and other stuff you hid. If we get to it first, maybe she'll live. If I were you, I'd talk some sense into her." The guy smacked Declan on the shoulder like they were buds and Declan would just go along.

Instead, Declan squeezed Skye's hand and tried to think of a plan to get them out of this.

The dirt road seemed to go on forever. If they had to run, he'd have to rely on Skye to lead them out of there to somewhere safe.

The van pulled in behind a long dark wood structure with several gates that should have led out to paddocks, but any fencing had been removed. He thought of the women and young girls brought here and held in those closed stalls.

No lights shone from the building. There were no cars in sight, but if they parked on the other side of the building, no one could see them. In order to find this place, you'd have to know about the nondescript dirt road.

Gabriel had chosen a good location to open his illegal brothel. He'd thought of traffic and how to keep the place somewhat secret.

He hadn't counted on Skye.

The van came to a stop and the dickhead in the front seat turned and glared at Skye. "End of the line, bitch."

"For you? I hope so." Skye hadn't lost her spunk. She didn't back down.

He had to give it to her, she wasn't going down without a fight. And neither was he.

The two guys behind him climbed out the side door and stood facing them.

The guy with the tattoo on his hand reached in and grabbed Declan's arm, pulling him out. "I've got him.

You bring her," he called to his friend, leading Declan away. Declan tried to get back to Skye, but the guy dug his fingers into his biceps, leaned in close, and whispered, "If you want to help her, go along."

Declan's heart stopped for a beat. He looked the guy in the eye and stilled at the directness and stark truth he saw in the dark depths. Declan didn't know why, but he believed the guy didn't mean him or Skye any harm.

"Declan. Wait," Skye called to him.

Those terror filled words clawed at his heart.

"They hurt her, I'm going to fucking kill you," he warned his captor.

Tattoo guy shouted over his shoulder, "Bring her along. Let's go. Jeremiah is waiting." He shoved Declan through the side door into what was a bare bones bar with a few tables surrounded by chairs, a wood bar with a couple taps and a row of stools. A few overhead lights left the place mottled with shadows and pools of light.

A couple guys sat at a table, wearing biker gear much like the men who took them from the motel. Another man stood by the bar, a glass in hand with a couple fingers of dark brown liquor.

The guy in the camo jacket stood from the table with a wide grin on his face. "Yes! You got her."

Skye fought the two guys dragging her in.

"Who is this?" the camo jacket guy asked.

Tattoo guy looked bored. "The guy who shot Beetle. I'll put him in a room until we deal with her."

Tattoo guy tugged him down the hall and into a dismal room that smelled like an outhouse and had a twin mattress on the floor covered in nothing but a faded quilt. The bucket with a lid in the corner accounted for the stench.

Declan couldn't imagine the poor woman who'd lived

in this squalor enjoyed her stay or wanted to be here any more than he did.

The guy who brought him in pressed his hand to Declan's chest and shoved him back against the wall. "Do you want to save your girlfriend?"

"I'll fucking kill you to do it."

"I'm not your enemy. I managed to warn those agents before the shots were fired. It could have been a hell of a lot worse."

"An agent is dead and Skye's father wasn't in good shape when we left, asshole."

The guy shoved him hard into the wall again. "I did my best. I didn't want those agents or anyone else to get hurt. The cavalry should be here soon. Until then, you and I need to get her the hell out of this without getting killed."

Declan's mind started catching up to what this guy was saying. "Are you a cop?"

"FBI." He spun Declan around and pulled the gun from Declan's back. "How the fuck do you think you got this gun?" The agent gave him an admiring nod. "Nice job pulling it off the agent on your way out the door without my dumb-fuck partner catching you."

Astonished, Declan smiled. "I thought you saw me do it."

"It was slick, but yeah, I saw it. If I was with them, you'd be dead. As it is, I needed you to come along. I can't take these guys alone. So are you really prepared to shoot your way out of this if it comes to it?"

Declan took the gun, popped the clip, checked the chamber, shoved the clip back in, and chambered the first round. "Ready." He wasn't as great with a handgun as he was with a rifle, but he'd do his best.

The undercover agent pulled an automatic rifle out from under the mattress.

"Got another one of those?"

"Sorry. No. But I do have another one of these." He pulled an semi-automatic pistol from his back.

Declan took it, shoved it into his waistband, and stuffed the extra clip the agent handed him into his back pocket.

"Don't shoot me," the agent warned.

"Don't worry about me. Save her," he ordered the agent.

"Don't be a fucking superhero. Shoot to protect her." The agent checked his weapon, then went to the door and looked back at Declan. "When we go out, stick close until we can split off. Backup should only be a couple minutes out if we're lucky."

Declan hadn't been lucky in a long time, not until Skye walked into his life, hungry and in need a safe place to stay.

He'd been starving for her. She'd filled him up and made his life infinitely better. She made him look toward the future with hope and a sense that all those dreams he had could come true.

He couldn't lose her now. Not when that future seemed so close and tangible so long as he had Skye by his side.

"Let's go get your girl." The agent walked out.

Declan nodded, knowing with Skye, life wouldn't be as boring and dismal as it used to be before she came along and moved into his life and heart.

It simply wouldn't be worth living if he lost her now.

He followed the agent out, staying right behind him so that the others in the bar area didn't see him until the last second and they kept the element of surprise.

Of course, the second he set eyes on Skye, she surprised the hell out of him again.

Chapter Twenty-Seven

SKYE STARED down Gabriel as he tossed back his drink, his eyes watering and throat constricting on the harsh liquid.

He hissed out a breath and took two unsteady steps toward her. "You ruined everything."

"You did that all on your own. You killed Lucy. You brought those girls here. You brought Prosperity to Sunrise." She didn't mean the good kind, but thankfully Gabriel got what she was saying. "The FBI proved I didn't kill her. They're coming for *you*. Why the hell are you still here?"

How dumb could he be?

"Because he owes me what you took." The big man in the camo jacket crossed his arms and set his hard glare on her, trying to intimidate her. It worked, but she tried not to let it show.

"If what you seek is peace and freedom, you won't find it at the end of one of those rifles."

"Sometimes men have to do bad things for the greater good," he shot back.

"Like holding young women against their will so that you can use and abuse them."

"That was your guy, sweetheart."

"Don't call me that," she snapped. "And he's nothing to me." She turned her gaze on Gabriel. "I never wanted you. But you couldn't take no for an answer. You tried to make the decision for me. You just wanted what you wanted, everyone be damned, including Lucy and your unborn baby."

"Yeah, well, you damned me, now, didn't you?"

"I hope you go to hell. But first I'd like you to spend a good long time alone in a cell with plenty of years to think about the lives you took. I hope you spend every second of every day thinking about Lucy, how much she loved you even though you threw it in her face, and about that unborn child you didn't want and never let take even a breath. I hope you don't have a single moment of peace until you accept responsibility for what you've done. Maybe you'll learn to atone." She choked back tears. "Because of you, an agent died tonight and my father was sh-shot. I don't know if he made it. Their lives are on you. *You* started this, but you can bet one way or another *I* will finish it."

The guy in the camo jacket took a menacing step closer. "Give us what we want before the cops get here and I'll let you go free."

They'd found out about where the FBI was hiding her family. She had no doubt he knew exactly when the cops planned the raid.

And she didn't believe for a second he'd let her go. "Oh, come on. I know you think he's stupid, but I'm not. You will never get those guns or make those bombs. You will never carry out your plot to take down a plane, bomb the New York Stock Exchange, or take out the targets you selected in San Francisco, Chicago, Washington DC, or New York City."

That menacing gaze swung to Gabriel. "Did you fucking tell her everything?"

"She took the plans from my office safe."

"And handed it all over to the FBI," she added.

Gabriel's eyes went wide the second he saw the guy in the camo jacket raise the gun and point it right at her.

She gripped the rope tied around her wrists and draped over the rafter, the other end held by one of the Prosperity men, lifted her legs, and shot her feet out, connecting with the guy's shoulder. The gun fired and the blast rang in her ears as she swung back and caught herself on her toes.

Gabriel squealed and clutched his bleeding arm.

The guy turned the gun on her again.

She stared down the barrel.

Another shot rang out, jolting her with a wash of panic, but she didn't get hit. The guy dropped into a hunch, holding his thigh, and the gun skittered across the floor. She kicked it away as the man who took Declan came out holding a rifle to his shoulder.

Declan walked up beside her, a pistol pointed at the guy bleeding from the leg. "You're lucky I didn't kill you."

The guy holding the other end of the rope tied to her let it loose. She dropped to her flat feet and yanked her hands down.

Declan made sure the other armed man kept everyone else in the room in his sights and turned, opened the knife from his belt, and cut her hands free, then spun back with the gun to make sure none of the other men made a move.

"Why the hell are you helping him?" the guy in the camo jacket asked the guy who came out with Declan.

"Too many innocent people have gotten hurt."

Skye thought it was something more, but didn't say anything about her suspicions. Agent Gunn had said he'd received inside information. She guessed from this man.

"I told you this was over the second they took her into custody. But you two"—the guy with the compass tattoo looked from the guy bleeding down his leg to Gabriel— "had to go after her despite the risks when the smart thing to do was get out." He shook his head. "Not that you would have gotten far, but we wouldn't have had to do it this way."

"FBI," the blare of a bullhorn announced. "Put the guns down and come out with your hands up."

The guy with the tattoo and rifle shook his head. "Told you."

"Take him down," the surprised man on the ground shouted to his other men.

All hell broke loose with the guy with the tattoo firing at the men who pulled their weapons.

Declan hooked his arm around her middle and pulled her along with him as he ducked and shoved her behind the bar. Bottles exploded over their heads, and glass and booze rained down on them.

Declan tried to help the other man, firing out from behind the bar. "Stay back."

She ignored that shouted order and tried to make herself as small a target as possible and protect Declan's back with her body.

One of the few small windows at the front shattered, and a bright flash and deafening bang went off, halting all gunfire and making all of them grab their ears and try to get their bearings.

With her eyes closed and hands over her ears, she

didn't know who grabbed her arm, but automatically rose and began to follow until her leg brushed Declan beside her and she realized it wasn't him pulling her out of the building. She felt his hand brush her leg as he made a grab for her, but it was too late as another flash and bang went off, making her stumble and close her eyes against the bright light and lingering fireworks that went off on the back of her eyelids.

She stumbled along as far as she could go before she fell to her knees, shaking her head, trying to clear the disorienting ringing in her ears and flashes in her vision.

A gun barrel pressed to the side of her head.

"Get up. Now." Gabriel stood over her, one hand held to his own head, blood running down the arm he used to hold the gun on her.

"FBI, drop the gun." Two men held guns on Gabriel.

He drew her up in front of him with his arm around her throat, held the gun to her head with his other hand, and pulled her back as the men closed in. "Stay back, or I'll kill her."

More lights came from behind them, but they were constant and not as bright. She couldn't hear the engine over the ringing in her head, but caught a glimpse of the front end of a truck when Gabriel's body shifted sideways as he dragged her toward the vehicle.

Joseph got out as Gabriel pulled her toward the driver's door.

"Take her," Gabriel ordered. "Get her in the truck. Let's go."

Joseph held up his hands and backed away. "No. I'm not part of this."

Her only chance was the officers and Declan headed toward her. "Shoot him!"

Joseph ran away, leaving her at Gabriel's mercy.

Declan ran toward her, yelling, "Don't shoot. You'll hit her."

Gabriel leveled the gun next to her. She planted her feet and shoved to the right, knocking his aim to the side, despite how much it hurt her throat when he yanked her back. But his shot went wide and missed Declan and the FBI guy standing in front of them about twenty feet away.

She locked eyes with Declan for a split second before Gabriel shoved her into the front seat of the truck, pushed her across the seat as he climbed in behind the wheel, and threw the truck in Reverse. He stomped on the gas pedal, sending her forward so fast she had to catch herself on the dashboard before she face-planted into it.

A couple shots pinged off the hood. One went right through the windshield but missed Gabriel by several inches. Unfortunately.

The last thing she heard when Gabriel cranked the wheel and spun the truck around was Declan's desperate shout. "Skye!"

Pissed off, hurting physically and mentally after what happened over the last hours, days, and weeks, she vowed that would not be the last time she heard Declan say her name.

Chapter Twenty-Eight

Declan DROPPED his empty gun, grabbed the under-cover agent next to him by the shirt, and shook him. "Why the fuck did you let him take her?"

"What do you want to do, run after the truck?" The agent held his hand out toward the oncoming vehicle. "Care to join us?"

Declan pushed the guy back a step and pulled the gun from his back. "Yeah."

"Great. Where is he taking her?"

Declan didn't really know where the hell they were right now, except on Sunrise property. He climbed into the SUV with the agent and asked, "What is up that way?"

"The orchard, fields of crops. Off to the left is the chicken barn. To the right is the Sunrise compound where everyone lives in the cabins."

Declan tried to think, though his brain was still a bit scrambled after the flash bangs went off one after the other right in front of him.

"What does Gabriel want from her?" the undercover agent asked.

"To kill her."

The agent shook his head. "Then he'd have shot her in

the head and been done with it. What else does he want from her?"

If he was Gabriel, he'd want to get the hell out of here. "He needs money, so he can leave and start over somewhere new."

"Okay. Does Skye have any money?"

"No. But Prosperity does."

"Prosperity is back the other way."

Declan shook his head. "The money is here. She told Agent Gunn that Prosperity had everything they needed to carry out their plot."

"Right. The guns and bomb material."

"I'm guessing there's money here, too."

"Shit. How much?"

"It's a hunch. But judging by how Skye held back divulging everything in one shot to Special Agent-in-Charge Gunn, I'm guessing she kept an ace up her sleeve just in case."

As fast as they drove after Gabriel and Skye, they still hadn't caught up, and Declan didn't see any sign of them or their taillights as they passed through rows and rows of some kind of vines. In the dark, he didn't know what he was seeing.

"Where would she hide it, Declan?" The agent's tone turned more urgent.

He thought out loud. "The guns are hidden in the old hayloft over The Stable we just left."

The agent's head fell back and he stared at the SUV ceiling, then busted up laughing. "Fucking brilliant. She hid them right where they spent all their time. They were so busy searching the property, they never thought to search the very building they were in."

Declan had to hand it to her. She'd outfoxed them at every turn.

"Where is the bomb stuff?"

"The one place Gabriel would never go. The chicken barn. He hates the chickens and especially the smell. She buried it all under a mountain of manure they collect and use to make mulch and compost. She used a backhoe to dig a hole, then filled it with all the bags of fertilizer and crates of other electronics and wiring stuff. Then she buried it and covered it in shit."

Despite the circumstances, the agent beside him and the two up front busted up laughing again.

"Where . . . where is the money?" the agent said between bursts of laughter.

"Probably with the chickens."

The driver caught his eye. "Because Gabriel is too chicken to go after it there."

Declan got the joke but had a hard time laughing with them when Skye was in danger.

The driver turned the wheel and took them down a dirt road between two fields of crops he couldn't really identify in the dark and headed for a huge structure straight ahead of them with a billion stars highlighting the peaked roof.

What he wouldn't give to be back in Montana with Skye on the ranch, staring up at that big sparkly sky and kissing her instead of chasing after the madman bent on killing her after he got what he wanted.

The dread from that thought clamped around his heart and squeezed until he could barely stand the pain.

"You know, I've spent the past two years with Prosperity and haven't been able to get close to taking them down. She did it without ever stepping foot on their compound. She did it without them ever knowing she was coming after them. She could have gotten away with ruining their plans if she hadn't taken those girls and run."

Declan admired that she'd taken the risk. "More than anything, she cares about people. She wanted to help those women. She did what she thought was right. She only ran because she thought Gabriel would kill her." Declan checked the gun in his hand as the car pulled to a stop twenty yards from the dark chicken barn. "And now he has her."

"I've never been in a chicken barn. So how do you think we should approach this place?"

Declan looked over the structure. He notched his chin toward the agents up front. "You two go around to the back and make sure they don't go out that way if they see us coming." He turned to the agent next to him. "It's basically one huge open room. Maybe it's divided into sections. I don't know. I haven't been inside. But there's an office or something at that end. There's no lights in the windows, but I'm guessing he didn't want to turn them on and alert us that they're in there."

The agents looked around. "I don't see their vehicle."

"It could be parked in one of the fields we passed and they walked in. Hell, they could be somewhere else."

The tattooed agent shook his head. "Don't second-guess yourself now. This is a good assumption."

"Not if it gets her killed because I guessed wrong."

The agent smacked the back of his hand into Declan's chest. "Let's go find out."

If he didn't find her here, he'd search every inch of the planet until he found her.

Damn, I love her.

If this all went south and he never got to tell her, he'd spend the rest of his days wondering what might have been, and whether she knew.

Chapter Twenty-Nine

"IF YOU fucking brought me here just to mess with me, I'll shoot you in the gut and let you bleed out for hours in agony."

If she didn't already know the depth of cruelty Gabriel was capable of, that right there told her exactly how ruthless he could be. He'd do it, too. She had no doubt.

But she wouldn't make it easy.

They walked along the chicken pen toward the office. She'd bought some time making him hide the truck near the plum orchard where anyone who came around the back side of the barn would see it but not from the front. She couldn't make her intent too obvious to Gabriel. She hoped the FBI surrounded the building, saw it, and knew she was inside. She hoped Declan had paid attention and knew the only thing Gabriel could do now was run.

"Where the hell did you hide the money?"

Just to mess with him, she took the long way to get there, too. "Well, the guns are in the loft over The Stable. You were literally under the guns every time you visited one of those girls and violated them."

She should have expected him to retaliate for her insolence, but the backhanded slap came out of nowhere, cutting her lip against her teeth. She spit blood right on his shoes. Like a child, he lashed out again and tried to kick her in the shin, but she saw it coming and sidestepped, making him miss.

She pushed him into the fencing separating them from the brood of laying hens, sleeping and sitting on their roosts. Wings fluttered. A few hens clucked their displeasure at being disturbed.

Gabriel jumped and glanced behind him but he never took the gun off her. "Stop fucking around and get the money so I can get out of here."

She reluctantly headed toward the office. "I love that you think you're actually going to get out of here. This place is crawling with FBI agents and more are coming for the guns and the bomb stuff. Which I buried out back under a pile of chicken shit, in case you're wondering."

"What the hell is wrong with you?" He glanced at a particularly disgruntled hen, his eyes wide and frightened of the six-pound bird.

Which gave her a very good idea.

"Me? What's wrong with you? You had a good life here. Why did you have to go and mess it up for everyone else if you were unhappy with it?"

"A good life," he scoffed. "Boring. The same thing happens here day after day, year after year. Nothing changes. I wanted more."

"We have what we need."

"There is so much more to enjoy in the world."

She knew that now. Declan had given her a glimpse of the wonderful life they could have together.

She rolled her eyes. "So you chose booze. And women. To start a war and hurt innocent people. That's the more you wanted?"

"No. It wasn't supposed to be this way."

"You hooked up with bad people and expected everything to go well? What did you think would happen?"

"I'd get paid and they'd leave."

She laughed right in his face. "You thought if it all went well, they'd simply leave. Are you serious? They'd have dragged us all in deeper. We'd be no better than them, hiding and supplying them. It's as good as condoning what they do when it goes against everything we stand for here at Sunrise."

"I wanted more for *us*." Repeating it didn't make it better or right. It didn't make her believe him.

"No, that's what I want. Along with everyone else here. I was working on making that happen in a bigger, more productive way. An honest way."

"Yeah, with the crops and contracts with businesses and your restaurant idea. It's more of the same. More hard work in the fields and with the fucking chickens."

"Yes, because this place and the people who work here are our biggest asset. What? You wanted to get rich selling sex with women you brought here under false pretenses and treated like shit? Was that your big plan?"

"We made money."

"Off hurting and exploiting those girls. You treated some of the young ladies you grew up with here like they were less than nothing to you. Lucy cared about you. She thought she loved you. She wanted to have your child and make a life with you, but you did worse than turn your back on her and your child, you callously and viciously killed them because . . . why? Why would you do that to a sweet girl who'd barely gotten a taste of life and love and the promise of a dream you made her believe in, then took away from her?"

"You have no idea how hard it's been since my dad died."

"Don't use his death as some lame excuse for what you've done. I miss him, too. Everyone at Sunrise does." Skye thought she heard a car outside and prayed Declan and the FBI finally found them.

"Everything is so easy for you."

She rolled her eyes. "Poor, poor Gabriel. Is too much expected of you?"

Frustration tightened all his muscles and made him lash out again. "I wanted to do something different here."

"So you went with prostitution and murder? You thought the community that works hard to provide for others would go along with that?"

Gabriel's eyes filled with rage. "Get me my fucking money!"

"You mean Prosperity's money. Do you think they'll let you get away with taking it?"

He grabbed her shoulder and shoved her forward. "Just get it and shut up."

"The truth hurts. Confronting what you've done isn't easy. But you should really just put that gun down and turn yourself in before you get yourself killed."

Gabriel huffed out a sigh. "Do you ever shut up?"

"Aren't you glad you didn't try to force me to marry you?"

Gabriel didn't like the sarcasm. "I'm wishing I killed you instead of Lucy."

She halted and smiled at Gabriel. "Thanks for saying that."

His eyes went wide at her grin. "What? Why?"

"Because *they* heard you admit to killing Lucy."

Gabriel scanned the area around them but didn't see

anyone lurking in the shadows. Neither did she, but she knew Declan was here. She felt him. And that meant the FBI was here, too.

"You're bluffing." Gabriel's gaze shot in every direction.

"No, she's not." Declan's voice rang out through the barn.

"I heard you loud and clear." Whoever that was, they sounded much closer.

Gabriel made a grab for her, but she expected the move, and dodged it. He leveled the gun right in her face. "Where is it?"

She cocked her chin toward the empty pen and nesting boxes behind him. "In there."

He kept the gun trained on her and reached forward and fisted his hand in the sweater Declan had bought her because she loved it. Gabriel dragged her forward and into the pen. Now, no matter where Gabriel stood, Declan and the other man, and whoever else came with them, had a clear shot at Gabriel. "I can't believe you said all that stuff just to stall."

"I stole all the stuff right out from under your nose, you think I'd just let you take that money and run?"

"I hate you." It permeated every word out of his mouth.

She leaned in and let all the hate she had for him fill her words. "The feeling is mutual."

Gabriel pulled her over to the nesting boxes, his gaze searching for chickens that might be hidden inside, but there weren't any in here. His fears still got to him. Just like she intended.

"Where is it?"

"Hidden in the shed out by the apple orchard."

He took her by the shoulders and shook her. "What?"

She shrugged. "I was never going to let you take the guns, the bomb stuff, or that money."

He stepped back and leveled the gun right at her chest. "You're lying. It's here. It has to be here."

She shook her head. "No. It's not. But they are."

Declan stood to her left. An agent stood to her right. She and Gabriel stood right between them.

Gabriel didn't even look at them. "I'm going to kill you."

"Maybe. But you won't kill anyone else. All those innocent people's lives you planned to take with Prosperity, they'll all live thanks to me."

"I hate you."

She batted the gun to the side and dropped to her knees and curled over to protect her head. Two shots rang out a split second before Gabriel crumpled to the ground. She uncovered her head and stared into his blank eyes as he lay dead in front of her. "I hate you more."

It wasn't her nature to wish harm on anyone, but Gabriel got exactly what he deserved for all the hurt and harm he'd caused.

She hoped Lucy rested in peace knowing Gabriel had paid for his crimes.

She was satisfied that she'd done all she could to free Sunrise from Gabriel and Prosperity's hold on them.

Now she wanted to find her mother and sister and make sure her father had made it. It hurt too much to think she might have missed her chance to say goodbye.

And she wanted Declan and his strength and love wrapped around her.

Chapter Thirty

DECLAN FELL to his knees behind Skye and wrapped his arms around her, drawing her close and burying his face in her hair. "Thank God you're okay."

Her hands grasped his arms and her nails bit into his skin. "It's over, right? They got everyone?"

"We got them," the Prosperity guy who turned out to be an undercover agent said, squatting next to them. "Thanks to you." He brushed his hand over Skye's hair, relief in his eyes that Skye made it out alive, too.

"Who are you?" She looked him up and down. "Besides Agent Gunn's inside source."

The guy with the compass tattoo grinned. "Mason Gunn. His brother. I've been undercover with Prosperity for two years. Jeremiah didn't trust anyone. When he partnered with Gabriel, I really didn't get it. I thought the guy would take them all down with his stupidity. But it took one smart, resourceful woman to topple a group of men who have little to no respect for women or anyone who doesn't believe in what they do." Mason glanced at Gabriel. "He turned out to be just as bad as the men who make up Prosperity. I could never get enough evidence to take them down. I gathered a piece here and there, but it just wasn't enough to stop them outright. You did it.

Thank you, Skye. You're one amazing woman to do all you did on your own."

Skye let out a huge sigh. "I saw those girls locked in those rooms and I just couldn't . . ." Skye shook her head. "This place used to be so peaceful and inclusive and respectful. He tainted it all."

"I have no doubt you'll wash away all the bad and put this place back to the way it used to be. The way it should be." Mason sighed, too. "I checked this place out as Gabriel and Jeremiah's connection tightened. Aside from what Gabriel and several of his men set up with those girls, this place seemed like a great place to live. The people care about each other and everyone contributes."

"It will be that way again."

Those words hit Declan right in the heart because he knew what that meant for him and Skye. She wouldn't rest until she made that statement a reality.

He loved her for it.

But it also meant they'd have to fight to stay together because she was needed here and he was needed at home, even if everything inside him needed her more.

"Come on, let's get out of here. The other agents will take care of Gabriel." Mason pressed his finger to his earpiece and listened. "Agent Gunn and his team just arrived. They want you to show them where you stashed everything. He's also got an update on your father. Sounds like he made it to the hospital and is in surgery, and he's reportedly stable."

Relief washed through Skye and loosened her tight muscles as he held her. "Thank God."

Mason stood and held out his hand to Skye. "We'll get you to him as soon as possible."

Skye took Mason's hand, stood on unsteady legs, and

launched herself into Declan's chest the second he hit his feet, too. He caught her in a tight hug and kissed her temple. "I got you, sweetheart."

"I can't believe it's over."

Mason shrugged. "I hate to tell you this, but sometimes the cleanup takes longer than the takedown."

Declan didn't want to hear that, especially when his thoughts were already heading in that dismal direction.

Chapter Thirty-One

SKYE SPENT an hour standing next to Declan, watching the scene play out as agents swarmed around the chicken barn, documenting the scene, and finally removing Gabriel's body. As the coroner's van drove away, she turned to Declan. They hadn't said much to each other, instead taking comfort in being close.

"Are you okay?" She tallied up all she'd put him through the last two days, including the fact he'd shot two people to save her, maybe more. She didn't know what happened during the shootout at The Stable after Gabriel grabbed her and dragged her out.

He rubbed his hands up and down her arms as the sun's first rays turned the dark sky gray. "I'm just glad you're okay."

She pressed her hand to his chest and looked him in the eye. "You saved my life."

He cupped her face. "I'll do whatever I have to, to keep you safe."

She pressed her lips tight and asked the hard question. "Does it weigh on you that you shot that man at your ranch and killed Gabriel? Was there anyone else at The Stable?"

Declan touched his forehead to hers. "I don't like that it had to be done, but I'd do it again to protect you." He closed his eyes for a moment and she gripped his shoulder tighter and kept one hand on his chest, offering what comfort she could while he gathered his thoughts. When he stared into her eyes again, she saw all the confusion and regret and determination in his eyes. "I'm sure it will hit me sooner or later. My brother is a soldier, trained for battle. I'm a rancher. I've had to put down sick and injured animals. But that's mercy. It's different than taking a man's life. I don't really know how to process it, except to say that I did it to protect you and save myself. I'll find a way to live with it because I know it was the right thing to do. I'd do anything to keep you safe. I—"

"There you are," Agent Gunn interrupted.

Skye really wanted to know what Declan was about to say.

Declan sighed and turned to Agent Gunn. "Looks like you took down all the bad guys."

Skye followed his gaze to the agents who arrived with Gabriel's men handcuffed and sitting in the back of a truck.

"We apprehended them at the Sunrise compound." Agent Gunn settled his gaze on her. "I'm afraid I need a little more help from you."

She nodded. "What can I do?"

"One of those men is desperate to talk to you." Agent Gunn pointed to the dark-haired man who leaped off the tailgate and stood with an agent holding his arm so he didn't go anywhere.

"Joseph. He's Gabriel's right-hand man."

"He confessed to everything, said he'd put it all in writing in a statement, but he asked to speak to you first."

She took Declan's hand and stepped away, but stopped when Agent Gunn called her name.

"Skye. You don't owe them anything."

"The man who is really responsible for all that went on here is dead because I led him to his death."

Declan squeezed her hand. "That's not true. Mason and I shot him."

"But I made it happen, bringing him here, stalling so you could get here, making sure I put him in exactly the right position for you to take him out."

"Because he was going to kill you."

"I know. I'll find a way to live with it because it was the right thing to do." She gave him back the exact words he'd said to her. "He would have kept hurting people if he'd lived." She glanced at the men in the back of the truck and Joseph in particular. "Those men aren't like Gabriel. They deserve to be punished for what they did, but they'll learn from their mistakes. They'll take responsibility. That's something Gabriel could never do. He always thought he was right and what he wanted mattered more than anything or anyone else. I showed him he was wrong."

"Yes, you did." Agent Gunn's eyes held all the admiration he put into those words.

Skye walked to Joseph with Declan right beside her, their fingers linked, their hearts connected like they had been for what seemed like a long time but had really only been a blink of an eye in the scheme of things.

Then again, she felt like she'd simply found where she belonged when she met him.

Joseph stood with his hands handcuffed at his back, his head bowed when she approached. "Skye. Are you okay?"

"A little banged up and exhausted, but I'll be fine."

"I heard about your dad." Remorse and worry filled his eyes and drew lines in his forehead.

"He'll make a full recovery." She had to believe that, because something good had to happen or she might crack clean open and all her grief, frustration, and anger would spill out and consume her.

Joseph looked at Declan, then back at her. "Can we talk in private?"

"No. Anything you have to say, you can say in front of him."

Joseph sucked in a breath. "This might be the last time I get a chance to say this, so . . . I'm sorry. For all of it. Especially for the way I treated you when we were together."

Declan looked down at her, waiting for some response.

She gave it to Joseph. "You mean when you pretended you liked me and that we had something special all so you could have sex with me?"

Joseph's eyes went wide. "I really did like you. I do. In fact, I knew I screwed up when I started seeing someone else and they just weren't . . . you."

"That only makes me feel sorry for whoever that girl was, because it seemed you went from me to a string of girls you never really cared about for long."

Joseph hung his head. "I'm sorry. To you and them."

"Yet you went along with Gabriel's plans. You participated in all those parties. You agreed to marry one of the girls Gabriel set you up with so you could all look like you were good family men. You let Gabriel set up

The Stable and never once spoke out about him or what was happening."

"I didn't know what to do. I never went there to . . . you know. I didn't. Neither did a few of the others."

"Very admirable." Sarcasm dripped off those words. "You guys brought those girls here. You held them against their will."

"Some of them were happy to have someplace to stay and regular meals."

The pathetic excuse soured her stomach.

"You think they were grateful to be locked up and used for sex because you fed them? You think it's okay to help Prosperity plot murder and destruction? You guys deserve the punishment that's coming."

She turned and started walking away with Declan.

"Skye, please, tell them I'm not like Gabriel."

She turned back, her hand still linked with Declan's, the only good man she knew these days. "You're not a murderer like him, but you are a coward. You could have helped those girls, but you didn't. You knew he killed Lucy, not me, but you didn't speak up about that either. You went along. You hid from your responsibility as a human being to help those in need. I hope when you get out of jail you're a better man than you are right now."

Agent Gunn joined them. "You didn't cut him any slack."

"He doesn't deserve it."

"Are you always this hard on the men in your life?" Agent Gunn teased, but she took it seriously.

"No. I respect and love Declan for being such a good man." Declan went still beside her but she went on without looking at him. "He's kind, hard-working, fiercely loyal to his friends and family, loves with his whole heart, and treated a perfect stranger like she was family. He treated me like I was good enough to welcome into his home, buy me what I needed, feed me, and give me a job all on my word that I'd work hard to pay him back."

"Skye, sweetheart, you don't owe me anything."

"Generous, compassionate, protective. He takes care of people, especially the ones he loves. I don't know a better man. I know the ones you rounded up here today don't come close to Declan. So what I said to Joseph is true. I hope he comes out of this even half the man Declan is. Maybe then he can do some good in this world and redeem himself."

Skye went up on tiptoe and kissed Declan. "That guy from the ATF on the tractor is making a bigger mess than he is uncovering the fertilizer and bomb stuff I hid. I'm going to take over and do it right." She fell back on her feet. "Please don't go anywhere."

"I'll be right here, sweetheart."

"I hope so." She wanted him to be right here, next to her, every day, all the time.

Declan watched her walk up to the guy on the tractor, say something, point to the pile he'd attacked, and the disarray of where he'd moved it, then waved him off the tractor.

"She's in love with you."

Declan didn't even bother looking at Agent Gunn to confirm the smile in those words. "I heard her."

"What are you going to do about it?"

"I don't know." That was the honest truth.

"Yeah, I guess it's complicated with you in Montana and her living here."

"Loving her is easy. Being with her, well, that's a whole other thing."

Chapter Thirty-Two

SKYE FINALLY made it to the hospital to see her father after she helped uncover and hand over everything she hid on the property at Sunrise, including the money she'd stashed in the shed out by the apple orchard. With her name cleared, everything in the FBI's hands, and all the men involved arrested, she could finally focus on her family.

Despite not having gone to sleep, like her, Declan insisted on driving her to the hospital. He held her hand as they approached her father's room. They hadn't done much talking in the truck. They both needed space and time to let everything that happened overnight and this morning sink in and settle.

"Hey, sweetheart, I'll let you go in alone and be with your family. I think I'll get a cup of coffee and sit in the waiting room."

"Call your family. They must be worried sick about you."

He'd charged his phone in the truck they borrowed from Sunrise to drive here. She'd seen the seven missed calls and twenty-something text message alerts he hadn't yet read.

"I will. But first . . ." He pulled her in for a soft kiss,

then brushed his fingers through her tangled hair. "I needed that."

"I need you," she confessed, like he didn't already know, but maybe he needed to hear it all the same.

"I'm hoping you've got someplace we can crash after you see your father."

She pressed her hand to his rough jaw, his beard stubble scratchy against her palm. "Yes, I do. I won't be long."

"Take your time. There's no rush. I'm sure they've been just as worried about you as you were about them."

Well, she had been kidnapped by a militia group and held hostage and nearly killed.

She worried about what Declan's family would say now about the stray he took in, who turned his life upside down. "Is your family going to hate me for getting you mixed up in all of this?"

"What? No. They're probably just as worried about you as they are about me."

She fisted her hands in his shirt at his sides and shook him a little. "I don't know how I would have gotten through this without you." She pressed her face into his neck, inhaled his earthy, sweaty, uniquely Declan scent. They both needed a shower and twelve hours of sleep, but right now she needed him to know that he'd made a difference in her life.

He'd risked his life to save hers and she was so damn grateful and in love with him that it was all too much to hold inside after the night they'd had. Tears cascaded down her cheeks, but she didn't lose it. Not yet. Later. She still had to see her dad, but with Declan, she could pop the lid on her emotions and let a little of them spill out.

Declan hugged her close. His strong arms banded around her, keeping her safe. Even with all the danger gone, she still needed to feel like nothing could get her, because Declan wouldn't let it. "Lord knows you've got every reason to cry, sweetheart, but it just kills me."

"I'm sorry. I don't know where this is coming from all of a sudden."

He kissed her on the temple. "It's okay. Just let it go. I'm right here."

She wanted to, but Declan had endured enough today. He didn't need her falling apart in his arms, though she knew he'd pick up the pieces if she did and find a way to make her feel better. The thing was, him just being here, holding her, it made all the difference in the world.

She sucked in a breath, held him in one long tight squeeze with her hands locked at his back, then sucked it up and let him go.

He immediately reached up and brushed the tears from her cheeks with his thumbs. "All better?"

"You make everything better."

"I feel the same way about you, sweetheart." He kissed her forehead and held it for a second before he stepped back. "Your family is waiting for you."

"So is yours. Call them." She nudged him toward the waiting area and took the few steps to enter her father's room. She stopped in the doorway and stared at her dad lying in the bed, IV lines in his arm, a white bandage covering his chest.

Her mother sat in the chair beside her father, her hand over his on the bed. Meadow sat in the corner of the room with her head resting on a pillow against the wall, her knees bent as she slept. They probably hadn't gotten much sleep last night waiting for her father to come out of surgery.

She should have been here.

But what she'd done was to help them, too.

She went to the side of the bed and touched her father's arm, careful to avoid the IV lines.

His eyes opened and went wide when he saw her. Then relief sent them closed again before he looked at her, the relief replaced with joy. "You're okay."

"Yes, Dad. I'm fine."

"What happened . . . after . . . they . . . took you?" His voice was weak, the words making him wince in pain, probably from breathing and moving his chest.

She kept her voice soft and tried to avoid waking her mother and sister. She didn't want to go into all the disturbing details, but told him what he really needed to know. "The guy from Prosperity and Gabriel tried to kill me. Declan saved me."

"Your new boyfriend?"

Is that what he was? "Yes."

Declan seemed like so much more than just a boyfriend. What they shared . . . she didn't know how to describe it.

Her mother came awake all at once. Tears cascaded down her cheeks. "You're awake." She rose and hugged him the best she could without causing pain or moving any of the monitors or lines connected to him. "I love you so much."

Her father patted her mother's shoulder, leaned his head to hers, closed his eyes, and just took in her mom's love. His relief was so deep that Skye saw it written all over his face and in the way his body relaxed even more into the bed.

She felt that way when Declan held her. Everything else washed away and nothing mattered but being with him.

Her mom sat back and stared at her dad, looking him over. "You look much better."

"I'm fine," he assured her, taking her hand.

Her mother turned to her. "When did you get here?"

"A few minutes ago."

"And?"

She didn't know what her mom expected her to say. "Gabriel is dead. Six other Sunrise men have been arrested, along with many of the men from Prosperity. The FBI took everything I hid at Sunrise as evidence. I may have to testify in the case, but more than likely they'll all plead out their cases and . . . we'll see what happens next, but it's pretty much over."

"Did you get Gabriel for killing Lucy?" Hope filled her mom's eyes.

"Yes. A federal agent heard him confess. The girls they brought to Sunrise have all been seen by doctors. Some will be going home to family. A few others have asked to stay at Sunrise for a real second chance, just like Gabriel promised and I'll deliver with the help of everyone at Sunrise."

Her mother relaxed. "That's good. Wonderful job, Skye. I'm so, so proud of you."

Stunned by her mom's unexpected praise, she wrapped her hands around the bar on the side of the bed to hold herself up. Her mother hadn't paid her a compliment in longer than she could remember. She'd certainly never said she was proud of Skye. "You are?" She couldn't help asking, because their last conversation had sounded like a whole lot of accusations that this was her fault.

"Of course we're proud of you. You stood up for what is right. You helped those girls and made those awful men pay for their misdeeds. Lucy's parents came by last night to sit with us while we waited for your father to come out of surgery. They are so grateful to you for getting justice for their daughter."

She didn't know what to say.

"They want to thank you when you return to Sunrise."

She knew she had to go back, but hearing her mother say that she'd return, like that was the only place she belonged, didn't sit quite right because she felt like she fit somewhere else, too.

With someone else.

Chapter Thirty-Three

DECLAN BLEW on the vending machine coffee, then took a sip. The caffeine fix wouldn't revive him for long. He needed to shut down his weary mind and body. Maybe then he could think clearly.

He thought about what happened next and didn't like the direction his thoughts took.

He knew what he needed to do, but he didn't like it or necessarily want to follow through with his plans. He wanted to talk to Skye and see what she wanted to do. But in his heart he already knew.

He didn't want to be without her, but he didn't see how they could be together. At least for a little while. After all Skye had been through, he wouldn't add to her burden by asking for more than she could give right now.

But it killed him to even think of going home without her.

He'd miss her terribly.

But he wasn't giving up on her, them, and what he wanted with her.

Time would tell how this all played out, but right now, he had to give her the space she needed to be with her family, her community at Sunrise, and time to figure out what she wanted to do next.

He called the rental car company first, ignored the knot in his stomach, and tried not to think about how hard it would be to leave her.

With his plans set, he called Drake. He needed to hear his brother's voice, tell him what happened and that he was okay, but also ask how Drake lived with the bad shit he'd done even if it had been for the right reasons.

"You okay?" Drake's deep voice held an edge of urgency.

"I'm good. All in one piece."

"I heard you put your sharpshooting skills to use."

"I learned from the best." But he hated that it had come to life and death and bullets.

Drake had always loved target practice. All three of them loved to try to one-up the other. In this case, Declan didn't mind that Drake was still a better shot and had a hell of a lot more experience shooting at people in his military career.

"It came in handy." Drake tried to make it seem normal. "You saved Skye." That's the only reason he'd resorted to using a gun to solve a problem. "That's all that matters, bro. How is she?"

Declan appreciated that Drake cared. "I'm not sure. We're both exhausted and . . . I don't know. It's been a long fucking night. Neither of us has slept. We're at the hospital right now."

"Are you hurt? Is she?"

"No." *Thank God.* "Her father was shot last night when some guys came to the motel and kidnapped me and her." He rubbed the heel of his hand into his scratchy eye, then raked his fingers through his mussed hair.

"Kidnapped. Jeez. You can tell me later how you got out of that. Is her dad going to make it?"

"Yeah. He's good. Out of surgery and on the mend. Skye . . . man, she just keeps going, taking on one thing after the next."

"The crash is coming. A person can only take so much." Drake knew from experience.

"I know. She's had a couple bad moments, but she powers through."

"What about you?"

Declan needed a second to get his racing heart under control and figure out how to breathe through the assault of memories and images racing through his mind.

"Declan, take a deep breath. Relax. You're alive. Skye is safe. However that happened, you'll get through it."

He needed Drake's assurance on that, because his brother had been through some shit and nearly didn't make it out alive. But he fought his way back.

Declan could do the same.

"After they kidnapped us, we ended up at this place, a bar, their hideout. Kinda. One of the guys was an undercover agent. We needed to save Skye before the leader of Prosperity killed her for stealing his shit. It was . . . intense. There was a shootout." He saw the two men drop to the ground when he'd had no choice but to shoot or be killed.

"In moments like that, you do what you have to do to survive. You don't think, you act. It's you or them." Drake sucked in a breath. "I'm glad it was you who survived. You have no idea . . . I can't wait to see you, bro."

"I plan on driving home tomorrow after I get some sleep and say goodbye to Skye."

"Goodbye?" Surprise filled Drake's voice. "Why?"

Declan pressed the heel of his hand to his forehead and the throbbing headache that made his eyes blur.

Maybe that was the exhaustion. Or the flash bangs and all the gunfire. "She's needed at home for a while." At least, he hoped it would only be a short time before he saw her again. "During the shootout, Gabriel managed to take Skye. Flash bangs and bullets flying . . . I lost her in all the chaos."

"Not your fault," Drake was quick to assure him.

"Yeah, well, he was about to shoot her in the chest when I took him out."

"Good. She'll feel better knowing that guy is never coming after her again." Drake stalled a beat, then added, "In time, you'll put everything that happened into perspective. It won't be so fresh and up front in your mind."

"It took you a long time to do that."

"I had stored up a lot of shit to unpack. I didn't let anyone in or talk about what happened. You've got me."

Yeah, and Drake had Adria, who'd been instrumental in getting Drake to claw his way out of the deep, dark pit he'd been in to a better life.

"I'm good," he assured Drake and himself. "I just need . . . time."

"Look, man, I can be there in a few hours. I'll drive you home."

Declan was already shaking his head. "Thanks, but I need tonight with Skye and the drive home tomorrow to just have some quiet time alone to let it all sink in before I get there." Because he belonged on the ranch and with his family. That was his life.

He didn't have a job where he could move locations. The ranch meant something to him. It had come to him from his father and he hoped to one day pass it down to the next generation of McGraths.

And he didn't expect Skye to uproot her life just to be

with him. He hoped they could work it out, but he'd never ask her to leave Sunrise if that's where she needed and wanted to be.

"Does Skye plan on coming back?"

"I don't know. Now isn't the time to make those kinds of decisions or even ask."

Drake sighed. "Declan, all you can do is tell her how you feel."

"She knows how I feel. I know how she feels."

But sometimes love wasn't enough.

"We'll see how it plays out." Declan took a big gulp of his rapidly cooling coffee. "Listen, let Tate know I'll be home sometime tomorrow afternoon or evening."

"If you need to stay longer with Skye . . ."

"She's got her work and I've got mine. It's best to do it this way." He didn't want to drag things out. He wanted her to reconnect with her family and sort out the issues and business at Sunrise without worrying about him or thinking she needed to divide her time between him and them.

He wouldn't ask her to choose. He didn't want her to think she had to for them to still have a relationship. He'd take whatever he could get, even if he feared the long distance thing would eventually doom them.

He'd try his hardest to keep that from happening, but . . .

"Get some rest. Things will look better when you've got a clear head."

Declan appreciated Drake's optimism. But looking at the real possibility he'd lose Skye only made him dread leaving her tomorrow without them really knowing how they'd handle the separation or how work and the people who needed them would make it harder to focus on each other.

"I'll see you tomorrow."

"If you need something before then, or change your mind about me coming to get you, just call. Whatever you need, man, we're here for you."

The only thing he really needed was time alone with Skye.

Declan said goodbye to his brother, bought Skye a coffee with milk the way she liked it, then headed to her father's room to check on everyone.

He stepped into the doorway just as Meadow busted up laughing. "Gabriel always hated the chickens. I can't believe you made him go in there. He must have been so pissed."

"Mad enough to kill her," Declan said from the doorway, finding none of what happened funny at all. But he got that her sister and family needed to stick to the lighter side of things at this point so they could try to put everything behind them.

Mr. Kennedy glanced over at him. "But you put him down before he could hurt my girl."

Declan wanted to say she was *his* girl, but held his tongue. He also bet Skye had a few bumps and bruises and aches and pains after the ordeal she'd been through.

Hell, his ears were still ringing after those flash bangs.

"I made sure she got out of there alive."

Unable to help himself or stay away from her, he closed the distance to the chair she leaned back in and brushed his hand down her hair. "You've got to be as tired as I am."

She nodded and leaned into his hand. "I thought we'd head back to Sunrise and get some sleep."

"Sounds good." He handed her the coffee. "Drink that so you can at least walk to the truck."

Mrs. Kennedy rose from her seat across the bed and came around to him. She wrapped him in a hug he never expected. "Thank you for taking care of Skye."

He gave Mrs. Kennedy's shoulders a pat. "I'd never let anything happen to her."

Mrs. Kennedy stepped back and held him by the arms. "I hear it in the way she talks about you. You're very important to her."

"She's very special to me." He didn't know what else to say but the truth. He'd never met anyone like Skye.

Skye stood and stretched, only half a cup of coffee left. "Do you and Meadow want to come with us back to Sunrise, so you can shower, change, maybe take a nap?"

"You two go on." Mrs. Kennedy waved her hand to shoo them out. "Sue and Beth will be here soon with lunch. We'll come back this evening once your father is settled for the night."

Skye went to her father, leaned over, and kissed his cheek. "Get some rest. I'll see you soon."

"Same goes to you."

"If you need anything, have Mom call me."

"She's all I need," he said.

Declan understood the man's sentiment and the look he gave his wife. Declan felt very much like that about Skye, who came to him and immediately took his hand.

"You two make a cute couple." Meadow beamed them a smile.

Skye bumped her shoulder against his. "I think she has a crush on you."

"What's not to like? He's hot and saved your life. More than once."

Skye shook her head at Meadow.

"I still want to hear about the helicopter ride," Meadow called as they headed out of the room.

In the hall, Skye looked sideways at him. "It's so easy for her to think we had some grand adventure now."

"She lived through the shootout at the motel and your father is going to be fine. You came back looking exactly how you left her, so for her, for a lot of people, it will seem like we survived a real-life action movie."

Her eyes narrowed. "I'm not exactly sure what you mean by that."

Of course she didn't. Most of the movies she saw were family-oriented films.

"I may look the same on the outside—aside from the fact I need a hot shower and clean clothes—but I don't feel that way on the inside. So much has changed for me. It's like . . . I don't know. I don't want to waste this next part of my life now that I survived coming so close to death."

He released her hand and hooked his arm around her shoulders, drawing her into his side. "I know exactly what you mean."

They stepped into the elevator. She went into his arms and held tight the second the elevator doors closed, leaving them alone in the small, quiet box. He savored every second of holding her close. He'd take the next few hours to remind her of all they had shared together, all they could have for their future, and hope it was enough of a foundation to build on despite what came next for both of them.

Chapter Thirty-Four

Skye waved to everyone they passed as Declan drove toward her cabin on the property. Many of them should be out doing their chores and tending to the fields, but she couldn't blame them for milling around and conversing with each other about all that happened.

She wondered if Agent Gunn and all the FBI agents who converged on Sunrise had taken all the evidence she'd literally buried and left the people here to get back to their lives without the drama and interruptions.

"Hey, where am I going?"

She pointed to the last cabin with the pot of purple veronica blooming by the front door.

"You live in that dinky little thing?"

She smiled. "It's all mine."

No doubt he'd find the accommodations sparse. But she had what she needed.

Declan parked the truck and stared at her front door. "Please tell me you have a bed bigger than a twin."

She wanted to tease, but the man looked ready to drop. "I have a queen-size bed. Your big feet might hang off but there's room for both of us."

He leaned over and kissed her. "Thank you, God." He

grabbed the sack of sandwiches they picked up at a shop in town.

She didn't know what she wanted to do first. Fall face-first into bed, take a shower, or eat. Her body needed the sustenance, but it also wanted to keel over.

Declan slipped out the door and held his hand out, waiting for her to slide over and join him. She did and fell to her feet on the ground with a thud.

"Come on. You're as tired as I am."

"It comes and goes at this point. I think the caffeine helped, but I used it all up."

They walked to her door. She opened it without a key, because why would anyone break into her place? She didn't have anything worth taking. If they needed clothes or the few dishes and utensils she owned that bad, they could have them.

"I knew you'd be a neat freak." Declan took in the perfectly made bed with the purple quilt her mother and some of the other ladies made her when she moved into her own place. She loved the floral pattern stitched into the soft fabric.

The cabin didn't boast much space. She had a small sink and counter and a mini-fridge. They all ate at the hall together, and she only kept snacks and fruit here. The only other door in the place led to her bathroom with the stall shower, pedestal sink, and toilet.

Declan set the sack of food on the table in her kitchen area and turned to her. "Do you want to eat first?"

"I think I want to get out of these grimy clothes and take a shower."

"Let me help." He took the hem of her shirt and pulled it up and over her head. He tossed it on a chair, then hooked his fingers in her waistband and undid her jeans. His gaze never left hers. "I've had a couple moments over the last two days where I thought I'd never get to be with you like this again."

"All that is over, but we're not." She hoped he agreed with that, because he'd been oddly quiet and introspective since they took down Gabriel.

He undid her bra at her back, slid it down her arms, and stared at her breasts. "I don't think I'll ever get my fill of you."

"Yeah?" She slipped her hands under his T and up his chest, taking the shirt up with them. She pulled it the rest of the way over his head. "You are a sight to behold." She ran her hands over his chest and rippling muscles, noting a bruise here and there marring his gorgeous golden skin.

She reached down and dragged off her boots and socks, hopping from one foot to the other as he did the same.

"Is your shower going to be big enough for the two of us?"

"Only if you stand real close to me."

"Count on it." He hooked his hand at her side and drew her into his chest for a deep, searing kiss that nearly buckled her knees, but Declan was there to hold her up. Her breasts pressed to his bare chest and she moaned at the sheer pleasure of being skin to skin with him again.

She undid his jeans as he pushed hers down her hips.

They both kicked the last of their clothes away. They took each other in like they had to reassure themselves they were still here, still in desperate need of each other.

He held his hand out to her. She took it and fell into him. He walked her backward toward the bathroom, his mouth fused to hers, his tongue sliding into her mouth, mating like their bodies desperately wanted to do.

Declan stopped all of a sudden. "Shit. Condom. Turn the shower on. I'll be right back." He dashed out of the bathroom.

She turned on the taps, stepped into the small stall, and let the warm water heat and pound her sore muscles. She tipped her head back and let it rain down her head and hair. Declan stepped in and took her peaked nipple into his mouth at the same time his arms went around her back.

From there, it was all hands and mouths and a desperate need to reaffirm they were still alive and together.

Declan slid his hand down between then, found her soft folds and sank one finger deep. She bit his shoulder and slid her tongue over the small hurt.

"Damn, I want you so bad," he growled at her neck, then thrust two fingers inside her.

She groaned and pressed her hips into his hand. "I want *you* inside me."

He removed his fingers and the loss nearly made her beg him to do it again, but then he hoisted her up his body, kissed her hard and deep as she wrapped her legs around his waist, and he thrust into her, pinning her back to the wall.

He stopped and just stayed there, his body joined with hers, his face pressed to her wet hair. "We belong together," he whispered in her ear.

She believed that all the way to her soul and hugged him tighter.

And then he moved, pulling out and pushing into her in long deep strokes. He took his time, drawing out every sweep of his body in and against hers. She didn't know how he found the strength to hold her up and make love to her slow and sweet, with an intensity that pulsed between them and amplified every kiss and touch and stroke of their bodies moving together in perfect harmony.

She melted into him until he quickened the pace and thrust harder, deeper. Her body tightened around his and she convulsed around his hard cock until he bucked against her one more time and spilled his seed with a satisfying moan.

They stayed locked together for a long moment.

Declan had his hands on her ass and lifted her off him, then held her until she had her feet under her. "You good?"

"Fantastic."

He smiled down at her. "Hang on, I'm not done taking care of you."

She cocked an eyebrow and watched him discard the condom in the wastebasket outside the shower door, then turn them so she was under the hot spray. He ran his hand through her hair, getting it nice and wet, then poured shampoo into his hand and rubbed it over her scalp, massaging the soap into her hair as he gathered it on top of her head.

She gave herself over to his amazing hands and the sweet gesture as he washed her from head to toe with long sweeps of his soapy hands gliding over her body. She'd never felt so pampered and cared for in all her life.

When he finished with her and was satisfied she'd been rinsed clean, he took his turn under the spray, and she let her hands glide over every muscle, giving back some of what he'd given her while he scrubbed his golden hair because she couldn't reach without him bending down. She didn't mind having complete access to his whole body. She stroked her fingers over his arms, shoulders, chest, and ripped belly, down his legs, and up his back after she turned him around to do that side. Just to tempt him and prolong the buzz of awareness and connection they shared, she slipped her hands around his waist, took his flaccid penis in her hands, and stroked him while she kissed her way across his back and down his spine.

His hands found hers and pulled them away as he grew thick and long in her palms. He slipped free of her grasp and turned to her, cupping her face and leaning down for another sultry kiss. "You drive a man to madness, you know that?"

"I just want to feel this way for a while longer."

"I know just what you mean." He turned off the cooling water and pulled her out of the stall. He took the towel from the bar and dried her off, then put the towel over her head and wrung out the water from her hair.

He barely ran the towel over himself before he took her by the hand and led her out to the quiet cabin room and to her bed. He pulled the comforter back and drew her down to lie with him on the cool sheets.

Goose bumps broke out on her skin. He started at her shoulder and kissed them away, trailing kisses to her chest, and taking her nipple in his mouth and sucking it hard and deep. She arched into him, holding his head to her with her fingers sliding through his damp hair.

"Every time I touch you, I want more." He kissed his way to her other breast and licked her aching nipple, then dragged his tongue down her belly, over her mound, along her soft folds and seam until he buried it inside her as he pushed her thighs wide. "You taste so damn good. I could do this for hours." His head dipped and his tongue licked all the way up to her clit. He circled it, then sucked it gently into his mouth. She shattered from the sheer ecstasy of it. He kissed her thigh, then looked up at her. "You like that as much as I do. But you're going to have to build up your stamina."

She used her legs to knock him onto his back beside her. She lay on her side, slid her hand down his tight abs, and wrapped her fingers around his thick dick.

He hissed and thrust his hard length against her palm. "*You* like that."

"I like being inside you more."

She liked that, too, but she'd never had the freedom to touch a man the way Declan allowed her access to him. So she worked her hand up and down his length, thought about how he'd used his mouth on her, and figured she could return the favor. She rolled to her knees beside him, planted her hands on both sides of his hips, and, not really knowing what she was doing, took him right into her mouth with a slide of her tongue down the length of him. His hand landed on her ass, one finger sliding into her wet core. Her body instantly bucked back into his hand as she slid his length out of her mouth and then back down. As she moved, he squeezed her ass and sank his finger deep.

"I'm not going to last if you keep doing that thing with your tongue."

She sucked her way back up to his tip and circled it, then let her tongue go soft and flat and used it to cup the head as she swept it side to side.

"Fuck me," Declan groaned out.

She was doing her best to drive him as crazy as he made her for him.

He gave her a soft smack on the bottom. "Come here."

She released his pulsing cock and turned to him. The second she let him go, he dragged her over his body and sank his tongue into her mouth, stroking and licking as the kiss spun out.

Declan broke the kiss, his eyes barely opened and filled

with heat and need. He grabbed another condom he'd left lying on the bed, tore it open, and handed it to her.

She straddled his legs and rolled the condom down his length.

"I love it when you touch me." He leaned up, grabbed her under the arms, and pulled her forward for another searing kiss. She eased back, felt the round head at her entrance, and sank down on him. She'd never done this either, but found the rhythm she liked and just the right amount of friction as she circled her hips against his.

She rode him, watching as his eyes closed and his hands clamped onto her hips, urging her on but never taking over. He let her have her way with him. And something inside her connected to him on such a deep level, they not only moved together but she felt him breathe and the beat of his heart echo inside her. She lost herself in making love to him until her body needed the sweet release she felt building inside him.

She rose up and sank down hard again and again, trying to find that sweet spot. He moved his hand and swept his finger over her clit, and a wave of pleasure rushed through her. Declan grabbed her hips, drew her down hard on his shaft, and pulsed inside her, setting off another round of aftershocks through her body until she collapsed on top of him, completely spent and lost in the love washing over them.

Declan tugged the blanket up and over them and wrapped his arms around her as sleep crept in.

The last thing she heard in the quiet cabin was Declan's exhaled breath and his whispered, "I love you."

Chapter Thirty-Five

DECLAN STARED at the empty bed and thought about all he and Skye shared last night. After the shower and falling asleep holding her in his arms, he'd woken up and made love to her again before they had a middle-of-the-night dinner in bed. They'd been just as ravenous for each other as the sandwiches. He simply couldn't get enough of her.

He woke her this morning with soft kisses and caresses that had her moaning and reaching for him before she ever opened her eyes. Every tempting touch and kiss led to another until they were desperate for release but reluctant to end what always seemed so perfect when they came together.

Though he knew it was coming, when the knock on the door came and someone from Sunrise drew her out of bed and back into work and the community, he'd wanted to hold her close in that bed and leave the outside world on the other side of the door as long as possible.

Forever if he could.

But that wasn't realistic.

So when she left to check on something on the farm this morning and said, "I'll be right back," he'd known she meant it, but her responsibilities and desire to be with the others would take over. She'd be compelled to ease everyone's minds and get them all back to the routine they needed to get past everything that happened.

Skye needed that, too.

She'd had a restless night's sleep. He did, too, despite their exhaustion.

In time, the nightmares and memories would fade.

Right now, they both needed something to take their minds off all the tragedy and horror they'd seen. He needed to stop thinking about *what* he'd done and focus on why he'd done it.

He'd do anything for Skye.

She made everything in his life better.

She did that for the people of Sunrise.

He imagined they'd be reluctant to let her go.

He sure was. But the rental agency had delivered his car, and he had a long drive ahead of him to get back to the ranch where he belonged. Where he was needed. Where his family was waiting for him to come home and carry on.

Because that's what he'd always done.

Sunrise needed Skye to help them move on.

He glanced around the small cabin, knew he'd imagine her here and sleeping in that bed every second they were apart.

He missed her already.

But he couldn't put off the inevitable.

He headed to the door, wishing for more nights like he and Skye shared last night and at the ranch.

He hoped they had more nights like that soon.

She'd visit. He'd come to see her.

This isn't over.

It wasn't the way they wanted it to be, but they both had their responsibilities and obligations.

He wanted her to be happy. And right now that meant she needed to stay.

He opened the front door and spotted the purple flowers. He picked one, went back into the cabin, and found a pad of paper on her small desk in the corner. He scribbled a note and left it on the bed along with the flower. Something nice for her to come home to tonight and make her think of him. Because he'd be thinking about her.

He left the cabin and walked down the road, checking out the large and small cabins lining this part of the farm. They stood not more than ten feet apart. They made him think of the early settlers' quarters. Simple. Efficient. Families living and working together.

He passed the main hall. He'd skipped breakfast. He'd grab some drive-thru on the way home. Right now, he heard the din of children gathered for their lessons. Three teachers, including Skye's parents, homeschooled the kids from grade school to high school. Education and reading in addition to learning how to tend the farm were just a way of life here.

Without TV, cell phones, and the internet available every single second of the day, the kids grew up working on their studies, doing chores, and playing with each other.

The same, but a little different, than life on the ranch.

He could see why Skye loved it here and why she fought so hard to keep this way of life untainted and in harmony for everyone who lived here.

Several people he didn't know waved to him on his

way to the big house that served as the council meeting place, the office, and the head of the council's quarters.

With Gabriel gone, he wondered who'd take his place. Skye?

Maybe. She'd be a good choice. She had such a beautiful spirit and everyone's best interests at heart. They'd be lucky to have her serve on the council.

He was lucky to have her in his life.

The ache in his chest only got worse the closer he got to her and the goodbye he didn't want to say.

Declan stood at the bottom of the steps as a young man came out of the house.

"Hey, you must be Declan. I heard you were instrumental in saving Skye."

"She did most of the work, taking on Gabriel and the others."

"Yeah, but you shot him." The guy ran his hand along the side of his neck. "I can't believe he's gone." He tilted his head. "Most people are glad he won't be . . . doing the things he was doing. He kept things interesting, that's for sure. Anyway, Skye's inside with the remaining council members."

"Thanks."

"Hey, you sticking around?"

Declan looked at the guy, wondering why he asked, and zeroing in on the way the guy eyed him. He had a thing for Skye. Declan knew about Joseph, the dickhead she liked when she was younger, who got what he wanted and moved on. Skye didn't say anything about dating anyone lately. In fact, she'd made it clear she hadn't dated anyone in a long time. Still, the thought of leaving and this guy moving in on her made his hands fist.

"I'm headed home, but Skye and I will stay in close contact." Declan gave the guy a back off look.

"Oh. Uh, okay then." He raised his hand and pointed his thumb toward the men gathering by one of the barns. "I gotta go. Vegetable picking."

Declan didn't bother to respond and walked up the steps to the door. He entered without knocking, because it seemed this was the community's place and everyone was welcome. He followed the sounds of voices to the left and stood in the open doorway of the large office.

Skye stood behind the large desk, her hands planted on top, as she stared down at a calendar. "We've got three farmers markets scheduled over the next month." She looked up at the four men seated in front of her. "Why isn't Marie here? She oversees the flowers. She'd be the best person to ask about what's coming into bloom and how many bouquets we'll have for each market."

"You always plan all the farmers market trips," one of the men responded.

"I know, it's just that we need to get Marie and the others who supervise the orchards and vegetables involved so that it's not all left up to one person to organize everything." Skye traced her finger over the calendar, then looked up at the men, and past them to him. A brilliant smile lit her face. "Declan. Hey." She looked at the clock on the wall and frowned. "I'm so sorry. I meant to find you quite a while ago."

He appreciated the apology and the I'm-happy-to-see-you look in her eyes. "Can I have a few minutes alone with you?"

The men didn't look pleased to give up their time with her, especially when they were trying to make plans for the upcoming events and coordinating logistics on the farm. He got it, but he needed to talk to Skye before he left to be sure they were on the same page.

The men stood. One came forward. In his sixties, dressed in jeans and a plaid shirt, deep lines spreading out from the corners of his eyes and weathered skin, he looked like the quintessential farmer. He slapped a hand on Declan's shoulder. "No amount of thanks will convey how grateful we are for what you did to stop those men and bring Skye home safe and sound."

The other men nodded and offered their few words of thanks to him as they all filed out the door. He was touched. Their words reinforced just how much everyone here loved and valued Skye.

They'd take care of her in his absence. It eased his mind, but it wouldn't make him miss her less.

She came around the desk, but stopped short of coming to him. Whatever she saw in his face filled her eyes with concern. "I'm sorry I left you alone at the cabin for so long. I thought I could answer a few questions, reassure people, then get back there and—"

He cut her off by simply holding up his hand to stop her. "It's okay, Skye. Everyone is happy to have you home. They want things to get back to normal."

She sighed and took a step closer to him. "It's going to take a little time for everyone to settle down, but they'll get back to their routine and everything will be fine again."

He stuffed his hands in his pockets so he didn't reach for her and not get out what he needed to say. But first, he started with what was most important to her. "How is your dad?"

Her smile said it all. "Better. Getting stronger by the minute. He should be released in a couple days. Mom and Meadow are with him. I hope to see him in a couple hours." She glanced over her shoulder. "I just have a few things to do that can't wait . . . then . . ."

"I won't keep you long."

She tilted her head and studied him. "Declan, is everything okay?"

"This is just harder than I thought it would be." He closed the distance and stood in front of her with his hands on her hips because he needed to touch her.

One more time.

He could do this.

Her hands went to his chest and her gaze met his, full of hope, but also knowing what was about to come. "You're needed at home." Worry lines crinkled her forehead. She fisted his shirt in her hands and held on to him.

He nodded. "The rental agency left a car parked out front for me."

Her lips pressed tight. "I hoped you'd be able to stay a couple of days."

"I wish I could, but I've left Tate shorthanded. As you pointed out, without me there and enough people to cover, things are falling way behind." He gave her a self-deprecating smile. "I need to learn to delegate."

She smiled, but it didn't have the usual brightness. "You're good at everything. I'm sure you can master that." Her gaze fell to his chest.

He drew her closer so their bodies brushed against each other. Such sweet torture. "It's okay, Skye. We're good, sweetheart."

Her watery eyes met his. "Do you mean that?"

"You're needed here, right? I'll be back next weekend. Maybe you can come up and see me the weekend after that?" They'd make this work for now.

Her frown deepened. "I won't be here next weekend.

The farmers market is too far away to drive in the morning, so we usually go the day before and stay overnight. In fact, the ones over the next few weeks, they're all big ones. Lots of planning and packing up and"—she raked her fingers through her long hair, then looked up at him— "this isn't what I thought would happen."

"It's not what I want either. We'll figure it out. Maybe I can come during the week instead of the weekend."

"Aren't you guys getting the herd ready for winter?"

He cupped her face. "What happened to the woman who makes everything seem possible? I want to talk to her about how we are not going to let distance come between us."

"I'm just going to miss you so much. If my father wasn't in the hospital and this place wasn't in such chaos with all that's happened . . ."

He kissed her softly, knowing she wanted to be everything to him and everyone else. She didn't know how to be everywhere and everything to everybody. Neither did he. "I love you. Does that help ease your mind that I'm not leaving and never coming back, that I want you with me every second of the day but understand you have your life, too?"

Her eyes pleaded with him. "I don't want you to go. And I know it's not fair to ask you to stay."

"I feel the same. All I want to do is take you home with me."

She slammed into his chest, wrapped her arms around his neck, and held on tight. "I love you, too. Why does this have to be so complicated?"

"Let's not think of it that way." He brushed his hands down her hair and tugged on the ends, so she'd look up at him. "We can do this. We'll make it happen. As soon as I get home, I'll send you a new phone. We'll talk, text, video chat. No matter what, we'll stay in contact with each other."

"I'm sure I can get my own phone." She scrunched her lips.

"Let me take care of it." He knew what to buy and what she needed. "I'll set it all up, so it'll be easy for you to figure out."

She nodded. "We should come up with a schedule. That way we know the other will be there."

"Whatever you want, sweetheart."

"I just need a little time to get Sunrise back on track. It's all a mess right now, but given a couple weeks, I can fix everything."

He loved her optimism, but saw the uncertainty in her eyes. "I know you can."

"I'll come to Montana. We'll be together, if that's what you want."

"Never doubt how much I love you and want to be with you."

She hugged him tighter. "I'm afraid if I let you go I'll never see you again."

After everything they'd been through the last few days, he got that. "You can't get rid of me, sweetheart."

She had his heart. She stood front and center in all the hopes and dreams he had for the future. Everything he wanted for the rest of his life included her.

She whispered his greatest wish. "I want to keep you."

"I'm yours, sweetheart. Never doubt that." He leaned back, cupped her face, and kissed her. It started soft and sweet, a reminder of how easy and wonderful their connection was, but then it deepened and the want and need they felt for each other took over. If she didn't feel how much he wanted to stay, he didn't know what else to say or do.

It took everything he had to kiss her one last time and make himself release her. "This isn't goodbye. I'll see you soon."

Her hands held his wrists until he backed away and she had to let him go. Tears welled in her eyes and slipped down her cheeks. He hated to see her cry, but he didn't know how to do this without it hurting both of them.

"Declan," she called just as he stepped out of the office.

He turned back and stared at her beautiful face. "Yeah, sweetheart?"

"Thank you. For saving my life. For showing me the best of what life can be."

"Being with you is the best thing that ever happened to me."

"Me too." More tears poured from her eyes, though she tried to hold it together.

Somehow, this felt more like the goodbye he didn't want, so he made sure she knew he was coming back. "I'll see you next Wednesday." He didn't know what the hell was happening at the ranch or with his brothers right now, but he'd make it happen.

They wanted him to be happy. That meant they'd have to cover for him so he could carve out time to be with Skye.

He rushed back to her, kissed her one last time on the lips, then on her forehead. "Don't work too hard, sweetheart. Tell your family I wish I'd met them under better circumstances, but I'm looking forward to seeing them again."

"Really?" More than anything else he'd said, that made her eyes light with hope and expectation.

Family mattered to both of them. That's what made this so hard.

He kissed her again, because he couldn't help himself, even if he was dragging this out.

She fisted her hand in his shirt and pulled him in for one more kiss. "I wouldn't have gotten through any of this without you."

"You don't have to get through anything from now on without me. This is the way things are right now, but it doesn't have to be this way forever."

"It won't be. I'll finish what I need to do here, and then we'll figure out us."

"Nothing to figure out. Just come as soon as you can."

"I will. I promise."

"Until then, we'll visit each other. It'll be like dating." Though they were more connected than that, even if they still had a lot to learn about each other.

He took her hand from his shirt, pressed her palm to his face because he loved the feel of her against him, gave her the best smile he could muster, then let her go and walked out, leaving a huge piece of himself with her.

He waved to those who waved to him on his way to the rental car. Everyone at Sunrise really was friendly, but right now he needed to get on the road before he couldn't leave Skye at all.

He stopped after two hours to get some food and stretch his legs. By the time he made it back to the ranch after stopping in town to check on his sisters and their shop and buying a few surprises he immediately dropped in the mail for Skye, it was late afternoon.

Road-weary, missing Skye more than ever, and tired of fighting his need to turn the car around and go back to her, he climbed out of the rental car he'd need to return tomorrow and stood in the yard.

He looked around the huge spread and stared off into the distance at the orchard Skye had spent so much time tending.

The place didn't feel the same anymore. Nothing did, because he didn't feel the same.

He missed her.

While his mind should be on work and finding Tate, he just didn't have it in him to jump back into the thick of things here at the ranch.

Besides, he was still wearing the same clothes he'd been in since they left in a helicopter.

He gave one last wistful glance at the orchard in the distance and headed up to the house. He smelled her the second he walked in the door. He missed the smell of something good cooking in the kitchen. He missed hearing her cleaning this and fussing over that. He headed up the stairs, passing the photos of his family from years gone by, and reminded himself this was home. This is where he belonged.

He stopped by her room and stared at her brush on the dresser along with a discarded hair tie. He preferred her hair down. If she were here right now, he'd run his fingers through the long, silky strands. His fingertips itched to feel it slide against his skin.

He wondered if he should pack up her stuff and take it to her next Wednesday.

Nah. She could use it when she visited here.

He left the spare room, headed to his, stripped off his shirt, and tossed it in the laundry basket, thinking of that first night she'd been here and done what he asked and made herself useful. She'd washed his clothes and left them piled on his bed.

He stared at the bed and remembered making love to her and how he'd be sleeping without her tonight and too many nights to come until they were together again.

The house, his bed, it all felt empty.

He'd been alone a while now, but he'd never felt this lonely.

He headed for the shower, thinking of how he'd made love to Skye last night at her place. His dick swelled with the images swirling though his head, but he made a bee-line for the phone on his bedside table when it rang.

"Hello."

"Hey. It's so good to hear your voice."

He sighed and sank onto the side of the bed, relieved Skye had called him even though he'd just left her a few hours ago.

"How was the drive home?"

"Not bad, except it took me away from you."

"I miss you, too."

"How's your dad?"

"Really good. The doctors said he's healing well. Mom is fussing over him like crazy, and he's loving it. Meadow is back at Sunrise with me. I only have a few minutes before I need to head up to the hall. I'm giving an update to everyone before dinner to try to put them all at ease. There's a lot of wild rumors running rampant, so I want to tell everyone what really happened and let them ask questions."

He worried recounting the events would only remind her of the trauma. "Are you sure you're up to it after everything you've been through? It's got to be so fresh still." And maybe he should have stayed longer to be sure she was okay.

"Talking about it with everyone, letting them know exactly what happened and why I did what I did, will help. I think. Plus, they're all talking about the gorgeous cowboy who stayed with me last night and saved my life."

The humor and pride in her voice made him smile. "All I can think about is you."

"Regret leaving me already?" She teased and flirted, but she needed the reassurance.

"It started even before I left you."

"It hit me, too, after everything calmed down and I was standing with you and watching the FBI do their thing. I knew you'd have to go home, but I wanted you to stay."

"I wish I could, but after I grab a quick shower, I'm headed to check in with Tate and see where we're at here." They shared the fact that on a farm or ranch, there was always work to be done.

Her soft sigh resonated through him. "Yeah. I need to hurry to my meeting, too. Everyone here wants to know we're back to business as usual." She went quiet for a moment. "Declan?"

"Yeah, sweetheart?"

"You'll really be here next week?" Hope filled those words and a desperation he felt, too.

"Count on it."

"I don't know if I can wait that long to see you." The shyness in that confession made him grin.

"Me either. You should get a present tomorrow."

"The phone?" Hope filled her voice.

"And something else, so that you know I'm always thinking about you and want you with me."

"I can't wait to get it." The smallest things made her happy.

He liked making her happy. A lot.

Meadow called out to Skye in the background.

Skye sighed. "I'm sorry. I have to go."

"I'll talk to you tomorrow when you get your phone. Have a good night, sweetheart."

"You too. I'll call you as soon as I get the phone. Promise. Bye."

And just like that, she was gone again and he was back to missing her, but he smiled because she'd called to make sure he made it home.

They could do this long-distance thing. No problem.

Except the lonely shower, filled with memories of her wet and sliding against him, and his empty bed after he finally caught up with Tate and spent several hours working so he could sleep, only made missing her worse.

Wednesday couldn't come soon enough.

He didn't want to think of how many days or weeks it would take her to put Sunrise to rights and come to him. More days than he wanted to endure without her in his arms.

He fell asleep with one thought ringing in his head.

I can't live without her.

Chapter Thirty-Six

SKYE HAD gotten quite adept at using her cell phone with all the bells and whistles. She couldn't believe Declan bought the phone for her the second he got home and sent it overnight to her. Over the last six weeks, they'd called and texted constantly. But it was never enough.

Declan kept his Wednesday visit with her, but he had to turn around the next day and head home for work.

The week after, he came down sick with the flu, so they didn't see each. He didn't want her to get sick, too.

The following week she was so swamped with fulfilling a huge floral order for a new contract she'd won with a distributor that they hadn't seen each other at all.

She went up the fourth week to see him for two whole days. They went to a movie and had dinner with his family. They all made her feel included. So much so, she'd wanted desperately to extend her stay, but Meadow begged her to come back and help her convince their parents that going to college wasn't the same as turning her back on everything she'd been raised with or the community.

At nineteen, Meadow wanted to spread her wings.

After that trip to Montana, Declan came the last two weeks, but only for one night each. Every time they were together, they crammed in as many conversations as possible and made love like they hadn't seen each other in forever. It seemed that way to both of them. But something was off the last time she'd said goodbye to him.

That had been six days ago and because of both their schedules and obligations, she wouldn't see him again for another *month*. They'd never gone that long without an in-person visit and it worried her. It made her sad.

Especially since she sensed Declan's growing frustration with how little they did see each other.

She held up the phone and took a selfie of her sitting in the chair on her little porch with baby Cara sleeping on her chest. She texted the photo to Declan.

SKYE: The newest Sunrise member

Bess had the baby last week. She stopped by to show Skye and let her know that after everything that had happened, she was moving on and enjoying being a new mother.

SKYE: Her name is Cara. She's the sweetest.
SKYE: I want one

She texted that before she really thought about how that might sound to Declan.

DECLAN: Cute baby
DECLAN: If you were here, we could practice making one of those

She bit her lip, thinking of all the ways she and Declan liked to practice. Her whole body tingled with the memories of his hands and mouth on her.

SKYE: Do you want kids?
DECLAN: YES!
DECLAN: Without you here, guess I'll have to settle for being an uncle soon

She loved Trinity, Adria, and Liz. They were all so nice to her. They really were a close family. Adria's and Liz's babies would grow up together, playing and riding horses on the ranch.

She imagined Declan envisioned his own children doing the same.

She knew he wanted everything his brothers had with their wives. They'd spent a lot of time on their calls and texts sharing their pasts and what they wanted for the future. He wanted a partner at home and on the ranch. She wanted to be that for him. But she also wanted to continue to work and be a part of Sunrise.

SKYE: You would be such a good father
DECLAN: I need a wife first
DECLAN: But my girlfriend is amazing
DECLAN: I just wish I saw her more often

She felt Declan's growing frustration, though he tried to hide it and gloss over it with how much he missed her and trying to connect with her the best they could over the phone and through texts. She loved their video chats, though they often got cut off or froze up because her cell service and his sucked. Calls and texts just worked better.

The door to her cabin opened and Bess walked out. "Thanks for holding her while I used the restroom."

Skye set her phone on her thigh. "No problem. She's perfect."

Bess smiled. "It's not ideal to be my age and a mother, but everyone here has been wonderful. Everyone is so ready to lend a hand and help in any way they can."

"That's what we're here for." Skye patted the baby's back and inhaled her powder scent. She really did want a family of her own.

The man you love is in another state.

She talked to him more by text message than in person.

Something needed to change, or she'd lose him.

She'd told him she'd set Sunrise right, then be with him in Montana.

She'd promised weeks, and it had been months.

How long do you expect him to wait?

Time got away from her. Work overwhelmed her. She hated that she hadn't kept her promise. She'd done what she'd always done and put Sunrise first, even though this time she wanted something for herself more than she wanted anything else.

DECLAN: Vet's here gotta go
SKYE: ♥ u

She waited for a text back from him that didn't come. She didn't blame him. He had things to do. But she wished it wasn't like this. She understood why people felt disconnected despite their devices and the ability to reach out at any time to someone else. It was superficial. She wanted to see Declan's face, hear his voice, know based on those things that he was okay, or if something was upsetting him and he was holding back.

He was. She felt it despite being so far away from him.

"You miss him a lot, don't you?"

"More every day."

Bess stared at her beautiful baby. "You're lucky to have found someone you love who loves you so much he'd risk his life to save yours."

What am I doing here when I really want to be with him?

It was past seven o'clock. If she left now she wouldn't get to him until after midnight and she had to be back to leave with everyone tomorrow at ten a.m., which meant she'd have to leave by five, five thirty in the morning.

She stood and handed the baby back to Bess. "Um, I have to go."

"It's late. You've already put in a long day. Where are you going now?"

"To see Declan."

"Don't you have that thing tomorrow?"

"Yes. But the drive back and forth is worth the few hours I'll get to be with him." And the time alone on the road would allow her to focus on what she wanted for her life and how she planned to live it. It meant some big changes that on the surface seemed scary because she'd only ever known life here at Sunrise.

But she loved being at the McGrath ranch, too.

And it didn't have to be all or nothing or even split evenly. It certainly wasn't right now and she'd like a lot more time with Declan than without him.

She'd slowly been implementing changes to how the Sunrise farm was managed. She'd gone slowly, allowing everyone to settle into the new system a step at a time. She'd accommodated the community while making Declan feel like he wasn't a priority. That had to hurt him.

She needed to speed things up if she ever wanted to be with Declan. Before she lost him. She'd find a way to set Sunrise up for success and have the life she wanted with the man she loved.

She just hoped his patience held out a while longer.

She brushed her hand over Cara's soft hair. "Thanks for bringing her by, but I need to go."

Bess smiled. "He's going to be so happy to see you."

Skye touched her hand to Bess's shoulder. With Adam behind bars for his crimes, Bess would be taking care of Cara on her own. "Take this time to think about what you want for you and Cara and your future. Her father made some terrible mistakes, but that doesn't mean he can't be a good father to Cara."

"He wrote me a letter, telling me he's sorry for what happened. I think he meant it. I think we could be friends."

"That's a great place to start." She hugged Bess and baby Cara all at once and barely waited long enough for Bess to wave goodbye and head home before she ran into the cabin and grabbed her purse, the keys to the truck she'd been using, and a change of clothes. She dashed out the door and climbed into the truck.

The gates were open and she was on her way with nothing but open road and time to think and make plans for what came next. She'd taken on way too much at Sunrise. She couldn't do it all. She didn't want to. But now that the responsibilities had landed in her lap, she'd taken a hard look at the processes and people working at Sunrise over the last few weeks and discovered they could do a lot better. She had a good idea of how, but it meant asking the community to hear her out, consider her ideas, and decide if what they truly wanted was to expand the business and hopefully feel like they were still connected to their community, their mission to serve others, and the farm.

Maybe Gabriel wasn't the only one who felt like the farm had become stagnant and monotonous.

She'd made some small changes over the last two years, not wanting to rock the boat too much, but maybe the storm they'd weathered had shown everyone they could navigate this new landscape with open minds and hearts and find a way to make everyone happy at Sunrise. Or at least make them all feel needed and useful, doing what made them happy.

By the time she pulled into Declan's dark driveway and parked outside the house, she'd exhausted her mind thinking of the monumental tasks ahead to change her life and still feel like she'd done her best by the people of Sunrise.

Yes, she was doing this for Declan, but mostly, she was doing it for herself. Because what she wanted and needed mattered, too.

And if her plans worked out, the McGraths and Sunrise would be working closely together.

She opened the truck door and used the overhead light to find the present Declan had included with her new phone. He'd said he sent it to her to let her know he wanted her with him. She palmed the key to his house hanging on the apple tree key chain. She stepped out of the truck and stared off into the distance at the orchard she'd spent so much of her time here tending. She bet Declan looked at those trees and thought of her.

She headed up to the house, unlocked the door, closed and locked it behind her, then took the stairs two at a time. Even in the dark, she found her way to his room because the pull was always there, tugging her to him.

She dropped her purse on the floor just inside his bedroom door, had her shirt and bra off before she got to the side of the bed, kicked off her shoes, shimmied off her panties and jeans, and lost the socks all in less than a minute flat.

She stared down at Declan lying on his back, one arm over his eyes and forehead, the other hand resting on his bare chest. God, he was a sight for sore eyes.

Before she climbed into bed with him, she took her phone from her jeans, set the alarm, placed it on the bedside table, and grabbed a condom from the drawer. Then she slipped into bed beside the man she loved.

The second her body touched his, he came awake, and stared up into her eyes. "Skye. You're here."

"I only have five hours before I have to drive back, but I plan to spend every second of it in your arms."

He rolled and pinned her beneath his warm, strong body. "I'm so happy to see you. I can't believe you're here."

She ran her hands up and down his back. "I know you're frustrated and impatient."

He kissed her softly. "It's not easy missing you all the time."

"I feel the same way." She locked eyes with him. "I'm going to be really busy the next several weeks, but then, I promise, things will be different." And this time, she'd keep that promise.

Whether he believed her or not, she didn't know. In the dark, it was hard to read the look in his eyes, but she understood all too well the kiss he gave her that tasted of his desperate need for her and the urgency in trying to show her how much he wanted her and hoped it would be enough to make her stay.

She didn't want to make any promises or set a date because her plans were just that. Until she started implementing them and figured out if the people at Sunrise would accept and apply them, she didn't know exactly how long it would take to settle her old life and start a new one with him.

If her plan worked, she'd have everything she wanted and be able to give Declan everything he wanted.

"Are you here with me?" Declan sensed her spinning thoughts.

"Do you want me to be here with you all the time?"

"That's all I think about. You and me. Here." He kissed her, then pressed his forehead to hers. "I know it's not fair to ask you to leave your home and the life you've made there."

"But if you had your way, I'd be here with you," she finished his thought and desire.

"Yes. God, yes." He kissed her hard and deep.

That's all she needed to know.

Now all she had to do was the hard part and make it happen. But oh how good it would be to spend every night with this man.

And for the love of this cowboy, she'd do everything possible to be here with him because she wanted it as much as he wanted her with him.

"I can't believe you drove all this way just to be with me for a few hours."

She kissed him, then smiled. "Worth it."

"I should thank you properly."

"I hoped you would."

"My pleasure."

That pleasure went both ways when they stopped thinking and talking and just enjoyed each other with hot kisses and soft strokes. His hands brought every nerve ending in her body to life.

She swept her hands down Declan's sides and up his back. "I need you."

Declan licked the tip of her breast, his warm breath fanning her nipple, drawing it tighter. "You just got here. I have five hours to convince you to stay."

"I wish I could." He thrust two fingers into her wet core and circled his thumb against that sweet little spot. "Soon," she swore.

He sank down her body, thrust those fingers deep again and licked her clit.

"I will. I promise."

"I want to hear how much you like this." He slipped his fingers free and drove his tongue into her, making her moan and grab a fistful of his hair to hold him to her. He licked and laved and drove her insane with his tongue as his thumb slowly drew circles over her clit until she was panting out his name and moaning for release. But the devilish man kept her right at the precipice until she begged, "Please, Declan." He sank one finger deep in her core and sucked her clit, setting off an explosive climax that sparked fireworks on the backs of her eyelids.

Declan kissed the inside of her thigh. "That's my girl."

The soft smile that spread across her lips only made him grin wider.

He shifted to her side, found the condom she'd tossed on the pillow, and tore it open with his teeth. She lay next to him completely relaxed and in a haze of replete ecstasy.

"You up for something different?"

"You said it, I'm your girl." Right now, she'd give him anything he wanted to make him feel as good as he made her feel.

He placed his big hand on her hip and turned her onto

her side. His big body spooned hers and all his warmth seeped into her in a wave of pleasure that made her sigh and press into him. His hand cupped her knee and his long length pressed against her backside. She wanted him inside her and shifted so his hard cock slid against her damp softness before he pulled back and thrust deep, filling her. She reached behind her, planted her hand on his hip, and held him close.

He kissed her shoulder and whispered in her ear. "I miss you every second of the day." He showed her how much, holding her close as he made love to her, his hand sweeping up and down her leg, up her side to her breast. He plucked her tight nipple, rubbed his palm over it, then cupped her breast, molding it in his hand as he thrust into her.

She lost herself in the rhythm of his body moving with hers, his breath at her ear, the feel of his big body against her, and the closeness they shared. That more than anything was what she missed. When they were together, everything felt right even when they were in dire circumstances. She trusted him and counted on him to be there. With him, she'd never have to face anything alone.

She wanted her day to start and end with him beside her.

She wanted to know every little thing about him.

She wanted a life with him.

She covered his hand at her breast and pushed her rump into his hips as he thrust deep. His breath came in deep groans. Pleasure built. Declan slipped his hand free of hers and slid his fingers down her belly to where they were joined. The pad of his middle finger grazed her clit, circled it as he pumped in and out of her. Her body tightened as the heat built inside her and that sweet friction set off a climactic explosion of pleasure.

Declan's hand gripped her hip and he thrust into her hard and deep once, twice, then spilled himself inside her, setting off another round of aftershocks that made her feel even closer to him.

He slid his arm around her middle and cuddled her close, though they were as close as humanly possible. He buried his face in her hair and sighed. In that soft sound she heard a world of frustration and wanting and wishing things were like this all the time and different all at once.

"Don't give up on us."

"I'm holding on, but it feels like everything else in our lives is pulling us apart." He held her even tighter.

She reached over her shoulder and brushed her fingers through his hair. "It's not going to be easy, but I need a little more time."

"I know you're doing the best you can. So am I. You showing up tonight after I wasn't the best boyfriend in the texts I sent you earlier . . . it floored me that you came all this way for a couple of hours."

"I know you want more than a few hours, or a couple of days."

"I want every day with you." He brushed her hair back and kissed her cheek. "Enough about all this. How are you? Your parents? Meadow? Sunrise?"

"Everything and everyone is fine and getting back to normal. But I don't want to talk about all that. I just want to be here with you." She shifted away from him and rolled over to face him. "I just want to look at you." She traced her fingers along his jaw. "You look tired."

"I spend my days thinking about you and my nights wishing you were here. In between that, I've been working my ass off to fill the time."

"I've been doing the same. My little cabin seems so huge and empty without you there."

"I can still smell you in the house and on the sheets."

"You should get that dog we talked about."

"For the chickens I don't have?"

"About that . . ."

He tapped her nose with his fingertip. "You still owe me a cost analysis."

"It's not worth the investment for you to do it here. You're a cattle rancher. Stick to that. I've got another plan for your sister's shop."

"Oh yeah?" Declan yawned, big and long. "Sorry. It's been a day."

"Just hold me, then, and get some sleep."

He wrapped his arms around her and pulled her partway onto his chest. She snuggled into his side and listened to the steady beat of his heart and his breathing even out and slow until he was asleep. It took her longer to quiet the thoughts in her head.

When her phone alarm went off, it seemed like ten seconds later, though it had been a few hours. She shut it off, hoping Declan slept through it, but the second she tried to get up, he held her tight.

"Don't go."

"I'll be back."

"Promise."

"Yes." And the next time she came back, she hoped to stay for good. She wanted to make this place her home, because nothing felt that way anymore without Declan.

Chapter Thirty-Seven

Declan STARED at his phone, wondering why Skye hadn't returned any of his texts or phone calls since yesterday.

DECLAN: Where are you
DECLAN: What's going on

Tate walked into the office and fell into the chair across the desk from him. "You look like shit."

"Fuck you." Declan wasn't in the mood.

"I take it this shit mood, like all the others, has something to do with Skye."

Declan stopped staring at his phone and trying to will a response from her and gazed across the desk at his brother. "What does that mean?"

"It means you spend more time miserable without her than you do happy when you're with her."

He didn't like that his family thought Skye made him unhappy. The situation did. Not her.

"How would you feel if Liz spent weeks away from you?" After Skye surprised him that night she drove all the way here just to see him for a few hours, they'd both gotten crazy busy. He'd managed to steal two days two weeks ago and go down to Wyoming, only to get more frustrated that she was in the middle of some big reorganization of Sunrise and worked from sunup to way past sundown. He spent those two days spending more time with her parents, helping them and the other Sunrise men build the new chicken barn, than he did with Skye.

He appreciated that they treated him like family and brought him in on their project like he belonged, but all it did was give Skye leave to run off to solve one problem or another and organize one shipment or harvest after the next.

When she was finally with him, they spent all their time in bed. There, everything was great.

But he felt her holding something back.

She worked too hard. He didn't understand the drive and urgency with which she did everything.

When he brought up his concerns, she made assurances and promises that everything was going to be fine. She was working on it. She wanted to be with him.

After that visit, he'd been reluctant to go back. He wanted her to come here, where there were no distractions for her. Where she could focus on him and them. He wanted to see her relaxed and happy, not frazzled and distracted.

Tate snapped his fingers in front of Declan's face. "Hey. I'm talking to you."

Declan shook himself out of his thoughts. "What?"

"I said, it sucks that you two live apart."

"I feel like I don't even know what's going on in her life right now. The first couple months were okay. We talked all the time. We weren't together but it was good to connect during those long conversations. Now, I can barely get in touch with her."

Tate winced. "Do you think she's blowing you off?"

"No." The immediate answer felt right, but then, he

second-guessed himself. "Last I spoke to her, she said the reorganization was going well, but it was taking longer than she thought to get everyone on board and follow the new order of things. She said Meadow was thinking of leaving Sunrise and her parents were really upset about it. She ends everything with how much she wants to be with me." That always reassured him. At least, it used to.

"So why isn't she here?"

"If I fucking knew that, I'd do whatever the hell I had to, to get her here."

"Have you actually asked her to move in?"

It shocked him to realize he'd never actually asked her. She knew that's what he wanted. They both wanted it, but they hadn't made a detailed plan to make it happen.

"Shit."

"Call her. Ask her to move here. There's a lot holding her there. Give her a reason to be here. A forever kind of reason. You love her, right?"

"Yes."

"What are you waiting for? Are you stalling because you're not sure?"

"I'm sure." He had the ring to prove it. He just needed to get on the same page with Skye about how they were going to make this work, because he didn't want to be married to someone who didn't live with him.

Tate leaned forward. "Have you considered moving to Sunrise? You could run that place with her."

He had thought about it. A lot. But he'd be the outsider. Though they were all friendly and appreciated what he'd done to rid them of Prosperity and Gabriel's influence and interference in what they did and stood for, he didn't think they'd appreciate him coming in and, not necessarily taking over, but leading, in a way. Though they had a lot going on with the farm, orchards, chickens, and flower businesses, none of that was his expertise. He ran cattle. That had been his whole life.

"I love the ranch. I don't want to leave it, or my family. My place has always been here. I've known that for a long time." Declan sank back in his chair. "So how am I supposed to ask her to leave her home and family to be with me when I don't know if I could give up my life here for her and we'd both end up happy?"

"If you don't ask, you'll never know what her answer is."

In his heart, he knew she'd say yes and that everything she was working so hard on somehow led to them being together even if he couldn't see it through her absence and lack of communication lately.

He held up his phone. "Something is up. She hasn't responded to me since yesterday morning." At the moment, he'd take a one-word text just to know she was okay.

"Call Sunrise, and see if she's buried in work in the office."

He scrolled to her contact info and hit the phone icon for the Sunrise number. It rang three times before someone picked up. "Sunrise Farms, this is Anne, how may I help you?"

Sunrise Farms. That was new.

"Hi Anne, this is Declan. I'm trying to reach Skye. Is she around?"

"I haven't seen her since the ambulance took her and Dave to the hospital yesterday afternoon."

His heart dropped, then double-timed it in his chest as a wave of fear swept through him. "What? What happened?"

"Oh. I thought you knew." Her light tone helped ease the urgency roiling inside him.

"She hasn't answered her phone."

"Maybe it got chewed up along with her jacket in the tractor when she broke her arm."

"She broke her arm!"

Tate leaned forward, trying to follow the conversation.

Declan tried to hold on to his temper. He couldn't believe Skye didn't call him. "Is she still in the hospital?"

"Oh, no. She came back last night wearing a cast. At least, that's what someone told me."

"How did this happen?"

"Dave was trying to fix the tiller on the tractor. Something went wrong and he got caught in the equipment. Mangled his leg pretty good. *He's* still in the hospital. Anyway, Skye saw what happened and ran over to help. She tried to pry him free, but her sleeve got caught and the thing wound around the tiller, and well, she tried to get the jacket off before she lost an arm, but she broke it in the process. Her arm. Not the tiller." Anne let out a whoosh of air. "Really scary. For both of them."

Declan raked his fingers through his hair. His heart thrashed in his chest. "Where is she right now?"

"Um, I'm not sure. She's never in one place too long. I could call Meadow. I think she was finishing packing before they leave."

"Meadow's leaving?"

"She's going to college. Skye found her a place to stay and a part-time job. Meadow starts school after the holidays, but she wanted to get settled ahead of time."

He didn't know any of this.

He wondered what else she'd kept from him if she hadn't even bothered to call him to tell him she'd broken her arm.

"Anne, I need you to find Skye and tell her to call me

back right now." His tone conveyed the order he issued without raising his voice.

"Uh, yeah, okay. It may take some time if she's out on the farm somewhere."

Frustrated and pissed, he tried not to take it out on Anne. "Tell her to call me back right away."

"Okay. Will do." Anne hung up.

Tate stared at him. "So she's okay?"

Declan picked up a pen and threw it against the wall, wishing he got the satisfying bang and destruction he needed but wouldn't make him feel any better. "How the fuck should I know when I can't get her on the phone and she doesn't bother to tell me she nearly got her arm chopped off in a tractor tiller?"

"Damn. So she's in the hospital with a broken arm?"

"She's back at the farm, probably doing too much and not taking care of herself."

"Listen, if you need to go down there, I've got you covered here."

"Anne said that Meadow is packing and leaving for college today. It sounded like Skye was taking her, so I don't even know if she'll be there."

Declan sat and fumed, though the worry eating away at his gut overrode all his other swirling feelings and thoughts.

Tate sat with him. Waiting. "Did you know the girls are talking to some supplier about organic chickens and vegetables? I overheard Trinity telling Adria that it's going to be a really big deal and that she's excited about the partnership."

Declan couldn't care less at the moment about Trinity and Adria's *Almost Homemade* business expansion. They were opening two more stores last he heard.

"Do you know anything about that, because I thought we were going to expand into chickens?"

Declan shook his head. "According to Skye, it's not cost-effective for us to do it here. She told me to stick to cattle."

"Do you think she's right?"

"She's been in the egg business a while and knows about raising chickens, so yeah, I think she knows what she's talking about."

The phone finally rang with an UNKNOWN number. He swiped to accept the call. "Hello."

"Hey, Declan, it's Meadow. I got a new phone." Her cheerful voice made him clamp his back teeth together to keep from snapping at her to put Skye on the phone.

"Nice. Where's Skye?"

"She was helping me pack, but I think the pain meds and too many nights getting four hours sleep has caught up to her. She fell asleep in a chair while she was folding a shirt. Seriously, like right in the middle of—"

"Meadow! Wake her up. I need to talk to her."

"Oh, Declan, I don't think that's a good idea. We've got a long drive ahead of us. She could use some—"

"Wake her up!" He didn't mean to be rude, but he needed to hear her voice. Now.

"O-kay." Meadow filled that word with all her annoyance.

He heard some rustling and Meadow's muffled voice before more rustling and Skye's soft voice. "Hey baby, how are you?"

He loved that sweet endearment and the happiness he heard in her voice, but he lost the battle to contain his anger. "You broke your fucking arm and you didn't call me! What the hell is going on, Skye?"

Stunned silence filled the line. "I understand you're upset."

"I'm pissed. I've been trying to contact you since yesterday. Nothing. Not a word from you. In fact, it's been harder and harder to get you on the phone."

"Well, it's going to be impossible now because my phone was destroyed yesterday when I saved Dave's life. And I'm sorry I've been busy lately, but I've been trying to be everything to everyone, including you, and you know what? It's not easy. In fact, it sucks, because I'm here, which means I fall short with you every damn day. I want to give you everything you want, but I can't do that from here. And I get you're frustrated by that. So. Am. I. You are more important to me than anything, but you don't see that when I'm here doing all this for you. I know it doesn't feel that way, but it's true. And I'm trying. I really am. I thought I'd have this all done weeks ago, but it keeps piling up and taking more and more to work it all out. But I don't even have time to explain that all to you right now because I have to go pick up the new business licenses and contracts and move my sister. So I'm sorry you haven't heard from me. I'm sorry for a lot of things." She sucked in a ragged breath, and he heard something that scared him. "You didn't even ask if I'm okay. I'm not, in case you want to know. I'm miserable. I don't have a second for myself. I give them all away to everyone here and to you. And I'm sorry, but your time is up. I have to go. People are depending on me. I can't let them down. I'm sorry I let *you* down even though I never meant to." The tears in those words tore his heart to shreds.

"Skye, wait." But she was already gone. "Fuck!" He tossed his phone on the desk and pressed the heels of his hands into his eye sockets. "Fuck!"

"I take it that didn't go well."

"I'm pretty sure I couldn't have handled that any worse." He met Tate's inquisitive gaze. "I made her cry." His stomach knotted. "I could hear it in her voice. She's trying so hard to please everyone and she's falling apart because no one's helping her. I haven't helped her. I've been asking more of her."

"That's not true."

He appreciated Tate's support. "Yes, it is. And I'm pretty sure she's got nothing left to give."

"She works too hard. Her arm's probably killing her. You know what it's like when you break a bone. She's tired. She misses you. She's just overwhelmed."

"I think she's been overwhelmed since Lucy's murder. She ran. She came here. I think I made that all easier for her to process. But once we were apart and the days stretched into weeks and months and everyone wants her to fix everything . . . I want her to fix this between us . . . It's too much to ask of her to do all on her own."

"She'll call you back. You'll work this out. You can't give up."

"I think what she needs right now is one less person asking her to do something for them. I want to make this right. I will make it right. But right now, she made it clear that I'm hurting her more than helping her. That's the last thing I want to do. So I'm going to give her whatever time she needs."

"Do you think that's really what she wants? Or does she want you to come to her and be there for her?"

"I don't know that she knows what she wants for herself right now." He hated to admit that after everything that happened to her, she was holding on to him because they were good together, when they were together, but maybe that's all it was. A distraction from everything else. A few moments to have something good in her life before she had to face all the nightmares and work and obligations. "I won't be one more person asking her to give and give and give when she's got nothing left."

"You don't know that."

"You didn't hear her, Tate. The utter exhaustion and weariness. I can't . . . I won't ask anything more of her. If she wants to be with me, she knows where I am. If she needs me, she knows all she has to do is call. Until then, she needs time to take care of Sunrise, her family, and hopefully herself."

"*You* need to take care of her."

"Don't you think if she wanted me to she would have called when they took her to the hospital? No one called me. Not her. Not her family." He scrubbed his hands over his face. "If something happened to me, wouldn't you call her, knowing I'd want her by my side?"

Tate's gaze fell to the floor. "Yeah. I guess so."

"I'm not giving up on her. I just think we both need to take a minute and decide what we really want. I love her. I want to build a life with her. Maybe that's too much to ask of her right now. I'm not a priority. At least, it doesn't feel that way."

"Have you made *her* a priority?"

"I could do better, but when I go visit her, she spends more time working than being with me. The couple of times she came here, I dropped everything to spend time with her."

"That's because me and the guys stepped up to cover for you."

"She's got over a hundred people working and living at that farm. Don't tell me she's the only one who can make a decision or pitch in when help is needed." The bitterness of those words left a sour taste in his mouth.

"They really do depend on her." Tate was finally getting it.

"I don't think even they knew how much they needed and depended on her until she left for a little while. She cares about all of them. She cares about the farm supporting and providing for them. When she talks about her plans for that place, it's daunting, but it's a good, solid plan to set them up for even more success than they've had over the years. Losing her and the vision she has for that place, it would be a big blow to the community. And that means something to Skye."

"They're all her family."

"Yes. And they've accepted me and treated me like I'm one of them when I'm there. But just like Skye feels obligated to that place and her people, I feel the same way about this place. So what do we do?"

"I don't know, man. I just know you've never been happier than when you're with her."

True. He was miserable without her. "I hate the way we left things."

"Call her back."

"And say what? She knows how I feel and what I want."

"Maybe right now, all she needs to know is that you love her."

Declan picked up his phone, pulled up the call log, and texted Meadow's number.

DECLAN: Meadow tell Skye I'm sorry, I love her, and to take all the time she needs
DECLAN: I'm here

He looked at Tate. "Now, I guess, I wait." He felt like he'd been waiting his whole life for her. Missing her these last months hadn't been easy. It would be worse now because of the way they'd left things. But he'd wait as long as it took.

Chapter Thirty-Eight

SKYE WOKE up to the same forwarded texts her sister re-sent her the last four days.

DECLAN: Meadow tell Skye I'm sorry, I love her, and to take all the time she needs
DECLAN: I'm here

Every morning at six, her phone alarm went off along with the chimes for the texts. She read them every day. And every day she got the same rush of love for the man who understood she needed a break, but that didn't mean she didn't love him. With that rush of love came the overwhelming urgency to get to him, because how long could she make him wait without it wearing on their relationship even more?

They had things to say and work out. This time, it had to be done in person.

MEADOW: GO. SEE. DECLAN!!!!
MEADOW: TODAY!!!

Why did I buy a new phone?
She felt Declan waiting for her and her sister's insis-

tence that she make things right with him. She worried and feared that maybe she'd hurt Declan and put him off too long for them to really work things out.

In her effort to do everything she could to be able to make a life with him, she'd somehow unintentionally told him he wasn't important.

She could tell him all day long she wanted to be with him, but when she didn't actually go see him, how was he supposed to believe it?

She'd never really had a serious relationship with a man. She was bound to make mistakes.

She had made them.

Declan apologized.

It was her turn.

She sat up in bed, wholly aware of how empty it felt without Declan. She'd slept as badly as she had every night for the last few months. Lack of sleep, worries, anxiety, and the aching pain in her broken arm added up to a lot of sleepless nights.

She was looking forward to calmer days and nights with Declan. She'd find peace with him just like she did every time they were together.

If he'd have her.

She was taking a big leap of faith that everything would work out with them. But it was worth it if she got what she wanted. What she hoped Declan *still* wanted.

The boxes she'd stacked by the front door reminded her that she'd made the decision, done everything possible to set up Sunrise for success and growth, and this was her time to find happiness.

But like all the other days over the last few months, she had a few things to tie up before she could do what she wanted.

Today was the day. Nothing would stop her from leaving for Montana.

She missed Declan so much. It had become a living thing inside her that grew each and every second until all she thought about now was him.

Anxious to get on the road, she took a quick shower and dressed comfortably in a pair of leggings and one of the soft sweaters Declan bought her, along with the boots he'd picked out for her.

She headed for the hall and coffee. She'd need it to get through this day.

When she walked into the hall, she stopped short as everyone stood before her and clapped beneath a banner that read, Thank You and Good Luck!

She checked behind her to make sure this amazing display of gratitude was for her, then faced the crowd again and smiled. They wanted to send her off with their blessing.

Her parents stepped forward from the crowd and her father addressed her, along with everyone else. "We are so proud of you, Skye. You saved this place from ruin. Your reorganization of the farm has changed the way we do things for the better. You've given our community hope and a step toward a bright and prosperous future. You've sacrificed a lot these last months and worked harder than anyone expected. We're sorry to see you go, but all of us support your decision. We know that your moving forward in your life doesn't mean you aren't very much connected to us and our community."

Tears trailed down her cheeks as she walked to her father and mother and took them both in a hug that they returned.

"Thank you, Mom and Dad. This means so much to me."

Her heart ached with love and missing them even though she hadn't even left yet.

"I don't know what we're going to do with you and Meadow living so far away."

Skye stepped back, but kept a hand on each of their shoulders. "We'll be back for visits all the time. And you'll be too busy running the poultry and egg business to miss us too much."

Her mom brushed a lock of Skye's hair behind her ear. "Declan is lucky to have you."

She hoped he still thought so. "If I don't go to him, I'll regret it the rest of my life. I love him very much."

Her father hugged her close. "Be happy, Skye. That's all we've ever wanted for you."

She leaned back and met her father's gaze. "Just being with him makes me happy. I love his ranch and family. It will be a good life." She glanced at her mother. "And I'll be back for a few days every month to check in on the business. We'll be in contact all the time."

It took two hours to get through breakfast and talk to everyone who came to say goodbye and wish her well. She appreciated everyone's support so much that it left her all at once overwhelmed and sad to leave.

She planned to leave at noon, but got pulled into some problems that came up at the new chicken barn and an order change in their new computer system that didn't get communicated to the crew.

Things happened. So she made sure the right people were on it and working through the issues. By the time she returned to say goodbye to her parents, it was almost two and she had a message from Declan's sister, Trinity, to call her ASAP.

She stopped by her cabin to put the boxes in the truck she'd borrow until she bought her own vehicle.

That was the other thing she'd set up at Sunrise. She turned the nonprofit into a real business with paid employees. They'd still live and work as a community, but everyone would be paid a fair and equal wage. Sunrise would still provide communal meals and housing. Surprisingly, very few people fought against the expansion or forming a true business.

They'd keep the best of what they were and embrace what they could be.

With her truck loaded and her belly fluttering with anticipation of leaving, she pulled out her phone and called Trinity.

"Hey, are you on your way?"

She'd told Trinity she was coming today, but swore her to secrecy. She wanted to surprise Declan. "Unfortunately, no. Not yet. I need to stop in town to pick up the contracts at the lawyer's office before I hit the road. I probably won't get there until . . . maybe seven. You didn't tell him, did you?"

"No. I can't wait to see his face. He's miserable without you."

"Same goes for me. I hope doing it this way works. Maybe I should call him first, so we can talk it all out before I get there."

"No. Surprising him like this . . . with a big gesture . . . that will show him how much you want to be with him."

"I hope so. It's been so long since everything was good between us."

"It's going to all work out now. Long distance things rarely work. I, for one, think you two are great together."

"Thanks. Everything okay at the shop?"

"Yes. Adria and I are excited about our new partnership. It's been tough keeping everything under wraps, but I think Tate and Declan are going to love how we've teamed up."

"Me too. Listen, I still need to say one final goodbye to my parents. So I better do that now or I'll never get out of here."

"See you tonight. We're having a big family dinner at Declan's place."

Great. Everyone would be there to witness her arrival and apology to Declan for what she'd put him through these last many months. She hoped he didn't kick her out.

"I'll see you soon." She hung up and went to find her parents. Goodbyes were hard, but she wanted to tell her parents again how much she appreciated their support and understanding.

And in a few hours, she'd be right where she'd wanted to be for months: with Declan.

Chapter Thirty-Nine

"COME ON, I look like I swallowed a basketball!" Adria rubbed her hand over her big belly. Twins took up a lot of room.

Declan couldn't wait to be an uncle. He'd like to be a dad. But that didn't look like it was in his immediate future.

He missed Skye more each day.

If he'd known sending her that text would make her go silent, he'd have begged her to call him instead. But he'd promised her the space she needed and he had to live with it, even if living with it was killing him.

Everyone around the table laughed with Adria about her ever growing baby bump. They'd had a great dinner. Trinity brought the food from *Almost Homemade*. He'd simply provided the space.

He pretty much figured they were trying to make him feel better and less alone. While he enjoyed having everyone at his table and filling the house with noise, it made him miss Skye all the more. She should be here with him. With all of them.

At first, he didn't believe his eyes. But there she was, standing in the opening between the dining room and living room with the key he gave her months ago in her hand, a duffel bag hanging from her shoulder, and looking more beautiful than he remembered. The hesitant look in her eyes shouldn't be there. She belonged here.

She was here.

"Get out!"

Her eyes went wide and his family all froze.

Skye's eyes fell with defeat as she stepped back and turned for the door.

He jumped up and grabbed her hand, pulling her back to him. "Not you." He turned to his family. "You." His gaze went back to Skye's stunned one. "We need to talk."

"It can wait until you're finished with your family dinner."

"It's waited too damn long already," he snapped, letting his impatience get the better of him.

This moment had been a long time coming. He wanted to clear the air, figure out where they really stood with each other, and go from there. Which meant he needed his family out of here, because if he had to beg her to stay, he was ready to hit his knees and plead his case.

Dinner done, plates empty, everyone at the table stood, ready to leave them alone without an argument.

Skye dropped her duffel bag in the entry hall and pulled out the folders tucked under her broken arm. "Before you go, Trinity and Adria, here's the contracts I promised."

"What contracts?" Declan looked to his sisters to explain.

Trinity smiled. "We're keeping the business in the family." Trinity opened the folder and flipped through pages. "This contract is for all our poultry and eggs from Sunrise Farms." Trinity signed her name and handed the pen to Adria while she opened the other folder and looked through the papers. "This one is for the organic produce and fruit we'll get direct from Sunrise Farms as well."

Declan turned to Skye, who stood back watching his sisters sign the contracts. "Is this why you came?" He couldn't believe she hadn't come to be with him.

She met his expectant gaze. "No."

His heart started beating again.

"And yes." Skye took the folders back from his sister.

Tate kissed Skye on the cheek. "It's good to see you." Liz hugged her and followed Tate out.

Drake kissed Skye on the head. "He's miserable without you. Welcome home."

Trinity and Adria both hugged her at the same time.

Skye held them both close. "Thank you for believing in my proposal and using Sunrise Farms as your supplier."

His sisters released Skye. Trinity spoke first. "Because you know us, you knew exactly what we were looking for in a partner."

Adria touched Skye's arm. "This is going to be good for us and Sunrise."

Adria followed Drake out.

Trinity turned to him. "She has been working her ass off to get back here to you. Listen to what she has to say."

He waited for the front door to close and they were finally alone. He started with the thing that had brought everything to a head between them. "How's your arm?"

She held up the dark blue cast and wiggled her fingers. "Better. It only aches some of the time. Usually when I overdo things."

"So, most of the time." That got him a soft smile, but it didn't reach her eyes.

"The cast comes off in a couple more weeks." The nerves in her voice made him anxious.

His heart raced. "What are you really doing here?"

She shifted from one foot to the other. "First, I owe you an apology."

"I don't want an apology. I want to know why you're here."

"I'm here because . . . *you're* here." She raked her fingers through her long hair. "I've been trying to get back here since you left Sunrise the day after everything went down there. I tried to make it clear to you that I wanted to be here with you, but I couldn't just leave my life and home behind without making sure I cleaned up the mess I made."

"You didn't do anything wrong. Gabriel made the mess."

"Yeah, well, someone had to fix things and everyone was looking to me to do it." The same frustration and weariness he'd heard in her voice these last months resonated through those words.

He tried to reassure her he understood. "I know that. It's why I came back here without you. I knew they needed you there."

"Yeah, well, *I* needed *you*."

He'd let her down. "Skye, I—"

"You were the best. You tried so hard. And I made it so difficult because I couldn't seem to be everything to everyone. I made you miserable. When you came to visit, I didn't stop everything like I should have and spend time with you. Worse, I actually put you to work." Tears gathered in her eyes.

"I didn't mind helping out."

"No. You resented not having enough time with me."

"Yes." Lying now only seemed stupid. They needed to get this all out in the open.

"And when I came to visit you here, my mind was there."

He agreed with a nod but let her know how he really felt. "You never stayed long enough."

She sucked in a big breath and let it out. "So here's the thing . . . I finally did it."

"Sunrise Farms. You turned the commune into a business. You expanded operations, reorganized the workers, set them up with fair and equal pay, put the right people in charge of the farm, poultry business, and flower operation. Apparently you partnered with *Almost Homemade*."

"It wasn't financially feasible for you to do it here," she reminded him. "Sunrise already had a thriving egg business. Adding the poultry business was a good fit and an easy expansion. How did you know about all this?"

"Meadow. After I texted you—well her—after you broke your arm, she called me from her new place in Bozeman." He smiled. "She got into the University of Montana." He was proud of Meadow for getting in and going after what she wanted.

"She wanted to go to college. And also be close to me."

That got his attention, because she'd only be close to Meadow if Skye lived here with him.

"What are you saying?" Hope filled his heart.

"It may not have looked like it, but I was doing all that work so I could be *here* with you."

"And you're done doing all that?" He was finally catching on, but it seemed too good to be true.

"Yes." She paused, then added, "And no."

Deflated, he crossed his arms over his chest, hoping his heart didn't rip right in half. "What does that mean?"

"Well, the business is up and running. Everyone is doing their part. But I'll have to go back a few days a month.

I was thinking a long four- to five-day weekend the first week of every month until I'm not needed so much. *If* that works for you. I can change when I go."

His arms fell limp at his sides. "Uh, I guess that would work."

"Okay. Good. Because most of what I own is in the truck."

His heart stopped. "You moved here?" The gears in his mind ground as his brain tried to process everything. "To live with me?"

She held up the key in her hand. "You gave me this so I could come anytime I wanted to. The text you sent said, *I'm here.* Wherever you are is where I want to be. I know it hasn't seemed that way, but it's been true all along."

"You're serious. This is real. You're actually staying."

She bit her lip. "If you want me to." She glanced back to the door. "Unless—"

He closed the distance, cupped her face, and kissed her like he'd wanted to since the second he saw her. He didn't need to say a word about how much he wanted her to stay because he let loose his need for her and kept kissing her until her arms went around his neck, her body molded to his, and she held on for dear life.

It took him a second to realize the wetness on his fingertips was her tears. He broke the kiss and stared into her bright, happy eyes. "Why are you crying?"

"Because I love you so much and I'm finally here."

He crushed her in a hug. "Then stay." That's what he should have said from the beginning.

She leaped into his chest and kissed him. Declan held her close and lost himself in the heat and need that swept through him. It had been so long since they'd been together. He didn't want to let her go.

Not now.

Not ever.

For weeks his life looked bleak without her. Now the dreams he had for their future looked like a reality they'd turn into a happy life.

Skye broke the kiss and pressed her forehead to his. This close, he couldn't miss the dark circles under her eyes or the weariness in them.

"I know I just got here. We probably have a lot more to talk about . . . but I really just want you to take me to bed."

He swept his thumbs over her cheeks. "Whatever you want, sweetheart."

"I just need you." She needed him to take care of her because she'd hit her limit of taking care of everyone else for a while. She needed time to recharge.

He'd give her that and everything else she needed.

He snagged the duffel bag she'd dropped, took her hand, and gently tugged to get her to come with him.

"Don't you need to clean up dinner?"

"The only thing I need to do is welcome you home." He left the dirty dishes and food out and walked right up the stairs with her following behind him.

Inside his room, he stopped outside the walk-in closet and opened the door, showing her that half of it stood empty and ready for her.

"Declan." She stared at the empty shelves and hanging bars.

"I didn't just tell you I wanted you here, Skye, I made room for you. I want you to make this your home. I want this place to be *our* place." To prove it, he dropped her bag in the closet, turned to her, helped her take off her jacket, grabbed a hanger from the rod, and hung it up.

She stared at her jacket in their closet, then met his gaze. "I have been waiting for this day to come."

"I've been waiting for you." He kissed her softly.

They didn't need to rush. She wasn't going anywhere. This was their place. Their time to be together.

He took the hem of her shirt and pulled it up and over her head. He tossed it on top of the pile filling the hamper. She shook out her long hair. He slipped his hands inside her leggings and panties and pushed his hands down her strong legs. They caught on the tops of her boots. She planted her hand on his shoulder and lifted one foot and then the other as he pulled off her boots, tossed them over his shoulder into the closet, and finished tugging off her pants, panties, and socks. They all went into the hamper. She tossed the bra and stood before him, beautiful and naked and softly smiling at him.

"You take my breath away." And because he wanted to be skin to skin with her, he quickly discarded all his clothes as she stood there watching him with hungry eyes.

Her patience disappeared the second he dropped the last sock and stood before her naked and ready to make love to her. She took him by the shoulders and pulled him close, her mouth landing on his in a desperate kiss that was tempting as hell.

He wrapped his arms around her and walked her back to the bed they'd made love in for the first time and they'd make love in for years to come. He gripped the cover, blanket, and sheet all at once and pulled them down, then laid her out on the bed. He lay beside her, kissing her like he had all night to do just that even as his hand mapped her body and she turned into him, getting closer.

He took his time, sweeping his hand over every soft

curve. She sighed and melted into him. This had always been good between them. Right now, he wanted to show her how happy he was to have her home and how much he loved and cherished her.

"I've missed you so much." She slid her hand down his chest and wrapped it around his aching cock. Her thumb found the bead of moisture and spread it over the sensitive head, making him groan and thrust into her hand.

He molded her breast to his hand, kissed her neck, and plucked her tight nipple between his fingers. "I dream about you in our bed every damn night." He kissed his way to that pink bud, took it into his mouth, and sucked hard, loving her sigh and the clamp of her hand around his shaft, driving him on.

She draped her leg over his and rocked her hips into his thigh. He slipped his hand down her belly to her sweet center. His fingers slid over her slick folds and he drove one finger deep into her wet core. She rocked into his hand and slid her fingers over his balls then back up his hard dick.

"Declan."

He licked her nipple and thrust two fingers into her tight core.

"Please," she whispered.

He needed to be inside her as badly as she wanted him there. He hated to leave her for even a second, but rolled to his back, reached for the drawer beside him, found a condom, and tore it open with his teeth while she laid a trail of openmouthed kisses over his chest as her hand pumped up and down his shaft. He brushed her hand away and rolled on the condom just as she straddled his lap and took him deep. He thrust up, lifting his hips right off the bed and burying himself deep inside her. He settled back and she rocked her hips against his.

He ran his hands over her chest and breasts as she moved over him, her weight braced on her good arm. She traced her fingertips from her broken arm over his chest as she stared down at him. "You feel so good."

She felt amazing moving over him. She lost herself in the rhythm, her eyes closed, and her body rocking with his. He watched her, taking her in, loving her for loving him like this. So open. So honest in the way she enjoyed being with him.

With his hands free, he gripped her ass in one hand and drove her on. He cupped her breast in the other. He leaned up, took her nipple into his mouth, and sucked and laved and played with her breast, eliciting a string of soft sighs and moans.

He wallowed in the feel of her body moving over and against his. With his release riding him hard, he slipped his hand between them, and circled her clit with the pad of his finger as she rose up, then sank back down, her body tightening around his. She did it again and he felt the need building inside her, kept the soft caress going until she sank down on him again and her body clamped around his. He thrust deep once, twice, prolonging her orgasm and his until he sank into the bed and she collapsed on his chest, aftershocks making her core pulse.

He loved having her draped over him, their bodies and hearts connected. He wrapped his arms around her, held her close, and whispered, "I'm so happy you're home."

She lifted her head and brushed her fingers along his jaw. "I love you."

He kissed her softly. "I love you, too. So much."

She settled at his side, her body pressed along his, her arm draped over his chest. He held her with one arm around her back and brushed his fingers across her skin in soft sweeps that put her to sleep. She needed the rest. She'd worked damn hard to put Sunrise in order so she could come back to him.

Now that he had her here where she belonged, he planned to ensure she never wanted to leave again. He wouldn't mind the short visits she needed to make back there, so long as she called this place and him home from now on.

He settled into the quiet night, watching her sleep and planning how to make her a real part of his life and the ranch. He'd give her time to settle in, find her place here, one that made her happy. Then he'd make her his wife. Soon.

Because he couldn't wait to start his life with her.

He kissed her on the head and she snuggled closer.

Well, this was a good start. But she deserved a really great proposal and a happy life.

And he wanted to give her both.

Chapter Forty

SKYE COULDN'T remember ever being this happy. She'd been living with Declan at the ranch for the last six weeks and it was even better than she'd imagined. He'd welcomed her with open arms and empty drawers to fill with her things. Every decision, big or small, he asked her to weigh in on, whether it was what to have for dinner or what to name the dog they rescued at the shelter.

The shepherd Lab mix with the beautiful light brown eyes settled into ranch life and their home like she'd always belonged. Declan loved that Mandy followed him around everywhere he went, though he'd drawn the line at her sleeping in their bed.

He wanted Skye all to himself. And he proved that, making love to her most nights with the same passion and need he'd always shown her.

She didn't think things could get any better between them, but every day she woke up in his arms, happier than the day before and so grateful for the life she had here at Cedar Top Ranch with Declan and his family.

Though she missed hers.

Her parents had embraced their new role at Sunrise, and Meadow loved her new job and independence. She couldn't wait to start school after the holidays that were quickly coming up.

Skye couldn't wait to spend her first Thanksgiving and Christmas with Declan.

"Hey, what are you thinking about?" Declan rode his horse beside hers.

They tried to take a long ride once or twice a week to spend time together and be alone. The ranch was thriving and they were often busy, though Declan had hired a couple new guys and handed over the paperwork and office to her to run. She loved being a part of the business and helping him and Tate run things. They'd even taken several of her suggestions for streamlining processes and implemented them. Plus, she still worked as the intermediary between Sunrise and *Almost Homemade*. The new arrangement for shipping food had been implemented and everything was running smoothly.

To her surprise, Sunrise ran without her. She'd set it up for success and everyone was getting on just fine, though she did field several phone calls and problems a week, and the last time she went back, she only stayed three days.

She turned to Declan as they rode down the hill back into the pasture leading to the stables and house. "I was just thinking about how nice it's been living here. I feel like I'm a part of this place."

"I'm happy to hear you say that. I love having you here."

The first few weeks had been filled with dozens of calls and that one trip back. She'd felt Declan's reservations and worries that Sunrise would pull her back and away from him again. "I'm exactly where I want to be. With you." She gave him a warm smile, which he returned, melting her heart.

"Good. Because I have a surprise for you." Declan waved up to the house that came into view.

She gasped and put her hand to her gaping mouth as tears filled her eyes.

His family and hers stood on the porch and steps, waiting for their return.

"What are they doing here?"

Declan reined his horse in by one of the ranch hands waiting by the stables. He dismounted and looked up at her. "They're here for us." He took her by the hips, plucked her right off her mount, and set her in front of him. He brushed his fingers across her wet cheek. "I have another surprise for you. Come with me."

He took her hand and led her toward the house.

Up close, she could see that the two dozen vases of white roses at the front of the house were arranged in a heart. Mandy sat like a good girl in the center, waiting patiently for them to come to her.

Declan led her right to the center of the heart, and grinned at their family quietly lining the stairs and porch, watching with wide smiles.

She waved at Meadow and her parents and saw the love and excitement in their eyes.

Declan squeezed her hand to get her attention. He took her other hand and made her turn to him. "I love you."

"I love you, too." She looked around, her heart pounding, her mind trying to figure out what was going on, but she knew in her heart, and couldn't wait to hear what Declan said next.

"This is our home. This is our family." He glanced at everyone, then back to her. "This is the place I want us to have a family of our own. You are the woman I want, the partner I need, the love of my life. I want to spend every day of the rest of my life with you." Declan dropped to one knee, pulled a gorgeous ring from his pocket, and held it up with one hand while he clasped her hand in his. "Living with you these last weeks has made me so happy. Will you marry me and make me happy the rest of my life as my beautiful wife?"

Tears slipped over her lashes, and the smile she couldn't contain spread across her face. "Yes!" She leaned down and kissed him. "Yes."

He slipped the ring on her finger. The sparkling diamond was a far better accessory than the cast she'd had removed a week ago.

Declan rose, wrapped his arms around her waist, hauled her up against his body and off her feet, and kissed her again. Mandy ran around them, barking her excitement.

Their family cheered, and Declan spun her in a quick circle that made her head spin and her heart soar.

"Look over here," the ranch hand called.

She and Declan glanced over, huge smiles on their faces as the guy took pictures with his phone.

Declan set her back on her feet, kissed her again, and finally gave Mandy a pat as she happily danced around their legs, as excited for them as everyone else.

They were enveloped by their families and congratulations.

Overwhelmed, Skye hugged her sister tight. "I've missed you."

Meadow held her by the shoulders. "Look how happy you are." Meadow took her in from head to foot and back up again. "This place is great, but I can see it's Declan who makes you smile."

"All day. Every day."

Her mother stepped up to them. "Then I have no doubt you'll be happy for the rest of your life." Her mother hugged her close.

"How long can you stay?"

"Declan invited us to stay for the weekend."

"He did?"

Her father hugged her next. "He knew you'd want your family here for this big occasion."

Declan wrapped his arms around her from behind and hugged her to his chest. "Mind if I have a moment alone with my fiancée?"

Her mother put her hand on Declan's arm. "We are so happy for both of you. Welcome to the family."

"Thank you. I'll always take care of her." He meant the solemn promise.

"You always have," her father said, following her mother and Meadow and the entire McGrath family into the house.

She turned in Declan's arms and stared up at him. "Oh my God, you asked me to marry you."

His huge smile made her heart soar. "I know. You said yes."

She squeezed his biceps and smiled up at him. "I can't wait to be your wife."

"You kind of started the day you got here. You walked into my life and made it better the second we met."

"You took me in and had my back."

He tightened his hold on her hips and drew her closer. "Always." He took her hand and admired the ring on her finger. "This is my promise that I will always be yours. I will always love you."

"When I ran away from Sunrise, I thought I was running away from something bad, but maybe I was running to the best thing that ever happened to me."

He pulled her in for a long, deep kiss. There was nothing better than the love of a man who would always stand beside her and support her through all the ups and downs they were sure to face over their lifetimes. And they would have a lifetime, because after all they'd been through together, they could get through anything. They loved each other, and nothing could tear them apart when they loved with their whole hearts.

Keep reading for a sneak peek at
the next book in the McGrath series

TRUE LOVE COWBOY

by Jennifer Ryan

Coming August 2021
from Avon Books

Prologue

4 months, 3 weeks, and 6 days ago . . .

TRINITY MCGRATH walked out the back door of *Almost Homemade* with a trash bag in hand, a smile on her face because they'd had their best sales week to date, and her heart overflowing with happiness because all the hard work was paying off. She and Adria should celebrate. Lost in thoughts of decadent desserts, because Adria was pregnant and couldn't drink champagne, she casually walked across the parking lot, oblivious to everything around her until a blinding white-hot pain exploded through her brain. Brilliant white stars burst on the backs of her eyelids. She dropped the bag and fell to her knees, tearing her black stretch pants and leaving stinging scrapes across her skin. She caught herself on her hands, sending a jolt of pain up her arms. Instinctively, she reached up to touch the swelling lump on the side of her head, but someone grabbed her arm and hauled her up to her feet. Dizziness made her wobble. At first she didn't understand what happened, but then her attacker's fingers dug into her biceps, bruising, punishing, and then she glanced up at his mask-covered face and met the deadly intent in his eyes and she knew exactly who had come for her.

"Cooperate or I'll kill you."

She didn't need to see the gun to believe him, or to actually see his face.

He'd killed before. And now he wanted her brother Tate's girlfriend.

He planned to use her to lure Liz into whatever trap he'd set for her.

Trinity didn't want to help him kill the love of Tate's life.

She didn't want to get hurt either, but she refused to go quietly and struggled to get free. She opened her mouth to scream, but he spun her away from him, hooked his arm around her shoulder, and clamped his hand over her mouth, cutting off the call for help.

"Shut up, or die. I don't need you alive to do what I need to do. I just need you to be missing." Those chilling words stopped her heart.

In that moment of shock, he pulled her phone from her apron and tossed it into a nearby bush. He shoved her toward a silver sedan with the trunk already open. She dug in her heels, trying to delay him long enough for someone, anyone, to see them and stop him before he shoved her into the car and did God knows what to her.

All her attempts to get free failed. He was too strong, she too dizzy and off balance from the blow to the head. She felt weak and ineffectual and doomed to fail and it scared her and pissed her off.

But she rallied, planted her foot on the bumper, and pushed back, trying to offset his determination to shove her into the trunk. She thought she had him for a moment, but he bashed her in the head again with the butt of the gun. Stars burst in her eyes and before she knew it, he pulled her head down, twisted her sideways, and toppled her over the lip of the trunk and into the compartment. He slammed the lid, leaving her in complete darkness.

Stunned, it took her a second to react, then she pushed and kicked, trying to get the trunk to open, but her efforts were all futile. A panic like nothing she'd ever felt seized her mind and body. She couldn't think clearly. Perhaps that had more to do with the head injuries. Her brain throbbed along with her pounding heartbeat, but she tried to force herself to think through the terror.

Trunks have a release!

She'd heard that somewhere. Owner of an SUV, she didn't know where to locate the lever or whatever, but she rolled to her side and spotted the glow-in-the-dark pull tab lying on the carpet beside her.

She picked it up and threw it against the wall. "No!"

He'd cut the line.

She banged her fist against the trunk top. "Let me out of here!"

The car engine started, creating an eerie thrumming sound.

Tears clogged her throat and streamed down the sides of her face as she stared into the darkness.

Clint backed out of the spot, hit the brakes, sending her rolling into the back of the trunk, then he stomped on the gas and rolled her the other way. She tried to brace herself, but she didn't have much room to maneuver. And so she clamped her jaw tight, braced her hands where she could find a hold, and tried to remain as still as possible so her head didn't spin and her sour stomach didn't pitch with every stop, start, and curve.

Where was he taking her? She had no clue and quickly lost track of time in the dark. Was she stuffed in the trunk ten minutes? An hour? She didn't know. But at one point the car stopped, the door opened but didn't close, then nothing for a minute before a car alarm went off, the horn blaring over and over again. The car door slammed, the engine revved, they sat idling. The horn alarm stopped. She assumed they were waiting in a parking lot or something, though she didn't hear any sound of other people or rush of cars on a street. Just the incessant noise of the engine running. She gave herself time to breathe, let the fear settle, her mind clear, so she could find the ability to think clearly and form a plan to get out of this.

All at once the car lurched forward, tires squealing. She braced herself with both hands and feet against the walls. The car jolted as something thumped against the vehicle. Whatever it was bumped against the top of the car and over the trunk with muffled sounds of distress.

At first she wondered if they'd hit an animal, but her mind quickly turned to darker thoughts. Those muffled sounds were human, not animal.

Clint shouted, "Take that, motherfucker!"

Her heart stopped. Clint had a short hit list. And two people she loved topped it.

Did he hit Tate?

Liz?

"You won't fuck with me again!"

Trinity's stomach dropped and her heart broke with the devastating thoughts running through her head and the nightmarish images filling her mind.

"She's mine now."

The words were muffled, but she heard them clearly.

He'd hit Tate. Now he'd go after Liz.

And what did that mean for Trinity?

She didn't know.

More muffled words came from the front of the car but

she couldn't make them out. She guessed he was talking to himself or someone on the phone. Was he luring Liz to him, using Trinity as bait? Probably.

"Let me out of here!" She hoped whoever was on the call heard her, but doubted it. "Help me! Please, someone get me out of here!"

It didn't take long for the temperature to rise in the confined space or for it to feel like she had no air. She tried to calm down, reminded herself there was plenty of air for her to breathe, but the panic seized her again and she lost it.

She kicked and screamed, hoping someone heard her. But the car drove on, making her efforts futile—and a little crazy.

"You have to let me out of here!"

Her captor ignored her.

She fell silent, shaking with fear, lost in her dark thoughts, trying to come up with a plan for when he opened the trunk.

He wouldn't just leave her in here. Right?

He had to open the trunk.

Oh God, he just had to.

The fear grew that this tiny, dark space would become her coffin.

The sudden sharp turn startled her. So did the abrupt stop.

She cracked her stinging and scraped knee on the wheel well and her elbow on the trunk lid as she flew one way, then rolled back.

The engine died and the car door slammed. Footsteps crunched over gravel headed toward the back of the car. She braced herself, ready to fight for her life. She turned so that when the trunk opened she could use her legs and kick, though the confined space didn't bode well for her success.

It didn't help. The moment the trunk went up, the bright light temporarily blinded her and sent a bolt of pain through her brain. She caught a blurry image of Clint, still wearing the mask, taking a picture of her on his phone.

Creepy.

She kicked at him, but it didn't do her a damn bit of good. Clint stood back, the gun pointed down at her. She had no defense against rocket-fast bullets.

He tucked the phone in his pocket. "You wanted out. Get out."

The words didn't compute at first, then she simply didn't know what to do. Was she safer in the trunk or getting out?

Would he just shoot her and leave her on the side of the road?

He waved the gun at her. "Get the fuck out!"

She slowly sat up, slipping one leg over the edge of the trunk and bumper. Her head spun from the bright light and the dizziness that hadn't waned. Woozy and nauseous, she clamped a hand on the edge of the car and tried to steady herself and stop the world spinning.

Clint grabbed her arm and pulled her out, making her stumble several steps until she fell to her knees in the dirt. A sharp rock jutted into her shin but she didn't dare move. Clint stood next to her, the gun pointed at her head.

"Count to a hundred."

She glanced up at him through squinted eyes, completely confused.

He lifted his foot, planted it on the side of her shoulder, and shoved her over. "On your knees. Count!"

She ignored the stinging scrapes on her hands and knees

from when he abducted her in the parking lot and the new ones that ran along her wrist and arm from him kicking her to the ground. She rose back up to her knees and glared at him. "If you're going to shoot me, just do it already."

She didn't want to die. She simply didn't want to be taunted and tortured with some countdown.

"If you don't start counting, I will shoot you, you mouthy bitch." He sidestepped and stood behind her.

She wished for a car to drive by, for someone to see them and stop Clint, or simply call the cops to help her. But the country road remained empty of traffic and her odds of living sank with each passing second no one found her.

Did anyone know she was missing at all?

"Do it now! Count!" His voice cracked on the screamed command as he lost his shit.

So she swallowed all the pleas and words she wanted to use to bargain for her life and started with, "One."

Gravel crunched as he shifted his weight and she waited for the blast of the gun, her heart pounding so hard it echoed in her ears.

"Two. Three," she bit out, body tensed and expecting the inevitable.

Out of nowhere, the gun butt bashed into her already swollen and bruised temple, sending her down to the dirt and rocks again. Blinding pain burst through her head, blood poured into her eye. What she could see of the world turned red and closed into a pinpoint of light.

In the distance, the car door slammed with an echoing sound. The engine rumbled to life. The car tore out of there, the tires spitting dirt and gravel that pelted her back and head.

The blinding light went black.

Chapter One

Today . . .

TRINITY STOOD at the *Almost Homemade* prep counter, earbuds in, hips shaking to the brand new Ashley McBryde song she already loved, while she chopped fresh broccoli for the next batch of Chicken and Broccoli Fettuccini Alfredo. Someone's hand touched her shoulder. Instinct made her jump and spin around all at once, her heart pounding in time to the thumping beat blasting in her ears, hands up to ward off an attack. She caught her breath and held it until she focused on her sister-in-law and partner, Adria.

Her mind took her back to the dark trunk where she couldn't see and death seemed inevitable.

Adria was saying something, but the words didn't compute.

Nothing got through the rising panic.

It took her a second, and Adria's disgruntled frown, to realize she couldn't hear because of the music that finally broke through the thumping of her heart.

She pulled out her earbuds, silently scolded herself for not standing on the other side of the counter where no one could sneak up behind her and bring back the nightmare, and reminded herself to breathe. "What?"

Adria held the ringing phone out to her. "I have to pee. Take this. It's for you anyway." Adria passed off the phone and rushed to the bathroom. Pregnant with twins, she did that at least twenty times a day.

Trinity picked up on the next ring, hoping the customer wasn't too upset for having to wait. "*Almost Homemade.* This is Trinity. How may I help you?"

Many of the customers ordered online, but some folks still preferred a personal touch and called in their pick-up orders.

"Hey, sweet girl."

Trinity smiled and the nightmare that threatened to send her into a panic attack receded from her mind. Focus on something else, her therapist had told her. Easier said than done most of the time, but she loved Mr. Crawford. He always made her smile. "My favorite customer."

"What's it going to take to get a beautiful woman like you to come visit an old-timer like me?" Mr. Crawford coughed. The deep, wet sound concerned her.

"Hey now, are you okay?"

It took Mr. Crawford a few extra seconds to catch his breath. "To tell you the truth, sweet girl—" Several more coughs cut off his words. "I could use some of your amazing soup. Maybe some other stuff." He coughed again. "You know what I like, right?" Those few sentences took all his breath.

They didn't do delivery service, but for a few select seniors, they made an exception. She and Adria had made it part of their mission to feed their neighbors. That meant helping those who were housebound, unable to drive themselves, or sick and in need of a good, healthy meal.

Mr. Crawford didn't need to be any of those—though he limited his driving and did seem sick today—because she liked visiting Mr. Crawford and hearing all about his favorite person in the whole wide world. Little Emmy. His pride and joy.

It didn't matter if Trinity only had a minute or an hour to spend with him, he couldn't wait to share pictures and stories of his beloved granddaughter.

"Isn't your son coming home this week?" She remembered him saying something about it the last time she dropped off an order.

"He'll be here tomorrow or the next day. He's always so busy. Something always comes up and delays him."

She understood that all too well. She and Adria had opened two other *Almost Homemade* sites. Because Adria was pregnant and wanted to stay close to home, that meant Trinity did a lot of the on-site setup and check-ins to make sure the managers were running things the way they wanted.

"How about I double up the food? That way you'll be prepared. If he doesn't show for a few days, you'll still have plenty for yourself."

Mr. Crawford had another fit of coughs. "Yes," he choked out.

"Perhaps I can drive you to urgent care so they can take a look at you and do something about that cough."

"Ah, sweet girl, I don't want to put you out. I thank you for delivering the meals."

"Nonsense. You're not only my best customer, you're my favorite. I want to make sure you're okay."

"Well . . ."

"I won't take no for an answer. Give me an hour to put the food together and another half hour to drive out to your place." She'd try to get there sooner, but she needed to make sure Adria and their team were prepared to close up shop without her tonight.

"You're a good girl, Trinity. I wish my boy had someone like you."

With her schedule, she had no time for dating. And meeting new people made her antsy and suspicious. Her last date probably thought her a whack-job for questioning everything he told her because she'd been looking for some hidden agenda.

"I'm sure Emmy's mom takes good care of your son."

"She can't even take care of herself these days." The exasperated words came out with a string of coughs and gasps for air.

Trinity didn't want to get into private family business. Still, she'd seen pictures of Mr. Crawford's son. Jon? She was pretty sure that was his name. Mr. Crawford was so proud of the businessman, who was the first in the family to graduate college and leave their small town and make it big in California.

"I'm sorry to hear that Emmy's mom is having a difficult time." What else could she say? She didn't want to dive too deep into that. None of her business. "*I* am going to take care of you. If you're able, make a nice hot cup of tea or even just hot water to help with that cough. I'll be there as soon as I can."

Mr. Crawford paused. "Thank you, sweet girl. Without you, and with Jon away, I don't know what I'd do." Deep emotion roughened his voice.

"Everything is going to be okay."

Mr. Crawford let out another string of harsh coughs

before he caught his breath again. "See you soon." He hung up.

Trinity didn't want to keep him waiting. He needed to be seen by a doctor.

Adria walked out of the bathroom wiping her hands on a paper towel. "Do you need help putting Mr. Crawford's order together?"

She nodded. "We need to do it quickly. He's sick, and I don't like the sound of him."

Adria frowned. "Poor thing. You think he'll be okay?"

"I hope so. Still . . . I want to get out there and check on him. I think I'll take him to see the doctor, too."

"Of course. But I'm worried about you, too."

Trinity paused, leaving the vegetables she'd been chopping on the cutting board next to a pot. "Why are you worried about me?" Her heartbeat picked up and she tried to keep her breathing even and not give away any sign that Adria made her anxious.

"It's been months since you were kidnapped and you're still so jumpy. I know it was traumatic . . . I just hoped you'd feel safer by now."

Trinity couldn't help it.

Adria held up her hand to stave off any ridiculous excuse Trinity thought up, like she always did when Adria voiced her concerns. "I haven't said anything to Drake or Declan and Tate because you've been seeing a psychologist, but . . . I don't know. I hate seeing you so . . . uneasy all the time." Adria touched her arm, and Trinity tried not to flinch, but Adria felt the movement. "You hide it well. Especially around your brothers, and especially Tate and Liz, but still, I see it because I'm with you all the time here at work."

She couldn't hide it from her best friend. "I appreciate the concern. I'm dealing with it the best I can."

"Are you taking the antianxiety meds the doctor prescribed?"

"When I need them." Probably not as often as she should, but she didn't want to be dependent on the drug to get through the day. She understood now what Drake had faced when he returned from the military a wounded warrior wrestling with the demons clawing at his mind every damn second.

She beat hers into submission most days, but she still had trouble sleeping, didn't like anyone sneaking up on her, and she absolutely couldn't stand an enclosed space.

Sometimes even the massive shop kitchen seemed too small and closing in on her.

"How much sleep do you get a night now?"

In the beginning, she hadn't slept for days at a time. Now, she was lucky to get a nice four or five hours.

The dark and quiet were not her friends anymore.

Sometimes she thought her mind was a trap she'd fall into and couldn't escape.

But Adria would only worry more if she spilled that disturbing tidbit. "Mr. Crawford really needs that order. I don't want to keep him waiting."

"You don't want to talk about what happened and how badly you're still dealing with it."

"I'm doing the best I can," she snapped.

Adria wrapped her in a hug. "I know that. I just wish there was something I could do, some way that I could take this away from you."

Trinity hugged her sister-in-law and took in her warmth and understanding. "This helps. Knowing you care and that you're looking out for me, that's all I need. The therapist said it would take time. Believe it or not, this is me better than I was those first few weeks."

Adria leaned back and looked her in the eye. "I wish you would share this with the family. If Tate and Liz knew, they'd help you, too. Maybe talking to them would help. They survived that asshole just like you did."

"They went through far more than I did and they've come out of it stronger and happier. I don't want to bother them with this or make them relive that terrible ordeal."

"They'd do it for you," Adria pushed.

"I'm fine. Now help me get Mr. Crawford's order together. He needs my help right now, and I don't want to let him down."

She'd been scrambling to keep it together every day and not lose it the way she did those first few days where Adria had to hold her while she cried uncontrollably in the bathroom, then help her upstairs to the little apartment above their shop and tuck her into bed where she didn't sleep, but lay curled in a ball of frozen fear.

Adria pressed her lips together, studied Trinity's face for a long five seconds, then nodded. "Okay." She pulled a tablet out of the front of her apron. "What should we put in the order?"

Trinity felt the tears of relief prick her eyes and blinked them away. She didn't deserve a friend like Adria, but she worked damn hard to keep her. It felt like a marathon to keep her shit together every minute of the day and not screw anything up when the anxiety made it hard to remember things, fear made her want to hide away, and baseless suspicions made her hyper aware of the people around her and turned ordinary people into a threat.

She wished that one day she didn't feel this way. That somehow she could put the past behind her and move on instead of reliving it every day in some way that stole all the joy out of everything.

What she wouldn't give to have her life back and to find the kind of love and understanding Tate and Liz shared that had seen them through the worst time in their lives.

She hoped she made it to that day.

Maybe someday someone would come along and be the distraction—and hopefully more—she needed to put the past behind her.